M.R. Mackenzie was ⌐                               ʼudied
at Glasgow Universitу                             ιn Film
Studies.

In addition to writing,                    ᴜ producer and has
overseen releases of films ι              ᴄιaimed directors, among
them Dario Argento, Joe Dᴀ        ᴜ Nakata and Jacques Tourneur.
Writing as Michael Mackenzie,  ᴌ has contributed chapters to books on
cult cinema and regularly provides video essays and liner notes for new
releases of celebrated films. He used to work in a library, before leaving
to spend more time with books.

In 2019, his first novel, *In the Silence*, was shortlisted for the Bloody
Scotland Scottish Crime Debut of the Year and longlisted for the
McIlvanney Prize. His third novel, *The Library Murders*, was featured in
Crime Time's Best of the Year 2020 list.

## Praise for M.R. Mackenzie

'Brings a fresh new voice to the field of Tartan Noir.'
JAMES OSWALD

'Writes with precision and passion.' CARO RAMSAY

'Splendidly written stuff.' BARRY FORSHAW, *CRIME TIME*

'An immersive slow burn of a tale, peppered with
disquieting fire-crackers of revelation.' MORGAN CRY

'Mackenzie has come up with something that defies easy
definition and is truly original.'
PAUL BURKE, *NB MAGAZINE*

'Up there with the best contemporary authors working today.'
DAVID B. LYONS

## Also by M.R. Mackenzie

\* To get this free Anna Scavolini short story
and keep up to date with all the latest news,
subscribe to the M.R. Mackenzie Mailing List
at **mrmackenzieauthor.com/mailinglist**

# M.R. MACKENZIE

# THE SHADOW MEN

AN **ANNA SCAVOLINI** MYSTERY

**MAD**HOUSE

Cover design by
Tim Barber / Dissect Designs

Typeset in 10pt Minion Pro

First published in 2021 by Mad House

ISBN: 978-1-9160948-2-6

Version 1.0

www.mrmackenzieauthor.com
facebook.com/MRMackenzieAuthor
@landofwhimsy

A suspicious mind conjures its own demons.

Ancient Japanese proverb


It's true that I do not know exactly who my enemies are.
But that of course is exactly why I'm paranoid.

Edward Abbey

# Harbinger

Autumn 2015 roared in on Glasgow with biblical fury. It had been a mild, dry summer with rainfall well below the historical average, but as September arrived, the heavens opened their reserves and spared no effort in making up for lost time. Gale-force winds pummelled the city, the Clyde threatened to burst its banks, and flood warnings were issued for low-lying areas. Mother Nature, it seemed, was determined to inflict a reckoning for sins as yet unatoned for – a reckoning which, judging by the unrelenting ferocity of the assault, would not be complete until blood had been spilled.

On the night of Tuesday the eighth of September, Mother Nature got her wish.

Gil McLaren hadn't wanted to be out tonight. As far as he was concerned, there was no such thing as a good time to be asked to work the 1900–0700 shift, but a night like this one made him crave his warm bed and electric blanket all the more fervently.

The call had come through at 0045: *Road traffic accident on the M8. Driver killed on impact. No other persons in the vehicle. Road Policing shift sergeant required to coordinate at scene.*

As he roared up the dual carriageway, tail-lights of the car in front shimmering on rain-slick tarmac, he took one hand off the wheel and slid it inside his coat, feeling the contours of the hip-flask in his breast pocket. Only the challenge of simultaneously unscrewing the lid and maintaining control of the wheel stopped him from helping himself there and then.

Hopefully, if the locus was as chaotic as he was anticipating, he'd manage to secure a crafty swig once he got there.

Up ahead, the flashing lights of a stationary police car blocked one lane, while a constable in a hi-viz jacket occupied the other – a last defence against any driver who'd ignored the 'ROAD AHEAD CLOSED' sign some way back. McLaren leaned forward, peering past the swishing wipers to get his first glimpse of the scene that awaited him. The unfortunate vehicle, a blue hatchback, had careened off to the right, the metal barrier having done nothing to halt its trajectory. That task had finally been accomplished by the granite pillar supporting the A814 overpass as it crossed over the M8 before curving round and joining the main expressway some two hundred yards further back.

The cop in the hi-viz jacket waved him through. He continued for another fifty yards before coming to a standstill. He steeled himself, his hand once more straying automatically to his breast pocket. Then, suppressing the urge, he pulled on his peaked cap – less a nod to protocol, more a forlorn attempt to keep his head dry – and got out.

There were three other cop cars present; six officers in total milling about in their waterproofs. No sign yet of the Ambulance Service – but they could afford to take their time. As McLaren tramped towards the mangled hatchback, one of the plods – a babyfaced lunk who looked like he probably got carded at off-licence checkouts on a regular basis – approached and fell into eager step with him.

'Looks like a straightforward case of the perils of driving in adverse weather, sir. Consensus is the brakes were to blame.'

'That right, is it?'

'Aye. One of the lads was saying these old Honda Civics are notorious for it. Rainwater gets on the discs and then they don't kick in when you need 'em to.'

'I'll be sure to convey your hypothesis to the Fatal Accident Inquiry.'

The plod grinned eagerly. Either he was thick as mince or McLaren was losing his sarcastic edge in his old age.

They halted in front of the hatchback. There wasn't much left of its front end, and the driver hadn't fared much better. His face – which, judging by the blood splatter, had bounced off the steering wheel upon impact – resembled battered roadkill. And yet, as McLaren gazed at the man's ruined features, it dawned on him that he'd seen them somewhere before. The gears of his mind, impeded by a lack of sleep and a surfeit of something else, cranked slowly as he tried to match the face to a name, and to recall the context in which he'd previously encountered both. As these three disparate elements finally aligned, like pictures on a slot machine, a trickle that wasn't rainwater ran down his back.

He stirred, becoming aware of a hubbub developing behind him. He turned as an unmarked black sedan drew up, waved through by the hi-viz-jacketed officer on traffic control duty. The driver scrambled out, unfurling an umbrella. Holding it aloft, he hurried round to open the rear door. A figure stepped out: short, unimposing, his unassuming presence belying the waves his arrival had created.

'What's the Chief doing at an RTA?' McLaren heard one of the plods asking in an awed whisper.

Peter Strickland, Assistant Chief Constable (West of Scotland), strode across the tarmac towards McLaren, his driver hurrying after him, umbrella shielding him from the rain. The babyfaced PC quickly melted away. All around McLaren, a newfound spirit of industriousness had taken hold, as officers who five minutes ago had been catching flies all suddenly seemed to find tasks which demanded their urgent attention.

Strickland came to a halt facing McLaren. He took in the sight of the totalled hatchback, then gazed at McLaren with his sad, hangdog eyes, and shook his head ruefully.

'My God, this is a rotten business. No way for a man to go.'

'Yes, sir,' McLaren agreed obediently.

Strickland took the umbrella from his minder, dismissing him with a barely perceptible nod, then turned to McLaren with an inviting hand.

'Shall we?'

Mystified, McLaren allowed himself to be led along the road, away from prying ears.

'You look tired, Gil.' Strickland's hand hovered behind the small of McLaren's back, guiding him.

'It's one in the morning, sir.'

Strickland smiled slightly, conceding the point. 'And no time for an old sea-dog to be abroad. This job makes old men of us all sooner or later. It's a youngster's game, perhaps more so now than ever.'

'I cope, sir,' said McLaren, the response mechanical, unfelt.

Strickland slowed to a standstill. The two men met each other's eyes – one small and slight, the other a stocky, ungainly giant. And yet there was no doubting where the balance of power lay.

Strickland sighed. 'I thought we'd turned a corner with you, Gil. You promised me you'd turned over a new leaf.'

'Sir, I don't know what—'

'Please don't embarrass us both by denying it. Every man and his dog knows it's still happening.' The same reproachful look. The same bitter disappointment. 'I can *smell* it on you.'

McLaren was suddenly acutely aware of the hip-flask in his breast pocket, burning a hole in the fabric, scalding his skin. He opened his mouth to – what? Protest his innocence? Come clean and throw himself at Strickland's mercy?

Strickland beat him to it. 'I don't hold it against you, you know.'

His manner was sympathetic, but tinged with a weary disgust which he couldn't quite manage to conceal – like a grown-up child who's come home to discover an elderly, infirm parent lying in their own filth and too incapacitated to do anything about it.

'It's simply who you are,' he continued, his tone philosophical. 'I know it, you know it, so let's not make a song and dance about it. Better to cash one's chips on one's own terms and leave the table with some degree of dignity than to lose everything and be escorted out by the in-house muscle. Better to avoid any unnecessary embarrassment – both to oneself *and* to the house.'

Until now, Strickland's tone had been philosophical – speaking, it seemed, more to himself than to McLaren. Now, his expression intensified, those hangdog eyes suddenly sharp and piercing.

'Do we understand one another?'

McLaren swallowed heavily. Oh, he understood. He understood all too well.

'Yes, sir.'

Strickland smiled. He patted McLaren's arm kindly: the level-headed child telling the embarrassed older man that there's no need to worry – they'll take care of the mess.

'Time to call it a night, I think. You're no good to anyone – not in your present state. Go on – home to your bed. We'll soldier on without you.'

The conversation over, Strickland turned to go. His driver was by his side in an instant, hair plastered to his forehead from exposure to the elements. Taking command of the umbrella once more, he escorted his master back to the sedan, deftly thrusting the rear door open for him while simultaneously shielding him from the downpour. McLaren watched, rainwater running into his eyes from the brim of his hat, as the sedan performed a one-eighty-degree turn and departed the scene, rear lights receding into the distance.

McLaren remained there a little longer, watching the plods hurrying to and fro. Already, it was as if he no longer existed. A bystander at his own incident scene, his presence immaterial to the smooth running of the operation. A relic of the past. An unperson.

He realised it came as something of a relief. It wasn't so much that he was leaving with his dignity intact. That had been expunged long ago, along with his self-esteem, self-respect and belief that what he was doing made any sort of difference, let alone one for the better. But at least it was an end of sorts; a line drawn in the sand, a laying to rest of the ghosts of the past. He took out the hip-flask and, in full view of his colleagues, downed a hearty draught. No one paid him the slightest attention.

He screwed the cap back on, turned and squelched back towards his waiting car.

On a street corner near the city centre, soaked by both the rain and the periodic splashes from vehicles howling past at full speed, a man waits, clutching the strap of the laden rucksack weighing his shoulders down. He's been standing there for over an hour, his windbreaker barely protecting him from the thundering downpour.

The person for whom he is waiting will not come tonight, nor indeed any night. Factors and forces beyond his control have put paid to that, though he doesn't know it yet. It is now 2 a.m. – more than forty-five minutes past the agreed rendezvous time.

And yet still he waits.

PART ONE

# The Missing

# 1

# Vasilico

The figure had been standing at the back of the lecture hall for at least the last ten minutes, leaving Anna wondering what precisely he thought he was doing here. There was something purposeful about his presence; something unapologetic, as if he had a God-given right to be here.

What made it doubly frustrating was that she couldn't see his face. The room was built in the old theatre style, with two columns of benches on an incline running down to the stage where she currently stood. As such, he was standing the equivalent of two or three storeys above her, and every time she looked up at him her eyes caught the full glare of the ceiling-mounted lights pointed at the stage, all but blinding her in the process. All she could tell was that he was male, that he was wearing a suit, and that he was tall and broad-shouldered. Beyond that, he was just a hazy, ill-defined shape. A shadow.

In the pocket of her slacks, her phone hummed: her two-minute warning.

'So,' she addressed her assembled first-years, 'we return to our original question: what *is* criminology? We must be able to define our topic before we can successfully study it. And before we can define criminology, we must first answer another, more fundamental question: what is *crime*?

'It's tempting to think we all have a solid understanding of what constitutes a criminal act – some innate knowledge that we're all somehow imbued with. But in reality, there are multiple variables at play. There are acts which are considered crimes in some jurisdictions but not in others. Some acts *were* criminal in the past but no longer are, and vice versa. Who decides what is a crime and what isn't? Governments? Academics? Broad public sentiment? And how do we approach legislation like the Nuremberg Laws, duly enacted according to the rules of the German constitution but themselves now considered to be crimes against humanity?' She raised her shoulders in an exaggerated shrug. 'I'm not posing these questions because I have definitive answers for you. I'm posing them to give you some idea of the complexity of your chosen topic of study.

'Over the next several weeks, I want you to do your best to clear your minds of what you think you know about crime, about criminals and about their victims. Let go of your assumptions, be willing to embrace new and sometimes challenging ideas. If you were hoping for an easy ride, this is not the class for you. But, if you're willing to park your preconceptions at the door and approach the subject as open-mindedly as possible, you should find the next three months both stimulating and intellectually satisfying.'

Sensing that she was done, and no doubt as aware of the hour as her, the students began to gather their belongings. It took a few minutes for the room to clear. As the last remaining stragglers headed for the exit, the stranger strolled down the steps towards her.

'Dr Anna Scavolini?'

Anna glanced up from jamming her laptop into her shoulder-bag. 'That's right.'

'Oh, super.' The man grinned, flashing twin rows of even teeth. 'And there I was worrying I'd come to the wrong place. An *honour* to make your acquaintance. Detective Chief Inspector Vasilico, Major Investigations Team.'

He was, as she'd already surmised, tall, and in his mid-thirties. He was also impeccably groomed, his suit clearly expensive and cut to measure, hinting at the well-honed muscles that lay beneath it. She eyed his outstretched warrant card with some suspicion. As far as she was concerned, anyone prepared to launch such a transparent charm offensive had to have an ulterior motive.

'What can I do for you, Detective?'

'I was rather hoping you'd consent to sparing a few minutes of your no doubt invaluable time.'

'As long as it really is just a few minutes. I've an appointment I can't be late for.'

'Naturally. Rest assured, I've not the slightest intention of detaining you any longer than *absolutely* necessary.' His extended pause gave immediate lie to this claim. 'Derek Sullivan. What can you tell me about him?'

Anna zipped her bag shut and turned to face him. 'He's one of my postgrad students. Been doing a part-time Masters in Criminology with us for the past year.'

'And presumably you're aware that, in addition to being a part-time student, he's also a serving police constable?'

Anna nodded. 'The department has a partnership with the police – providing opportunities for officers to expand their knowledge-base and develop their analytical skills. Derek's one of four who are with us at the moment. Why? Is he in some sort of trouble?'

'That rather depends. When was the last time you saw him?'

'We had a supervision meeting just over three weeks ago. Since then, we haven't had any contact.'

'And is that normal?'

'More or less. We're scheduled to meet once a month, and he attends group lectures in between, some of which I teach. I don't remember seeing him at any of mine since our last supervision – but then, his attendance has always been . . . ' She hesitated, unable to shake the feeling that she was somehow betraying a confidence. ' . . . *spotty.*' She put one hand on her hip, gazing up at him entreatingly. 'Look, I'm really not sure what I can realistically tell you unless you give me something more to go on.'

Vasilico was silent for a moment, as if considering how much he should say. At length, he exhaled a breath.

'Derek Sullivan was last seen leaving work just over a fortnight ago. He failed to report for duty on Friday the eleventh of September, and since then has made no contact with his colleagues, friends or family.'

The silence that followed was so absolute Anna could hear the creaking of the building's foundations.

'I'm sorry to hear that,' she said eventually, not knowing what else *to* say.

'As you can no doubt appreciate, the more time that passes, the more concerned we grow about his wellbeing. I take it from your somewhat tongue-tied reaction that he hasn't made contact with *you*.'

'No, and I wouldn't expect him to.' Anna shrugged helplessly. 'I really didn't know him all that well. To be honest, I find it hard to believe there's not someone better placed to answer your questions than me.'

Vasilico winced, as if this pained him on a personal level. 'That's just it. I'm not sure there is.'

'You'll have to explain.'

'If I asked you to describe Derek, what would you tell me?'

It was a trickier question to answer than she'd anticipated. 'Quiet, I suppose,' she said after a moment. 'Not especially talkative or outgoing. From what I gather, he kept himself to himself.'

'Then we're on the same page. Over the last few days, I've spoken to more of his squadmates than I've eaten hot dinners, and they all described him in more or less the same terms as you: quiet, preferred his own company, didn't go in for socialising out of hours with the other lads.'

'That's not a crime.'

'No. Does make it markedly harder to build up a picture of his movements, though.'

Anna studied Vasilico's face, taking in the knitted brows, the pensive frown. She still wasn't sure she altogether trusted him, and there was an overbearing slickness about him that set her teeth on edge, but he seemed sincere in his concern for the missing constable, and she found herself wishing she could do something more to help them both.

'Well,' he said, stirring, 'I suppose it always *was* a long shot. I shan't detain you further. I appreciate you taking the time to . . . ' He stopped, frowning for a moment as if he'd lost his train of thought, then smiled knowingly. 'I've just realised.'

'What?'

He wagged a knowing finger at her. 'I know where I know you from.'

'Oh?'

'You're *the* Anna Scavolini. The one who wrote that screed in the *Tribune* about the toxicity of police culture – how we're all a bunch of unreconstructed bully-boys who go around breaking skulls and trampling on folk's constitutional rights. What was that phrase again? "To be the law is not to be above the law"?'

There seemed little point in denying it – not least since she stood by every word. A few months earlier, the *Glasgow Tribune* had invited her to contribute to a package of articles about the changing face of the modern police force – though, as she'd insisted in the piece she subsequently penned, the words 'changing' and 'modern' could scarcely be less appropriate when applied to the Strathkelvin Police Force, the body which served the entire Greater Glasgow area. She'd been forthright in her language, highlighting both the moral conservatism that multiple studies had shown to characterise law enforcement officials in general, and a string of recent scandals that had dogged the Strathkelvin force in particular. The former included accusations of an aggressively macho 'canteen culture' which ostracised and targeted those who failed to fit in; the latter the heavy-handed treatment of protesters at a recent climate change rally, which had left one teenager with a fractured zygoma, as well as the burial of a report on institutional sectarianism within the force, the contents of which had only come to light following a lengthy Freedom of Information battle. She'd ended by calling for – amongst other measures – a root-and-branch overhaul of internal and external complaints procedures, and the establishment of a new supervisory body consisting solely of non-police officers to review all operational policies. '*The Strathkelvin Police Force*,' she'd concluded, '*is the oldest in the world, but it's time they joined the rest of us in the twenty-first century.*'

'Yes, I rather enjoyed that.' Vasilico was still smiling – an arch, self-satisfied smile that left her with an overwhelming urge to wipe it from his face by any available means. 'You'll be pleased to know you made waves at HQ. Wouldn't *believe* how exercised the head honchos were by it. I gather the phrase "set public relations back to the Palaeolithic Age" was uttered.'

'I'm glad it provided you with some amusement,' Anna said, not sure which irritated her more: his implied belittlement of her or his seemingly blasé attitude to the serious charges levelled against the organisation he worked for.

Vasilico raised his hands in a gesture of truce. 'Of course. Forgive me. Rest assured, we treat all accusations of misconduct with the utmost seriousness. Tricky though it may be to believe, the vast majority of us are in fact fine, upstanding individuals.'

'Present company included, naturally.'

Vasilico chuckled. 'Perhaps the problem is one of perspective. *Walk a mile in another man's shoes* and all that. Now don't mistake me,' he added quickly, forestalling whatever objection he'd anticipated her making. 'I understand the need for accountability and due process. But I also understand the practicalities – that, in life-or-death situations, it's not always possible to dot every "i", say "please" and "thank you".'

This time, it was Anna's turn to smile, though hers was considerably more saccharine. 'Or perhaps you're just too close to the action, Detective. Perhaps you lack the necessary distance to see what's screamingly obvious to the rest of us.'

Vasilico threw back his head and laughed – a rich, deep laugh that reverberated in the high rafters. '*Touché*. I suppose I should have known better than to get into a battle of words with someone who bandies them for a living. And now I really *have* exhausted my welcome.' He gestured to the stairs with a grandiose sweep. 'Go! Attend your appointment, and let it not be said that the officers of the Strathkelvin Police Force are guilty of preventing citizens from going about their lawful business.'

Anna turned to go, hiding the involuntary smile that was threatening her lips. As she shouldered her bag, a thought occurred to her. She turned to Vasilico once more.

'If there's any news about Derek Sullivan . . . '

' . . . I assure you, you'll be among the first to hear it.' Vasilico paused, fixing her with an earnest look. 'We'll bring him home safe – just you watch.'

Anna smiled, this time not entirely insincerely. 'Don't make promises you can't keep, Detective,' she said, and headed up the stairs.

## 2

# Twenty-Two Weeks

'All right now, this may feel a little cold.'

*Cold and more than a little invasive* was Anna's considered assessment as she lay, shirt open, slacks unbuttoned and lowered to her hips, while the sonographer pressed the plastic probe to her exposed stomach, under the watchful eye of Dr Nuala Byrne. She watched as a fuzzy black-and-white image took shape on the portable monitor nearby: the flickering, somehow not entirely corporeal form of the tiny humanoid creature growing inside her.

'You get a good view of the brain and other internal organs at the twenty-week scan,' Nuala explained as the sonographer continued to move the probe this way and that, pressing a little firmer here, a little lighter there. 'The further gone you are, the thicker the bones become, and the less effective the ultrasound is.'

It was actually Anna's twenty-second week, and the tail-end of it at that, but she had a feeling such pedantry would be ill-received, not to mention draw unnecessary attention to how late she'd left it to book an appointment. So she said nothing and gave a neutral grunt instead, hoping it conveyed polite interest, unbridled joy or whatever was the correct sentiment with which to respond to such information.

Nuala peered over the sonographer's shoulder, examining the image on the monitor. 'This is all looking very positive,' she purred in that soft, lilting voice that supposedly made her such a hit with nervous mums-to-be. 'Baby's skull is developing nicely, and we can rule out both spina bifida and cleft palate ... '

*Baby.* Why did those in the healthcare profession feel such a compulsive need to omit the definite article? Was it some aversion to basic grammar? Or was it just another part of the infantilising process, treating the mother as every bit as simple-minded and in need of wrapping in cotton wool as her offspring?

'. . . and the brain, kidneys and other internal organs all look as they should.' Nuala paused to glance at the laptop angled towards her on the nearby desk. 'You've had all the standard antenatal screening tests: Down syndrome, Patau's and Edwards' syndromes and so forth.'

'All clear,' said Anna, conscious that none of this information was new to either of them.

'Would you like a picture to take home?' The sonographer's finger hovered over the console under the monitor.

Anna shook her head.

'Sure? It's all part of the service.'

'I'm sure.'

'I'll save one for you anyway. If you change your mind, you can let us know.'

Before Anna could lodge any objection, the young woman had already tapped a button.

'Right then,' the sonographer said brightly, 'all done. You can get cleaned up.'

As Anna took the proffered tissue and wiped the sticky gel from her stomach, Nuala swivelled round to face her laptop, her long fingers dancing across the keyboard as she wrote up her notes, while the sonographer, her role in the proceedings completed, gathered her things and slipped out, shutting the door to the consulting room behind her with a soft click.

'Have you given any thought to prospective birthing partners?' Nuala asked as Anna sat up to button her shirt.

'I've had thoughts. Nothing definitive, though.'

'What about the father?' Nuala's piercing eyes glanced up at her from behind her tortoiseshell glasses. 'How involved is he?'

'He's not part of the picture.'

'Is that by choice? Forgive me, I don't mean to pry, but you shouldn't underestimate the value of support, be it emotional or—'

'It's less complicated this way.'

Awkward silence. Nuala's lips puckered, her disapproval clear even if she wasn't voicing it.

'Fair enough – though I'd strongly advise settling on a birthing partner sooner rather than later. Things always go more smoothly when they're involved as early as possible.'

'Noted.' Anna stood to tuck in her shirt.

'Now.' Nuala crossed one leg over the other and steepled her fingers together, swivelling round to face Anna. 'We also need to talk about how you're managing your condition.'

*Here it comes.*

'Am I right in thinking you're still off the lithium?'

'That's right.'

'Even though, beyond the first trimester, the concerns about heart defects no longer apply.' It was a statement of fact, not a question. 'All things considered, I'm of the view that it would be safe to resume your normal dosage now. In fact, from the point of view of your own mental wellbeing, I'd strongly recommend it.'

Anna had been ready for this. 'The baby's brain continues to develop right up until birth, so there are ample grounds to believe that taking lithium at *any* stage in the pregnancy could potentially cause lasting developmental defects. Plus, I know what being pregnant does to your body. Your hormones, fluid levels, kidney functions are all over the place . . .'

'We can monitor these things—'

' . . . all of which' – Anna, speaking calmly but firmly, raised her voice over Nuala's – 'impact the amount of lithium in the bloodstream, putting the mother at risk of overdose or any number of other side effects. And there's the increased risk of stillbirth.'

'A *tiny* increase.'

'But an increase all the same. Besides, I'm planning on breastfeeding.'

'You still could, potentially. You'd need to have Baby's lithium levels and kidney function tested frequently, but the risk—'

'Is more than I'm prepared to countenance.'

'What about the risk of a severe manic or depressive episode? Are you prepared to countenance *that*? The risk of a post-delivery relapse is dangerously high in mothers with bipolar disorder. Lithium won't eliminate that risk, but it *will* reduce it considerably. We need to balance the dangers associated with taking it against those of *not* taking it.'

Anna sighed inwardly. Why did it always feel like she was under attack whenever she visited a medical professional? No matter how rigorously she researched her options, weighing up risk and reward with the same diligence she applied to her professional life, her choices were invariably met with judgement, disapproval and the implication that she didn't know her own mind.

'Let me ask you this,' she said. 'Imagine you're a psychiatrist and I come to you as a pregnant woman newly diagnosed as bipolar and with no prior history of treatment. In that scenario, would you be advising me to start taking lithium?'

'Well . . . ' Nuala met her eyes, though it took some effort.

'You know as well as I do that you wouldn't. I can quote the SIGN guidelines chapter and verse. I know all the recommendations for health practitioners. I've reduced my dose gradually, in consultation with both my GP and my psychiatrist. I've been completely lithium-free for three months now, without any hint of a change to my mood levels. I know what I'm doing.'

Nuala gave Anna a hard look, consternation writ large. 'It's your decision,' she said eventually, 'and one I respect, though I will be recording my reservations in my notes.'

*But of course you will,* Anna thought.

They ran through a few more points of order: whether Anna had been experiencing any back or hip pain (a little), whether she was getting enough sleep and exercise (she was), whether the morning sickness had cleared up (it had). The whole performance left her feeling like a child waiting to be granted permission to leave the table. *Yes, I have eaten all my greens. May I please go out and play now?*

'In that case,' said Nuala, 'I think we're done here. I'll see you again at twenty-eight weeks.' She wagged a chiding finger at Anna. 'And remember what I said about a birthing partner. I'll be expecting an answer next time I see you.'

As Anna walked up the hill towards the university, she replayed the conversation with Nuala in her mind, wondering whether things would have gone more smoothly if she'd succeeded in reining in her combative side. On the face of it, Nuala's concerns were far from unfounded, and Anna supposed that, if the boot had been on the other foot and she'd been the one dispensing medical advice, she'd have raised precisely the same concerns. Plus, she supposed medics were all too used to patients who either knew nothing and had to have their hands held every step of the way, or came armed with reams of crap they'd read online about how the MMR jag caused autism and whatnot. But she wasn't one of those people. She knew the difference between peer-reviewed research and the deluded ravings of the tinfoil hat brigade. She just wished the likes of Nuala Byrne could see that, and that this wasn't some mad flight of fancy on her part.

As she turned up the steps to the university's rear entrance, still slick from the near-endless downpour of the past few weeks, her phone vibrated in her pocket. She slowed to check the screen. *Unknown number.*

'Hello?'

'Dr Scavolini, it's Paul Vasilico.' She recognised the detective's smooth, languorous drawl instantly. 'We spoke earlier, remember?'

'What do you want?'

'Always straight to the point. I admire that about you, Dr Scavolini. I was calling to ask if you'd be interested in attending Monday's case review of the Derek Sullivan investigation.'

Anna came to an abrupt standstill halfway up the steps, wondering whether she'd heard correctly.

'In what capacity?'

'As his university tutor, for a start. Someone with direct experience of the man.'

'But I've already told you everything I know about him – which is next to nothing.'

'Rack your brains over the weekend. See if there's anything you can dredge up that you've overlooked. And even if there isn't, your presence would still be greatly appreciated. You're a criminologist, aren't you? You can add your professional insight to the cacophony of white noise.'

'I'm honestly not sure what you think I can realistically contribute,' she said, her irritation growing rapidly. 'My specialty is the criminal justice system and its impact on women. I've only the most rudimentary knowledge of the current thinking on missing persons. Some don't even regard it as part of the discipline of criminology—'

'Which, to be frank, still leaves you at an advantage over half the people who'll be in that room on Monday morning. Come on, what have you got to lose?'

'My time, for a start. I'm not sure if you noticed, Detective, but I do have a job, with contracted office hours and fixed commitments. I can't just decide to roll in late when I feel like it.'

'Ah, I'm sure you can spare an hour or two from your *incredibly* demanding schedule.' He paused. 'Unless, of course, you're afraid.'

'I *beg* your pardon?' she all but spluttered. 'What could I possibly have to be afraid of?'

'Of having your preconceptions challenged, for one thing. Of discovering that we're not all power-crazed, truncheon-wielding sadists – just a bunch of regular Joes doing our bit to make the world a better place.' He chuckled. 'Come on – humour me. If it all turns out to be a colossal waste of your time, I'll buy you coffee afterwards.'

'I can't drink coffee. I'm pregnant.'

It was her last throw of the dice – a last-ditch attempt to come up with something, *anything*, to give her an excuse to bow out with her pride intact – and she immediately regretted saying it. Her pregnancy was hardly something she'd taken to shouting about from the rooftops, even to people she actually *liked*. That couldn't continue indefinitely, but she was determined to cling to that last sliver of privacy until her bump got too big to hide beneath the loose tops and long cardigans she'd taken to wearing of late. All of which made her outburst all the more out-of-character, not to mention ill-advised.

Vasilico gave a low whistle. 'You kept that quiet! In that case, warmest congratulations are most assuredly in order. And if it comes to it, I'm sure we'll be able to rustle you up a decaf.'

He was persistent, she had to give him that.

'Take some time to think about it, and get back to me when you're good and ready. You'll get me on this number anytime, day or night. Toodle-oo the noo.'

With that, he rang off, leaving her grappling with a mixture of exasperation and sheer disbelief.

\* \* \*

It was getting dark by the time Anna parked her Citroën hatchback at the kerb and climbed the steps to her house on Clarence Drive, a stone's throw from the busy West End thoroughfare of Hyndland Road. The house itself had once been part of a much larger property, built in the old Victorian-era townhouse style. But after falling into rack and ruin during the latter part of the twentieth century, a shrewd developer had bought it for a song, done it up and split it into several smaller properties, resulting in a row of tall, narrow residences, highly prized – and highly priced – both for their location and faded elegance. Shortly after she'd come home to Glasgow four years ago, Anna, having fallen in love with its high ceilings and large bay windows, had used the money left to her by her late father to put down a deposit, and was now forking over the better part of her salary on the monthly mortgage payments.

In times past, light would have been spilling out onto the street and the smell of cooking would have greeted her as she stepped into the hallway – accompanied, more often than not, by a gentle voice calling her name. Now, the house was in darkness, the oven was cold, and the only communication that greeted her as she crossed the threshold was the pile of mail on the doormat. She scooped it up and rifled through it on the way to the kitchen. It was mostly just circulars – one, as was periodically the case, addressed to Daniel Goldblatt. She used to make a point of sending them back with a note explaining that Daniel Goldblatt no longer lived here, but that only seemed to serve as an invitation for them to send yet more unwanted excreta addressed to him. So into the recycling bin it went. Out of sight, out of mind.

Later, she lay soaking in the bath, soothing her aching back and swollen ankles, gazing at the small, firm lump that was her stomach, protruding above the water like the tip of an iceberg.

*Congratulations.* It always struck her as laughable that people said that to women when they fell pregnant. It suggested there was some skill involved in the act, when in reality, unless there was some sort of biological impediment, it was no great achievement.

*In fact, it can happen without you even intending it . . .*

The real challenge, as far as she was concerned, was successfully raising a human being who wasn't a mental and emotional fuck-up – which, based on all the evidence before her, was inordinately difficult to do.

*And speaking of fuck-ups . . .*

Derek Sullivan loomed large in her mind. Truthfully, she'd been somewhat more circumspect with Vasilico than she hoped he realised. She'd described Derek as quiet, but that had only been the half of it. She'd had misgivings about the arrangement between the university and the police force from the outset, feeling that it laid the door wide open to her department's objectivity towards the actions of its newfound partners being fatally compromised. Adding an extra student to her roster of supervisory responsibilities would have been an inconvenience at the best of times, but Derek had ensured that their every interaction had been like pulling wisdom teeth. She recalled their drawn-out, monosyllabic supervision meetings; her repeated entreaties to him to identify a research topic for his dissertation; his singularly underwhelming attempts to put pen to paper. At first, she'd thought he was just introverted, though it hadn't taken her long to revise that assessment to 'lazy and feckless'.

She thought back to the last time she'd seen him, some three weeks earlier. As usual, he hadn't done any of the preparatory work, and in fact had seemed even more closed-off than normal. Even now, she could picture him slouched in a chair in her office, arms folded, glowering at the floor, as if he actively resented being there. Well, now he was gone, and a part of her couldn't help but feel just a tiny bit glad that he was no longer her problem.

Except it wasn't really as simple as that, was it? It was one thing to be relieved at no longer having to deal with an uncooperative student, but what if something serious had happened to him?

Her thoughts turned to Vasilico's invitation to attend Monday's briefing. On the face of it, it seemed like an utter waste of her time. Vasilico was, it seemed, labouring under the belief that she was in a position to provide some startling insight that would crack the case wide open. She wasn't sure whether he was deluded or desperate, but either way he seemed determined to use every trick in the book to cajole her into attending. Worse still, he'd known exactly how to push her buttons, appealing to the part of her that, above all else, refused to suffer the indignity of appearing afraid of having her beliefs challenged.

*It's only an hour – two at most. A small price to pay in order to save face.*

'What d'you think, Trouble?' she asked the bump. 'What should I do?'

*This is ridiculous,* she told herself. *I'm having a one-way conversation with a barely sentient foetus.*

Besides, she already knew the answer. Had known it, in fact, since before Vasilico had even ended his call to her. She just hadn't wanted to give him the satisfaction of providing him with an answer then and there.

Ten minutes later, she was out of the bath and dialling his number.

# 3

# Lion's Den

Anna emerged from High Street Station and gazed up at the dilapidated multi-storey building across the road that served as the headquarters for the Strathkelvin Police Force's Major Investigations Team. With its multiple protruding blocks of brick and glass, it reminded her of something Picasso might have come up with in his cubist period, if he'd been an architect, and a particularly tasteless one at that.

As she crossed the road, a sudden gust of wind buffeted her, causing her to almost miss her step. When you were as short as she was, it really didn't take much to knock you over, and the recent changes to her body had affected her centre of gravity with a vengeance. The weather was just so damn changeable at the moment: massive downpours one minute, bright sunshine the next, and even hailstones – *hailstones*, for crying out loud! Wild weather like this always made her feel heady and giddy, her synapses tingling at the thought of the endless possibilities the world held. It wasn't an unpleasant sensation, but it did leave her feeling that she might be on the verge of losing control – and, as one well-kent playwright had once put it, that way madness lay.

Vasilico was waiting for her in the foyer, beaming in a way that made her think of an overeager estate agent.

'Anna, you made it! I'm so glad. It *is* OK to call you Anna, isn't it?'

She said yes, it was, even if she privately doubted she'd be calling him Paul anytime soon.

In short order, she found herself following him up several flights of stairs, a laminated pass hanging round her neck bearing the word 'VISITOR' in bold red. He buzzed them through a set of Formica doors and led her into a rather dingy open-plan office, clusters of cubicle desks arranged haphazardly throughout the long, low-ceilinged room. The overhead strip lighting gave everything a jaundiced look, including the various individuals dotted throughout the room, staring at computer screens, cradling phones to their ears or, in some cases, doing both.

'Welcome to the nerve centre,' said Vasilico, giving one of the broad, sweeping hand gestures that Anna was quickly coming to realise were an integral part of his communication toolkit. 'This is where the proverbial magic happens.'

Her eyes skittered over the two dozen or so concentration-bowed heads stationed throughout the room. A couple glanced in her direction. Most, however, paid her no attention.

'Has there been any news?' she asked, as they made their way through the bullpen. 'About Derek, I mean.'

'I wish,' said Vasilico. 'He's like the Invisible Man – here one minute, gone the next. But you'll hear all about it in due course.'

At the far end of the bullpen, they came to the door to a small conference room, outside which stood a short, Crimplene-suited man with one arm raised, wrist angled towards his face as he glared at a flashy-looking Rolex.

'Cutting it a little fine, aren't we?' he sniffed. He was in his mid-forties, with an officious manner and a neatly trimmed pencil beard – so styled, Anna suspected, to create the illusion that he had a neck.

Vasilico shrugged breezily. 'Helps build anticipation. You should try it sometime, Sean.' He glanced over the little man's shoulder into the room. 'Besides, I count at least six vacant seats, so it's a comfort to know there are people out there even tardier than I.'

The man gave a thin smile that failed to reach his eyes.

'Detective Superintendent De Groot, head of Major Investigations,' Vasilico explained to Anna. 'Sean, this is Dr Anna Scavolini, the woman I told you about. She's kindly offered to aid our efforts in tracking down our lost boy.'

'Hmm, yes.' De Groot regarded Anna with close-set little eyes. It was hard to shake the feeling that he was looking down on her, even though any height advantage he had over her was negligible. 'Well, that remains to be seen, doesn't it? Personally, I fail to see what assistance a university lecturer can possibly bring to bear on a missing person investigation. But then, it seems my views count for naught within my own department, so I suppose I shall just have to lump it, shan't I?'

Anna wasn't sure she entirely disagreed with his assessment, though the manner in which he'd chosen to express it would have exposed him as a venal, thin-skinned little man even if his entire demeanour hadn't done that job already. She got the distinct impression some sort of power-play was being waged between the two men, with her the pawn in the middle.

De Groot gave Vasilico a sharp look. 'Five more minutes. Then, regardless of who's here, we start.'

'It might not show,' Vasilico stage-whispered to Anna as De Groot moved off, 'but really he's as thrilled to have you here as I am.'

Anna doubted that very much, but said nothing.

They headed into the cramped, windowless room. A flatscreen monitor was mounted on the far wall, while a large oval table encircled by twenty or so chairs occupied most of the floor. The place was already tightly packed, the overwhelming majority of the assembled throng men. Most were dressed in suits, of varying degrees of quality, though a handful wore the regulation Police Scotland black T-shirt and trousers uniform. Glasses were being filled from water jugs, jackets hung on the backs of seats, and the air crackled with conversation. Anna, installing herself in an empty chair at the back of the room, tried to tune into what was being said.

Many of the conversations, she quickly realised, were the same ones that occurred in every workplace on a Monday morning – How are the kids? Get up to anything special at the weekend? – and incorporated a range of accents, ranging from the cut-glass to the resolutely working-class. She watched as Vasilico, who seemed to have forgotten about her as soon as they'd stepped into the room, clapped a hand on the back of a man of similar age – almost as tall and well-polished as himself and, like him, impeccably dressed – who, turning, gave an exaggerated, mock-horrified grimace before breaking into a broad grin and shaking him warmly by the hand. She couldn't help but be struck by the discordance between all the jollity on display and the seriousness of the matter they were gathered to discuss.

As she retrieved her water bottle from her bag and set it on the table, she became aware of a change in the room's mood. The hubbub hadn't died out completely, but it *had* grown quieter, more guarded. She looked up and immediately saw why: De Groot had arrived and was taking his place at the head of the table. Vasilico broke off his conversation and slid into the chair next to him. As those who were still standing hurried to find seats of their own, Anna found herself flanked by two uniformed officers, securing the last remaining empty chairs. One glanced at her and nodded a gruff greeting. She smiled awkwardly, certain that he was wondering just who the hell she was and what she was doing here.

'Good morning,' said De Groot, as silence fell. 'As most of us in this room will know, a decision was taken last week to hold weekly case reviews into Operation Griffin, to ensure appropriate allocation of resources and that nothing has been overlooked. Most of you are already familiar with the particulars of the case, but for the benefit of those joining us today for the first time, I'll invite DCI Vasilico, as senior investigating officer, to provide a summary of developments so far.'

Vasilico got to his feet, his poise and projection of self-confidence putting Anna in mind of a politician at the despatch box.

'Before we get underway, it may interest you to know that we have a visitor.' He extended a hand towards Anna's end of the table. 'This is Anna Scavolini, whose name I imagine will be familiar to most of you. For those who've spent the last few months under a rock, Anna is one of our fiercest critics.'

Anna was instantly aware of every eye in the room homing in on her with laser-like focus, many of them bristling with undisguised animosity. Vasilico's tone had been good-natured, but he would need to have been utterly naïve not to have anticipated the effect of his words, and she very much doubted he was that. He could hardly have made it feel more like she'd stepped into the lion's den if he'd tried.

'I'd like you all to be on your best behaviour for her,' Vasilico went on, 'and to show her that, contrary to popular rumour, we really are a civilised bunch, and fully committed to the ideals of transparency and account-ability.'

Anna gritted her teeth and nodded a general greeting to the room.

Vasilico picked up a remote and, holding it aloft, clicked it. Anna turned to see that the screen on the wall behind her was now filled by a head-and-shoulders photograph of a man in his mid-twenties. He appeared much as she'd remembered him: stocky, with a round, slightly doughy face and the sort of hooded eyes that made it look like their owner never got enough sleep. The standard issue policeman's peaked cap obscured most of his hair, but a dark tuft was visible on either side, covering the tips of his ears. His mouth was a straight line, apart from the corners on either side, as if the person taking the picture had ordered him to smile and he was determined to do the bare minimum that would qualify.

'Derek Sullivan,' said Vasilico. 'Date of birth 15.03.1990. Became a probationer in March of 2013 and has spent the majority of his career to date based out of Cambridge Street Police Station in the city centre.'

He clicked again, and the image on the screen was replaced by a street-map of Glasgow, with various points of interest highlighted.

'On Tuesday the eighth of September, young Derek leaves Cambridge Street at the end of his shift, just shy of 1700 hours. He walks to Charing Cross Station and catches an eastbound train to his home in Garrowhill, as per his usual routine. He has the next two days off, during which he has no contact with his colleagues. So far, so unremarkable. It isn't until the following day, Friday the eleventh, when he fails to show up for work at 0700, that his absence is noticed.

'Initially, there's little cause for immediate concern. Derek is a notoriously poor timekeeper and has, on previous occasions, been reprimanded for tardiness. At around 0800, his senior officer, one Sergeant Dave Vickers, calls Derek's mobile to ask him "what the hell?", but it goes to voicemail. Being a forward-thinking sort, Vickers has already arranged cover, so at this point he wastes no further time on the matter. It's not until around 1600 hours, having tried Derek's number again and got no answer, that he dispatches a squad car to the boy's flat to try to rouse him. The attending officers chap the door but receive no response and can find no evidence of anyone being home. At this point, Vickers leaves Derek a final voicemail, telling him he'd better have a bloody good excuse when he finally deigns to show his face, and calls it a night.

'Saturday the twelfth rolls in – but alas, our boy does not. Once more, officers are dispatched to Garrowhill, with orders to do a spot of door-knocking to see if the neighbours can elaborate on his movements. This proves singularly unfruitful. Seems he kept himself to himself – a refrain which will be heard more than once as our story develops. In the meantime, Vickers manages to raise the boy's father – his next-of-kin; stays up at the top of Gardner Street, out Partick way – who confirms he hasn't heard so much as a sniff from his son in over a week.'

One of the uniformed officers – one of the few women in the room besides Anna – raised a hand. 'Is that normal for their relationship?'

'Seems so. Per Sullivan Senior, they only saw each other every once in a blue moon, if that. Of course, by now there's a growing realisation among the Cambridge Street faithful that this isn't simply a case of "Sullivan being Sullivan". And so, on Saturday night, our boy is officially designated a missing person.'

As Anna listened, two things became increasingly clear. One, Vasilico was very much enamoured of his own voice and positively relished having the floor. Two, initial progress in the investigation had been slow. *Painfully* slow. She was far from an expert in these matters, but she knew the first forty-eight hours were critical in any missing person investigation. After that, people's recollections of events grew increasingly unreliable. In this case, it seemed those precious forty-eight hours – and more besides – had been frittered away like loose change.

'The initial assessment,' Vasilico continued, 'deems him low-risk: no apparent likelihood of suicide, no mental or physical health conditions, no drug or alcohol dependency, no family conflict, no known financial problems. *And,*' he raised a finger to underscore his point, 'no prior history of absconding. A decision is taken to carry out routine enquiries and put out the usual social media boilerplate, plus circulate his details on the PNC and local information systems. They keep the father in the loop – let him know that, beyond the basics, no further active steps will be taken, but that the case will be subject to regular reviews, with the next one scheduled for twenty-eight days after the initial report.'

'What was the father's response to that decision?' asked another member of the audience – a plain-clothes officer this time.

'Singularly unperturbed,' Vasilico declared, with a slight raise of one eyebrow. 'You'd think we were dealing with a missing set of car keys for all the concern he showed, rather than the first and only fruit of his loins. We did try to interest him in fronting a media appeal, but he wasn't for biting.'

'Is that no a bit heartless?' said the female officer.

'If you met him, you'd understand,' said Vasilico. 'He's an old-fashioned sort of chap. Did things differently in his day, y'see. Odds are he's more concerned about the lad than he's letting on, but his is a generation not renowned for making a scene. No,' he continued, an almost amused glint in his eye, 'that particular intervention came slightly later, and from loftier quarters. I refer, of course, to our own dear Assistant Chief Constable. Word of the young lad's disappearance finally reached his noble ear on the night of Sunday the twentieth of September, almost two weeks after his last sighting.'

'For those who haven't worked it out yet,' put in De Groot, 'Derek Sullivan's father is the brother of *Hugh* Sullivan, formerly of this parish. The late Chief Superintendent is one of this force's most decorated heroes, and it would be a grave insult to his memory were it thought that his nephew's disappearance was being treated as an afterthought.'

'Yes, quite.'

Vasilico looked and sounded almost subdued, to the extent that Anna half-wondered if he was about to lead the entire room in a moment of reflection for the dearly departed Chief Superintendent. Then the moment passed and he continued:

'Thanks to this timely intervention, a case review is held first thing the following morning, with the ACC attending in person. He immediately orders efforts to be stepped up, transferring responsibility from our boy's local nick to the Major Investigations Team, with yours truly tasked with overall control.'

'With my oversight,' added De Groot quietly.

Vasilico gave De Groot a rather indulgent smile. Once again, it seemed to Anna that the two men were embroiled in some sort of power-play. She got an overwhelming sense that, despite De Groot being Vasilico's superior by rank, everyone in the room knew where the authority really lay.

'So,' Vasilico went on, 'with the oversight of Sean here, I undertake a root-and-branch re-evaluation of the case, interviewing the boy Derek's erstwhile colleagues, authorising a search of his flat, applying to access his bank accounts and trawling the city's CCTV archives to build up a picture of his movements prior to his disappearance – all the while keeping both the ACC and the boy's father fully appraised. His neighbours and landlord all paint a picture of a man of few words who kept himself to himself and rarely went out, except for work and his weekly shop and visit to the launderette.'

'What about relatives, friends, known associates?' said one of the other detectives. 'Anyone he could have gone to?'

'We've covered Daddy Dearest already, and he confirms he's not seen hide nor hair of Junior. Mum's deceased, and he's not in close contact with anyone from her side of the fam. As for friends, "loose acquaintances" might be the more appropriate designation. We've established that he did keep in touch with a few of the folk he used to kick around with at school. They get together every so often – birthdays, anniversaries, the usual jazz. But the ones we've spoken to all told us much the same thing: that our boy was on the periphery of the group; more of a hanger-on than the life and soul. Oh, he'd come to the odd knees-up or meal out when they remembered to invite him, but he'd just as often cry off – though God knows what else he had on, 'cept washing his hair. You get the sense that, if it hadn't been for the rest of them putting in the effort to keep him in their orbit, he'd have drifted away like an unmoored boat. And maybe that's precisely what happened.'

As Anna listened, she was struck by just what a profoundly lonely existence Vasilico's words conjured up. She felt a pang of pity for Derek in the depths of her stomach, accompanied by something else she couldn't altogether place.

'We've circulated his description to all emergency services,' said one of the uniformed officers, 'and we're in the process of canvassing the bus and taxi firms in case he caught a ride off one of them. And we've checked with all the local hospitals, hostels and guesthouses. So far, zip.'

'What about his passport?' asked the female officer. 'Is it accounted for?'

'Safe and sound in the desk drawer at his flat,' said Vasilico. 'So it's a reasonably safe bet he hasn't skipped the country. Needless to say, we've alerted the ports and airports regardless.'

'Credit cards? Bank accounts?'

'All being monitored, and no attempts made to access them since he went missing. No evidence of either crippling debt or unexplained riches.

He paid his rent on time, donated once a month to the SSPCA and Cancer Research, and withdrew fifty pounds from the cashpoint outside the Co-op on Baillieston Road once a week to cover his outgoings. He was, as they say, a creature of habit.'

'His computer and other electronic devices have been seized, I take it?' said another officer.

'Sent to the lab for analysis, postmarked "urgent". No social media presence to speak of, and the tech boys found nothing untoward on his hard drive, apart from a copious amount of pornography of the homosexual variety.'

Anna distinctly heard a handful of sniggers, mostly from the younger men in the room.

'Explains a lot,' said the detective Vasilico had been speaking to earlier. 'His colleagues did let it be known that he wasn't like other boys.'

'All right, Plessis,' said Vasilico, with a note of weary indulgence, 'less of that now. The man's proclivities are his business and his alone.'

The smirk lingered on Plessis' face for a moment, but his bravado seemed to have deflated. Anna, who couldn't help noting that Vasilico had been the only person in the room to step up to Derek's defence, found herself warming to him ever so slightly.

'Is there anything to suggest he had a lover?' she asked, interjecting for the first time. 'Someone he could have gone off with?'

'So far, we've found no evidence he was involved with anyone,' said Vasilico.

'But you're considering it as a possibility.'

'At this stage, we're considering *everything* a possibility,' snapped De Groot, promptly dashing any hope of Anna warming to *him* anytime soon.

'It's a good shout, though,' said Vasilico, flashing her a brief smile, which she found herself appreciating more than she felt comfortable admitting to herself. 'And now, if I may make some progress . . . '

He clicked the remote. The image on the screen changed to fuzzy nocturnal CCTV footage of an urban intersection. The colours were oversaturated, the frame rate choppy, vehicles jerking along the road like stop-motion models. A constant curtain of rain lashed across the ground, ripples visible in the deep puddles on the tarmac. In the bottom-left corner, under the glow of a streetlamp, stood a figure, a black rucksack strapped to his back. He was facing the intersection, side-on to the camera, his features obscured by the hood of his red windbreaker.

'Wait for it,' said Vasilico.

As if he'd heard, the figure looked round, his face upturned towards the camera. Vasilico paused the image, the fuzzy but unmistakable features of Derek Sullivan frozen in time.

'That,' said Vasilico, 'is the corner of Rose Street and West Graham Street, near Cowcaddens Subway Station, in the early hours of Wednesday the ninth of September. CCTV from Charing Cross and Garrowhill Stations tells us that, having returned to his flat after work on the night of the eighth, our boy then catches another train back into town several hours later and heads to this desolate and inhospitable place. As you can see, he's dressed in a red windbreaker, quite distinctive, along with blue denim jeans, white velcro trainers, and he's carrying what his colleagues inform us is the black Adidas rucksack he usually sported.' He resumed playback. 'He proceeds to stand at the same location for the better part of an hour, until . . .'

As if on cue, Sullivan vanished right before their eyes. One moment he was there, the next he was gone. Anna managed to stop herself before she let out an involuntary gasp.

'For the avoidance of doubt,' Vasilico went on, 'our boy wasn't suddenly beamed up by little green men. I think it's safe to say we all remember the inclement weather at the start of the month. You may *also* remember that, in the wee hours of the ninth, said inclement weather resulted in a major power cut which took out half the city – including, unfortunately, the Cowcaddens area.' He wound the footage back until Derek reappeared. 'The outage occurred at four minutes past two. By the time the cameras came back online close to three hours later, our boy was long gone.'

He froze the image once more, Sullivan's face upturned towards the camera. Still holding the remote, he circled round the desk to the screen.

'Why did he head back into town that night? Why did he spend nearly an hour – and, for all we know, considerably longer – standing on an exposed street corner on the wettest night of the year? And, in the time between the camera going offline and coming back on, where did he go? Was he waiting for someone? Did they rendezvous successfully and take off together? Who can say? All we know for certain is that *that*' – he jabbed the remote towards the screen – 'is the last known sighting of Derek Sullivan, dead or alive.'

The weight of his words hung heavily in the air. As Anna continued to stare at the frozen image, Vasilico pointed the remote at the screen and switched it off, the picture vanishing with a soft *foom*.

'The last signal from his phone places him at the corner of Rose Street and West Graham Street at seven minutes past two – at which point it goes dark, leading us to believe it was switched off shortly after the CCTV feed failed. Whether he switched it off himself or someone switched it off *for* him . . . well, that's the million-dollar question.'

He folded his arms behind his back and faced the assembled throng. 'So here's what we know. Derek Sullivan – by all accounts a reserved, stay-at-home type who preferred his own company and stuck rigidly to his daily routine – goes missing without any apparent cause, after making an out-of-character late-night trip into town for what may or may not have been a pre-arranged meeting. We're aware of no major upsets in his life, no financial irregularities, no reason whatsoever for him to up and vanish without warning.'

He arched his shoulders in a broad shrug. 'It's a puzzle all right. But before going any further, I reckon it's time we heard from someone who, unlike the rest of us, has actual firsthand experience of our boy and has generously agreed to share her unique perspective on the matter: his dissertation supervisor, Dr Anna Scavolini. Anna?'

# 4

# Duty of Care

For the second time that morning, Anna found herself the focus of every pair of eyes in the room. This time, though, their looks were inquisitive rather than hostile. Feeling unexpectedly apprehensive, she cleared her throat, straightened her back and addressed the sea of expectant faces:

'I . . . well, I can only tell you what little I was able to glean from our supervision meetings. Derek never spoke to me about his home life or any pursuits outside university – but then, I never spoke to him about mine. It really wasn't that kind of relationship.' She shrugged. 'With some students, particularly the postgrads, you ask after their families, trade notes on what you got up to at the weekend; perhaps even socialise with them outwith work. But with Derek, I always got the sense he preferred to keep things at arm's length.'

'What sort of a student was he?' asked Vasilico. 'Motivated? Hard-working? Conscientious?'

'He was . . . ' She sighed. They might as well have the truth. 'To be honest, I thought he was going to struggle to scrape a passing grade. Not every student who comes through our doors is a natural academic, but he'd been with us for over a year, and in all that time I didn't see any improvement in his output at all, or any evidence of him even *trying* to improve. In fact, I really couldn't understand why he'd put himself forward for the programme. As far as I could tell, he didn't have a scholarly bone in his body.'

'The view among his colleagues was that he saw it as time off for good behaviour,' said Plessis, scarcely able to conceal his mirth. 'In other words, a chance for a skive. Reading between the lines, I'd say the feeling was mutual – in spades. Every day he was away on secondment was a day off from having to carry him.'

'You mean to say they didn't go out of their way to make him feel welcome and valued?' Anna made no effort to hide her sarcasm. 'You do surprise me.'

Plessis looked at her sharply. 'Meaning what, exactly?'

Defiant, Anna met his gaze. 'Just that it would hardly be the first time someone was blackballed from the police force over a failure to . . . assimilate.'

'Nonetheless,' said Vasilico, stepping in before Plessis or anyone else could respond, 'his colleagues all gave variations on the same refrain: that he wasn't a team player; that his attention often appeared to be elsewhere; that he wasn't pulling his weight. I had wondered if this was because he was pouring his efforts into his academic sideline.'

'If he was, I saw no evidence of it,' said Anna, then instantly regretted her words.

'Sounds like his fellow beat bobbies weren't the only ones who failed to welcome him to the bosom of the family,' grinned Plessis.

Vasilico shot Plessis a warning look before turning again to Anna. 'At your last meeting, did he give any indication that he was worried about anything?'

Anna considered her response before answering. 'Well, he was withdrawn, uncommunicative, unengaged – but then, that wasn't anything out of the ordinary. We weren't making much headway, so we wrapped things up early.'

'Who wrapped things up early? Was it at his suggestion, or a mutual decision, or . . . ?'

'*I* wrapped things up,' said Anna, feeling another unexplained pang in her stomach. 'I didn't see the point in us both sitting there for the full hour staring at the walls. So I called it a day.'

'And that was the last time you saw him,' said De Groot quietly.

'Yes, that was the last time,' Anna retorted, aware of the rising note of defensiveness in her voice. 'Look, if I had any idea why he disappeared or where he might be, believe me, I'd tell you – but I'm as in the dark as you are. Maybe, if you hadn't been so slow to get moving—'

'All right, all right, *truce!*' exclaimed Vasilico, as De Groot opened his mouth to respond. 'We're not here to pass judgement or seek recriminations. I'm sure there are plenty of folk who, knowing what they know now, would change things they said and did – or didn't. The facts of the matter are that it's now nearly three weeks since Derek was last seen alive, and I doubt I'm making too much of a leap when I say that every person in this room, be they CID or uniform or civilian, wants to find him and bring him home.'

The silence that followed implied the tacit agreement of all and sundry.

It was Anna who finally spoke. 'Is it safe to assume that he was at a higher than average risk of foulplay – that, as a police officer, he could have made enemies of the wrong sorts of people?'

'You mean the sort who write hit-pieces in national newspapers?' suggested De Groot.

'I was thinking more of the criminal sort,' said Anna stiffly, refusing to rise to the bait. She turned to address Vasilico – the closest thing, she reckoned, to a genuine ally in this room. 'Could he have been the victim of some sort of reprisal attack – or maybe fallen into temptation and got himself mixed up in something he shouldn't have? I'm not suggesting he brought this on himself,' she added, forestalling what she anticipated as the inevitable response of a bunch of people who plainly regarded her as the enemy. 'I'm just asking if it's being considered as a possibility.'

'I've already pulled the notes relating to every case he was involved with in the last six months,' said Vasilico. 'So far, there's been nothing untoward. In any event, we're talking about an entry-level police constable here. Most of the cases he worked on were small fry: petty theft, breach of the peace and the like. The odds of him having ended up in the crosshairs of anyone with the wherewithal to make a man disappear off the face of the earth are pretty slim. That's way beyond the means of the average ned harbouring a grudge against the bobby who lifted him for shoplifting.'

Another heavy silence fell on the room, broken only by the creaking of seats as people shifted restlessly. Vasilico remained standing at the head of the table, massaging the bridge of his nose with a thumb and forefinger, lost in thought.

'There's another angle that hasn't been considered yet,' said Anna.

Vasilico turned to look at her. 'What's that?'

'That he *wanted* to disappear.'

She'd been waiting for someone to raise it as a possibility. The fact that it had become clear no one was going to do so had forced her hand.

'You're all taking it as a given that something bad must have happened,' she went on as close to twenty pairs of eyes bored into her once more. 'But maybe this was exactly what he wanted. By the sounds of it, he wasn't having a great time at work. Perhaps he decided "the hell with this", cleared out and is now living a much happier life somewhere far away from here.'

For a moment, no one spoke. It was as if she'd just denied God in front of an audience of devout believers.

'Oh well, that's it, then,' said Plessis. 'We should all just pack up and go home. Job done.'

'I'm just saying' – Anna turned to stare him down – 'that he's an adult, he's of sound mind, and he's not suspected of any crime. In trying to find him, we might not be doing him any favours.'

'It seems to me,' said De Groot, his tone unmistakably chilly, 'that for someone who was invited here to assist in locating a missing person, you seem extraordinarily at ease with the idea that he should remain missing.'

'People have a right not to be found,' said Anna, refusing to back down under the glare of those priggish little eyes.

'If he *did* leave of his own volition,' said Vasilico, his own tone conciliatory yet firm, 'then that *is* his prerogative, and we could hardly force him to return home against his will. But before we write him off as a lost cause, we need to know for sure that that is indeed what he wants. And we can't do that unless we find him, can we? Sort of a Catch-22 situation, really.' He gave an amiable smile. 'Now, shall we try to make some progress?'

They continued for a while longer, going over various points of business, but it seemed the meeting had reached the limits of its productivity. Anna sat in silence for the remainder of its duration, feeling she had nothing else of value to contribute and not trusting herself not to say something she'd regret. Vasilico brought things to a close by thanking the team for their attention and issuing instructions to the various officers under his command, the vast majority of them variations on *keep on doing what you're already doing*.

As people began to scrape back their chairs, Anna got to her feet. Not waiting for Vasilico to see her out, she shouldered her bag and made a beeline for the exit, coat hanging from one shoulder. She was standing at the top of the stairs, grappling to disentangle the visitor's pass from around her neck, when she heard the Formica doors opening behind her.

'Well,' said Vasilico amiably, 'that could've gone a whole lot worse.'

'You think?' Anna turned to him with an accusing glare. 'I could have done without you introducing me to them as their fiercest critic. Talk about giving them a perfect excuse to dismiss anything I had to say!'

'On reflection, that was perhaps a tad inconsiderate. Still, I confess to having rather enjoyed the spectacle of you putting that jumped-up little popinjay De Groot in his place. And there's something to be said for setting the cat among the pigeons every once in a while.'

'From where I was sitting, it felt more like being a pigeon among a whole army of cats,' said Anna glibly.

She fell silent as a couple of officers emerged from the bullpen, engaged in earnest conversation of their own. One of them exchanged a brief nod with Vasilico in passing. As they headed upstairs, Anna set off in the opposite direction, clattering down the steps with Vasilico hot on her heels.

'You know,' she said, without stopping to make sure he was keeping pace with her, 'I genuinely can't fathom why you insisted on my being present, unless this entire episode was just your way of teaching me a lesson.'

'Nothing so crass, I assure you,' said Vasilico, falling into step with her. 'Hard as it may be to believe, my overriding objective really *was* to draw on your knowledge and expertise. But if I had a secondary aim, it was to hopefully show you that we're really not such a rum lot after all.'

'And how d'you feel that turned out? It seemed to me the message being hammered home loud and clear was that, until a week ago, this investigation barely even deserved to be called as much.'

'Oh, come on now, that's hardly fair.'

'Isn't it?' She briefly halted, turning to look at him sharply, before continuing her descent. 'Seems to me Derek's so-called colleagues treated his disappearance as little more than an excuse to thank their lucky stars they were finally shot of him.'

'I'll admit that, when the history books are written, it won't go down as one of our prouder moments. I hope, though, that the lengths we've gone to in the past week to turn things around demonstrates a willingness on our part to learn from past mistakes.'

'And those jibes about his sexuality? The whole "not like other boys" schtick? Forgive me, but I didn't see much evidence of learning from past mistakes *there*.'

'Oh, *that*?' Vasilico laughed, though his nonchalance rang hollow. 'You don't want to go paying too much attention to what Plessis has to say. I doubt he'll ever be in line for a sensitivity award, but he's essentially harmless.'

'Let me guess,' said Anna, pace quickening as she came to the final flight of stairs; 'he's just another of those irksome bad apples who can't help but keep popping up despite their supposedly inconsequential number. You could hardly have come up with a better illustration of police locker room culture if you'd *tried*.'

She alighted on the ground floor and turned to face Vasilico, proffering her visitor's pass.

'You really don't like us, do you?' he said, a note of what sounded like genuine bewilderment in his voice as he accepted it from her.

Anna took a moment to consider her response. 'I don't like the way you brush off every criticism of your organisation as if it's nothing for me to worry my pretty little head about. And I especially don't like the way a young man who didn't fit in was bullied and cold-shouldered to the point that he saw no option but to run away.'

'We don't know that's what happened.'

Anna scoffed. 'Please! It would be obvious to any remotely objective observer that you lot completely failed in your duty of care to him.'

'And that's what you are, is it – an objective observer? Only, from where I'm standing, you're not without skin in this game yourself.'

'*Excuse* me?'

'I'm just saying, he was your student. Perhaps we weren't the only ones who were deficient in our duty of care.'

For a long moment, Anna stood and faced Vasilico, unblinking. Despite the heat of her glare, he didn't appear remotely ruffled.

'Goodbye, Detective,' she said eventually. 'Thank you for providing me with this insight into the inner workings of the police service. It's been *enlightening*.'

As she alighted on the pavement outside, the uneasy feeling in the pit of her stomach rose up to engulf her. She recalled, with a sudden, aching clarity, the precise details of her final encounter with Derek Sullivan – details which had until now evaded her, or which she herself had subconsciously been suppressing. He'd been characteristically unprepared for the tutorial, with no answers to any of the questions and action points she'd asked him to address beforehand. Shortly before she'd drawn the meeting to an unscheduled close, she'd told him in no uncertain terms just how she felt.

'I don't know why you even come along to these sessions if you're not prepared to put in the effort,' she'd said. 'As it stands, it would be a considerably more productive use of my time and yours if you didn't bother.'

She knew now what that unfamiliar feeling had been all along. *Guilt.* Guilt at having allowed her frustrations to get the better of her. At having as good as told him she didn't want to see him again. At having been so unreceptive to his state of mind that she hadn't even *attempted* to find out what was troubling him. It wasn't curiosity that had compelled her to attend the briefing, or even a desire to save face. It was a deep-rooted, nagging fear that this situation was partly of her own making, coupled with a desire to do something, *anything*, to atone for her own failings. She could dress it up however she liked, but Vasilico was right: she'd let Derek down every bit as much as any of his colleagues, and now he was gone, and she had no choice but to admit that at least some of the blame lay squarely at her door.

# 5

# Partners

'So I'm just after speaking to Yvonne. She reckons there's definitely going to be cuts to next year's research budget.'

'Oh?' Anna half-glanced up from her screen as Sophie Hennessy stepped into the cramped little office they shared on the second floor of the Department of Law and Social Sciences. 'And just why, pray tell, would Yvonne be privy to that information before the rest of us?'

Sophie shrugged. 'Search me, but she sounded like she knew what she was talking about. And assuming she's right, it means there's going to be an absolute bloodbath come January, what with everyone jockeying for their share of the money-pot.' She settled behind her own desk, which faced Anna's on the other side of the room. 'If I were you, I'd get all my funding applications in good and early, seeing as you'll not be here when it all kicks off.'

Anna gave a sympathetic 'mm' to cover up for the fact that she wasn't really paying attention.

'I mean, if your workload's anything like mine, you'll have squillions of things to be getting on with already, but you know what they say: the early bird catches the worm.'

'Duly noted.'

Sophie frowned in consternation, clearly of the opinion that Anna wasn't treating the matter with the gravity it deserved. Her disapproval melted away, however, as her eyes alighted on Anna's desk.

'Ooh, Jaffa Cakes! Gie's one – I'm gaggin'.'

Anna tossed the half-empty packet – a parting gift from a student who'd doled them out at a group tutorial earlier that day – across the room to her. Sophie caught it deftly and helped herself to one, clenching it between her teeth as she logged into her computer, while Anna returned her attention to her own screen and to the journal article she'd been reading when Sophie came in.

> Verhoeven et al (2000) identify four categories of missing person:
> (1) those who leave of their own accord; (2) those in an at-risk
> category that leaves them vulnerable to falling through the social
> security net, e.g. former prisoners, the homeless and those with
> alcohol/drug dependencies or mental health issues . . .

'Sooo,' Sophie's voice cut through the dense wall of text, 'how'd it go?'

Anna looked up. 'How'd what go?'

'Your chat with Hugh.' Sophie pulled an exasperated face, as if she couldn't believe Anna could be so obtuse. 'About scheduling your mat leave?'

'Oh, that.' Anna shrugged dismissively. 'It went fine. We agreed I'd see out the end of the semester and start my leave at the Christmas holidays.'

'I hope you didn't let him guilt-trip you into that.' Disapproval was writ large on Sophie's face. 'You're not obligated to work right up till you're about to pop just to make life easier for *him*, you know.'

'He didn't guilt-trip me. It was *my* idea. It'll let me see my teaching commitments through and make the handover as smooth as possible.'

'Fair enough,' said Sophie, patently unconvinced, 'but just remember you're within your rights to start at any point from week twenty-nine onwards.'

Anna nodded and said nothing, aware that getting Sophie off your case invariably involved doing as little as possible to contradict her. It helped that they generally saw eye to eye on most matters and, as a result, had always got on well – a fairly essential condition for sharing an office. It was just that Sophie could be a bit . . . full-on.

As the room fell silent apart from the sound of Sophie nibbling on her Jaffa Cake, Anna resumed reading.

. . . (3) those who drop off the radar unintentionally, whether because they fail to inform friends or relatives of their whereabouts or because they suffer from a memory disorder such as dementia or amnesia; and (4) those who go missing as a result of deliberate and malicious action by another person . . .

'Know whether it's a girl or a boy yet?'

Anna sighed inwardly. Accepting that Sophie was determined for the two of them to have A CONVERSATION and that she wasn't going to get any peace until she indulged her, she minimised the article and turned to give her officemate her full attention.

'Just going to wait and see what comes out on the day.'

'Mm, that's nice.' Sophie nodded approvingly. 'Matthew was desperate to know as soon as we found out we were expecting, but I never understood the massive urgency. I mean, what difference is it going to make? It's not as if you can say to the doctor, "That's not what I wanted. Can you change it to the other kind?"'

Sophie had given birth to a screaming, bouncing baby boy, Cosmo, in June the previous year, and was now a fount of knowledge on the subject, dishing out if-I-were-you's and if-you-ask-me's as if they were going out of fashion. Anna had been doing her best to receive her advice with good grace, even though there were times when she was sorely tempted to point out that she *wasn't* Sophie and that she *hadn't* asked her. Now was definitely one of those times. And now Sophie was grinning at her with those big, searching eyes of hers (eyes that had always struck Anna as slightly too large for her narrow, elongated face), giving her the sort of meaningful look that leaves you feeling like you're the only person in the room who hasn't understood a really obvious joke.

'What?' she said, a little more defensively than she'd intended.

'Nothing. Just . . . ' Sophie clenched her fists against her chest and gave a silent squeal of excitement. 'Aaah! You're going to be mummy!'

Anna forced herself to smile. 'Yeah. It's going to be wild.'

Sophie sighed wistfully. 'I know it's a cliché, but it really is the most magical thing in the world. Just wait – once you're a parent, your outlook changes on *everything*.' A thought occurred to her. 'So have you chosen a birthing partner yet?'

'It's in hand.'

Was it fuck! Truth be told, Anna hadn't given the matter more than a moment's thought since Nuala Byrne had raised it nearly a month ago. There had been far too many other things clamouring for her attention – like poring over journal articles on subjects that were beyond her expertise or remit.

'*Well*,' said Sophie loftily, ' – and I don't want you to feel like I'm putting you under any pressure to say yes to this – but if you can't find someone who fits the bill, I'd be more than happy to step into the breach. I've been around the block myself, so to speak, and not to toot my own horn, but I reckon I've a pretty fair idea of what's involved.'

Anna had a sudden, nightmarish vision of herself in the delivery suite with Sophie's head thrust between her legs, issuing strident guidance on proper pelvic floor relaxation technique, and concluded that this was just about the *last* situation she wanted to find herself in, comparable only to having her own mother in the room for the blessed event. And even *that* might be preferable.

'We'll see,' she said, making a mental note to redouble her efforts to find someone – *anyone* – to save her from this fate.

Long after Sophie had closed down and gone home for the night, Anna remained at her desk, her angle-poise lamp creating a well of light in the otherwise darkened room. Not that she'd managed to make even a dent in her to-do list over the last several hours, despite her repeated efforts to knuckle down and make some proper headway. It didn't matter how many times she told herself she wasn't going to do it again; after a few minutes of forcing herself to give her undivided attention to the work she was actually being paid to do, her mind would invariably begin to drift and she'd find herself Alt-Tabbing back to JSTOR and clicking on just one more missing persons paper. And then, next thing she knew, another hour would have passed and the list of tasks requiring her urgent attention would be just as long as it had been before. Often longer.

She leaned back in her chair and rubbed her weary eyes with the heels of her hands. *All work and no play* indeed! When was the last time she'd been out with her friends; truly let her hair down? Even the rare occasions when she accepted an invitation to grab lunch or a coffee with a colleague invariably turned into excuses to talk shop. That was the trouble when your friends and co-workers were one and the same: the personal and the professional blended together until you could no longer reliably tell which was which. Daniel had been good for her in that respect. Whenever they'd visited a gallery or attended a wine tasting event or gone on a day out, it had invariably been his idea – all activities she'd genuinely enjoyed but would never have thought to initiate herself. He had, she realised in retrospect, made sure she had a life outside work to speak of. Since they'd gone their separate ways, her entire existence had telescoped to encompass her job and precious little besides.

She found her thoughts turning to Zoe, her sole remaining contact from her pre-uni days and just about the only friend she hadn't made through work. When was the last time they'd seen one another in the flesh, or even so much as exchanged an email or a text? For some time now, Zoe had been keeping an uncharacteristically low profile, ever since . . . well, the events three summers ago, the specifics of which Anna never had managed to get to the bottom of. At the time, she'd thought it best to give Zoe the space she needed, confident that she'd re-emerge and reconnect with her when she felt good and ready. But over two years had now passed, and Zoe remained as elusive as ever.

Curiosity getting the better of her, Anna opened a new browser tab and loaded Facebook. She'd been persuaded to sign up for an account a while back and had spent all of thirty seconds on it before concluding that it was a massive time-sink which her life would be greatly improved by avoiding. Zoe, on the other hand, was fully committed to the social media cause. A quick perusal of her page – on which, in a halfhearted bid for anonymity, she went by the name 'Fanny de Bergerac' – confirmed her as one of those people who felt the need to share every minor detail of their life with the whole world, from the latest Dr Weetabix video she'd watched on YouTube to whatever random thought had just come into her head. (Example: *How come Americans all have such massive teeth?*) In any event, Anna concluded from the plethora of duck-faced selfies and frequent talk of drunken shenanigans on nights out that Zoe, with her long flaming red hair and irrepressible gap-toothed grin, was still the life and soul of the party.

Which made the fact that she seemed to have been avoiding Anna like the clap all the more perplexing. Anna couldn't help wondering if she'd done something to offend her, or had inadvertently given the impression that she didn't want to see her. If things had been different, there was no question Zoe that would have been her natural choice for a birthing partner. If nothing else, she'd be able to help keep her mind off the pain and panic with a steady stream of dirty jokes and innuendos. Now, however, the ties that had once bound them together as tightly as lovers had frayed to the point that Anna couldn't think how she would even begin to make the approach to her.

She massaged her shoulders, turning her head this way and that as she tried to work out the crick in her neck. She glanced at the clock at the corner of her screen. 20:35. She'd burned enough oil for one day. Time to call it a night.

She shut up shop and let herself out of the department, crossing the deserted West Quadrangle in eerie solitude. The nights were rapidly drawing in now, and the ground was thick with soggy leaves as she tramped across the darkened grounds to her car.

Ten minutes later, as she sat behind the wheel, queuing at the last set of traffic lights on Hyndland Road before the turn-off to Clarence Drive, her mind wandered once more to the matter of Derek Sullivan. In the three weeks since she'd attended the case review, he'd seldom been far from her thoughts. She'd followed the progress on the case – or lack thereof – almost religiously, scanning the papers for news first thing in the morning, in addition to reading every piece of academic research on missing persons she could get her hands on. She now had a far deeper knowledge of the subject than someone who didn't study it for a living had any right to claim, and had amassed a laundry list of things she thought the police should be doing differently – from liaising more actively with their colleagues on a national level to harnessing the power of social media to reach people who didn't consume traditional news sources. More than once, she'd been tempted to pick up the phone and present her ideas to Vasilico. But something always stopped her. Partly it was because she suspected any attempts to tell him how to do his job were unlikely to be well-received, but partly too it was because the memory of how she'd left things with him still hung over her like a heavy cloud. Not for the first time in her life, she'd made a right arse of herself through her insistence on adopting the most dogmatic stance possible.

As she waited for the lights to change, her eyes strayed to two figures making their way along the pavement up ahead, one large, one small: a father and, clutching his hand, a girl of no more than three, dressed in a bright blue duffle coat and red wellington boots. *Just like Paddington Bear,* she thought, and smiled to herself. She watched as the girl stopped and turned to her father, saying something to him as she tugged on the hem of his coat. With a loving smile, he hoisted her off the ground and, placing her on his shoulders, continued on up the pavement. Anna watched them till they disappeared from view.

Her hand moved instinctively to her stomach, protruding below her swollen breasts like an oversized watermelon. In just a few short months, she'd be in the same position as that man: responsible for another life, obliged to respond to its every beck and call. She wondered if the man had a partner waiting for him at home – someone with whom to share the duties of childrearing – or if, like her, he was on his own.

Her thoughts strayed to another single parent–child relationship: that of Derek Sullivan and his father. She couldn't help but compare the affection she'd just witnessed between the man and his daughter with the elder Sullivan's purported indifference to his son's plight. *Singularly unperturbed* was how Vasilico had described him. She'd had enough experience of grief to know that it did strange things to a person, and yet she couldn't conceive of a scenario in which any father would simply shrug off his son's disappearance as a mere inconvenience. There had to be more to his apparent coldness than that, surely? *If you met him, you'd understand,* Vasilico had said. Perhaps, though she somehow doubted it. She *was* curious about him, though – there could be no denying that.

She remembered Vasilico mentioning that the elder Sullivan lived at the top of Gardner Street in the Partick area. Right now, she was almost as close to it as to her own home. More to the point, there was nothing waiting for her at the latter apart from a meal for one and, no doubt, several more hours in front of the computer, reading missing persons articles and feeling powerless. She had no idea whether he would open the door to her, far less agree to talk to her. And yet, wasn't it better to have tried and failed than to do nothing and wonder what might have been?

*Carpe diem,* she thought and, as the lights turned green, performed an unsignalled turn and set off back down the other side of Hyndland Road, serenaded by a barrage of irate horns.

# 6

# Fathers and Their Sons

There was only one Sullivan listed in the online phone directory as a resident of Gardner Street: a Mr Clive Sullivan, named as the occupant of a flat on the third floor of a corner tenement at the top of the hill, overlooking both Gardner Street itself and Partickhill Road. Anna parked at the kerb, headed into the building and tramped up the three flights of stone steps, trying her best to ignore the tall south-facing windows and the view they afforded of the steepest hill in Glasgow, falling away before her like the plunge of a rollercoaster track. She didn't have a great head for heights at the best of times, and the feelings of nausea that invariably accompanied such sights had only become worse since getting pregnant. Reaching her destination, she composed herself and rang the bell to flat 3/2.

The man who opened the door was of the old-school, stiff-upper-lip variety: in his late sixties, ramrod-straight, with a long thin face and a pencil moustache. The only thing missing was a military uniform.

'Can I help you?'

'Mr Sullivan? I'm sorry to trouble you so late.' Anna drew herself up to her full height – a futile attempt to compensate for his imposing stature. 'My name's Anna Scavolini. I'm a senior lecturer in the Department of Law and Social Sciences at Glasgow University. I was your son's dissertation supervisor.'

'I see.' Clive Sullivan regarded her coolly, his expression nonplussed. 'And what does that have to do with me?'

Anna was so wrong-footed by this that it took her a moment to formulate anything approaching a coherent response. 'Derek was doing a part-time

Masters in Criminology with us,' she said – aware, even as she spoke, that this didn't even come close to answering the question.

'Yes, yes, I know,' Sullivan snapped. 'None of that explains what you're doing at my door at nine o'clock on a Monday night, though, does it?'

She was hard-pressed to disagree, not least because she couldn't even articulate to herself what she hoped to gain from this visit, beyond a desire to satisfy her own morbid curiosity about the man himself – and she could hardly tell him, *I came to find out whether you really* are *a heartless wreck of a human being*, could she?

In the silence which followed, and as Sullivan continued to gaze at her, something in his expression changed. It took her a moment to realise he was looking at her protruding stomach.

'Oh,' he said, sounding almost alarmed. 'Forgive me, I didn't know . . . Here I am making you stand on ceremony while . . . '

He trailed off with a vague gesture in the direction of her belly, then cleared his throat awkwardly.

'Perhaps you should come in and take the weight off your feet.'

The living room into which Sullivan ushered Anna looked like it hadn't been redecorated since the 1950s. It was neat, orderly and, for a living room, looked decidedly un-lived-in. Anna pictured its occupant spending his evenings sitting alone, watching *University Challenge* and listening to Radio 4. She certainly didn't imagine it saw much use for the entertaining of guests.

'I'm afraid I can't offer you any tea,' Sullivan said. 'I used up my last bag this morning and I haven't had a chance to get to the shops yet. If I'd known I would be having company . . . '

'It's all right,' said Anna, sensing a proud homeowner's embarrassment. 'Just water will be fine.'

While her host busied himself in the kitchen, Anna, left to her own devices, sized the place up. There was precious little of the personal touch in evidence, barring a handful of framed photographs on the mantelpiece. She moved over to inspect them more closely. One showed Sullivan sitting in a deckchair wearing a sunhat and polo shirt, his hands folded across his chest. A small wooden shed was visible behind him; at his feet, a row of vegetable crops poked into view at the bottom of the frame. He must rent an allotment somewhere. The location pictured certainly wasn't the tiny basement-level communal garden she'd passed on her way into the building.

She moved on to the other photographs. One showed Sullivan as a much younger man – albeit every bit as upright and severe-looking as he was now – on what was evidently his wedding day, standing outside a small church with his arm around his considerably more diminutive wife. In another, he was pictured standing side by side with another man, the latter slightly older and decked out in full police dress uniform. The physical resemblance was unmissable: the same long, thin face and military bearing. Anna concluded that this must be his brother, the late Chief Superintendent.

The final picture seemed, at first glance, to be a recreation of the second, albeit with one of the participants having been replaced. Clive Sullivan was again present, closer now to his present age. Standing next to him, wearing a uniform similar to that sported by his late uncle, was Derek, looking as awkward and uncomfortable as Anna had ever known him to be.

'That was the day he was sworn in.'

Anna almost jumped at the sound of the elder Sullivan's voice. She turned to find him standing just behind her, his arm extended as he offered her a glass of water.

'Thanks.' She accepted the glass and, as a show of gratitude, took a perfunctory sip.

Sullivan drew alongside her, arms folded behind his back as he gazed at the row of pictures. He nodded to the one of himself and his son. 'A proud day for us both,' he declared, 'and certainly my proudest as a father. "Finally," I said, "he's made something of himself".'

Anna was left in little doubt, both from the consternation implicit in Sullivan's tone and from what she knew about Derek's post-graduation fortunes, that those sentiments had been short-lived. Sullivan, however, chose not to elaborate, instead continuing to gaze at the picture in silence. In so many ways, father and son seemed to be the antithesis of one another. Where the younger man was short and stocky, the older was tall and thin. Where the father carried himself with the stern dignity of a man utterly secure in his understanding of his place in the world, the son oozed uncertainty from every pore, the nervous half-smile suggesting that he wasn't entirely sure how he'd ended up in his present situation. Anna had a strong suspicion that he'd inherited most of these traits, physical and otherwise, from his mother.

'Did he always want to join the police?' she asked, partly to fill the increasingly oppressive silence and partly in the hope that she might persuade Sullivan to open up about their relationship.

Sullivan made a noise at the back of his throat that was somewhere between a laugh and a cough. 'Chance would have been a fine thing! From the moment he was born, I can't recollect a single occasion when he exhibited anything approximating what I gather is known in the trade as a "calling". I suspect, if he'd been allowed to have his way, he'd simply have cruised through life in whatever fashion required the least amount of effort on his part. I indulged him till he graduated university. Then, when he showed no inclination of putting that *comparative literature* degree of his to practical use' – his voice dripped contempt as he uttered the words – 'I sat him down and told him that either he found a way to provide for himself or I'd find one for him. In the end, he elected to follow in my late brother's footsteps.'

Anna felt like asking whether, in this instance, *elected* meant *was browbeaten into*, but managed to restrain herself.

'And how did he find it?' she asked. 'Did he enjoy the work, do you think?'

'It put food on the table,' Sullivan replied, as if work wasn't something you were supposed to enjoy. He paused, before gesturing to the seating area. 'Shall we?'

Anna did as she was bidden, easing herself into a low, floral-patterned sofa while her host settled in an armchair as tall and straight-backed as himself. He looked at her expectantly, clearly still awaiting an answer to the question that had so flummoxed her on the doorstep.

'How are you bearing up, Mr Sullivan?' she asked, for lack of a better opening gambit.

Sullivan snorted contemptuously. 'What sort of a question is that?'

'Well, I mean, it must be a difficult time for you. A worrying time. I'd imagine anyone in your shoes would feel the same.'

'It is what it is. It's not as if there's anything I can do to affect the course of events, so there seems little point getting exercised about the situation.'

The rational part of Anna's mind recognised a certain cold, pragmatic logic in this philosophy. The part governed by normal human emotions wanted to grab him by the collar and shake some sense into him.

'I understand the police are keeping you informed about developments,' she said.

'Oh yes.' Sullivan's voice was heavy with sarcasm. 'Every Friday, at four on the dot, I have the pleasure of the company of two imbeciles from the Major Investigations Team, who are unable to provide me with any fresh information as to the whereabouts of my son, but nonetheless are at great pains to convey to me just how much they *care*.'

Anna could see how such platitudes would be of little comfort under the circumstances. In Sullivan's case, however, he seemed to possess an active contempt for anything approaching compassion that bordered on pathological.

'It was really Derek's work I wanted to talk to you about,' she said. 'I'm . . . well, I suppose I'm trying to build up more of a picture of his life in the weeks leading up to his disappearance.'

'Indeed? And might I ask why you've taken it upon yourself to undertake such an endeavour? Do you, by any chance, moonlight as a private investigator when you're not teaching at the university?'

'No, but he was my student. I'm concerned for his wellbeing.'

'I see. You're another one who *cares*.' That same sneering contempt again. After a moment, however, it passed, replaced by a weary fatalism. 'Well, it's up to you which particular lost causes you choose to attach yourself to. Though, if you ask me, you're wasting your time – as indeed are those who decided, in their wisdom, to divert precious resources to what is, in all likelihood, a futile endeavour.'

'What do *you* think happened to Derek, Mr Sullivan?' Anna asked. It wasn't so much that she believed he had any particular insight into what had become of his son, but she wanted to know why he was so convinced that looking for him was a waste of time.

'My son's a grown man,' said Sullivan. 'I'm not his keeper. He's free to come and go as he pleases. Free to make his own decisions.'

'I understand that,' said Anna, aware that her patience for both his callousness and his obfuscation, deliberate or otherwise, was stretched to breaking point. 'But you must have given some thought to what might have become of him. I mean, you're clearly of the opinion that whatever happened to him happened of his own volition.'

'Or as a result of choices he made. We're each responsible for our own actions and how we choose to respond to the circumstances in which we find ourselves. That's how you determine the measure of a man: how he acquits himself in the face of adversity.'

'And what adversity was Derek facing? I gather,' she went on, taking care to keep her tone relaxed and conversational, 'that he wasn't having the best time of it at work.'

Sullivan scoffed contemptuously. 'Told you that, did he, during one of your one-to-one tutoring sessions? He always was prone to making mountains out of molehills. I doubt very much that he was subjected to anything worse than what goes on every day in the average schoolyard.'

'With respect, Mr Sullivan,' said Anna, 'from what I gather it was rather more than just a spot of playground teasing. Would Derek—' She stopped herself, suspecting she already knew the answer to what she was going to ask.

'Yes?' Sullivan's sharp eyes bored into her.

'Would Derek have confided in you if he had a problem? I mean, if something was troubling him – I mean *really* troubling him – do you think he would have turned to you?'

'Well, I like to think so,' said Sullivan, haughtily and a little too quickly. 'I always made it clear that, if he ever found himself in any difficulty, financial or . . . or . . . ' He trailed off into a faltering, flustered mumble.

Anna couldn't think when she'd last witnessed such a transparent exercise in deliberately missing the point. 'Mr Sullivan,' she said firmly, 'that's not what I'm asking, and I think you know it. What I mean is, if he was having problems at work, would he have felt able to talk to you about them?'

'Well, I mean' – Sullivan continued to equivocate, his cheeks turning ruddy – 'that's not really how men are with one another, is it? I suppose it's different for you women when it comes to sharing your personal woes . . . '

'Again with respect, we're not talking about *men* here. We're talking about your son.'

'Well, you need a mother for that touchy-feely stuff, don't you?' Sullivan snapped, embarrassment giving way to exasperation. 'And his was taken from us long before her time. All I know is that I raised my son to the best of my abilities, and I taught him to do what was right and to never shirk his responsibilities. I taught him to speak out if he saw an injustice being committed . . . even if it came at personal cost.'

'Is that what happened?' said Anna, quietly but intently. 'Did Derek witness something and speak out?'

For a long stretch, Sullivan said nothing. He stared at Anna, poker-faced, the rasp of his breathing audible over the hum of the radiator.

'Mr Sullivan?'

After several moments, he deflated somewhat, his posture slackening, the bags under his eyes seeming to grow heavier.

'About six months into the job, Derek came to me about something that had happened at work. For most of his probation, he'd been partnered with a more experienced officer – a constable like him, but with several more years on the clock. One day, while they were out on patrol, his partner insisted they make a detour so he could take care of what he called some "business". He drove to a house on London Road and asked Derek to come in with him, telling him he wanted him there as backup.

'As soon as they crossed the threshold, it was obvious the place was a . . . ' – he lowered his voice, as if to spare Anna's blushes – ' . . . a brothel.' There were women in there wandering around without any . . . Well, anyway, Derek observed his partner collecting money from the woman who ran the place, and afterwards, when they came outside, he shoved a couple of fifties into Derek's pocket and told him, "That's for your support back there".

'A few days later, Derek told me everything and asked me what he should do. Naturally, I told him it was his duty to report the man. An officer of the law, collecting protection money from a whore-house? It couldn't be allowed to stand. So he went to his superior, told him what had happened and handed over the money. His superior thanked him for his candour and assured him he'd take care of the matter. He thought that would be the end of it, but it turned out it was just the beginning.'

Anna said nothing, not trusting herself to interrupt in case she inadvertently brought Sullivan's unexpected streak of forthcomingness to a premature end.

'Needless to say,' Sullivan went on, 'there was an internal investigation. Nothing official, all strictly off the record, but they hauled the pair of them in individually to give their version of events. His partner copped to what he'd been up to straight away, but he claimed Derek had been a willing participant and pointed to their splitting the proceeds as proof. And Derek could hardly deny having taken the money, or that he'd waited a number of days before raising the alarm. Proof, in their eyes, that he'd only come clean after his conscience had caught up with him.

'Of course, any fool could see that, guilty or innocent, Derek wasn't the one calling the shots. They split the pair of them up – moved the partner on to a different division while Derek remained at Cambridge Street. It was supposed to have been kept on the QT – less chance of it becoming a public scandal that way. But word got around, as it is wont to do. Nobody ever confronted him directly, and yet, from that moment on, he was a marked man to his colleagues. All the most unpleasant jobs seemed to come his way, and he was convinced his superiors were altering his shifts at minimal notice just to spite him. And, any time he entered the squad room or the canteen, the other officers would all go quiet, as if they'd been talking about him behind his back – or so he thought. And then there were the pranks.'

'Pranks?'

'On one occasion, someone urinated in his locker. On another, they left a dead rat in his sandwich box. There were other, similar incidents, but those should give you a flavour of how his integrity was rewarded.'

'And how did he respond to these . . . pranks?' asked Anna, somehow feeling that the word scarcely did justice to what Sullivan had described.

'Told him to tough it out, didn't I?' Sullivan retorted, as if it was the only reasonable course of action. 'I told him they were testing him, trying to find out where his limits lay, seeing if they could break him. I told him not to give them the satisfaction; said that if he just kept his head down and took it on the chin, sooner or later they'd realise they were on a hiding to nothing. Perhaps they'd even come to respect him for being made of sterner stuff than they'd realised. After all, that's all anyone ever wants, isn't it? The acceptance of one's peers.'

'Except that's not what happened, is it?' said Anna. She could see the chain of events with crystal clarity. 'Instead of accepting him, they ramped up their bullying, making his life a misery, until one day he'd had enough and decided his only option was to cut and run.'

Sullivan snorted contemptuously. Already, he seemed to have reverted to his previous state of indignant indifference. 'Well, in that case, he's even more of a weakling than I gave him credit for. You call it bullying; I call it a normal part of growing up. At least it was when I was his age.'

'Built character, did it?'

'It raised men rather than weaklings!' the old man snapped. He looked to Anna to be on the verge of spontaneously combusting. 'I wouldn't expect *you* to understand.'

'Oh, I think I understand just fine. Never mind basic human decency. Never mind love or compassion. The most important thing is keeping a stiff upper lip and taking your beatings like a man.'

'Well, since you're such an expert in childrearing, perhaps I should have delegated the task to you!' Sullivan retorted. 'Lord knows, his mother would probably have agreed with you.

'But then,' he mused, more softly now and seeming, to Anna, to be speaking more to himself than to her, 'perhaps that's where things went wrong. She always was a great one for indulging him – coddling him, wrapping him in cotton wool, letting him spend all his time indoors, reading and making models, while all the other boys his age were off having adventures and getting into scrapes.'

He sighed unhappily. 'Perhaps I should have put my foot down – insisted he had the same experiences as any other child his age. But she was forever telling me that he was different from the other boys – more sensitive, more in need of protecting from the big bad world. Then came the endless parade of shrinks and therapists, giving him a complex about himself, putting him on those pills, filling his head with—'

Anna looked up sharply. 'Pills? What pills?'

A look of alarm momentarily crossed Sullivan's face as he realised he'd said too much, before being replaced by a surly scowl. 'Never mind. Forget I said anything.'

Anna stared at him intently. 'Are you telling me Derek was on medication?'

But Sullivan was already shutting down, retreating to a state of pinch-lipped obstinance. 'I said forget it. It's not important.'

Anna was on her feet now, hauling herself upright despite the best efforts of the sofa's deep folds to suck her back in. 'Mr Sullivan, if Derek has some kind of condition that requires him to take medication, I'd say that's pretty pertinent to his current situation, wouldn't you?'

Sullivan glared up at her with a last burst of defiance. Then the fight seemed to go out of him and his shoulders slumped. 'All right. If you must know, in his mid-teens, one of the succession of quacks his mother insisted on taking him to see diagnosed him with something called schizoaffective disorder. It's a mental health condition. They say it means—'

'I know what it means,' said Anna.

The signs had been staring her in the face all along: the difficulty forming and maintaining relationships, the poor timekeeping and concentration, the lack of ordered thoughts when he put pen to paper . . . Certainly not enough to make a definitive diagnosis, but all signs that she, as someone with a mood disorder herself, should have been attuned to spot in someone else. At the very least, she ought to have *considered* the mental health angle as a possible explanation for the myriad problems Derek had exhibited. But her initial feelings of self-reproach quickly faded in the face of the cold fury now rising up inside her towards his father.

'This wasn't something he disclosed to his employers, I take it,' she said – though she knew the answer was a foregone conclusion.

'It was none of their business,' said Sullivan stiffly. 'He felt it was better they didn't find out.'

'I wonder where he could have got *that* idea from.'

Sullivan gave Anna a scornful look, his old combativeness rekindling. 'Isn't it obvious? Imagine you're a prospective employer and you've succeeded in whittling the list of applicants down to two more or less evenly matched candidates. Which one are you going to give the job to? I don't care what you parrot about diversity quotas and inclusivity and the Equality Act – it's not going to be the young lad who's mentioned in his personal statement that he's on mood stabilisers and has a history of paranoid delusions. Anyone who claims otherwise is a liar. And once he'd been formally accepted onto the training programme and they asked him if he had any health concerns they should be aware of and he looked them in the eye and still said "no" . . . well, there was no rowing back, was there?'

'And when he was reported missing, you didn't think that perhaps the circumstances had changed? That it might be a good idea now to tell them? Not even when the days turned into weeks?'

'Well, it's not something you talk about, is it?' Sullivan snapped. 'Oh, I know it's all the rage these days – being diagnosed with the latest trendy condition, assigning a label to everything. But there's such a thing as having a sense of dignity; of not making a scene; of not broadcasting your problems to the world and expecting it to bend over to accommodate you.'

A minute ago, Anna would have doubted there was anything left that could have shocked her about this strange, coldhearted man whose relationship with his son barely even deserved to be called as such. Now, however, she was so appalled she could barely form words. She could see it all clearly now. A young man with a mental health condition which predisposed him to negative thoughts and feelings of paranoia had been subjected to a campaign of covert bullying by his peers, and this, coupled with a lack of support from an emotionally hamstrung father, had pushed him over the edge.

'You were ashamed of him, weren't you?' she said. 'Even when you knew his life might be in danger, you still couldn't bring yourself to admit your own son might be "defective" in some way.'

For a long while, Sullivan said nothing. He sat with his head bowed, eyes fixed on the rug at his feet.

'I never believed it,' he said at last, a hint of something other than defensiveness entering his voice for the first time. 'I thought the doctors were just humouring his mother – telling her what she wanted to hear, feeding her a bunch of pat excuses designed to absolve her of any responsibility for his problems. Now, though? Now I don't know *what* to believe.' He looked up at Anna, the corners of his eyes quivering slightly. 'You hear things, don't you? About people with ... problems ... who listen to the demons inside their heads and go off and do something foolish.'

He appeared to have shrunk before her eyes – a wizened husk of a man dwarfed by the frame of his chair, his eyes sunken and hollow.

'Are you saying you think your son is dead?' she said quietly.

He didn't answer at once. He sat there, unspeaking, unmoving, as if he'd turned to stone. Anna was beginning to wonder whether he'd heard her when he finally expelled a deep, mournful breath.

'Well,' he said, with a weary fatalism that seemed to suck all the air out of the room, 'I suppose that scenario would be considerably less messy than some of the alternatives.'

Afterwards, Sullivan saw Anna to the door. She assumed they had nothing more to say to one another, but as she stepped out into the hallway, he cleared his throat awkwardly.

'I'm not sure it counts for anything,' he said, unable to meet her eye, 'but I gather he enjoyed his time on your course. Spoke about it in positively glowing terms, the few times it came up. He had nothing but praise for his tutors. You . . . well, it seems you made something of an impression on him.'

'That's . . . very kind of you to say.'

She had no intention of telling him the truth: that for most of the time Derek had spent under her tutelage, she'd wanted nothing more than to be shot of him. Far better to let him believe his son had had some measure of enjoyment amid what appeared to have been an otherwise dismally unhappy existence.

'He took care of my brother's effects.' Sullivan's words cut into her thoughts.

'I'm sorry?'

'When he died, back in July, it was . . . well, it was very sudden. The house needed emptying before it could be put on the market. Derek offered to take care of it, because I . . . well . . . '

It took Anna a moment to understand that he was trying to tell her he'd been unable to face the task himself; that Derek had stepped in to spare his father any further distress. It was, she suspected, his way of conveying that, in spite of all prior evidence to the contrary, a part of him at least was proud of his son.

'Oh,' she said. 'That was . . . that was good of him.'

'Yes,' Sullivan agreed, 'it was.'

For a moment, they stood facing each other on either side of the doorway, saying nothing. Then Sullivan muttered a brusque 'goodnight' and shut the door, leaving Anna standing alone in the cold, darkened hallway.

# 7

# Night Call

Once she was safely back inside her car with the heating turned up, Anna got out her phone and dialled Vasilico's number. He picked up a few rings later.

'Paul Vasilico.'

'Detective, it's Anna Scavolini.'

*'Anna!'* Vasilico's tone positively oozed delight, as if hers was just the voice he'd been hoping to hear. As if he'd been waiting all day for her call. 'To what do I owe?'

'I'm not interrupting anything, am I?' She could hear what sounded like papers being shuffled in the background.

'For you, I've got all the time in the world. What's on your mind?'

'It's . . . look, I think you'd be better hearing this in person. I'm in the car now. Can we meet somewhere?'

'Why don't you come up to the office?'

'Are you sure? There's not some rule against having civilians on the premises after hours?'

Vasilico laughed. 'Well, I won't let on if you don't. Come on up. I'll tell Gary to keep an eye out for you.'

Twenty minutes later, Anna rolled up at MIT headquarters on High Street. At the entrance, she found a middle-aged nightwatchman in a peaked cap and fleece waiting for her.

'He's upstairs,' he said, before Anna could get a word out. 'This way.'

Anna thought she detected more than a hint of resentment from him as she followed him into the building and across the darkened foyer, presumably at having been called away from whatever pressing responsibilities normally consumed him at this time of night to serve as Vasilico's personal lookout and doorman. They tramped upstairs to the third floor, where he buzzed open the door to the bullpen and stepped aside to let Anna go first.

The place was deserted, the deskchairs lying empty, the computer screens blank. A handful of desklamps had been left on, but the room was otherwise in darkness. There was no sign of Vasilico. Anna assumed the doorman was going to show her where she was meant to go, but when she turned to face him, she found that he'd already disappeared from sight, his footsteps receding down the stairs.

Just as she was wondering where Vasilico could possibly be and why he'd entrusted her delivery to such a surly individual instead of coming out to meet her himself, Anna spotted a glimmer of light coming from a half-open door at the far end of the room. She headed over and peered round the door into what turned out to be a tiny, cluttered office. Files and piles of papers occupied every available surface. At the heart of it all, seated behind a desk strewn with paperwork and empty carry-out cartons, was Vasilico, brows knotted in concentration as he pored over an open file. So intense was his concentration that he didn't realise he had an audience until Anna rapped on the doorframe.

He looked up, breaking into a delighted smile that belied his rumpled suit and five o'clock shadow. 'Well well, look at *you*. You're positively blossoming.'

'Positively ballooning, more like,' she said ruefully, stepping into the room.

She'd come here half-expecting – and, if she was being honest with herself, half-relishing – some sort of confrontation. They'd hardly parted on the warmest of terms the last time she'd been here, and the revelations from her conversation with Clive Sullivan had done nothing to improve her view of the organisation he served. And yet, as he leapt to his feet to clear a pile of papers from a nearby chair for her, she realised he'd already succeeded in disarming her, blunting her stomach for a fight with his winsome smile and easy repartee. As she sank into the now vacant seat, she reminded herself that Vasilico had had nothing to do with Derek's treatment; that, though he worked for an institution about which she felt ambivalent at best, he wasn't the enemy here.

She blew out a breath. 'I thought *my* hours were unsociable, but this is something else. Tell me, is it normal for a DCI to still be slaving away at half-ten at night when everyone else has gone home?'

'No, but these aren't exactly normal times.' Vasilico affected a grimace. 'De Groot's got a bee in his bonnet about something. I don't know – maybe it's because we're approaching six weeks since the boy Derek did his vanishing trick and still not a sausage. Either way, he's really stepped up the pressure, hence . . . ' He gestured to the mountains of paperwork around him. 'All this has to be gone through with a fine toothcomb in the off-chance we've missed something.'

His failure to come out and meet her in person now made sense. She'd been in his shoes enough times herself to know that, when you were up against a looming deadline, it was all too easy to let the social niceties fall by the wayside.

'Well,' she said, setting her bag down at her feet, 'I might be able to help you out there.'

Vasilico gazed back at her pleasantly. 'Oh yes? Do pray tell.'

By the time Anna reached the end of her account, Vasilico was almost apoplectic. She could see him seething silently, his jaw becoming tighter and tighter as he struggled to keep a lid on his growing anger. As she fell silent, he balled his fist and slammed it hard against the desk.

'What the *hell* was he playing at? What possessed him to keep something like this from us?'

Anna sighed helplessly. 'It's like you said yourself: he's of a different era. And he's proud. He clearly thinks it reflects negatively on him that his son—'

'I'm not talking about the old man!' Vasilico snapped. 'I'm talking about the son. *Our* Sullivan. Why the hell did he not tell his employers he was schizo?' He was on his feet, pacing, rubbing incessantly at the bridge of his nose.

'I don't know,' Anna said helplessly, privately suspecting that Derek would have had any number of reasons, many of them well-founded, for not disclosing his condition – not least the fact that, by law, he was under no obligation to do so.

'If you ask me,' Vasilico muttered, talking at least in part to himself, 'one's as bad as the other. It's like the two of them have conspired to make things as difficult as humanly possible for us.' He finally came to a halt, turning to face Anna with an imploring look. 'If we'd known he had mental health problems, we'd have had boots on the ground the moment he didn't show up for work. We would have *helped* him.'

'Would you? Or would he just have been making another rod for his own back? Another reason for his colleagues to shun him, to bully him, to grind him down?'

Vasilico said nothing, but Anna sensed, from the look in his eyes, that he was privately wondering the exact same thing.

'Did you know anything about this business with his partner?' she asked. 'Last time I was here, when you were giving me that whole spiel about transparency and accountability, were you quietly sitting on the fact that he'd been at the centre of yet another hushed-up corruption scandal?'

Vasilico didn't respond immediately. He remained on his feet, facing her from the opposite side of the table, his jaw set. 'I knew there'd been some trouble,' he said eventually. 'Some sort of disciplinary matter that had been dealt with unofficially. But I wasn't aware of the specifics.'

'And let me guess – you decided the best thing for it was to adopt a policy of "don't ask, don't tell". This is why you lot get a reputation for closing ranks, you know. It's like you can't help yourselves.'

Vasilico gave Anna a long, hard look, the seething resentment behind his expression unmistakeable.

'You know what this means, don't you?' she continued. 'It means we can't rule out the possibility of his disappearance being the result of some sort of reprisal for his whistleblowing.'

Vasilico's eyes didn't leave her. 'You're suggesting one of his colleagues could have . . . ?' He trailed off into silence, then shook his head. 'That doesn't add up. There's a world of difference between pissing in a man's locker and what *you're* suggesting. Besides, this business with his partner was – what, a couple of years back? Why wait until now to . . . ? No,' he went on, his tone more resolute, 'no, I fancy some sort of mental break-down is the most credible explanation.'

Anna was minded to agree, though she noted that once again Vasilico seemed markedly unwilling to countenance any suggestion of nefarious behaviour on the part of his colleagues.

Vasilico sighed and slammed down into his chair, so suddenly and violently that Anna flinched. 'Jesus *Christ*,' he hissed, 'what a clusterfuck.'

She gazed across at him, sitting there with his forehead resting on his hand, and felt a pang of sympathy for him. He was angry, exhausted, frustrated and, judging by his earlier comments about De Groot, under extreme pressure from his superiors to deliver a result. She recognised, too, that on some level he felt responsible for the present situation – whether because he believed he'd failed to show due diligence or simply because he took the view that, as senior investigating officer, every success or failure ultimately reflected on him.

'Hey.' She laid a hand on the desk, within touching distance of his arm. 'We all missed the mental health angle. I taught him for over a year and it never once crossed my mind.'

Vasilico gave a tired, thin smile and shook his head. 'If I'd only applied to access his medical records . . . '

'And what possible reason could you have had to do that? You can only act on the information available to you.'

Vasilico glowered at the desk in silence. Anna could tell he wasn't convinced.

'He'd have been taking regular antipsychotic medication,' she said, 'and his dad mentioned he'd been on mood stabilisers – probably lithium or carbamazapine. You should look into where he gets his prescription. Find out when it was last filled. You never know – he might still be collecting it.'

She was clutching at straws, looking for any possible glimmer of hope in a thoroughly hopeless situation, but she felt they could both do with a bit of cheering up right now.

Slowly, Vasilico's expression grew more resolved. 'Well, if there's one good thing to come from tonight's shenanigans, it's this: they'll have no excuse not to grant me additional resources now. No more half-measures. This is a clear, inarguable case of a vulnerable, at-risk individual, where-abouts unknown.'

He was on his feet again, shifting armfuls of paper to uncover his desk phone. Anna watched as he snatched up the receiver and dialled an extension. It cheered her in ways she hadn't anticipated to see him moving with determination and purpose once again.

'Maggie,' he said, when the recipient picked up, 'it's Vasilico. New information's come to light in the Derek Sullivan case. I'm convening an urgent meeting of all department heads for seven a.m. sharp tomorrow. Alert all the relevant parties.'

He ended the call, then turned to Anna, still holding the phone. 'I need to brief the ACC. He'll want to know.'

It took her a moment to realise he was asking her to give him some privacy. As she got to her feet and headed towards the door, he began to key in the number.

'Anna.'

She turned in the doorway to see him standing with the receiver clutched to his chest. He smiled at her and mouthed a silent 'thank you'. She acknowledged him with a nod and slipped out.

The cold air hit her like a tidal wave as she stepped out into the night. She halted under the shadow of the building, breathing in deeply as she collected her thoughts. Like Vasilico, she felt energised. Energised and strangely buoyant. There was no doubt that tonight's revelations meant Derek was at far greater risk of harm than either of them had previously thought possible, but she nonetheless felt the first stirrings of hope she'd experienced in a long time.

Finally, it seemed, things were going to move.

# 8

# A Long Drop

And move they did. The following morning, at the hastily convened meeting of department heads, the Derek Sullivan case was re-assessed and accorded the highest possible risk level. Anna wasn't present, but Vasilico relayed the gist of it to her in a phone call afterwards. He'd been granted substantial increases in both budget and manpower, which meant more boots pounding the streets; more doors being hammered; more jakeys being woken up in shop doorways to have pictures of 'our boy' shoved under their noses (his words). The police helicopter was scrambled, the Dog Unit was dispatched to comb the Cowcaddens area, and the media campaign was ramped up, with Derek's face plastered on the Wednesday editions of every local newspaper and a few of the nationals. That same day, a press conference was held, at which Vasilico made a fresh appeal for witnesses. Anna, watching it on the evening news, couldn't help but note Clive Sullivan's conspicuous absence, though this hardly came as a shock.

'We're desperately worried about our friend and colleague Derek Sullivan,' Vasilico told the assembled throng. 'I wish to make it clear to him, if he's watching or listening, that he's not in any trouble. Derek, we miss you and want you to come home.'

As he spoke, gazing earnestly into the camera, Anna was forced to concede that, as hollow as the words sounded given what she knew of how Derek's colleagues had treated him, Vasilico's technique was impressive.

Whether Derek, if he was still out there somewhere, would buy into it was another matter entirely.

'We look after each other in the Force,' Vasilico continued. 'We're a family. We all care deeply about our missing colleague and look forward to giving him the support he needs.'

As time passed, it became increasingly clear that a breakthrough wasn't going to happen anytime soon. The wave of hope that had briefly carried Anna on Monday night swiftly faded. She knew, given how much time had passed, that the odds of Derek being found alive and well somewhere in the city were vanishingly slim, and as October drew to a close, all the old feelings of guilt and self-recrimination returned. She found herself wondering if she'd given him shorter shrift than she would have given another student who had the same academic shortcomings but wasn't seconded from the police. Perhaps, on some subconscious level, she'd even *wanted* him to fail and be sent back to his employers with his tail between his legs, proof that the partnership scheme was an ill-thought-out waste of time.

Shortly after 1 p.m. on the first Friday of November, Anna was sitting alone at a table in the little café at the top of Woodlands Road, munching her way through an extra-large black bean burrito (extra beans, extra guacamole). On the other side of the café, the entrance door opened and closed, accompanied by a brief gust of cold air from the outside world. She looked up to see Vasilico making his way towards her, his relaxed stride suggesting that he was wholly unconcerned about his lateness.

'I swear,' he said, looking her up and down, 'you keep getting more pregnant every time I see you.'

'Sort of the way it works.'

He eyed the half-eaten burrito in front of her. 'Generous portion you've got there.'

Anna winced sheepishly. 'I was just going to have soup, but this caught my eye and I couldn't resist.'

'Well, I've heard of stranger cravings,' said Vasilico amiably, shrugging off his overcoat.

*Ain't that the truth.* She decided against mentioning that her current go-to comfort food was Golden Crunch Creams dipped in chocolate milk.

'That's your hormones talking,' Sophie Hennessy had said when she'd mentioned it the other day, nudging her and winking conspiratorially, as if this was Special Pregnancy Knowledge to which only a select few were entitled. 'No joke, while I was having Cosmo, I used to get wicked cravings for Oreos and mustard.'

She suppressed a shudder. If she ever found herself hankering after *that*, she'd know she was losing it completely.

'Are *you* eating?' she asked, as Vasilico settled in the seat opposite.

Vasilico shot another look at her plate and shook his head. 'Tempting though it would be to join you in fried bean heaven, I'll pass. I already grabbed a sandwich earlier, and not all of us are eating for two.' He attracted the attention of a passing barista. 'Americano, please. Black.'

As the barista departed with his order, Anna looked at him expectantly. 'Well? What's the latest news?'

Vasilico smiled. 'Always straight to the point. Fair enough. You're not the only one on the clock.' His expression turned serious. 'The short version is that there *is* no news. We managed to trace Derek's medication supply to a pharmacy in Garrowhill and established that his most recent prescription, due to have been filled on the twelfth of October, went uncollected.'

'Oh,' said Anna, unable to hide her disappointment, though it was what she'd already anticipated. 'No response to the public appeal, I take it?'

'Oh, there's been plenty of response – just none of it any use. That's the trouble with cases like this. Everyone loves the thought of doing their bit, but the end result is a slew of false positives, all of which have to be investigated and ruled out. And as for the cranks – the ones who deliberately make stuff up to get attention . . . don't get me started on *them*.'

He fell silent as the barista returned with his Americano, nodding his thanks to her. He took a sip, checked to make sure she was out of earshot, then continued:

'We checked in again with all the local hostels and homeless shelters. No joy there, either. If our boy's still alive, it's a safe bet he's a long way from Glasgow.'

Anna said nothing. She gazed down at her still-laden plate, her appetite gone.

Vasilico paused for another sip of his Americano. 'I also spoke to Sullivan Senior again.'

'And?'

'As anticipated, he wasn't exactly *thrilled* to be asked to provide chapter and verse, though he ultimately buckled and gave me more or less the same account he gave you. On which note,' he added, a hint of mirth entering his voice as he wagged a chiding finger at Anna, 'it was rather remiss of me not to take you to task for taking matters into your own hands with the old man. But then, I gather you have something of a history of overstepping the mark when it comes to police business.'

There were few things more certain to get Anna's back up than being treated like an errant child. 'In which case,' she replied, not missing a beat, 'it would be remiss of *me* not to point out that, if it wasn't for me "overstepping the mark", you lot would still be labouring under the belief that Derek Sullivan had a clean bill of mental health.' She shrugged. 'Perhaps it just rankles you that I was able to get my hands on information you missed.'

Vasilico smiled, genuinely amused. 'Game, set and match. Mind you,' he went on, as Anna pushed her unfinished meal to one side, 'there's a certain irony to be noted in all this.'

'Which is . . . ?'

'Well, I can't help but note that your determination to hamstring the police with all these new checks and balances is a touch hypocritical given your own fondness for going off piste.'

Anna scoffed. 'Oh, come on. The two aren't remotely comparable.'

'Right – the difference being that when you take the law into your own hands it's perfectly acceptable, but the moment we put so much as a foot out of line you run straight to the Sunday broadsheets claiming we're out of control.'

'Excuse me, but I didn't abuse my position in any way. I merely paid Clive Sullivan a visit in my capacity as his son's university tutor, expressing my concern for his wellbeing.' She shrugged, feigning nonchalance. 'We talked, and he happened to divulge information that proved pertinent to the case.'

'Oh, come *on*,' Vasilico chuckled. 'You can't seriously expect me to swallow that. Why don't you just admit you went there with the express intention of showing us up?'

'Is that how you feel? That I showed you up? That I made a dent in your ego?' She was the one doing the mocking now, mimicking his chiding tone from earlier. 'That's the thing about taking the time to talk to people and listen to what they have to say: sometimes you learn things that get missed when you go in all guns blazing. Did it ever occur to you,' she went on, casually tracing a circle on the tabletop with her finger, 'that the world would be a noticeably better place if there were a few less trigger-happy police officers in it and a few more people willing to take a more . . . enlightened approach?'

Vasilico threw back his head and laughed. 'A *splendid* idea. Absolutely faultless. Let's solve all the world's problems by talking and listening. But allow me to go one better: why not just do away with the police altogether and leave it to the academics and special-interest agitators to enforce law and order?'

Anna rolled her eyes. 'That's a strawman and you know it. I've never claimed to want a world with *no* police.'

'All right, then – just one where we're stripped of all our agency and drowning in red tape. Because if there's one thing I've learned, it's that people with your agenda are never satisfied. There's always one more layer of bureaucracy that needs to be added.'

'And if there's one thing *I've* learned,' Anna shot back, 'it's that those most eager to accord themselves power are invariably the least qualified to wield it fairly.'

'You know,' Vasilico jabbed a finger at her, giving no indication that he'd listened to a word she'd said, 'perhaps we should ask the public – who, incidentally, are *overwhelmingly* favourable in their view of the police – who they'd rather turn to to resolve their problems if they get mugged or duffed up or burgled: their local beat bobby or their local professor of gender studies.'

Anna sighed and tilted her eyes towards the ceiling. 'Be serious.'

But Vasilico wasn't finished. 'In fact,' he continued, his voice rising as he became increasingly exercised, 'I've got an even better idea. Perhaps you should try going and living in a country that doesn't *have* a properly functioning police force. I guarantee you wouldn't last a week. Because the cold, hard reality is that it's thanks to my colleagues and I that you're free to write your articles denigrating us instead of spending every waking moment worrying that some random sicko's going to pull a knife on you next time you step out of your ivory tower.' He paused to let his words sink in. 'I came here today as a favour, you know,' he said after a moment, his voice once more at its normal level. 'I didn't have to keep you in the loop.'

'And I'm grateful for that,' said Anna quietly, feeling a stab of resentment towards him for compelling her to say it.

'You've a queer way of showing it.' He frowned at her, as if trying to make sense of her. 'Actually, I don't think you realise just how much capacity your words have to hurt people. Now me, I can take it. I've had worse thrown at me. But have you ever stopped to consider just how galling it is for the men and women who devote themselves to keeping the citizens of this city safe – who put their lives on the line day in, day out – to have to read diatribes decrying them all as thugs and bullies?' He drained his cup and set it down. 'We don't ask for anyone's thanks, but it would be nice if, every now and then, our efforts were acknowledged.'

Vasilico fell silent. The noise of the café continued around them, but he and Anna sat, saying nothing, neither looking at the other. Anna wondered how it was that they'd come to be arguing about this. She wasn't sure which of them had started it, but she recognised that she'd done nothing to defuse the situation.

She looked at her watch. Realising it was later than she'd anticipated, she eased herself upright and set about tugging on her coat.

Vasilico stirred. 'Off somewhere?'

'I've got an appointment at two. My twenty-eight-week scan.'

'Whereabouts?'

'The Western.' She'd calculated that it was likely to take at least twenty-five minutes to walk there in her condition – and most likely longer.

'Well, let me give you a lift, then,' said Vasilico, getting to his feet, their earlier war of words seemingly forgotten.

'Oh, no,' she said immediately, 'it's really not necessary.'

'Perhaps not,' he said genially, 'but I insist nonetheless.'

In the end, she concluded that it was more efficient just to accept Vasilico's offer than to waste time rebuffing him. She followed him round the corner to Woodlands Drive, where he directed her to a gleaming black Porsche sportscar which even she, with her near-total ignorance of all things vehicular, recognised as a considerably more extravagant mode of transportation than was typically afforded by a DCI's salary. He opened the passenger door for her with a flourish before jogging round to the driver's side and slipping behind the wheel.

'I'm not sure if you're aware,' he said as they headed up Gibson Street, past St Silas Church and the north gate of Kelvingrove Park, 'but you've a tendency to respond to criticism by arguing a more extreme version of what you've already articulated.'

'Look who's talking, Mr "Go and Live in a Country with No Cops".'

Vasilico laughed. 'It's like – I don't know, someone disagrees with you and you see it as your duty not to win them over but to shock them by saying something even more outrageous.'

Anna said nothing. It was something she'd long recognised as her Achilles' heel, but despite her best efforts seemed to keep allowing herself to be tripped up by. As such, the observation was far from welcome.

Truthfully, she still didn't quite know what to make of Vasilico. There were times when she came close to liking him, and other times when she found him utterly insufferable – and even occasions where she found herself experiencing both emotions simultaneously. He was capable of being both carelessly flippant and deadly serious, shifting between the two registers so seamlessly that she wasn't always aware of him doing it. She was left with a feeling that none of this was by accident – that he knew exactly what he was doing and was fully exploiting it to his advantage. And she wasn't sure she could bring herself to trust someone so fully in command of their own delivery.

They drove in silence for a while, heading south down the Kelvin Way. They'd turned onto Sauchiehall Street and had just passed the Kelvingrove Art Gallery when Vasilico's phone began to ring. With one hand still on the wheel, he reached into his pocket and, retrieving it, put it to his ear.

'Vasilico.'

Anna watched, half-amused by the sight of a serving police officer indulging in this flagrant spot of lawbreaking. She was gearing up to give him a ribbing about it when she noticed the tightening of his jaw and the look of anxiety that had entered his eyes.

'I understand,' he said, his voice flat. 'I'll be there ASAP.'

As he ended the call, Anna, her own sense of unease deepening, watched him intently.

'What is it?'

He didn't respond, continuing to drive in silence for another fifteen seconds or so before pulling over to the kerb, the entrance to the Western Infirmary's car park visible less than fifty metres ahead of them.

'It's about Derek, isn't it?' said Anna, when Vasilico continued to sit in silence.

For several agonising seconds, Vasilico said nothing. 'They think they've found something,' he said eventually. 'On the Erskine Bridge. I need to get there right away.' He turned to face her, as if only just realising she was there. 'I'll update you as soon as I can.'

'Let me come with you,' said Anna, the words out of her mouth before she even had time to think.

'I'm positive I didn't hear that right.'

She let her silence do the talking.

'Oh, you are something *else*, Anna Scavolini.' Vasilico shook his head in exasperated disbelief. 'I've met some chancers in my time, but you elevate the art to a whole new level.'

'He was my student,' said Anna, warming to her own reasoning. 'You can't pretend I haven't got skin in the game. I had a duty of care to him just as much as you lot did – you said so yourself. If it's bad news, I'd rather find out now than spend the next several hours fretting by the phone, wondering what it's going to be.'

Vasilico regarded her in studied silence. 'What about your scan?' he said after a moment.

'I'll reschedule,' she said breezily, trying not to think about the tongue-lashing she was going to get from Nuala Byrne.

Vasilico considered this. 'You stay in the car. You say nothing. You *do* nothing. You don't get involved in any way.'

'Deal.'

They journeyed in silence, Vasilico driving like the clappers, swerving around every vehicle in their path and running every red light they hit. Anna, sitting next to him, fingers digging into the upholstery of her seat, wondered what the procedure was if they got pulled over. Would Vasilico just flash his warrant card and be sent on his way with a salute and a *sorry, sir, my mistake*? She never did find out, for they remained unimpeded for the entire ten-mile journey, arriving at their destination just twenty minutes later, the bridge's distinctive cable-stayed pylons looming into view ahead of them sooner than Anna had anticipated.

For as long as it had been in existence, the Erskine Bridge had been one of Scotland's most sought-after suicide hotspots. Multiple efforts had been made over the years to deter people from using it to end their lives, from the multiple phone boxes and signs bearing the number for the Samaritans strategically placed at various points on the footpath, to the high fencing that had been installed a few years back. But even that, Anna surmised, wouldn't stop a determined jumper. You just needed to hoist yourself up, and then, once you were over the top, there was nothing left except a long drop to the River Clyde below.

Just over a third of the way across the bridge, a couple of police cars and an unmarked one – another sportscar – were parked next to the barrier separating the footbridge from the road. An officer in a hi-viz jacket stood sentry nearby, directing the oncoming traffic to go around them. Vasilico pulled up behind them and got out, his long legs easily clearing the barrier as he advanced towards a trio of uniformed officers and another in plain clothes whom Anna recognised as Plessis, clustered together a few metres beyond the furthest car.

She watched for a moment, then undid her seatbelt and got out. She knew Vasilico had told her to stay in the car, but she needed air and a stretch – and besides, it wasn't as if she was going to follow him. As she paced back and forth, hands in the small of her back, she kept one eye on Vasilico and his colleagues as they conversed urgently, their words obscured by the howling wind and roar of passing traffic. She clocked their grave expressions, then watched as Plessis handed Vasilico a large, see-through evidence bag containing what looked to be an item of clothing. Vasilico's back was to her, so she only glimpsed it briefly as he took it, but that was more than enough time for her to clock the item's colour.

She had a sudden, achingly clear vision of Vasilico, standing in the conference room at MIT headquarters, gesturing to a fuzzy CCTV image displayed on the wall-mounted screen. She heard his words too, as clearly as if he was standing next to her speaking them now.

*As you can see, he's dressed in a red windbreaker, quite distinctive . . .*

As her heart plunged into her gut, Vasilico turned and glanced over his shoulder at her. Their eyes met and, seeming to read her mind, he gave a soft, almost imperceptible nod of confirmation.

Anna closed her eyes in resignation.

PART TWO

# Lost Boys

# 9

# Bad Dreams

*Friday 6 November*

It all started, appropriately enough, with a funeral – or rather at the oversubscribed, booze-soaked purvey that followed. *Richard Alexander Deans, 1981–2015.* Taken before his time. Gone but not forgotten.

Zoe hadn't planned on being there. She hadn't spoken to Richie in God knows how long, and it wasn't as if they'd been bosom buddies back in the day. At best, they'd orbited around each other like different planets in the same solar system. But the notification had popped up on Facebook – a general invite to all friends and former classmates – and she'd decided to give it a look-see, just for the sheer hell of it. It got her the afternoon off work, and there was bound to be free booze on offer. There might even be some good craic, though she was beginning to realise the latter was in seriously short supply – at least while *she* was within earshot.

She was conscious, as she pushed through the throng of mourners, packed like sardines into the function room at the Great Western Guesthouse, that she was deliberately and consistently being given the cold shoulder. It didn't take a genius to work out why. Her status as Victor Callahan's older sister made her about as welcome as a ham sandwich at Ramadan. If she had to guess, she'd say they thought it was in poor taste that the sister of the Kelvingrove Killer, responsible for the deaths of three of their number, had turned up at the funeral for another former Willow Bank pupil whose life had been cut tragically short. The few who deigned to talk to her were clearly doing so through gritted teeth, exchanging strained pleasantries because the social niceties their upbringing had instilled in them didn't allow them to say what they *really* thought.

Bunch of uptight, repressed, two-faced pricks.

She was just about to call it a day and make tracks when she heard a high-pitched, girlish squeal behind her.

'Zoe? Zoe Callahan? It *is*, isn't it? Ohmygod, how *are* you?'

And then, striding towards her in a flurry of blonde hair, jangling bracelets and makeup applied with a trowel was a genuinely friendly face: Lucy Foster, life and soul of every party she graced with her presence, voted Runner-Up Prom Queen two years running. Transferring her Diamanté clutch bag from one hand to the other, she leaned in to give Zoe a delicate embrace, doing the air-kissing thing Zoe never had managed to get the hang of.

'It's so mad seeing you here! I didn't realise you and Richie were buddy-buddies.'

Zoe gave a louche smile, playing to expectations. 'Ye know me, Luce. Any excuse for a bevvy.'

Lucy was the living proof that book-smarts were not the same as intelligence. She'd left school with straight A's, but that didn't stop her being as thick as two decidedly short planks. Zoe had met several of her type among the ranks of the privately educated. Most, in her estimation, were so up themselves she'd have crossed the street to avoid them. But not Lucy. She'd always been kind to those who lived a less charmed life than herself, and not just in a patronising, 'white man's burden' sort of way. She was brash and couthy and endearingly un-self-aware. For those reasons, Zoe had always liked her.

After several attempts to make themselves heard, Lucy suggested they go someplace where they could have a proper catch-up. They were among the only women present, and Lucy was clearly feeling a bit overwhelmed by all the testosterone in the air – or as she put it, 'It's an absolute cockfest in here, dontchathink?' They headed out to the considerably less crowded bar, where Lucy ordered them both a shandy – 'My pleasure, darling' – and they got down to business.

At first, Lucy ploughed Zoe for information about her recent exploits – 'Is it true you're a lesbian now? How thrilling!' – and Zoe, acutely aware that her current fortunes were nothing to write home about, found herself embellishing her rather meagre existence, saying she'd tried her hand at a number of business ventures (technically true) but now worked in an upmarket restaurant (half-true) as an assistant manager (categorically false). Lucy, of course, had landed on her feet, securing a well-paying gig with a publishing firm straight out of uni – though all that had changed since she'd got back with Gregor Fraser, her old boyfriend from high school, and had decided to carve out a new career as a full-time mum. Their union had resulted in three gorgeous children; she showed Zoe pictures to confirm the fact of their gorgeousness.

After a while, talk inevitably turned to the reason they were both there. 'It's a sin what happened,' Lucy declared solemnly. 'Literally, if you believe in that sort of stuff.'

'How's that, then?'

'Well, you know what St Augustine said. I'd have thought you of all people would be up on that – you being of the, well, Catholic persuasion.'

(Lucy had excelled in RE class.)

'Aye, but that's about suicide, in't it?'

She caught Lucy's meaningful look. Her eyes widened.

'*No*,' she breathed.

Zoe, like everyone else, had listened to the minister's solemn eulogy, bigging Richie up as the greatest thing since sliced bread and recounting all sorts of amusing anecdotes from his childhood and teenage years in the same dour, passionless tone normally reserved for reading out the Shipping Forecast or the bingo numbers. He'd been more than a little vague about the cause of death, stating only that Richie had died suddenly and after what he referred to as 'a short and unexpected illness'. It had seemed unnecessarily evasive at the time, but she hadn't, until now, given any further thought to what lay behind it.

'"Illness" is the line his folks are spinning,' Lucy went on, 'and to be fair, who can blame them? But *I* heard from Sarah Carmichael who heard it from Iain Albright that his poor girlfriend came home to find him suspended from the light fixture in the living room.' She mimed hanging herself and made a gagging sound. 'Plus, by all accounts the autopsy showed he'd taken a bumload of pills beforehand.'

Zoe smiled incredulously. She was having trouble buying it. For one thing, Lucy had a tendency to believe everything she heard, so it was advisable to take her gossip with an entire shaker's worth of salt. For another, she had vivid memories of Richie Deans as something of a class clown, with a braying donkey's laugh and a talent for sowing mischief. To go from that to taking his own life simply didn't compute.

*Yeah, but what you see isn't always what you get. You never know what's hidden behind a smile – isn't that right, Zoe?*

'Are ye *sure* about this?' she said. 'I mean, could someone no just've got the wrang end of the stick?'

Lucy regarded her primly, as if to say *you know me better than that*. 'According to my Gregor, things hadn't been right with him for a while. He'd've liked to have been here today, only he couldn't get the afternoon off.' She took a sip from her glass – fortifying herself, it seemed to Zoe. 'Anyway, about six months ago, Richie calls up him out of the blue, saying can they meet up? Now, Gregor hadn't heard from Richie in *yonks*. But he's a decent sort, my hubby – you know, accommodating. So of course he says, "Absolutely, Richie. Name the time and place".'

'Couple nights later, they hook up at Elysium on Candleriggs. Know it? Their Caipirinhas are to *die* for.' Her eyes momentarily glazed over at the very thought. 'And straight away, it's obvious there's something Richie wants to get off his chest. And, after a whole lot of humming and hawing, he comes out and tells Gregor that, for about the last year or thereabouts, he's been having these dreams.'

Zoe found herself leaning in closer. 'What sorta dreams?'

Lucy gave her a knowing look. 'Well, *he* says "dreams", but the more he talks, the clearer it becomes that we're not talking about stuff his unconscious mind just magicked out of thin air. They're from ye olden days. You know, at Willow Bank.' Her eyes narrowed defensively. 'I'm just telling you what Gregor told me. I'm not making any of this up, I swear.'

'I believe you,' said Zoe.

And it was true. Lucy might repeat every half-baked Chinese whisper that reached her ears, but she hadn't the gumption to invent.

'So he describes these dreams – or memories, or whatever you want to call them. And it's nasty stuff – stuff to make the hair on the back of your neck stand up. There's this one he keeps having where he's in the headmaster's office . . . you remember how it was down at the end of that really long corridor in the east wing, right? And there's this older guy there with him

– not the head or any of the other teachers, just this random bloke – and he's making Richie . . . you know, *do* things.' She nodded towards her lap, as if the meaning wasn't already obvious.

'Jesus fucking Christ,' Zoe breathed, her shandy long forgotten.

'Quite. Anyway, Richie goes on and describes a bunch of other dreams he's had, all of them equally hair-raising.' Lucy exhaled a theatrical breath. 'Well, I tell you, Gregor was properly freaked out. I mean, no bullshitting, I would be too. He tells Richie to seek proper help – *urges* him, tells him he needs to talk to someone who's paid to listen to this sort of crap. But Richie's not having it. Says it was hard enough telling this to a mate. Can't *imagine* sharing it with a total rando. And besides, he still can't be sure these are real memories. What'd really help, he says, is if someone else could back him up. And he asks Gregor if *he* remembers anything like that.

'By this point, Gregor just wants to get the fuck out of there. He says no, absolutely not, if anything like that'd happened to him he'd've had the entire police force down on the place in two seconds flat. And he more or less tells Richie not to contact him again – says he doesn't need this in his life. Which, by the way, seriously not cool, and I said as much to him at the time.

'Anyway, they go their separate ways, and Gregor does his best to put what he's heard to the back of his mind . . . and then, next thing you know, silly Richie's only gone and offed himself.'

Lucy fell silent, her story at an end. Zoe knew this was her cue to say something, but she was lost for words. She sat there, picking at the damp beermat under her glass, feeling uncomfortable and vaguely embarrassed, like if Lucy had just shared details of her wanking habits with her or something.

'D'you remember that business at Netherfield Academy?' Lucy asked suddenly, jolting Zoe out of her trance.

Zoe looked up. 'Course I do. I havnae been living under a rock. Every man and his dug's heard about Netherfield.'

'Right,' said Lucy, clearly intent on explaining it to her anyway. 'A bunch of parents went to the school board, accusing various teachers of inappropriate conduct, and when the board didn't do anything, they went to the police.'

'But they never proved any of it, right? It was all just rumours and accusations.'

'It was a *lot* of accusations, all from different sources. All saying the same things about the same people. And the investigation was a clusterfuck. You must remember those pics in the papers of the head detective coming out of the pub half-cut.'

Zoe did, vaguely. That period in her life – collectively referred to as her student years – had been something of a blur, with one all-night bender blending into another to the extent that it was a miracle she'd ever made it to any of her classes, let alone come out the other end with a halfway decent degree. However, even she had had a modicum of awareness of the national scandal unfolding at the time, as cock-up after cock-up came to light, ultimately resulting in the biggest institutional sex abuse investigation in Scottish history collapsing without a single charge being brought.

'Anyway,' said Lucy, 'I got to thinking. All that stuff kicked off not long after we were all at Willow Bank. Mind how one of the accusations that kept coming up about Netherfield was that one of the gym teachers had been getting handsy with the boys in the changing rooms?'

Zoe nodded, taking her at her word.

'Couple of weeks after his night out with Richie, my Gregor remembered something. You remember the showers at Willow Bank? The girls had individual stalls, but the boys just had this one long row of shower-heads where they all got washed at once. And the boys' PE teacher, McCluskey – he used to stand there and watch them. To make sure there was no monkeying around, supposedly – but I mean, come *on*.

'Anyway, Gregor says he remembers, this one time, there was another bloke there as well. Not a teacher or anything to do with the school, just this random bloke in a suit standing there with McCluskey watching a bunch of naked teenage boys showering. He never interfered with them or got himself off or anything – just, y'know, stood there and watched, like it was a meat market or something.'

'You're kidding.'

'Nuh-uh, swear to absolute God. Gregor says he remembers finding the whole thing really weird – I mean, you *would*, wouldn't you? But no one else was saying anything, so he just kept schtum. Most likely everyone else was thinking the same thing – waiting for someone else to speak up.'

She paused for a moment. '*You* ever hear about anything like that? Like from your brother, maybe?'

Zoe shook her head. It wasn't the sort of thing she'd have forgotten.

'Me either,' said Lucy. 'But here's the thing: what happened to Richie, assuming it actually did happen – he'd blocked it out for a good fifteen years, and as far as we know the only person he ever talked to about it was my Gregor.'

She downed the last remnants of her shandy and leaned in closer. Laying a hand on Zoe's thigh, she stared at her intently, lowering her voice to a whisper.

'What if it wasn't only Netherfield? What if it was also happening at Willow Bank? And what if there's a whole lot of other boys out there besides Richie who had the same things done to them and then buried it?'

# 10

# Delve

With Lucy's words still echoing inside her head, Zoe caught a train out to Mount Vernon in the east of the city and made for the Corner Bar & Grill – where, for the last six months, she'd found gainful employment as a member of the waiting staff. As she stepped into the rear courtyard, she spotted her colleague Craig, a gangly youth in his early twenties, nursing a cigarette on the back step. He raised a hand in greeting. She returned his wave and loped over to join him.

'Hey-ho, Craigyboy. Sent ye to the naughty step again, have they?'

Craig smiled sheepishly and held up his severely depleted cigarette. 'Malcolm Malcolm made me go out back. New rule: no smoking where the punters can see you. So how'd it go?'

Zoe shrugged. 'Ach, y'know what like funerals are. Sadness 'n' gladness, tears 'n' cheers. They're all much of a muchness.'

Craig grinned. 'Right enough, yeah. Any excuse for a skive.'

Zoe affected an easy smile and joined him on the step, budging him up with an arse-nudge. She'd not had more than a second or two to collect her thoughts, however, when a shadow fell on the pair of them. She looked up to see the Corner's short, rotund proprietor standing in the doorway behind them, mopping perspiration from his rosy features. His eyes alighted on Zoe.

'Look sharp, Red. I need you out front. I'm not paying you to sit out here on your backside chewing the fat.' He flashed Craig, who was doing his best to make himself as small as possible, an acrid look. 'That goes for you too, Rankine. Break was over almost a minute ago.'

Craig instantly leapt to his feet, tossing his cigarette and practically saluting before scurrying indoors, limbs flapping every which way.

Zoe followed, albeit at a more relaxed pace. One of the distinct advantages afforded by age was the ability to see tinpot dictators like Malcolm Stilwell for the blowhards they were. They loved throwing their weight around almost as much as the sound of their own voices, but, when push came to shove, were more to be mocked than feared. And mock him she did, in subtle ways to his face and more overtly behind his back – like imitating his haughty West-Endy drawl and referring to him as 'Malcolm Malcolm', because he sounded so much like the Limmy character of the same name. She'd even managed to get Craig in on the act, young impressionable lad that he was, though he took considerably more care to make sure Malcolm didn't catch him in the act. In a job like this, you had to get your kicks where you could.

Still, all things considered, it wasn't the worst gig in the world to have. She was vastly overqualified for the work she was doing, and dealing with the whims and foibles of the public often left her wanting to bash her head against a brick wall. But it was fast-paced and varied, and yes, she had to admit there was a certain pride that came from knowing that the quality of the service she provided played as significant a role as the food itself in determining whether or not customers left with a satisfied taste in their mouths. It might not be much, but given how close she'd come to hitting rock bottom just a couple of years ago, she was positively flying high.

And yet she couldn't help noticing that, ever since her conversation with Lucy, that familiar sense of foreboding was once again gnawing away at her insides.

At 10.30, the Corner shut its doors for the night. Once Malcolm Malcolm was satisfied that everything had been left spick and span for the following day, Zoe, freed from the bonds of work until Monday, bade her colleagues goodnight and set off to catch her train home.

Back at the flat on Dumbarton Road, she carefully folded and put away her uniform, then showered, changed into some comfy clothes, fixed herself a late meal for one and set herself up on the living room sofa with the space heater on and her laptop open on her knees. She clicked through to Google, typed in 'Netherfield Academy abuse' and hit Enter. The screen filled with result after result after result. She clicked the first link and began to read, continuing long into the night.

Over the next couple of days, Zoe spent almost every waking moment on the sofa, getting up only to stretch her legs, make food or answer the call of nature. She even said no to Malcolm Malcolm's offer of an extra shift on Saturday, despite knowing it was the busiest night of the week and that she was turning down a king's ransom in tips.

Working methodically, she devoured every article on the Netherfield allegations she could get her hands on, absorbing the finer details, of which she'd previously only had a sketchy understanding. Back in 2002, following multiple complaints from the parents of pupils at the prestigious South Lanarkshire boys' secondary school, Strathkelvin Police had launched a major inquiry, interviewing dozens of students, staff and other assorted hangers-on. The details of the complaints varied, but the gist was the same: several members of staff stood accused of sexually abusing the boys in their care, with the earliest allegations going back more than a decade.

The depths of the investigation's apparent incompetence seemed mind-boggling to Zoe, from the accounts of botched interviews, to transcripts and evidence going missing, to the now-infamous photos of the senior investigating officer – one DCI Tom Cadogan, a big bulky man with jowls like a bloodhound's – emerging bleary-eyed and discombobulated from the boozer next to the cop shop following a three-hour liquid lunch. He'd been publicly tarred and feathered, with the press placing the blame for the investigation's collapse squarely on his shoulders and his masters in the Major Investigations Team seemingly only too happy for him to serve as the fall guy. Articles published in the wake of the fall-out mentioned that he'd been demoted and bumped back to uniform. Netherfield, mean-while, had trucked along for a few more years, but the rumours continued to linger around it like a bad smell and, faced with plummeting admissions, it eventually closed its doors in 2012.

From there, and with a certain inevitably, Zoe's thoughts turned again to Willow Bank. Could Lucy have been right? Was it really possible that the school where she'd spent six of the best years of her life had been another hotbed of filth and depravity? With little else to go on, she ran a search for Joe McCluskey, the handsy PE teacher whose name Lucy had brought up. It turned out he'd been struck off the teaching register a couple of years after Zoe had gone on to university, when it came to light that he'd been forcing boys to take cold showers as a punishment measure – a fate that, if there was even a passing truth to the rumours, seemed comparable to Al Capone getting done for tax-dodging.

Aside from McCluskey, Zoe could find nothing to suggest that any of the staff at Willow Bank had been involved in anything dodgy, with no public accusations of impropriety from either current or former pupils. She began to suspect that, as had so often been the case, Lucy had simply got carried away listening to gossip and rumour and that Richie Deans really *had* just succumbed to some mystery illness.

And yet she couldn't let it lie.

Having exhausted the official sources, Zoe began to explore the various blogs and message boards dedicated to the Netherfield case – a veritable rabbit-hole of anecdotal evidence, speculation and conspiracy. These were home to a disorienting mixture of firsthand testimony (or so its authors claimed) and unsubstantiated, swivel-eyed lunacy, with a definite emphasis on the latter. A veritable army of cellar dwellers had taken the events at Netherfield as licence to give their imaginations free rein, invariably falling back on the clarion call of 'freedom of expression' when challenged to back up their claims. Zoe loved a good conspiracy theory as much as the next person, but while she was happy to while away hours watching YouTube videos about how the moon landings were faked and how Denver Airport was a secret Illuminati temple, the crucial difference was that she didn't actually *believe* any of them. Or at least she took them with a large enough pinch of salt to know that whatever truths might be contained within them were the equivalent of chunks of corn in a pile of steaming horse manure. These nut-jobs seemed to think the onus was on their critics to prove that Netherfield *hadn't* been the epicentre of a worldwide ring of shapeshifting paedophile reptiles sacrificing children in order to summon Baphomet, rather than the other way round.

On Sunday morning, three days after she'd first begun to delve into the Netherfield case, Zoe found herself on a website called 'Justice for Conor' – a tacky-looking amateur blog which at first appeared to contain nothing more than the unfiltered rantings of yet another fruit loop. All the signs were there, from the links to articles on the cancer-giving properties of 4G signal masts to the ubiquitous 'profound' quote on the masthead: *It's easier to fool people than to convince them that they have been fooled* – *Mark Twain*. As she continued to read, however, she began to wonder.

The site's author was a Gillian Crowley, whose son Conor – a pupil at Netherfield and one of the complainants in the abuse scandal – had taken his own life in his late teens. In a lengthy introductory post, his mother alleged that the case's collapse had been the primary motivating factor in his suicide. She now dedicated her life to shining a light on cases of child abuse ('exposing the monsters who stole our children') not just at Netherfield but around the world. To that end, she invited victims and their loved ones to write in about their own experiences, many of which she published on the blog. All the entries were open to comments, with the largely anonymous userbase flooding the site with expressions of their outrage and disgust. 'OMG death penalty NOW!!!!' was the top-rated comment on the most recent article – a piece about a clerical worker who'd mislaid vital paperwork relating to an ongoing investigation into an allegation of indecent assault at a school in Chippenham.

Netherfield, the site's introduction claimed,

> is only the visible tip of a huge iceberg. Through the 1990's and early 2000's, abuse of teen-aged boys was wide spread in several schools in the west of Scotland. The real scandal runs far deeper though, with the abusers not only evading Justice but prospering in privilidged positions in Society which they continue to exploit to their own wicked ends. Judges, Politicians, Media personalities, even a former Solicitor general. All of these and more are implicated. I dare not name these powerfull and well connected men publically, but one way or another they will face JUSTICE, in this life or the next.

Taken at face value, it seemed so far-fetched as to be almost laughable, and Zoe was strongly inclined to suspect that the poor woman, driven mad by grief, had lost the ability to separate myth from fact and had turned into one of those crop-circle-chasing zoomers who inhabited the comments sections of so many YouTube videos.

And yet, if there was even a chance it was true . . .

At the bottom of the page was a form inviting visitors to contact the site's author directly.

**HAVE YOU OR SOME ONE YOU KNOW EXPERIENCED ABUSE, OR HAVE QUESTIONS ABOUT WHAT I HAVE DISCOVERED? GET IN TOUCH HERE. ALL CORRESPONDINCE IS PRIVATE & CONFIDENTIAL. I WILL NEVER PUBLISH ANY THING WITHOUT YOUR PERMISSION.**

Zoe hesitated for a solid minute before clicking the form and beginning to type.

# 11

# Whispers and Shadows

All things considered, living alone did have its perks. Having gone straight from sharing a roof with her late brother to moving in with her ex, Carol, life inside someone else's pocket was, until just over two years ago, the only existence Zoe had ever known. There were downsides to the bachelorette life, to be sure – coming home to a cold, empty flat after a long day at the coalface for one. But then, for much of the last year or so of their relationship, she and Carol had more or less lived separate lives anyway, working different shift patterns and often only briefly crossing paths as one came in the door and the other went out. And there were undeniable upsides too – like being able to pick her nose in peace without getting a lecture about what a filthy habit it was, or letting the dishes pile up in the sink without being harangued about not doing her share of the housework. But best of all was the freedom to come and go as she pleased, without having to explain to a 'just asking' Carol why she'd suddenly decided to don her parka and head out on an impromptu jaunt on a chilly November morning.

Late autumn had long been Zoe's favourite time of the year. The trees were alive with colour, the ground crunchy with freshly shed leaves, the air sharp and crisp, the cloying stickiness of summer a distant memory. For that reason, and because she had a mission to give her purpose and meaning, there was a spring in her step as she headed round to the bus terminus outside Partick Station.

Her destination was Pollokshields, a residential area on the Southside. Having grown up and spent most of her life north of the Clyde, the lands south of the river had always had an air of mystery for her, filled with unfamiliar streets whose names meant nothing to her. The old joke was that, if you were crossing the river, it was wise to have your passport ready for inspection. She hoped it wouldn't come to that. Still, when the bus driver – a chatty sort who knew her by sight – casually asked what was taking her there, she was nonetheless momentarily tongue-tied, before clumsily spinning a yarn about visiting her cousin who lived out there. She figured it was easier than telling him the truth.

The Coffee Cave was on Nithsdale Road, a short walk from the bus stop. She was the first to arrive; a brief sweep of the cosy little shop with its handwritten menus and depressed-looking French bulldog lying in its basket by the till confirmed that none of the three punters already in situ was Gillian Crowley, all of them being either too young, too old or too male.

She was halfway through her salted caramel mocha when Gillian finally arrived – a big, blustery woman in her fifties with wild, frizzy hair, wearing mismatched clothes that looked to have been procured exclusively from charity shops. Zoe got instant 'crazy cat lady' vibes, but was determined not to prejudge her. After all, some of the soundest people out there were crazy cat ladies.

'I watched you go in,' Gillian said, once she'd collapsed into the seat opposite and ordered a flat white from the proprietor, 'but I decided to give you a few minutes. I had to be sure it was just you.'

'Aye, fair play. Are you—'

Gillian raised a hand, silencing her. Then, as Zoe watched, she took out her phone, tapped the screen a couple of times and placed it on the table between them.

'I want to make you aware,' she said, over-enunciating for the benefit of the phone, 'that I shall be recording our conversation for my own archives. If you're unhappy with that, we'll conclude this meeting and go our separate ways. Deal?'

'Deal,' said Zoe, knowing she didn't have much choice in the matter.

Gillian shook off her thick woollen coat. 'I took a big risk agreeing to meet you, you know,' she said, in a tone that suggested Zoe ought to be profoundly grateful. 'They've set traps for me before.'

Zoe swallowed her desire to ask who 'they' were.

'When I got your email, I thought this might be another entrapment scheme,' Gillian continued, pausing to nod her thanks to the proprietor as he deposited her coffee on the table, then waiting till he was out of earshot once more. 'But I decided that, on balance, you seemed genuine.' She folded her hands on the table. 'So, you think someone you know was a victim of institutional child abuse.'

'Knew,' Zoe corrected her. 'And no even that well, really. We just went to the same school. I was a year ahead of him. He, uh . . . well, I was at his funeral the other week.'

Gillian's features became deathly still. 'And you think he killed himself because of what was done to him back in the day.'

Zoe, not really sure *what* she thought, half-nodded and half-shrugged.

'A lot of the victims shared that fate,' said Gillian. 'Others are in prison, or took to the bottle, or something stronger.' She shook her head sadly. 'All these schools, these centres of excellence, promising to nurture the talents of the best and the brightest. Instead, they created a generation of lost boys.' She raised the cup to her lips and blew on it before taking a long, contemplative sip.

Zoe bit her lip, her mood uncertain. She wished she'd come here with a plan – a predetermined set of questions to ask. God knows she had plenty. But now that she was here, with Gillian sitting in front of her, her mind was blank. She decided to dive straight in, starting with the matter that had been consuming her for the past week and more.

'What I dinnae get is how could they have got away with it for so long – and at all they different schools? Surely someone must've spoke out?'

Gillian lowered her cup and gave her a kindly look, as if she felt for Zoe in her naïveté. 'It's no great mystery if you actually stop and think about it. For a start, they picked their targets carefully. Always the loners, the outcasts, the ones from dysfunctional backgrounds. They made for easy prey – desperate for affection, willing to do pretty much anything to get it. I don't know if you were aware, but at Netherfield they used to have what they called "after-school clubs". The school took in a mix of day and boarding pupils, but they were forever holding extracurricular events, often at weekends, and the day pupils were encouraged to stay over so they could attend.'

'What sort of events?'

'Sport, mainly. Team-building stuff, designed to foster a spirit of healthy competition and camaraderie. In reality it was an excuse to get a bunch of young boys away from their parents at an isolated location. Then the staff involved would invite their pervert friends in to have their fun – folk with no connection to the school and absolutely no business being there.'

Zoe had read about this in the press coverage. Netherfield Academy had operated out of an eighteenth-century manor house in the middle of nowhere, but there were a couple of residential houses on the narrow lane leading to its gates, and the elderly couple living in one had reported hearing cars coming and going from the school, late at night and at weekends.

'What about witnesses, but? I don't care *how* careful they pricks were when it came tae picking and choosing. Someone somewhere must've seen something.'

'Someone probably did. A whole *lot* of someones, I'd imagine. As for why they didn't speak up, who can say? Perhaps they convinced themselves they were mistaken – that they either misinterpreted something perfectly innocent or else imagined the whole thing. Or maybe they *wanted* to say something but decided the repercussions were too great. Don't underestimate the sense of loyalty their staff feel to the institutions they serve. These schools have reputations to uphold. They depend on a regular supply of parents willing to pay exorbitant fees to send their kids there. Did you know there's no legal requirement for these places to inform the authorities about suspected abuse?'

Zoe shook her head.

'Well, it's true. Scandalous, but true. But then, it should come as no surprise that one pillar of the Establishment helps prop up another.'

'How d'ye mean?'

Gillian scoffed. 'You think it's a coincidence the law favours the abusers? Who do you think their friends were – the ones they invited along to these "events" to have their wicked way? I'll tell you who: politicians, judges, lawyers, civil servants – the very foundations of respectable society. They've been scratching each other's backs since the dawn of civilisation.

And believe me, if they have to choose between doing the right thing and protecting their own, they're not going to think twice.'

'But what about the parents? If I found out any kiddo of mine had been interfered with, I'd raise blue murder, and it wouldnae matter *how* well-connected the basturts were.'

'Some of us *did*,' said Gillian pointedly. 'A bunch of us Netherfield parents clubbed together, made a whole lot of noise, forced them to sit up and pay attention – for all the good it ultimately did. And we were that rare example that actually made it into the public eye. I've received firsthand testimony regarding over a dozen schools in the West of Scotland that never appeared on the front page of any newspaper. Whitecraigs, Maxwell Park, St Christopher's . . . ' She glanced at Zoe. 'Which one did you and your friend go to?'

'Willow Bank.'

Gillian gave her a sympathetic look. 'Willow Bank was the worst of the lot. I've heard stories about that place that would make your toenails curl. I don't publish them all. There are some things you're better off not knowing.'

Zoe didn't doubt it. She also knew that, if Gillian was speaking truthfully, she'd accumulated a mountain of evidence of serious wrongdoing over the years and had done nothing with it except use it as fodder for an obscure blog with a sideline in conspiracies about mobile phone masts.

'Have ye ever tried taking any of this to the papers?' she asked, trying to make it sound like a genuine question rather than an accusation of negligence.

Gillian scoffed. 'Seriously? Have you any idea what a narrow, parochial little outfit the Scottish Establishment actually *is*? Spend even a short while digging into the backgrounds of the men who've risen to the top and you'll find they all went to the same schools, send their *kids* to the same schools, drink in the same clubs, rub shoulders at the same charity dos. The papers are every bit as much a part of it as the judiciary or the civil service or anyone else.'

'What about the police?'

At this, Gillian threw back her head and laughed out loud. 'Oh sweetie, why do you think no charges were ever brought at Netherfield?'

'I thought that was cos the cop in charge was a feckless alkie,' said Zoe sheepishly, feeling she must have missed something obvious.

'That's what *they* want you to think.' Gillian tapped the side of her nose in a way that Zoe assumed was supposed to convey great meaning. 'The reality is, that investigation was sabotaged from day one. Oh, they made a show of taking our concerns seriously, but there were dark, dark forces at work behind the scenes, fixing it to make sure no one was ever brought to book. Believe me, these scumbags wouldn't be able to do half the things they do without the tacit approval or active cooperation of law enforcement.'

Zoe shifted in her seat. Gillian was losing her. She had her own reasons for being wary of the police, but the idea that they would intentionally botch an investigation to protect a bunch of child molesters was a stretch too far. The level of cooperation it would have required, the sheer number of people who'd have to have been in on it, blew any shred of credibility the claim might have held.

'So here's what I don't get,' she said, no longer attempting to disguise her incredulity. 'Ye say this lot are all-powerful, that they've infiltrated every corner of the Establishment, that they'll dae anything to protect their pervy pals. How come they havnae put a stop tae *you*?'

Gillian's expression grew stony. If her lips had become any thinner, they'd have disappeared altogether.

'I mean, here you are, large as life, writing yer blog, leaking all their dirty secrets, 'stead of lying in a ditch somewhere wi a bullet in yer back.'

Silence.

'Y'know, I done some digging of my own before I came here. Know what I found? That you were arrested back in 2003. Got a caution for harassing that cop who headed up the Netherfield case. You were sending him threatening letters, showing up at his hoose, following him down the street shouting dug's abuse at him.'

'And you believed it?' Gillian's voice dripped contempt. 'Doesn't say much for your critical faculties, does it?'

'Oh, right – so ye didnae harass that guy?'

'All I ever wanted was an honest, face-to-face conversation,' Gillian snapped. 'It was the least he owed me. I was sure he could have told me what really went on behind closed doors – who was pulling the strings, who leant on him to take the fall. But he refused to talk to me. Ended up taking out a restraining order against me. Against *me*!'

'I also read ye were sectioned,' said Zoe quietly.

'Oh, here we go.' Gillian rolled her eyes. 'The old "crazy lady" schtick. I might have known. You know it's been standard practice since time immemorial for the Establishment to publicly discredit anyone who makes life uncomfortable for them? They mock, they belittle, and when that doesn't work, they smear you.'

'All lies, was it?'

'I was declared sane, you know.' Gillian thumped her chest with a balled fist. '*Sane*. A leading independent psychiatrist assessed me. Confirmed I was of sound mind. But I can see that's not good enough for you, oh *no*! You read a couple of hit-pieces from the lamestream media and all of a sudden you think you know everything about me. Well, let me tell you something, missy.' She jabbed a finger across the table, the nail coming to rest a couple of inches from Zoe's eye. 'I don't owe you an explanation for anything. I'm here talking to you because I thought you reached out to me in good faith. But if all you've come here to do is denigrate me and my efforts to uncover the truth, then you can fuck off.'

Over by the till, the shop's proprietor looked up from his newspaper and glanced in their direction. The French bulldog raised its head, farted, then sighed contentedly and went back to sleep.

'Awright.' Zoe raised both hands in a peace gesture. 'I'm sorry. I wasnae having a go. S'a lot to take in, is all.'

For a few more seconds, Gillian just glowered at her. Then, slowly, she lowered her outstretched finger, though she continued to give Zoe the evil eye.

'Tell me about Conor,' said Zoe, scrabbling to get Gillian back onside. 'What was he like?'

'He was . . . ' Gillian sighed and gazed down into the remains of her coffee, seemingly unable to find the words. 'He was everything.'

Zoe saw what must have happened with aching clarity. That Conor had been abused, she was in no real doubt. Probably, too, there *had* been widespread abuse at Netherfield that had gone unpunished through a combination of sloppiness and genuine malice. But all the rest – the cabal of perverts greasing each other's wheels from positions of social and political power? These were just the mad ravings of a grieving woman desperate to give her son's death meaning by recasting him as the victim of a grand conspiracy. In turn, her own sense of victimhood, and the fact that no one had taken her seriously, had pushed her into the arms of the sort of folk who spent their days ranting about chemtrails. They were probably the only ones who'd ever made her feel listened to.

'How'd he end up at Netherfield?' she asked. 'I mean, it's a . . . ' She trailed off, struggling to find a non-offensive way to say it. She had no reason to assume Gillian was on poverty row, but Netherfield had had a reputation for being the sort of place even the landed gentry had to scrimp and save to send their offspring to.

Gillian laughed drily. 'I could ask the same of someone like you stalking the corridors of Willow Bank. Bet you were the token blue-collar girl there.'

Zoe acknowledged this with a dry smile.

'"Life opportunities for boys from underprivileged backgrounds",' they called it.'

'Huh?'

'By law, these schools have to subsidise the education of a certain number of children from lower-income families each year, or lose their cushy tax-exempt status. I figured it was too good an opportunity to pass up. Conor was an . . . unruly child. I thought sending him to that place would do him a power of good – you know, instil good values and discipline. And I regret it. There's not a day goes by that I don't pay for that decision.' She gave another deep, mournful sigh that seemed to reverberate through her entire body.

'He never did make friends easily, and that only seemed to get worse at Netherfield. The other boys shut him out. Not the right sort, you see – not that I imagine he did himself any favours in that regard. He could be an obstreperous wee so-and-so. But it wasn't just the bursary boys who were targeted for abuse. I've been contacted by folk who didn't have two brass pennies to rub together and by folk who've never wanted for anything in their lives.'

Zoe said nothing. Somewhere, at the back of her mind, a thought was starting to take shape. It was embryonic, underdeveloped, but it was there, fermenting below the surface.

'You asked me earlier if I ever took any of this to the press,' Gillian went on. 'In the early days, I tried. You wouldn't believe the number of doors I had slammed in my face. I spoke to countless journalists, showed them the material I'd collated, tried to get them to pursue the matter – but it was always the same story. They'd nod their heads, make all the right noises, say "Leave it with me and I'll be in touch", and then that would be the last I'd ever hear from them. Then, earlier this year, I got an email out of the blue from an investigative journalist – Matt Pinnock. Heard of him?'

Zoe shook her head.

'No reason you should. He's not with any of the major papers. Too willing to speak truth to power. But he's done good work in the independent media, exposing a bunch of scandals the mainstream outlets refused to touch. He told me he'd read my blog and was interested in what I'd uncovered, and asked if we could meet.

'Right from our first conversation, I could tell he had his head screwed on. He grilled me for hours, checking and double-checking all the facts. Once he was satisfied everything was kosher, he agreed to take the case on. He was going to write an article that lifted the lid on everything that'd been going on in these schools. We were going to nail the buggers to the wall once and for all. I began reaching out to the people who'd got in touch, asking them if they'd be willing to go on the record. A lot refused, but a few said yes – more than I'd expected. And Matt unearthed a few of his own, some of whom agreed to be interviewed on condition of anonymity. He even managed to track down Cadogan.'

'The cop who led the Netherfield investigation?'

Gillian nodded. 'After the whole sectioning fiasco, I was forbidden to have any further contact with him. Of course, there are ways of keeping tabs on a man that don't involve direct contact. By the time I picked up his trail again, he'd moved down in the world: sold his nice suburban house, broken up with his nice suburban wife. A couple of years later, he upped sticks again and I lost track of him. I tried all the usual techniques for tracking a person down – the phone book, the voters' roll, querying various credit agencies – but it was as if he'd ceased to exist.'

*Or perhaps he skipped the country on account of being hounded by a pure madwumman*, thought Zoe.

'So where did Pinnock find him?'

'Wouldn't tell me. Worried I'd show up at his door and start haranguing him, I imagine. Not that it would've done a bit of good, mind you, since

Cadogan wouldn't give him the time of day. Kept giving him "no comment" and "I have nothing to say". Can't say I was too surprised. If he wouldn't talk to me back in the day, why would he spill the goods to some journalist asking him to go on the record thirteen years after the fact? Besides, not long after, Matt managed to turn up something even better: a high-placed source who was going to get him proof that would put everything beyond doubt.'

'What sort of proof?'

'Again, he didn't say. And I don't suppose we'll ever know. Just a few days after he told me, Matt died in a car crash.'

Zoe sat up a little straighter. Suddenly, all this talk of Establishment conspiracies no longer sounded quite so crazy.

'That's convenient,' she said.

'Very. You remember that spell of bad weather at the beginning of September? His car skidded off the road and he died at the wheel. Failed brakes, the FAI claimed. It was all very Willie MacRae.'

'Who?'

Gillian waved her hand as if it didn't matter. 'A couple of weeks before he died, someone broke into his flat. They didn't take any valuables, but they made off with his computer and his notes on the case. I told him at the time he needed to start taking better precautions, but he kept insisting it was fine. Well, now we know who was right, don't we?'

There was a smugness to Gillian's tone that Zoe found decidedly distasteful under the circumstances. 'So I'm guessing all his notes are gone,' she said, managing, with some effort, to keep her eyes on the prize.

'It would be wise to assume his killers have since got their hands on anything they didn't make off with at the time of the burglary. Of course,' she went on, a trifle grandly, 'I've collated copious research notes of my own over the years. And I wasn't resting on my laurels while Matt was doing his thing. While he was speaking to the victims, I was in the process of drawing up a master list of suspects, based on the testimony of the people who've contacted me over the years via the blog.'

'Have ye got it on ye?'

For a moment, Gillian hesitated. She eyed Zoe with a frown, as if gauging her trustworthiness. 'Yes,' she said slowly.

'Can I see?'

Once more, Gillian hesitated, before reaching into the folds of one of her many layers and drawing out a dog-eared scrap of paper. She passed it across the table.

'I had thought about going public with it – publishing it on the blog. But I can't see what it would achieve. Without Matt's research, without the victims' testimonies, it's just an unsubstantiated list of names.'

Zoe was about to point out that this hadn't stopped her before, but then she thought better of it. She unfolded the page and ran her eyes down the handwritten list. Most of the names were completely alien to her. A few she *had* heard of, but they seemed so far-fetched that she once more came close to dismissing the whole thing out of hand. A top solicitor-advocate; a daytime TV personality; a Scots-born Hollywood movie star; a former Glasgow MP deposed in the recent general election, of whose existence even the politically inattentive Zoe had been aware . . . And then there were the names of former Willow Bank teachers – names she'd almost forgotten, but the memories associated with which came flooding back instantly. Joe McCluskey was there, and a geography teacher she'd never had but about whom, she now remembered, rumours had abounded that he was a total lech.

A few lines from the bottom, a name leapt out at her in flashing neon.

'Jesus. *Broadhurst* was at it?'

Adam Campbell Broadhurst, headmaster of Willow Bank Academy, 1982–2004. Scourge of the delinquent and the unruly; a tall, stiff-backed man with a long, severe face and a penchant for ruling with an iron fist. And now, it seemed, a kiddie-fiddler as well.

Gillian's expression was grave. 'Both at it and facilitating it in others, if my sources are to be believed. From what I've gathered, he presided over a culture of silence, with pupils and staff alike too afraid to say anything.'

It didn't seem much of a stretch. They'd *all* been scared of him. Zoe remembered the one and only time she'd been summoned to his office – for some minor misdemeanour, the specifics long forgotten. He'd barely even spoken to her and hadn't once raised his voice, and yet the whole encounter had been so terrifying that, to this day, she considered it a miracle she'd left that room with her pants still dry.

'He was headmaster at Willow Bank for over two decades.' Gillian's voice jolted her back to the present. 'That's by far the longest reign enjoyed by any of the suspects. In my correspondence, his name came up more times than any other.'

Zoe said nothing. She felt hollowed out and empty, as if she'd just endured a marathon puking session. Before now, all this talk of abuse had seemed somehow abstract, diminished by the multiple degrees of separation through which she was experiencing it. Broadhurst changed that. There was something powerfully tangible about his name, giving it all an immediacy it hadn't previously possessed. This was something that, if true, had been going on right under her own nose, affecting boys she'd sat next to in class, considered her friends, maybe even shared her own formative sexual experiences with.

As she sat there, caught in a tailspin of nausea, Gillian stirred. 'Well, I ought to be making a move. I volunteer at the Refugee Council on Tuesdays.'

She switched off her phone and got to her feet, pocketing it.

'Can I ask ye something?' Zoe said.

Gillian paused from gathering up her coat. 'By all means.'

'How d'ye do it? I mean, how d'ye keep going, knowing what happened tae Conor, knowing he took his own life? How d'ye manage tae find a reason to carry on?'

Gillian stood, brows pursed tight, mulling Zoe's question over. 'I take things one step at a time,' she said eventually. 'I get out of bed in the morning – that's a victory. I brush my teeth, I wash my face – another victory. I put on my clothes, I open the door and I step outside – all victories. Little victories, but victories nonetheless. And, for a great many years, the thought that one day I might be able to avenge what was done to him was a powerful motivator.' A heavy, sorrowful breath racked her. 'But I know now that day will never come. No one cares enough to do anything, and those responsible are too well-protected. That's why I'm getting out.'

'Out?'

'Out of campaigning. Out of Scotland. Out of all . . . ' She made a vague gesture with her hand. ' . . . this. My sister lives out in Melbourne. For years she's been saying I should come out and join her. I wonder if it's time I took her up on that offer.'

'Aye? Well, good luck, whatever ye decide tae do.'

Gillian gave a slight, head-tilted smile. 'And the same to you.'

With that, she turned and headed for the exit. The bulldog raised its doleful head as the bell above the door tinkled, then shut its eyes once more.

Zoe remained where she was, mulling over everything she'd heard. It wasn't until several minutes later, when she too began to think about making tracks, that she realised she was still holding Gillian's list of names, and understood the meaning behind her parting words.

## 12

# Maternal Instinct

*Thursday 19 November*

'So let's take a look at the actual mechanics of breastfeeding.'

The midwife, a middle-aged, Falstaffian caricature oozing warmhearted practicality, waddled over to the whiteboard and started to draw. As the illustration took shape, an array of titters and whispers broke out among the fifteen or so women and men assembled on chairs or floor-mats in the small, overheated room on the ground floor of the Hyndland Community Centre. Anna, perched on an uncomfortable plastic chair at the back of the room, rolled her eyes in disbelief. It was like being back in first-year biology class.

'Now,' the midwife continued, 'I doubt this particular part of the female anatomy requires an introduction for anyone in this room, but just in case, this' – she tapped the grotesquely large and swollen appendage with her pen – 'is the mother's breast, brimming with all the nutrients Baby needs. Here we see the areola' – *Was there any need to make it so detailed?* Anna thought – 'and here, behind it, this little circle represents the zone where the milk gathers. And *here*' – she drew a series of lines – 'we have all the little ducts that carry the milk down. Now, can anyone tell me what's missing from this picture? Anyone?' She looked around expectantly. '*Baby*, of course.'

Several of her pupils gave audible sighs. *Of course, why didn't we think of that?*

Anna's phone began to vibrate in her pocket. As surreptitiously as possible, she slipped it out and glanced at the screen. *Vasilico.* What did *he* want? She rejected the call and pocketed her phone again, making a mental note to call him back later.

A further ripple of laughter broke out. Anna looked up to see that the midwife had drawn a giant head with a gaping mouth like Pac-Man advancing towards the poor, defenceless breast.

'So here's the thing.' The midwife put down her pen and, picking up a small plastic doll from the array of props strewn on the nearby table, turned to face the class. 'A lot of people think, "Breast, nipple, baby's mouth. How hard can it be?" Turns out, it's a little more involved than that. Here's what not to do.'

To Anna's alarm and much hilarity from the others, she proceeded to demonstrate, smashing the doll's face into her own ample bosom. One of the handful of men present – doting husband accompanying expecting wife – gave a mock wolf-whistle, earning him a nudge in the ribs and a chiding 'Silly!' from his significant other.

The midwife beamed, positively revelling in the attention. 'So what happens when you clamp down here?' She pointed to the nipple on the whiteboard. 'Can anyone guess?'

'Nothing?' suggested one woman – a large, bottle-blonde lady in her early forties who looked like she'd done this at least a couple of times before.

'Well, not *nothing*,' said the midwife, the beatific smile that seemed to be the only expression of which she was capable growing even wider. '*Something* happens. Does anyone know?'

One of the mums-to-be in the front row – a girl who looked about seventeen, in oversized dungarees and dreadlocks – raised her hand. 'Feels like nipple clamps,' she said, to yet more giggling and laughter.

'*Exactly*. It hurts like billy-o. Gold star for Sasha. *Someone*'s speaking from experience.'

Sasha looked around at her peers with a superior smirk. Anna wondered whether this meant she had prior experience of breastfeeding or nipple clamps. Perhaps both.

The midwife returned to her terrifying rendition of an engorged breast. 'Whereas if *this* gets compressed' – she tapped the collection zone behind the nipple – 'whatever's in *here*' – pointing to the ducts – 'comes down, and whatever's in *here*' – the collection zone again – 'comes shooting out.'

With considerable vigour, she drew multiple jets of milk squirting out of the nipple, straight into Pac-Man's expectant mouth. The fortysomething woman said something to one of the others mums, and a whole bunch of them exploded with laughter.

'So really,' said the midwife, 'when it comes to feeding, the most important thing to master is what we call The Latch.'

*The Latch.* There it was – that dreaded phrase. *It's all about The Latch.* Just thinking about it was enough to make Anna's own boobs ache in anticipation. She'd heard all the stories, of course – about how it was such a beautiful experience; how, while it was suckling, the baby became an extension of you – but all she could think about was the fact that, a few weeks from now, she was going to have a freshly birthed little humanoid clamping its gums onto one of the most sensitive parts of her anatomy.

Her phone hummed again. Chancing another look at the screen, she saw she had a text from Vasilico:

**Call me when you get this. V**

The midwife droned on about familiarising yourself with the mechanics, making it all sound painfully technical – or just plain painful. Strictly speaking, Anna knew it all already. Her bookshelves back home were crammed with well-thumbed baby manuals, each of which she'd read cover to cover and annotated with multiple colour-coded post-its. She didn't need to be here. She was just humouring Nuala, who, at the belatedly rescheduled twenty-eight-week scan, had been decidedly insistent about her going. It wasn't *compulsory*, of course not, but these classes were offered to all expectant mothers and she was *strongly* encouraged to make use of them – which presumably meant that if you didn't, a black mark would go against your name in a file marked 'DIFFICULT WOMAN', which would only lead to problems further down the line. Anna was quickly learning that, when it came to matters of childbirth and child-rearing, it was easiest just to nod and at least *pretend* to go with the flow.

She gazed around at the other mums, hanging on the midwife's every word, laughing at all the appropriate junctures, and observed just how at ease they all looked – as if they *belonged* here. To look at them, you'd think their whole lives had been leading up to this very moment; that motherhood was the purpose for which they'd always been destined. Anna wished she shared their sense of purpose. She'd never been someone who naturally got excited about babies, the vital neural pathway that every other woman appeared to possess seemingly absent in her. When colleagues showed photos of their or their relatives' newborns around the office, she of course smiled and made the appropriate noises, but in reality they might as well have been showing off pictures of their new fridge-freezer for all the impact it had on her. Not for the first time, she wondered how she'd reached this juncture – how she'd ended up so far down the rabbit hole.

*You* know *why, Anna. Because you made a decision to go through with this, come hell or high water, because you knew you wouldn't be able to face the alternative.*

Afterwards, Anna joined the procession towards the door. Impatient though she was to call Vasilico back and find out what he wanted, she was resigned to going nowhere in a hurry. Most of the women were, like her, in their third trimester, many of them even larger than her – and she was approaching the size of a baby elephant. And when everyone, yourself included, took up twice as much space as normal, slipping surreptitiously through a gap between two bodies simply was not a realistic proposition.

As she waited for a few would-be mums to stop dawdling and blabbering, she spotted the midwife approaching.

'How are you bearing up, Anna?'

She did her best to affect a perky smile. 'Fine. Yeah, I'm grand, thanks.'

'Feel you got something out of our little session?'

*Oh, sure – two hours of my life I'll never get back.* 'It was very informative. Thanks.'

The midwife beamed. 'I'm so glad. And will we be seeing you next week?'

'Well . . . '

'It's really important you keep coming,' she continued, before Anna could decide how to respond. 'I know they're not for everyone. That it can seem like most of the stuff we're covering is plain old common sense. That it can be a bit awkward, not knowing anyone else . . . '

*She means 'being the only person without a partner or a friend with them',* Anna thought.

' . . . but all the research shows that antenatal classes have an over-whelmingly positive impact on the birthing experience.'

*Experience?* She made it sound like a package tour, or an amusement park ride.

'And for those of us that are on our own, it can really help to establish a support network of other mums – folk who're going through the same thing as you, who understand your hopes and fears.'

'I'll certainly bear that in mind.'

The midwife beamed. 'I'm so happy to hear that.' She placed a reassuring hand on Anna's arm. 'And don't worry if you're not feeling the way everyone expects you to just yet,' she said in a low, kindly voice. 'Those maternal instincts will kick in soon enough.'

Anna smiled stiffly and took her leave, considerably less than thrilled that it was that obvious.

As she emerged from the centre, she got out her phone and dialled Vasilico's number. He picked up almost immediately.

'Anna, thanks for giving me a bell. Didn't catch you at a bad time, did I?'

'It wasn't anything important. So what's up?'

In the moment it took for Vasilico to reply, Anna pictured him pursing his lips, weighing up his response.

'This is going to sound slightly bizarre, but when you left for work this morning, had the postman been?'

'Yes. Why?'

'Any unusual communiqués?'

'Not that I'm aware of,' said Anna, wondering where this was all going. 'What sort of unusual communiqués did you have in mind?'

'I've just received, via recorded delivery, an invite to a memorial service a fortnight today. From Old Man Sullivan, to be precise.'

'A memorial service for *Derek*?'

Anna was aware, as she spoke, of how slow on the uptake she sounded, but she was still having trouble believing what she was hearing. In the two weeks since Derek's windbreaker had been found, tangled in the railings of the Erskine Bridge, his initials written on the inner tag, the police Dive and Marine Unit had scoured the river and its banks in search of a body. Someone had once told Anna the Clyde was such a popular spot for disposing of murder weapons that, if you drained it, you'd be able to solve ninety-five percent of the city's homicides overnight. They hadn't actually *drained* the river, but they'd done just about everything short of that, and yet had failed to turn up any conclusive proof that Derek had met the same fate as many a jumper before him.

'But I don't . . . ' Anna trailed off, struggling to articulate her thoughts. 'I mean, what's going through the man's *head*?'

'All the head honchos have had invites,' Vasilico continued. 'De Groot, yours truly, even the ACC. I must admit, my curiosity is well and truly aroused. You definitely haven't received an invitation?'

'No.' Anna glanced up briefly to nod a distracted goodbye to one of the other women from the class, waddling out of the community centre arm-in-arm with her devoted partner. 'Should I feel overlooked, d'you think?'

'That's a matter of perspective, I suppose – though possibly a moot point. I was calling to ask, in the off-chance that you *weren't* on the invite list, whether you cared to accompany me as my plus-one.'

Despite herself, Anna let out an incredulous chortle. 'Are you asking me on a *date*, Detective?'

'Well, I wouldn't call it *that*.' Vasilico, to her ears, sounded almost flustered, if such a thing was even possible. 'I figured you'd want to be there – him being your former pupil, after all. Plus, if you do decide to opt in, there's no sense taking two cars when one will do nicely. Got that pesky ozone layer to look out for.'

'The ozone layer. *Right*.' Anna smiled knowingly, even though she knew he couldn't see her face. 'Well, it's very kind of you to offer. I'm not saying yes or no, but I'll give it some thought and get back to you.'

'I could not, in good conscience, ask for more. Keep in touch!'

He ended the call, leaving Anna to consider her options. The whole notion of a memorial service for someone whose death hadn't even been established struck her as in incredibly poor taste, to the extent that she felt that even deigning to grace it with her presence would be affording it a legitimacy it didn't deserve. And yet she couldn't deny that, like Vasilico, her curiosity was piqued. Just what was Derek's father playing at – and why now?

*A fortnight today* . . . If nothing else, it would mean one less antenatal class to endure.

# 13

# Care

*Saturday 21 November*

Zoe's feet ached as she climbed the stairs to her flat – the aftereffects of another manic, nonstop shift at the Corner. Inside, she shrugged off her coat, cranked up the heating and tramped through to the living room. She'd been intending to fix herself a late evening meal, but as she neared the sofa, she found the draw of her laptop too great to resist. With a sigh, she plonked herself down and opened the lid. She wasn't all that hungry anyway.

In the last few days, she'd thrown herself into her work, taking every extra shift going in an attempt to keep herself busy and her mind occupied. Predictably, what little time she'd had to herself had been spent brooding, wondering just how much of Gillian's account she actually believed. Given some of the loopier ideas the woman espoused, it was all too tempting to dismiss the entire thing out of hand.

But then, maybe that was just what they wanted her to think – whoever *they* were. Maybe she was allowing the parts of Gillian's worldview that were obviously crazy to serve as a convenient excuse to dismiss the parts that had a ring of credibility – in other words, the stuff about Netherfield and the other schools. If there really *was* a grand, overarching conspiracy to protect a cabal of well-connected paedophiles, then it probably suited the conspirators down to the ground that their most prominent accuser happened to be a mad banshee who banged on about chemtrails and the Illuminati.

When she'd got home from their meet-up at the Coffee Cave, there had been an email from Gillian waiting for her: a massive, unordered dump of Word documents which, the accompanying message explained, constituted all the testimonies Gillian had received over the years relating to abuse at schools in Scotland, albeit with the names of the complainants, their abusers and the schools themselves redacted. It would be a betrayal of their trust, Gillian explained, to allow them to be identified. As such, Zoe had immediately recognised the testimonies as being of little practical use, except as a galvanising force – which, perhaps, had been Gillian's intention in sending them all along. She'd spent the entire night reading the whole lot from start to finish – a deeply unpleasant task, yet compulsive in that way that accounts of extremes of human suffering so often are.

And then there was the dead journalist, Pinnock. Zoe had spent some time looking into him as well, reading various investigative pieces he'd written for campaigning websites of one hue or another. A lot of the causes he'd involved himself in were what might be termed 'fringe', but he seemed on balance to be the real deal. She tried telling herself that there were any number of perfectly logical explanations as to why his car had gone spinning off the road, not least the official one . . . but it didn't feel right. Pinnock's involvement, and the overly convenient nature of his demise, lent credence to Gillian's story.

Over the last few days, she'd begun to question her own recollections of her time at Willow Bank. She'd spent some time reading up on the phenomenon of collective amnesia – when a group of people all forgot something too painful to acknowledge, like soldiers who'd witnessed or participated in atrocities during a war. Via the Willow Bank Alumni Facebook group, she'd made tentative contact with a few friends from the old days, many of them folk she'd lost touch with years ago. The resulting conversations had been awkward, the people she reached out to invariably figuring out pretty quickly that she had an ulterior motive for ringing them up out of the blue after fifteen years. Most, when she revealed her true purpose, responded with variations on *don't be so bloody ridiculous*, as if the very idea that anything remotely untoward could have happened at Willow *Bank* was too outrageous to countenance. She found the men to be the most forthright in their denials. The women were less vociferous, but nonetheless made it clear that these were questions she shouldn't be asking. One, Keri Barnes, who'd sat next to her in fourth-year Modern Studies, told her that even if anything like that *had* been going on, it would do no one the slightest bit of good to go raking it up now.

'Let the past be the past,' she'd implored Zoe. 'No one'll thank you for going round opening up old wounds.'

At the centre of it all was Broadhurst – the lightning rod for all her disgust and ire. She could picture him now, striding the school corridors, his old-fashioned black gown billowing behind him as pupils scattered to make way for him. Tapping his name into Google, she discovered that he'd left the education sector altogether after his time at Willow Bank came to an end, reinventing himself as an executive at a successful firm of property developers with offices in the city centre. Now Adam Broadhurst MBE, he seemed only to have grown in stature, his aloof gaze in the photo on the company website that of a man who considered himself beyond reproach. *You can't touch me,* it seemed to say. *I'm powerful and well-connected, and you're not.*

Zoe closed her laptop with a tired, frustrated sigh. Life would be a whole lot easier if she could stop caring this much about things she couldn't control. It was all too much, the scale of the problem too overwhelming. The feelings she was now experiencing were similar to the ones she'd gone through in the aftermath of the previous year's referendum. The months leading up to that historic vote – the so-called Summer of Independence – had been a giddy, intoxicating time in Scotland, and in spite of her avowedly apolitical nature, she'd nonetheless found herself swept along on the tide of a hopeful, peaceful revolution that dared to dream of a better, more just future. For a brief time, it had become her everything – the panacea that was going to cure society of all its ills and give newfound meaning to her life. Everything else had gone on hold: hobbies; career aspirations, such as they were; even the friendships she'd cultivated.

Then had come the morning of the nineteenth of September, and it was all over. Hope had lost to fear. It was as if she'd suffered a bereavement – only somehow worse, because there was no body, no funeral, nothing tangible to grieve over. She remembered standing on Dumbarton Road on the drab, cheerless morning after the declaration, in the shadow of one of the many food banks that scarred this, one of the most resource-rich countries in the world, thinking, *This is it. This is the best we can ever aspire to*. And, faced with the prospect of no hope, no future, just the same grey mediocrity stretching out in front of her for the rest of her life, it had been easier just to switch off, completely cutting herself off from the national question and current affairs in general. To convince herself she didn't care. Apathy had embraced her with its warm, inviting caress.

But she couldn't do that now. Not with this. The independence cause had been important to her – but it was, on some level, an abstract. Liberty, fairness and self-determination were powerful ideas, but you couldn't reach out and touch them. This, on the other hand, was something that stirred her on a deeply personal level. And as she sat there, the ache gradually receding from her battered feet, she knew there was no way she could pretend this didn't matter to her. One way or another, she had to do something.

She opened the laptop again. There was Broadhurst, gazing back at her, just as she'd left him. Challenging her to look the other way. She clicked the 'Upcoming Events' link on the side of the page. His company was doing up an area in Scotstounhill, with a public consultation scheduled for the following Monday. Among the list of attendees, Broadhurst's name called to her like a beacon.

There was nothing in the small print saying you had to be a local resident to attend. And besides, all she wanted was to get a feel for the man – to listen to him speak; to get a sense of what sort of vibes he gave off. Just to satisfy her own curiosity – nothing more.

And so, a little before seven o'clock on Monday night, Zoe arrived outside Scotstounhill Primary School – a venue which seemed somehow strangely appropriate under the circumstances. Standing on the other side of the road, out of the range of the nearest streetlamp, she watched as people headed into the building in dribs and drabs. She gave it until a few minutes before the meeting was about to start. Then, tagging along behind a trio of chatty women in their forties, she made her way into the assembly hall.

Inside, several rows of chairs, about half of them occupied, had been set out facing a long table at the front of the room, behind which four people in suits – one woman and three men – were sat. A fifth seat was empty, with no sign of Broadhurst. Zoe, crouched low in the back row behind the chatty women, began to fear that he'd stood them up and that the first order of business when the meeting started would be to convey his apologies. However, as the clock struck the hour, a side door towards the front of the hall opened and a man strode out – suited like the other dignitaries, six foot three or thereabouts, with grey-white hair in a taper cut.

With his straight-backed posture and long, confident stride, it was like watching him pacing the corridors of Willow Bank all over again. Zoe had to remind herself to exhale as Adam Broadhurst made his way over to the table, laid a hand on the shoulder of the man nearest him, muttered something to him in a voice that was drowned out by the continued snatches of conversation from the audience pews, then slipped into the empty seat.

That, it seemed, was their cue to begin. The man at the far end of the table – a short-arse with an oily-looking face and a decidedly unsubtle combover – got to his feet and raised his hands, silencing the chatter from the audience pews.

'Thank you all for coming out on such a dreich night. I'm Chris Norman, MP for Glasgow North-West. With me is Myra Canning, councillor for the Scotstounhill ward, and these three gentlemen are here on behalf of Excalibur Developments.' He gestured to Broadhurst and company. 'We've got a lot of business to get through tonight and I know many of you have concerns you wish to raise. But before I open up to the floor, I'd like to give our guests the opportunity to state their case, which will hopefully cover some of the questions you may have and allay some of your fears. Gentlemen?'

There was some hushed, hurried debate between the three men. Then, one of them – the one Broadhurst had spoken to as he came in – got to his feet and began his address.

For the next half-hour, Zoe sat and listened as Excalibur Developments' nominated spokesman extolled the virtues of the new homes his company was building and the opportunities they would bring to the local area. This was followed by a handful of questions and an abundance of open-ended diatribes from a bunch of irate locals who of *course* had no objection to the building of more affordable housing but surely there were other places it could be built and anyway what was it going to do to the value of existing properties in the area? Broadhurst himself said very little, letting his colleagues set out their stall and field the questions from the floor. He sat, hands folded on the table in front of him, sometimes with his eyes half-closed, as if he was meditating. Once or twice, he interjected in a low, virtually inaudible voice to remind one of his colleagues of some detail or other they'd overlooked, but for the most part he was less an active participant than an ever-present guiding hand, there to give them purpose and moral support. Clearly he hadn't lost his touch for instilling discipline via the silent treatment.

When the meeting finally drew to a close, Zoe, feeling decidedly unfulfilled, got to her feet and joined the exodus from the assembly hall. A number of people had congregated in the foyer, seemingly intent on continuing the post-game discussion long into the night. As Zoe struggled to force a path through the multiple bodies packed into the narrow hallway, a voice – a man's – rose above the hubbub behind her.

'Excuse me!'

At first, she assumed he was addressing someone else and kept walking, but as the same shout was repeated, something gave her pause. There was something familiar about that voice, like the half-remembered melody of a song she hadn't heard in years. And she knew, even before she turned, why she recognised it.

'I spotted you sitting at the back,' said Adam Broadhurst, standing before her with an expression that wasn't unfriendly. 'You were one of my girls, weren't you? At Willow Bank?'

Zoe just stood there, tongue-tied, trying to force a response from the part of her brain that normally made dealing with social situations second nature to her. Her heart was racing, her mind an empty vacuum. It was like being fifteen all over again, standing to attention before him, waiting for him to pass sentence on her. How could it be that this man still had so much hold over her, a decade and a half after she'd ceased to be his pupil?

Broadhurst tilted his head slightly, studying her. 'I know the face, but I can't place the name . . . '

'It's Zoe Callahan.'

*Je-SUS!* What possessed her to blurt that out? *Ya absolute* turnip, *Zoe*. She should have made something up. But then, she somehow suspected he'd have immediately seen through any lie. He always did have a knack for sniffing out bullshit. It could have been worse, she supposed. At least she hadn't called him 'sir'.

'Of course, of course.' He nodded approvingly, as if she'd passed some test he'd set for her. 'The girl from Ruchill.'

Yes, because of course her defining characteristic was that she came from a scheme.

He chuckled softly to himself, as if reminiscing about a particularly fond memory. 'I remember now. We used to have such a terrible time trying to improve your elocution. Never did manage to hammer the blue-collar Scots out of you, as I recall.'

'Aye,' said Zoe stiffly, indignation briefly overcoming her lingering fear of the man, 'ma granny wis aye throwin good money efter bad.'

'Well, well, well – fancy running into you here of all places. And what have you been doing with yourself since you left us?'

She decided to tell the truth in the most blunt, unvarnished way possible, hoping it would prick his pride knowing that one of 'his' girls had amounted to so little.

'Waiting tables and cleaning toilets, mainly.'

If Broadhurst was at all disappointed, he gave no sign. 'Well, we all have to earn a living somehow. And you're based in Scotstounhill now . . . ?'

'Naw really. I was just kinda in the neighbourhood.'

'And you chose to attend a hustings about a local housing develop-ment?' Broadhurst's tone was more bemused than mocking, but regardless, she didn't like it.

'Aye, takes aw sorts.'

She had no idea what she'd expected to get out of coming here. It wasn't as if, just by being in the same room, breathing the same air as him, she'd have been able to determine whether or not he'd really done the things he was accused of. *They don't all wear a dirty mac and have a lazy eye, Zoe.*

Now Broadhurst was stroking his chin thoughtfully. 'Of course, you were Victor's older sister, weren't you? It was tragic what became of him – truly tragic.'

She made no attempt to spare his blushes by sugarcoating it. 'Aye, one a skivvy and the ither a murderer. Easy tae see how yese never used our family as wan o' yer success stories in the school pamphlet.'

Broadhurst attempted a small, polite laugh, but it came out sounding more like an uncomfortable cough. They stood there facing one another, neither speaking. The silence between them grew and grew until it was clear that even Broadhurst was becoming uncomfortable.

'Well, I'd best be getting on,' he said. 'You know how it is: never enough hours in the day to do everything you need to. It was nice to run into you again, Zoe.'

As he turned to go, Zoe felt an urge bubbling up inside her to confront him – to ask him straight out if he still buggered little boys and made them suck his wrinkly old dick. That would give the concerned citizens of Scotstounhill something to *really* worry about. But she couldn't. As she tried to speak, she found her voice catching in her throat, preventing her from getting out anything more than a strangled breath, drowned out by the sounds of conversation around her. It was fear that prevented her – fear and, she was forced to admit, a lingering sense of deference towards the man who, for the six years she'd spent at Willow Bank, had been more powerful in her eyes than God, the Devil and Darth Vader all rolled into one.

As she watched Broadhurst retreating into the crowd, she realised she was glad her fear had got the better of her. It would have been monumentally stupid to have let him know she was onto him. And yet that fact did nothing to stop her from feeling totally, utterly craven – a miserable, pathetic failure who'd let an old man cow her because of who he'd once been.

There was nothing for it but to head for home. Defeated and dejected, she trudged towards the door.

# 14

# Adult Games

*Monday 30 November*

The girl barrelled out of the department store, anti-theft alarm pealing behind her. She took off across the concourse, confident that the over-weight, ruddy-cheeked security guard hadn't a hope of keeping up with her. She smashed through the entrance doors of the shopping centre and set off down Buchanan Street, weaving through the crowds with practised ease. Down the slope she went, past Paperchase and the Gap, past the Tartan House and its all-day cacophony of bagpipe music, before ducking into one of the many narrow lanes that criss-crossed the city centre. She stopped to catch her breath, giggling with delight at her own wile, then unzipped her battered denim jacket and drew out the designer handbag she'd swiped.

As she stood admiring it, a long shadow fell on her. She froze, the laughter dying in her throat, and slowly turned to face the tall, suited figure who now stood in the mouth of the lane, blocking her only means of escape.

'Well, well, well,' he drawled, amusement writ large across his chiselled features, 'Mandy *Burns*. Last time our paths crossed, you were just a doe-eyed waif turning tricks in the East End. See you've graduated to shoplifting now?'

Zoe lay on her back, one arm tucked behind her head, and wondered how much longer this could possibly take. Craig continued to grind and thrust, going at it with both a stamina and an enthusiasm that seriously outstripped either his skill or imagination.

If she was being honest with herself, there'd been something in the air between them for weeks now: the sly glances, the nervous half-smiles, the sitting just a little bit closer than necessary to one another on the back step during break-time. Indeed, she'd had half an inkling something like this might happen when he'd invited her back to his parents' place during their lunch hour to listen to the new track he and his bandmates had just recorded. And, after they'd listened to the track and Zoe had told some polite lies to the tune of them really being in with a chance of landing a deal, the inevitable had duly happened. Was *still* happening. He'd been going at it for a good fifteen minutes now, which had given her plenty of time to regret her choices.

Finally, the humping, which had been increasing in both pace and ferocity for some time, reached its peak. He gave a strained cry that sounded more like that of a wildebeest in its death throes than a man in his prime reaching sexual ecstasy, and went limp, rolling off her and panting for breath.

'You're amazing,' he told her between gasps. 'Absolutely amazing.'

She smiled, taking the compliment with good grace but unable to think up anything to reciprocate it that would have sounded halfway believable.

As they lay side by side, him still panting, her noticing she was still wearing her left sock and that it had a hole in it, she reflected that fornication with the opposite sex really wasn't all it was cracked up to be. After she and Carol had gone their separate ways, she'd dived fairly quickly into a couple of brief relationships with men – trying, she now realised, to convince herself that that period in her life was well and truly over. Of late, though, she'd concluded that she was more enamoured by the *idea* of getting pumped by a bloke than the actual act of it happening. On paper, there was something firm and decisive about it, like pounding a punchbag or hammering a nail into a wall. But the reality always seemed to fail to live up to expectations. She felt like telling Craig it wasn't him, it was her – but then, one look at his expression of satisfied bliss was enough for her to realise there was no way she could shatter his illusions. Let the boy think he done good.

She watched as he manoeuvred himself upright and, sitting on the end of the bed, prised the loaded condom from his still-twitching knob. (Another delight you didn't have to contend with when you weren't doing it with a guy.) He tied it off, took a wad of tissues from the box on the dresser and wrapped them round it – so his parents wouldn't find it, presumably – then got up and deposited it in the wastebasket by the far wall, before turning to face her.

'You OK?'

'Hmm? Oh aye, just peachy.'

'You seem a bit . . . distracted.'

*Oh God,* she thought, *he's going to ask, 'Wasn't I good?'* And there was no way of answering that question that didn't involve lying to a degree that was beyond her skill.

'I was just thinking.'

'Oh yeah? What about?'

'Stuff.'

'Stuff? Like what?' He perched on the end of the bed and gazed at her expectantly, genuinely interested.

''Bout, well . . . '

*Fuck it.* She might as well tell him. It would give her a chance to work through the thoughts inside her head. She pushed herself up into a sitting position, the better to articulate them.

'OK, so it's like this. Let's say, hypothetically speaking, there was this person, and he done something bad – I mean *really* bad, as in hurt a buncha people. And you knew. Right?'

Craig nodded, a vacant look in his eyes.

'And say this'd all happened years ago and he'd never answered for it and was still walking round, free as a streaker's bawsack.'

Another nod.

'But like, he's powerful. Got powerful mates – folk who'll back him up. And if you said anything, it'd be your word against his.'

Another nod, this time accompanied by a deep 'mm', to show how seriously he was taking this.

'Well, what would ye do?'

Craig pursed his lips and continued to sit there, absentmindedly stroking himself down there, as if he was hoping the act would provide inspiration.

She wanted to yell at him to leave it alone, but she sensed it wouldn't help matters.

Eventually, he gave a dopey shrug. 'Dunno really. S'pose, if it's someone powerful, someone folk're gonna believe over you, there's not a whole lot you *can* do.'

Zoe bit her lip, saying nothing. She wondered if that was actually true – if powerful people really were that untouchable – or if it was just a case of too many folk *assuming* it was the case, creating a self-fulfilling prophecy where everyone tiptoed around them, afraid to face up to them, when in reality they'd fold at the slightest push, like the wee man behind the curtain in *The Wizard of Oz*.

'Right,' she said eventually, 'but d'ye reckon, in cases like that, where ye know they're never gonnae face justice the normal way, d'ye reckon there's ever a case for going outside the system – y'know, taking matters into yer own hands?'

For a long moment, Craig stared at her, his eyes wide. 'Zoe,' he said, his voice an awed whisper, 'are you thinking about doing Malcolm Malcolm in?'

'What?' Zoe blinked at him in disbelief. 'No! Malcolm *Malcolm*? What the fuck? D'ye reckon I'm some sorta nutjob?'

'Course not, no,' said Craig, chastened.

'Christ on a bike, Craig! I said we were talking hypothetically.'

'Right, right, sure, yeah.' Craig was nodding vigorously, backtracking for all he was worth. 'So I mean, yeah, hypothetically, I guess . . . '

Zoe sighed. 'Forget it. It disnae matter.'

She lay back, scraping her hands down her face. Her head hurt from all this thinking. She raised her arm, checking her watch – which, like her left sock, had remained on in the rush to get down to business. Still another ten minutes before they were due back.

'Hey, Craig – wanna do something for me?'

He looked up like an excited puppy, eager to make amends. 'What?'

Rather than spell it out, she reached out, grabbed his head with both hands and shoved it between her legs, figuring he'd at least have the gumption to work out what she expected from him. As he set to work like a duck taking to water, she sank back, shut her eyes and tried very hard for the next five minutes – or however long it was going to take – to forget.

\* \* \*

Several hours later, Zoe swallowed a yawn, tossed the bowl of instanoodles into the microwave and perched on her kitchen worktop, watching as the display counted down the five minutes to Sriracha-chicken-flavoured goodness. The Corner had been unusually busy for a Monday night, and her brain was fried. Mind you, the frenetic pace had meant there had been mercifully few opportunities for her and Craig to be alone together. She dreaded to think how she was going to respond when he inevitably enquired about the prospect of a repeat performance. Perhaps if he agreed they'd stick to oral in future . . .

She wondered what had possessed her to start wittering on to him about punishing bad people and all that other crap. The lack of anyone else in her life with whom she could talk these things through, she supposed. Once upon a time, Anna would have been the obvious person to turn to – Anna, who was sensible and level-headed and smart and basically all the things Zoe wasn't. In fact, around the time she'd rung up a bunch of random ex-classmates and asked them if they'd been aware of anything dodgy going on back in the old days, she'd contemplated calling Anna and sounding her out, on the basis that if anyone could offer a more nuanced perspective on the matter, it was surely her oldest and bestest friend. She'd actually got as far as keying in her number before realising she couldn't possibly lay this at her door. Anna had more than enough to be dealing with at the moment, what with having a bun in the oven and all – a state of affairs Zoe *still* couldn't wrap her head around. The pair of them hadn't exchanged more than a quick text or two since Anna had told her her big news, and Zoe wasn't sure whose fault it was that they'd become so distant of late. Hers, probably. Most things usually were.

As the microwave pinged, she heard a soft thud in the hallway. Stepping out of the kitchen, she spotted a padded envelope lying on the doormat.

*Bit late for a delivery.*

She picked it up and inspected it. No name and address on it. She took the door off the chain and stepped outside, the stone floor chilly under her bare feet. There was no sign of anyone in the stairwell – not even the sound of fleeing footsteps. Whoever had posted the parcel was long gone.

She headed back into the flat, tore open the envelope and slid a hand inside. She felt something hard, flat and round. A CD, maybe, or a DVD?

She slid it out. It *was* a DVD – one of those burnable thingies with a blank label so you could write what was on it. Only, just like the envelope, no one had.

'The fuck . . . ?'

Her noodles forgotten, she padded through to the living room, popped the DVD into the player and switched on the TV. A menu appeared on the screen – one of those generic 'My Home Movies'-type affairs, with only one item on the list: a video with a runtime of eight minutes and forty-seven seconds called 'Untitled'. The thumbnail, a black square, offered no clues as to its content. She highlighted it and pressed Play.

The screen went blank. For a couple of seconds, nothing happened, then dancing fuzz filled the screen, accompanied by an overpowering static sound that had her scrambling for the volume control. A few more seconds, then an image finally appeared.

It was old, shot on VHS and clearly copied multiple times, riddled with tracking errors and alternating between black-and-white and severely bleeding colours. A date was burned into the bottom corner: 15.05.97. In the middle of the frame, the top of his head cropped off just below his hairline, stood a boy. The camera was stationary but at a slight angle, which gave the footage a canted, vaguely queasy appearance.

Making it doubly queasy was the fact that the boy was wearing nothing but boxer shorts.

From his overall proportions, she concluded that he was young – fourteen or fifteen at most. She wondered if this was some sort of medical exam. But no, the setting was all wrong. She could see a low bookshelf behind the boy, and the wallpaper was a diffuse pastel hue – more like an office or a study than a doctor's surgery. The boy looked puzzled, as if he was trying to work out why he was there. With his fists balled by his sides, his head held high and his narrow chest puffed out, he appeared defiant – determined not to let himself be intimidated by the situation.

Someone fiddled with the camera, adjusting its height and angle. The overall results weren't much better than before, but the operator appeared satisfied.

'See now?' A man's voice, offscreen. 'Nothing to be scared of.'

Zoe recognised the voice immediately. It had been in her thoughts more often than not since she'd last heard it, a week ago to the day. And she now realised why she recognised the room. She'd stood there herself once, in almost the exact same spot the boy now occupied.

'Why don't you tell us your name and how old you are?' Broadhurst's voice continued – smooth, reassuring, but still with that authoritative edge which left you no option but to obey.

'Josh . . . ' began the boy, eyes moving towards something out of view to the left.

'Don't look at him,' said Broadhurst sharply. 'Face the camera.'

The boy did as he was told. Staring into the lens, almost as if he was looking directly at Zoe, he began again.

'Joshua Manning.'

His tone, like his body language, seemed designed to project an air of defiance, which she suspected belied how he really felt.

'And how old are you, Joshua?'

'Fourteen.'

'And aren't you growing up fast!' It was an observation, not a question.

Silence for a moment, a low hum – Computer? Air-conditioner? – the only audible sound. Joshua shifted uncomfortably from one foot to the other.

'Well, go on, Joshua.' Broadhurst sounded somewhat exasperated. 'Tell us about yourself. What are your favourite subjects? What hobbies do you have?'

'Em . . . ' Joshua's eyes drifted to the side again, either to Broadhurst or the other offscreen presence he'd been instructed not to look at. Realising his mistake, he once again directed his gaze to the camera. 'I like PE, History, Modern Studies . . . English is OK, I guess. Hobbies . . . I like football, basketball, hockey . . . '

'An active lad, then.' Broadhurst evidently approved. 'No couch potato, you, eh? That's what we like – a healthy mind and a healthy body.'

There was a creaking sound off-camera. Joshua's gaze shifted upwards, indicating that Broadhurst had stood up.

'So,' Broadhurst mused, 'you like playing games. Are there any other games you like, I wonder? *Adult* games, that is.'

Joshua stared in Broadhurst's direction, his expression blank.

'There's no need to be coy. We've all gone through the same changes, experienced the same urges. We know just what it's like at your age:

hormones racing, overflowing with pent-up desires. Why don't you show us what you do to relieve those urges?'

Throughout this speech, Joshua's cheeks had grown increasingly red. Now, a look of blind panic entered his eyes. All trace of defiance had vanished.

'There's no shame in it, you know.' Broadhurst's tone was silky-smooth, almost sensual. 'Every boy does it at some point in his life. Some only do it once in a while, others every chance they get. It's why the Good Lord gave you that part of your anatomy.'

Joshua's previously clenched hands moved to his groin area, cupping the part in question defensively.

'No need to be shy, now. It's just us here. No one else is going to come through that door.'

*No one's coming to save you.* The boy seemed to understand this all too clearly. As Broadhurst fell silent, the look in his eyes was one of utter despair. For a few seconds, he didn't move. Then, with what almost amounted to resignation, he began to do as he'd been instructed.

Until now, Zoe had sat perched on the edge of the sofa, watching with a mixture of horror and morbid fascination. Now, however, she was galvanised into action. No fucking way was she going to watch this. Lurching across the floor to the DVD player, she hit the Eject button.

As the TV went blank and silence fell once more, she remained sprawled on the floor, acutely aware of her heavy breathing and thundering heart. What sick fuck would send her this? And *why*?

She reached for the envelope, checking it for some sign of the sender's identity. Not that she expected to find anything. She didn't imagine the sort of people who posted home movies of child abuse through folk's doors tended to include a return address.

There was something else inside. She tipped the envelope upside down. A bundle of photographs fell onto the floor – a dozen or so, held together by a rubber band. She tore it off and began to rifle through them. The first two were of the boy from the video – one shot from a distance outdoors, almost like a paparazzi snap; the other a professional, head-and-shoulders affair. Yearbook photo, maybe. The next was of another boy, about the same age, again taken unawares. A couple more, both boys she didn't recognise.

She continued to rifle. Another boy, and another. The implication of all these pictures was painfully clear. A couple more, one, two. She was nearing the end of the stack. She came to the last picture, and found herself gazing down at a face she knew better than any other on the planet. It didn't matter that he'd been dead for nearly six years; when she shut her eyes, she could still picture every contour of that face. Every freckle. Every imperfection.

She opened her eyes again. Her brother Victor continued to stare back at her from his yearbook photograph with that familiar, uncomfortable half-smile he always gave in awkward or formal situations.

She was on her feet in an instant. She bolted across the hallway to the bathroom, dropped to her knees and hugged the toilet bowl, moments before spewing the contents of her stomach into it.

# 15

# The Quiet Man

*Thursday 3 December*

Anna emerged from her house, shrugging on her coat, and made her way down to the street, where Vasilico's Porsche was idling at the kerb, its freshly waxed bodywork gleaming in the midmorning light.

'Quite the lodgings you've got there,' he remarked as she eased herself into the passenger seat. 'I didn't realise university lecturers were *that* well-paid.'

'We're not,' she said, stretching the seatbelt across her protruding belly.

'Mr Scavolini must be on quite the little earner, then.'

'There's no Mr Scavolini,' she said shortly. She'd slept badly the previous night, her rapidly ballooning stomach making it impossible to find a comfortable position. Add to that the absence of her much-missed morning caffeine fix and it was hardly surprising she was a little tetchy.

'In that case, the only possible conclusion to draw is that you have seriously wealthy benefactors.'

Turning, she fixed him with a stiff glare. 'Just drive.'

With an amused grin, Vasilico revved the engine and pulled out into the road.

They drove north up Cleveden Road and on into Kelvinside, the portable police radio on the dashboard emitting a continuous stream of low-volume chatter. As Anna's mind tuned into the words, she realised they related to a live incident: the serious assault of a woman in the Finnieston area and the ongoing efforts to apprehend the as yet still at large perpetrators. She caught the words *kicked multiple times* and *fractured jaw*, and decided she'd heard enough.

'Would you mind turning that off?'

Vasilico glanced up from the road, momentarily confused. Then, as he followed her gaze to the radio, recognition dawned.

'Of course.' He flicked a switch, silencing it. 'Sorry – I didn't think. I just . . . well, I like having it on in the background. Keeps me abreast of what's going on, and . . . ' He shrugged sheepishly. 'Well, it's company of a sort.'

'It doesn't bother you, listening to a constant running commentary of the violence people do to one another?'

He frowned, considering the question. 'Guess I've never really thought about it in those terms. I'm not focusing on the viscera of it per se. I tend to see it more in the abstract – like pieces on a chessboard, or drawing pins on a map.'

'Isn't that a bit dehumanising?'

She meant it as a casual enquiry rather than a criticism, but she saw instantly from the narrowing of his eyes that he'd taken it as the latter.

'I'm not sure there's an alternative,' he said. 'You don't last long in this line of work without developing a certain sense of healthy detachment. But then, I can see how that might sound slightly insensitive if you don't have much direct experience of humanity's innate capacity for cruelty.'

'I'm not some naïve little girl, you know. I'm more than aware of humanity's capacity for cruelty.'

Vasilico gave a dry chuckle and said nothing.

'What?'

'Nothing. It's just . . . ' He glanced in her direction with a rather strained smile. 'Forgive me, but it's one thing to read about something in a textbook and quite another to witness it firsthand.'

'Oh, I see. *Those that can, do. Those that can't, teach.* Is that it?'

'Not at all. Hard as it might be to believe, I really do have nothing but the healthiest respect for the contributions you and your colleagues make to the discourse on criminal justice.'

She smiled thinly. 'Just as long as I remember it's *you* and *your* colleagues who actually get results, right?'

'Well . . . ' He gave a vague shrug, neither a confirmation nor an outright denial.

'There's an interesting dichotomy to law enforcement, you know,' Anna said.

'Oh yes?' said Vasilico, in the tone of a parent humouring a precocious child. 'What's that, then?'

'It simply isn't all that effective. If it was – if your methods *actually* resulted in a meaningful reduction in criminality – you'd be out of a job overnight.'

'Well then,' said Vasilico, with a deep, philosophical sigh, 'I suppose I'll just have to wait for the day when you publish that paper that solves all crime everywhere in one fell swoop, so I can retire early to a beach in Malibu.'

Anna didn't trust herself to respond. Instead, she rested her chin on her knuckle and gazed out the window as they continued on up into Kelvindale, only too aware of Vasilico smirking away to himself just beyond her field of vision.

The venue for the memorial service was St Martin's, a small Presbyterian church just east of the River Kelvin. When Vasilico pulled into the grounds at a quarter to eleven, a small crowd was already gathered outside the entrance to the nondescript-looking single-storey building – a couple of them, Anna noticed, with professional video cameras on their shoulders.

'Who tipped off the media?' said Vasilico, articulating the very thought that was going through Anna's own head.

As they got out of the car, Anna continued to observe the crowd at the entrance, noting the way they were clustered together like a single contiguous body, conversing with an ease that implied familiarity. She concluded that they were *all* press – or, if they weren't, that they must all know each other from some other context. She and Vasilico hung back near the car – or rather, Vasilico hung back and Anna, noticing that he'd come to a halt, did likewise, on the basis that she didn't fancy braving the media scrum alone.

As the minutes slowly ticked down towards eleven, more cars began to trickle into the grounds, most of them parking at the opposite end from Anna and Vasilico, where there were more available spaces. Several of the men and women who emerged from them were in police uniform, and those that weren't still had that unmistakeable look which marked them out as law enforcement from a mile away. Among them were a few Anna recognised from the briefing she'd attended at MIT headquarters back in September. There was no sign yet of any conventional mourners: no friends, no family.

Among the vehicles to arrive was a black sedan with tinted windows. It came to a halt some way off from the other cars, spread diagonally across two parking spaces. The driver got out, opened the back door and stood back, almost like a soldier at attention, as two men got out. The first was De Groot, his tie knotted so tightly that Anna was amazed blood was still circulating above his non-existent neck. Behind him followed a slight, meek-looking man in his mid-fifties, wearing a cheap, ill-fitting suit and with sad, hangdog eyes like a Basset Hound's. De Groot looked in Anna's direction, his beady little eyes seeming to grow even smaller as he glowered at her, while the other man – who Anna couldn't help but think resembled a down-at-heel lawyer, or at least a caricature of one – gave a brief nod to Vasilico, which he returned.

Anna was about to ask Vasilico who the unfamiliar man was when another, considerably less ostentatious car pulled into the grounds: an old Volvo bearing the insignia of a local taxi firm. It came to a halt in the middle of the grounds, the back door opened and Clive Sullivan emerged. A silence fell, every pair of eyes trained on him as he paused to lean against the roof of the cab, as if steeling himself. Then, with the veneer of a proud soldier determined to cling to his dignity to the bitter end, he walked stiffly but defiantly across the car park towards the church. The media scrum, who'd seemingly been caught napping, sprang into action, a round of flashbulbs going off as he strode through them, ignoring their cacophony of questions. He made his way up the short flight of steps; then, standing on the low porch, he faced the assembled crowd.

Eventually, it seemed to dawn on them that Sullivan was waiting for quiet. The barrage of voices gradually died away, until only the rustle of dead leaves skittering across the concrete could be heard.

'Thank you all for coming,' he said, his voice thin and reedy in the open air, but nonetheless unwavering. 'I wish to make a brief statement.'

He took a piece of paper out of his pocket, unfolded it and, head bowed slightly, began to read from it.

'My son, Derek Sullivan, has been missing now for twelve weeks. For much of that time, I refused to abandon the hope that he was alive and well somewhere.'

*Bullshit,* thought Anna. By her side, she heard Vasilico swallowing hard and guessed he was harbouring similar thoughts.

'Just under a month ago, I was informed by the police that an item of clothing belonging to my son had been found caught in the railings of the Erskine Bridge. While no body has yet been recovered, I now believe that the time has come to think the previously unthinkable. In the course of his short life, my son battled a variety of demons, some real, others imagined. It is my belief that he succumbed to the latter and that the most likely explanation is that he took his own life.'

Sullivan paused to inhale a deep breath. 'Fate, it seems, is a cruel mistress. We all endure a degree of tragedy in our lives, and yet it's hard not to look back on the last several years and feel that I've been dealt more than my fair share. Cancer took my wife from me before she reached her sixtieth year. Then, earlier this year, the same evil disease also claimed my older brother – a formidable man whose legacy should be familiar to everyone here. And now it seems my son, my last surviving relative, has joined them.'

Listening, Anna chewed the inside of her mouth pensively. 'Is it just me,' she murmured to Vasilico, 'or does this all feel like a show that's being staged for our benefit?'

'It's not just you,' he replied.

'I would like to offer my sincerest thanks,' Sullivan continued, 'to those of you in the media who have publicised my son's plight, and to the police officers who have been unceasing in their efforts to find and bring him home. But you can stand down now, all of you.' He lifted his head from his notes and gazed out at the various faces assembled before him. 'You've devoted enough resources to this. It's time to stop.'

He fell silent for a moment, allowing his words to hang in the air. As he did so, his gaze briefly strayed to Anna and Vasilico. If he was in any way surprised to see Anna there, his eyes didn't betray it.

'Today is about drawing a line in the sand,' he went on. 'About saying a final goodbye. I ask that my decision be respected – that you allow this to be the end of the matter.' He refolded his notes and slipped them into the inner pocket of his jacket. 'I have nothing further to say.'

With that, he turned and headed into the church, ignoring the flurry of questions that erupted from the press pack.

A church usher stepped out onto the porch. Raising her voice over the din, she announced that those who had received invitations were now requested to take their seats for the service of remembrance. A couple of the reporters closest to the steps immediately tried to chance their arm but were swiftly rebuffed by the usher, who placed herself firmly between them and the entrance. As the various police officers began to head towards the building, Vasilico grunted a gruff 'shall we?' to Anna, and they joined the procession.

The service itself offered few surprises: the usual procession of hymns and prayers, a brief Bible reading and a summation of Derek's life, delivered by the minister in the dour, Calvinistic mode Anna remembered so well from the religious services she'd been obliged to attend as a schoolgirl. (A succession of teachers had been unmoved by her protestations that, as a child of Jewish parents and an atheist to boot, the requirement that she participate in Church of Scotland worship was doubly unjust.) There were around thirty guests altogether, and Anna, stealing a glance behind her from her seat next to Vasilico in the second row, once again concluded that, apart from Sullivan and the minister, she was the only civilian present. There was no sign of anyone of Derek's own age – none of the schoolfriends he'd supposedly kept in touch with. As the minister droned on about his childhood love of model aeroplanes and Enid Blyton novels, her overriding impression was once again that this was a show and they were the hand-picked audience – brought here to make sure they received, loud and clear, the message Sullivan wanted them to hear.

When the service was over, they headed outside, congregating in the grounds in little clusters, like schoolchildren at playtime. Watching the various officers milling around with their hands in their pockets, Anna strongly suspected that they were as bemused by the whole affair as her. Near the church entrance, Sullivan was deep in conversation with the minister and with the small, meek man who'd arrived in the sedan, the latter nodding understandingly to every word uttered by Sullivan, his drooping eyes radiating sympathy. A couple of members of the press were still hanging around on the periphery: a ratty-looking man armed with a Dictaphone and a portly one sporting a camera equipped with a telephoto lens. Both were clearly intent on securing an audience with Sullivan, but for the time being were being kept at a safe distance by a stolid-looking plain-clothes officer, who seemed to have taken it upon himself to assume bodyguard duty.

Having missed out on the opportunity earlier, Anna once more turned to ask Vasilico who the man talking to Sullivan was, only to discover that the DCI was nowhere to be seen. She looked around, slightly unnerved. Throughout Sullivan's valedictory to the press and the subsequent church service, she'd sensed him growing increasingly irate by her side, like a ticking bomb counting down to detonation. Before she could set off in search of him, however, a short, squat shape moved into view in front of her and she found herself face to face with Sean De Groot.

'Dr Scavolini,' he said, his lips parted in the thin veneer of a smile. 'How nice to see you again.'

'The feeling's mutual,' she said, through gritted teeth.

'Though I must confess to being ever so slightly puzzled as to your continued . . . affiliation with the Sullivan affair.'

'I came to pay my respects,' said Anna, wondering why she felt she had to justify herself to this self-important little prig. 'Same as you, I imagine.'

De Groot made a noise at the back of his throat, almost but not quite a scoff. 'I think we both know your involvement extends far beyond today's little gathering. Yes,' he went on, before Anna could formulate a response, 'my DCI seems to have taken quite a shine to you – even to the point of hosting out-of-hours consultations with you in his office.'

As Anna stood there, wondering how De Groot could possibly have found out about *that*, Vasilico rematerialised by her side. He stank of tobacco and was breathing hard through his nostrils, like a bull preparing to charge.

'Look at him,' he spat, shaking his head in disgust. 'Who does he think he's kidding?'

Anna followed his gaze to the church steps, where Sullivan was now in earnest discussion with an older man, whom she assumed was a retired cop – perhaps a contemporary of his late brother. She watched as he laid a consoling hand on Sullivan's upper arm.

'To hell with this,' muttered Vasilico, and set off across the concrete towards them.

'Where are you going?' De Groot shouted after him, to no response. 'Oi! I'm talking to you!'

With rising panic, Anna set off after Vasilico, moving as fast as her condition allowed. She shouted at him to wait, but he didn't seem to hear her. Clearly a man on a mission, he barged up to Sullivan, elbowing his way past the older cop.

'Are you happy with yourself?' he demanded, pushing himself right up into Sullivan's face. 'Are you proud of everything you've accomplished?'

'I *beg* your pardon!' said Sullivan, as Anna came to a breathless halt by Vasilico's side.

The third man, clearly not wanting any part in this, backed off surreptitiously, though he might as well not have existed for all the heed paid by Vasilico and Sullivan. They stood facing one another, mere centimetres apart, oblivious to the growing audience of onlookers who'd ceased their conversations to watch the unfolding spectacle.

'If you have something to say,' said Sullivan, glaring at Vasilico, 'then say it.'

'Vasilico, just leave it,' Anna hissed, tugging on his arm.

Ignoring her, Vasilico continued to square up to Sullivan, fists clenched. 'All right, then,' he said, 'I think this whole circus is a ploy on your part to deflect from your own responsibility for what happened to your son. From the word go, you refused to lift so much as a finger to help find him, no matter how many times I urged you to make a direct appeal. On top of that, you sat on the fact that he had a chronic mental health condition – a condition which, by all accounts, you never once took seriously – preferring to let the clock run down rather than admit you'd fathered a fuck-up.'

Sullivan blinked several times, his mouth opening and closing in apoplexy. 'How . . . how *dare* you! I've never once regarded my son in that way.'

'Then you've a *unique* way of showing it.' Vasilico gave an ugly smirk. 'Those were some fine words back there for our friends in the media, but we both know the truth, don't we? You didn't give two shits about Derek and his so-called "demons", in life or in death. And now you have the gall to arrange this . . . this *performance*, to make sure the whole world knows you've written him off like a used condom wrapper. Well, message received loud and clear!'

'I think you've said enough,' Anna hissed, reaching for his arm again.

But once again Vasilico paid her not the slightest bit of attention, if indeed he was even aware of her. 'You never give up on a loved one!' he yelled, spittle flying from his mouth as he jabbed a finger in Sullivan's face. '*Never!*'

'PAUL!' a voice behind them roared.

An eerie silence settled on the church grounds. Slowly, Vasilico turned. Anna, doing likewise, saw that the shout had originated from De Groot, standing a little way off, his face beet-red as he struggled to contain his rage. Every pair of eyes in the vicinity was fixed on Vasilico, their expressions ranging from shock to consternation. Towards the back of the crowd, Anna spotted the meek-looking man in the rumpled suit, his hangdog eyes radiating bitter disappointment.

The silence was broken by the click of a shutter. The man with the telephoto lens, stationed on the periphery of the car park, lowered his camera, the moment captured for posterity. As a couple of imposing-looking officers began to move towards him, he beat a hasty retreat, shoes slapping on the tarmac as he high-tailed it up the driveway and out of sight.

Vasilico turned to face Sullivan again, but before he could say anything, Sullivan beat him to it.

'Do you want to know what *I* believe?' he said, glaring at Vasilico with vengeful eyes. 'I believe you hounded my son to his grave.' He looked past Vasilico to the assembled crowd, raising his voice so they could all hear him. 'You people – you made his life a misery, tormenting him, ostracising him, making him feel less than worthless. And why? Because he had the nerve to do the right thing. Because he stood up for what was just.'

His eyes returned to Vasilico. 'And you – yes, you, Detective Chief Inspector Vasilico – don't think that I hold you blameless. The newspaper splashes, the gaudy television appeals, the army of officers pounding the streets day and night . . . All your doing. All your responsibility. *You* left him with nowhere to hide; no other way out except . . . '

He fell silent, swallowing a deep, shuddering breath. 'I l—' he began, then stopped himself. 'I . . . cared . . . about my son. I may not be as *adept* at expressing my emotions as you, Detective Chief Inspector, but I cared about him to a degree you couldn't possibly imagine.'

With that, he turned and began to walk back towards the church, his back stiff and straight, his steps slow but deliberate. As the crowd parted to let him through, Vasilico, his face a mask of bitter rage, straightened his lapels. Then, with every set of eyes still on him, he too strode off, heading up the driveway towards Kelvindale Road.

As De Groot made to follow him, his face like puce, Anna held up a hand, warning him off. 'Let me talk to him.'

Then, before De Groot could make any objection, she turned and set off after Vasilico.

At the mouth of the driveway, she halted and looked in both directions before spotting him, perched on a low wall about seventy metres down the road, lighting a fresh cigarette. She stood watching him for a moment, then sucked in a breath and made her way down the slope towards him. He glanced up momentarily as she halted in front of him, then lowered his head again and carried on smoking.

'Just what the hell was *that*?' she demanded.

'What? He didn't make you want to smack his face as well? If I'd had to spend another minute breathing the same air as that desiccated old fossil, I wouldn't have been responsible for my actions.'

'Believe me, I noticed. Fancy telling me what your beef is with him?'

Vasilico snorted. 'I thought I made my views pretty clear. For a man with his son's blood on his hands, he doesn't half act like his shit don't stink.'

'Oh, come on.' Anna rolled her eyes. 'In every single one of our dealings to date, you've been Mr Unflappable – slick, suave, the perfect model of professionalism. And then, today, you decide to throw it all down the drain and get into a schoolyard slanging match with a grieving father? I'm not stupid, Vasilico. What happened back there was deeply, deeply personal.'

Vasilico said nothing. He continued to stare off into the distance, twin plumes of smoke escaping from his nostrils as he let out a long breath. Gazing down at the half-finished cigarette pinched between his fingers, Anna felt an unexpected pang of disappointment. She considered it a vile habit, to the extent that it was a deal-breaker for her in any relationship. She reminded herself that she wasn't *in* a relationship with him, nor was she going to be. Still, she couldn't help but feel strangely let down, as if an assumption she hadn't even realised she'd made about him had been proven false.

Vasilico continued to sit in silence. Then, just when Anna was on the verge of conceding defeat, he stirred and took out his wallet. He opened it and produced a small, dog-eared picture, which he handed to Anna. It showed a boy in his early teens, dressed in T-shirt and shorts, with a mop of sandy hair and a long, aquiline nose that was instantly familiar.

'That's my brother,' he said – though she'd already guessed as much. 'Luke. When I was twelve and he was a couple of years older than me, he died suddenly in his sleep. Cause was an undiagnosed brain aneurysm. Most likely, it was something that'd been there since birth – in other words, a ticking time bomb. I was the one who found the body.'

'Christ,' murmured Anna, not sure anything else really covered it.

'I was all right, at the time. Felt I didn't have much choice. My mum fell to bits, though. She'd raised us on our own since before I was five, and . . . well, I suppose I saw it as my duty to be the man of the house now that Luke was gone. And, for a while, we managed to truck on. But then, just after I turned fifteen, things came to a head and I had what might loosely be termed a breakdown.

'They put it down to a combination of the stress I'd been putting myself under and a delayed reaction to finding the body. I was hospitalised and diagnosed with major depression and put on an intensive course of anti-depressants and CBT. I don't think it's anything of an exaggeration to say that it's thanks to that course of intervention that my mum didn't have to bury *two* sons rather than one.

'When I got out of hospital, my uncle – my mum's brother – moved us both in with him. He got me back on track; practically raised me as his own. I owe him everything – him and the docs and good old Prozac.'

He took another drag on his cigarette. 'Point is, I've been to the same sort of places Derek Sullivan must have been to. I know how dark it is down there. How lonely. How hopeless.' Still clutching the cigarette between his fingers, he jabbed a trembling arm in the direction of the church grounds. 'And seeing that . . . that *prick* wittering on about fate and tragedy and what have you when he's half the reason the lad jumped off the Erskine Bridge – gimme a break!' He tossed the now severely depleted cigarette, watching it spark as it glanced off the ground.

Anna lowered herself gingerly onto the wall next to him, legs wide apart to balance herself. 'We don't know any of that for sure,' she said gently, as she handed back the photo. 'We still haven't established what happened to Derek or why – no matter what his father might say.'

Vasilico returned the photo to his wallet and turned to her with a wan smile. 'I think it's about time we faced facts, don't you? Neither you nor I believes he's coming home.'

Anna said nothing. She wished she could disagree with him, but she knew he was speaking the truth.

Vasilico grimaced apologetically. 'Sorry to land that hot mess in your lap. It's not something I make a habit of shouting from the rooftops.'

'It's OK,' she said, wishing it didn't feel quite so much as if the onus was now on her to share her own story – a sort of mental health *you show me yours, I'll show you mine*. 'I'm glad you felt able to tell me.'

Vasilico shrugged slightly. 'It helps that you're a good listener.'

It took Anna a moment to realise he was alluding to one of their earlier conversations: the one in the café on Woodlands Road, when she'd opined that the world would be a better place if more people took a more enlightened approach to resolving their problems. She smiled, acknowledging the reference.

'Still,' she said carefully, 'it must be difficult, you being a police officer.'

'How so?'

'Well,' she shrugged, 'I mean, it's such a stoic, macho culture. You're conditioned not to talk about your feelings, not to show any vulnerability, not to seek help if you're having problems. I'm not having another go,' she added, raising her hands in a peace gesture as she sensed Vasilico stiffening beside her. 'I'm just trying to put it in context.'

Vasilico smiled – a small, rather bittersweet smile, but a smile nonetheless, and the mood seemed to lift slightly. 'It's not all bad, you know.'

'I'm sure it's not,' she said, unable to pretend to be convinced.

'I wish I could make you see!' He sighed in frustration, rubbing at the back of his neck like he was trying to work out a knot. 'Yes, there's an element of chauvinism running through it – and believe me, there's stuff about it that I wish I could change. But there's also camaraderie. A feeling that you belong to something bigger than yourself. That you're a family.'

'I'll take your word for it.'

Vasilico looked at her with a mixture of exasperation and compassion. 'What *happened* to you?' he said, his tone beseeching. 'There must be something – some experience in your past that's given you such a negative view of us and everything we do.'

Anna sat, staring straight ahead to avoid his gaze. The problem with having a personal story, AN EVENT, was that it allowed people to dismiss your convictions as driven purely by emotion rather than something you'd arrived at rationally – when, in reality, the two couldn't always be separated so easily.

She sighed inwardly. If she didn't answer, it was just going to hang in the air as unfinished business, tainting every subsequent interaction they had. And besides, having cajoled him into divulging his own personal demons, it seemed hypocritical, not to mention cowardly, to refuse to reciprocate in kind.

'You're familiar with the Kelvingrove Park Murders?' she said.

'Of course.'

'About six years ago, I got caught up in the investigation. I was a witness to the first murder, and . . . well, I knew the victim, sort of. Anyway, one of the detectives took a serious dislike to me; convinced himself I was sticking my nose where it didn't belong.' She rolled her eyes, forestalling the inevitable wry comment from Vasilico. 'I know, I know – big surprise, right? There was a misunderstanding, and officers were sent to bring me in – by force, if necessary. I panicked, and in the process of trying to get away I did what anyone in my shoes would have done: I fought back.'

She blew out a heavy breath. 'After they got me back to the station, they treated me to the works. They stripped me, they manhandled me, and then they left me in a freezing cold room for hours, naked, with nothing to cover myself with. It was only the arrival of the senior investigating officer that put a stop to it.'

Vasilico stared at her in disbelief, his eyes flaring with righteous anger. 'Who were they, the officers who did this to you? What were their names?'

Anna laughed humourlessly. 'You see? There you go, doing what you lot always do. You want to make it about individuals instead of facing up to the fact that the problem is systemic. Just a few more bad apples – right?' She shook her head. 'It doesn't matter who they were. The point is, the system within which they operated provided them with both the means to do it and the confidence that they'd suffer no repercussions.'

For several moments, Vasilico just gazed at her, saying nothing. He looked genuinely pained, as if her disillusionment, and the reason for it, hurt him on a genuinely physical level.

'I know you'll just say I'm missing the point,' he said eventually, 'but I swear to you, Anna, I would never do something like that – not to you, not to anyone.'

Anna met his gaze, unblinking. 'And yet these things, and far worse, continue to happen. And it's at least in part because too many people who insist their hands are clean nonetheless turn a blind eye to what's going on around them. They don't call it the blue wall of silence for nothing.'

Vasilico's shoulders sagged. He sighed in disappointment and frustration, his head bowed low.

'Are you familiar with Marcus Aurelius?' Anna asked.

Vasilico looked up with a hint of a smile. 'Wasn't he in that film with Russell Crowe?'

'Sort of. He wrote that "often injustice lies in what you *aren't* doing, not only in what you *are* doing". Not doing evil isn't enough – you have to actively fight it when you see it, or else you're complicit.' She shifted her position on the wall, turning to face him directly. 'Say you have a hundred cops, and out of them, perhaps – what, three are crooked? If the other ninety-seven say and do nothing about the three crooked ones, you haven't got ninety-seven good cops and three bad. You've got a hundred bad ones.'

Vasilico looked unconvinced but said nothing.

Anna sighed, running her hands over her face. She felt tired and emotionally drained. 'I know you have this idea that I hate the police; that I want to burn the whole institution to the ground and piss on its ashes. I don't. I accept that it serves a vital function and that, as individuals, a lot of you really are genuinely good people motivated by the best intentions – maybe even the majority of you. But you work for a system which allows for the most egregious abuses of power and of the trust people place in you to keep them safe. And until that situation changes, I won't stop talking about its shortcomings.'

Vasilico said nothing, but he gave a slight smile and dipped his head in acknowledgement. It seemed to Anna that they'd reached something of an entente – that, even though they both knew that their respective positions were ultimately incompatible, they'd nonetheless arrived at an understanding as to where the other was coming from. They'd agreed to disagree.

They were still sitting side by side when Anna heard footsteps approaching. Vasilico got swiftly to his feet, rubbing down the creases in his trouser-legs, and Anna turned to see De Groot making his way towards them. He came to a halt facing them, less red-faced now but no less livid.

'I've just spent the last fifteen minutes trying to douse the flames of your creation,' he said, ignoring Anna and addressing Vasilico. 'Clive Sullivan is, understandably, most aggrieved about both the manner in which you spoke to him and the insinuations you made. I hardly need labour just how grievous a breach of conduct your behaviour today constitutes. Bad enough that you should behave like that towards any member of the public, but the brother of one of our most decorated heroes and a man grieving the loss of his son to boot? It's beyond words.'

Anna, now on her feet, glanced up the road and spotted a figure standing at the entrance to the church grounds. It was the meek-looking man whose identity had preoccupied her for so much of the morning. He was watching them, his expression unreadable.

'OK, OK.' Vasilico held up both hands to placate De Groot. 'I was out of order – I admit it. Don't know what came over me. Won't happen again.'

'Too bloody right it won't.' De Groot's eyes burned with feverish intensity. 'Any repeat behaviour of this sort and I'll have you, Vasilico. You hear me? I'll *have* you.'

'Message received loud and clear. I'll go to the old man right now and apologise, if it'll make you happy.'

'You'll do no such thing. As of this moment, you're to have no further contact with Clive Sullivan. The man's suffered enough. He's to be left in peace. If I hear you've been within so much as a mile of him, you'll be out the door so fast you won't know what's hit you.' He shook his head, face dripping with disdain. 'You're just fortunate he doesn't wish to make a formal complaint.'

Anna assumed De Groot was done, but he scarcely paused for breath before turning to her. 'And as for you, I don't expect our paths to cross again, Dr Scavolini, in relation to this or any other matter. Do we understand one another?'

Anna understood him just fine. She too was getting the 'or else' treatment.

'Perfectly,' she said stiffly.

De Groot gave a curt nod. Then, in a manoeuvre that would have made Anna laugh under different circumstances, he pirouetted on his heels and strode off, making his way back up the pavement to rejoin the meek-looking man. The pair of them headed back down to the church grounds together, soon disappearing from view.

Vasilico, who'd resumed his seat on the wall following De Groot's departure, remained there for another minute or so, toying with a fresh, as yet unlit, cigarette. Then, seemingly changing his mind about smoking it, he pocketed it and got to his feet.

'Come on,' he said, turning to Anna. 'I reckon that's more than enough excitement for a woman in your condition. Let's get you home.'

They drove in silence, each preoccupied by their own thoughts. They'd turned onto Cleveden Road and were passing the local secondary school when Anna finally broke the silence.

'I've been wondering . . . who was that short, melancholy-looking man who was at the service?'

Vasilico stirred, his eyes not leaving the road. 'Hmm? Who?'

'He arrived with De Groot and sat next to him in the church. Afterwards, he went and spoke to Sullivan, and then, when De Groot was laying into you, he was watching the whole thing from the end of the road.'

'Oh, him.' Vasilico's tone was one of disinterest. 'That's the ACC.'

Anna half-wondered if he was pulling her leg. That bland, diffident-looking man in the discount suit had been the Assistant Chief Constable? She wasn't sure why it came as such a shock. There was no earthly reason why the most powerful police officer in the West of Scotland *shouldn't* look like a put-upon office administrator. And yet, the image she'd constructed in her head, from Vasilico's various passing references to him, had been of someone vastly more imposing and more overtly distinguished.

'Huh,' she said.

Vasilico glanced briefly at her. 'What's that?'

'Nothing.'

She fell silent for a moment, then decided to risk bringing up the very matter that had driven Vasilico to such apoplexy earlier.

'What d'you suppose today was really about? What was Sullivan trying to accomplish?'

'Does it really matter now? You heard De Groot. I've been ordered to let it go.'

Anna stared at him incredulously. 'You're seriously going to throw in the towel just because of what *he* said? No offence, but that seems a little out of character.'

'None taken.' He gave her one of his long-suffering, vaguely patronising smiles. 'What you seem to be forgetting is that, unlike you, I'm a sworn officer of the law. We have rules and a hierarchy. When a superior gives an order, you obey. Unlike you, we don't get to just swan around doing whatever we like.'

Anna said nothing. It occurred to her, now that she thought about it, that Vasilico's willingness to let the matter drop might have less do to with De Groot's own admonitions than with the presence of that slight, innocuous figure standing on the periphery. *Beware the quiet man . . .*

'It just doesn't feel right,' she said. 'Sullivan knows more than he's letting on, I'm sure of it.'

Vasilico sighed. 'I know. Look, I'll see if I can have some of my boys keep an eye on him. It won't be round-the-clock surveillance, and heaven alone knows how I'm going to keep it on the down-low, but . . . ' He shot Anna a sly look. 'Well, De Groot said *I* was to keep my distance from the old fart. He didn't say *anything* about letting others do my dirty work.' He smiled. 'Reckon you can square that with your high ideals?'

'I reckon I'll just have to,' said Anna, with a slight smile of her own.

The staging of a clandestine police operation was hardly her dream scenario, but she knew it was either this or nothing. She had her own thoughts and suspicions about why Sullivan had acted the way he had today, but for the time being, that was all they were: thoughts and suspicions. She resolved not to give voice to them just yet – not till she'd had time to properly develop them.

'So tell me' – Vasilico's voice broke into her thoughts – 'd'you really think I'm slick and suave?'

She turned to look at him, saw the playful glint in his eye, and groaned inwardly. She *had* called him that, hadn't she?

'In my defence,' she said, 'I was talking down a man in a highly volatile state of mind. You don't want to go putting too much stock in the veracity of what I said.'

'Uh-huh. Mr Unflappable, that's what you called me. *Slick, suave, the perfect model of professionalism.* I might get that put on a business card.'

'Oh God!' She mimed puking. 'What have I unleashed?'

'Blame it on the pregnancy hormones if you like.'

She glanced sidelong at him, caught his eye and felt her own lips curling into an involuntary smile. She decided to admit defeat.

'Fine. Hormones it is.'

And with that, she leaned back in her seat, shutting her eyes and folding her arms over her distended stomach, determined not to utter another word for the remainder of the journey, lest she say anything else she would later regret.

# 16

# Memory

Down on her hands and knees, Zoe rummaged through the mountain of boxes and other odds and ends that covered every inch of the hallway cupboard. She was sure what she was looking for was here somewhere. No way would she have chucked it out.

She finally spotted it: a battered shoebox, its lid held on by a rubber band. The shoes it had once contained were long gone. In their place was a thick pile of photographs – a mixture of digital printouts and ones developed the old-fashioned way, printed on glossy 4x6 paper. All told, a chronicle of her life from the cradle to the point when the concept of taking photos with an actual camera and having them developed had been replaced by the ubiquitous smartphone and gigabytes upon gigabytes of slapdash snaps, all uploaded automatically to the cloud and promptly forgotten. The ones in this box, and the memories they represented, were somehow more tangible. More real.

Curled up on the sofa, she began to sift through them, losing herself down memory lane. They were in no particular order. One moment she'd be in her student years, reliving drunken nights out in the pubs and clubs of the West End and city centre; the next, back to that brief, all but forgotten period when her parents were still alive – a time where, in her mind, it was always summer and the magic hour lasted all day. At times, she had tears running down her face unchecked; at others, deep belly laughs bubbled up inside her as one picture after another triggered memories of long-forgotten escapades. Anna featured in a bunch of them, and these she set aside, thinking that Anna might welcome the chance to look at them and perhaps make a selection to keep for herself – though when such an opportunity would ever arise was anyone's guess.

The ones of Victor she separated out as well, gathering them into a little pile on the coffee table. There weren't a whole lot of them. He'd hated having his picture taken. Most of what existed were either semi-official affairs – ones taken at school events where participation was mandatory, or the times their granny had made them put on their Sunday best and dragged them down the road to the little studio where she got a discount because she played bingo with the owner's aunt – or impromptu snaps taken when he was unawares.

A few weren't too bad, though. One in particular, taken by her when they were both in their early twenties, stirred something deep within her. They'd been on a day out somewhere, the specifics lost to the mists of time – but she remembered them getting the train home late in the afternoon, both dog-tired after spending all day on the hop. He'd been asleep in the seat opposite her, head resting on the window, and she'd noticed the way the light was catching his face, accentuating its sharp angles, giving his normally pallid flesh a warm golden glow. On a whim, she'd grabbed her camera and snapped a picture of him. The sound of the shutter had roused him and, after blinking in confusion, he'd glared at her and demanded to know what the fuck she'd just done. He'd sulked the whole way home, assuming the sullen, distrustful outer shell behind which he retreated whenever he felt threatened or mocked. For a few brief moments, though, there'd been something innocent and pure about him, dozing by the window with the sun on his cheeks, and she'd succeeded in capturing that little-seen side of him onto celluloid, preserving it forever. It had been years since she'd last seen that picture, and she was damned if she was going to shove it back into a dank cupboard to be forgotten for another decade.

As she crammed the photo into a battered frame that had once contained a picture of her and Carol, her phone pinged: a text from Craig, asking if she was up to anything and when she'd next be in at work. She ignored it. Of late, she'd been picking up fewer shifts at the Corner – partly because she simply didn't have the inclination or headspace to deal with eight hours or more on her feet, smiling and making nice with the punters, and partly to avoid running into *him*. Whenever they ended up on shift together, he kept trying to catch her eye, giving her these sly little smiles, the meaning behind which she could easily guess. She hadn't the heart to tell him that she'd rather have her anus bleached than subject herself to a rerun of their afternoon getaway. It wasn't just that he was a lousy lay – though, in fairness, his skills with his tongue weren't completely unsalvageable. It was also that she'd belatedly come to find the age difference between them decidedly icky. He was, according to the letter of the law, a consenting adult, but in so many respects he was still just a big, daft boy. The two situations might not be remotely comparable, but that DVD of Broadhurst and that poor kid had well and truly taken the shine off shagging someone more than ten years her junior.

She'd hidden the DVD, along with the photos, at the bottom of her sock drawer, but when she closed her eyes she could still see it, seared into her mind as if the image was physically imprinted on her eyelids. Since the night it had dropped through her letterbox, she'd existed in a state of mental and emotional paralysis, not knowing how to respond. She had, of course, thought about doing the sensible thing and taking it to the police. But each time she told herself she was going to do it, she managed to come up with a laundry list of reasons why it was a seriously bad idea.

Top of that list was the simple fact that she didn't want to have anything to do with them if she could help it. She still felt like she'd dodged a bullet with the Dominic Ryland business three summers back, and to this day she couldn't be sure how much the cops had worked out about her role in what had happened to him. *Knew but couldn't prove it* was her strong suspicion, and she still periodically caught herself stopping to look over her shoulder when she was out and about, a part of her convinced it was only a matter of time before they collared her for the part she'd played in arranging for gangsters to beat an up-and-coming politician within an inch of his life.

There was also the question of whether she could even trust them to do the right thing with anything she took to them. She might not be fully on board with Gillian Crowley's belief in an all-powerful, all-reaching conspiracy with its tentacles in every organ of the state, but the more examples she encountered of these animals somehow getting away with their crimes, the more convinced she became that it couldn't simply be down to incompetence on the part of those tasked with bringing them to justice. The other day, she'd come across a blog post about a social worker who, convinced his colleague was abusing one of their charges, had set up a hidden camera to capture hard evidence of the crime. He duly handed the footage over to the authorities, only to find himself charged with the production and possession of child pornography. The abuser, meanwhile, got off on the grounds that the quality was insufficient for a reliable identification. Would that be her fate too if she took the DVD to the cops? She'd watched it, hadn't she? She'd sat in her living room and watched bona fide kiddie porn, even if she *had* switched it off before the kid actually finished rubbing one out. *And* she'd had it in her possession for nearly a fortnight. It was the perfect Catch-22 situation: the more time that passed, the harder it became to justify not having gone to the police with it, and the harder it became to justify, the more reluctant it made her to go to them.

She wondered if it had come from Broadhurst himself. Had he somehow got wind of what she was up to? Was he taunting her – telling her, *I know you know what I did, and I want you to know that I know you know*? The envelope had appeared on her doormat within a week of their encounter at the hustings, which was one coincidence more than she was prepared to dismiss. Plus, he knew Victor was her brother, and even a mentally impaired chimp would have been able to work out what the presence of his photo in that little collection would do to her. On its own, it wasn't *proof* – or so she kept telling herself. But someone clearly wanted her to think Broadhurst had—

*Stop it, Zoe. Don't think about it.*

She couldn't help it. In the days following the delivery, she'd started to go through something akin to the five stages of grief. First had come denial. There was no way something like that could have happened to Victor – just no fucking way. *Not my brother.*

Then had come anger – a powerful, all-consuming rage that, with no clear target at which to direct it, she quickly turned on herself. If it *had* happened, it had happened right under her nose. How could she have been so thick? It was *her* fault. She should have seen it.

Then had come bargaining – her attempts to rationalise things, listing all the reasons why it *couldn't* have happened. She was his sister. She'd have known – of course she would. And Victor was a lifelong recluse, who'd avoided after-school clubs and activities – where, if you believed Gillian Crowley, the bulk of the abuse had supposedly taken place – like the Black Death.

And yet surely the very nature of his being an outsider and an introvert would have made him a prime target for these sick fucks? What was it Gillian had said? *Always the loners, the outcasts, the ones from dysfunctional backgrounds.* Easy prey, she'd called them. The ones least likely to share their problems with others.

'But I'd have known . . . '

*Would you, Zoe? Or maybe you just chose to ignore the signs, too wrapped up in your own trivial existence to see what was staring you in the face.*

She stirred and arched her aching shoulders. How long had she been in that position, sat there on the sofa with the laptop on her knees? It was dark in the flat, and cold, though the heat generated by the laptop had kept her thighs nice and toasty. She'd been trying, without success, to track down Cadogan, the detective responsible for the botched investigation into Netherfield. Not that she was in any way surprised that her efforts hadn't borne fruit. If Gillian, who lived and breathed this sort of thing, had already exhausted all the means at her disposal to find him, what chance did a mere amateur like her have?

She got up, knee-joints cracking from stiffness. As she headed over to shut the curtains, she noticed a small, forlorn figure standing on the pavement across the road: a young woman, early-to-mid-twenties, wearing a denim jacket and a skirt far too short for this time of year, bare legs trembling in the cold. As Zoe stood watching her, the girl lifted her head and gazed up at her. Their eyes met briefly, then the girl quickly looked away, staring at the ground as if it was the most interesting thing she'd ever seen.

*Poor wee cow,* Zoe thought. She'd seen her a couple of times before over the last week or so, always hanging around Dumbarton Road late at night. Zoe had concluded that she must either be homeless or didn't feel safe going home. She was sure there must be better places to while away the hours on a cold December night than the scruffy end of Partick – but at that particular moment in time, she couldn't think of any.

Her eye was drawn to the coating of frost at the bottom of the window. Over the last few days, the temperature had dropped like a flasher's drawers. It was chilly enough indoors, and that was with the heating on. God knows what it must be like out there without even a single-glazed window between you and the elements.

Shrugging on her parka, she let herself out of the flat and headed downstairs. As she stepped out into the street, the girl, who hadn't moved, started and looked around in wide-eyed panic, as if searching for an escape route. Finding none, she stood her ground, shoulders drawing up defensively, as Zoe crossed over to her.

'I'm no lookin fer any trouble,' she said, before Zoe could get a word out.

'That's good.' Zoe affected a cheery tone. 'Me neither. Whatcha doing standing out here?'

The girl glowered sullenly at Zoe, suspicion oozing from every pore. 'Waiting on ma boyfriend.'

'Picking ye up, is he?'

'Aye. Said I wis tae wait here for him.'

At least she wasn't homeless.

'He say when he'd be?'

'Soon. He's got work and that.'

Zoe checked her watch. What sort of job did this boyfriend do that caused him to still be at it at two in the morning? She supposed it wasn't any of her business. Either way, it didn't change the fact that this girl was in serious danger of her wee tits dropping off from frostbite if she stood out here much longer.

'Right, well, c'mon. Ye can wait for him at mine.'

The girl stared at Zoe, piggy little nose curling distrustfully.

Zoe jerked her head, as if ordering a dog to heel. 'C'mon – it's baltic oot here.'

She turned and set off, heading back across the road towards the flat. At first, she heard nothing but her own footsteps. Then, as she reached the pavement on the other side, she heard slow, hesitant shuffling behind her as the girl began to follow.

* * *

Back inside the flat, Zoe ushered her through to the living room.

'Make yersel at home. Want something to drink? Coffee? Hot chocolate?'

'Hot chocolate sounds good, aye.' The girl's voice had a dazed quality to it.

Zoe headed through to the kitchen, where she poured milk into a saucepan and put it on the stove to warm through.

*So what's the plan, Zoe? You planning on taking in every waif and stray in Glasgow, or just the ones on your own doorstep?*

*Fuck off, brain. I'm being nice, that's all.*

Returning to the living room, she found the girl still on her feet, arms drawn into her sides as if she was afraid to come into physical contact with anything in the room.

'Have a seat.' Zoe gestured to the sofa. 'Be ready in a min.'

The girl didn't move. Her eyes swept the room, taking in every nook and cranny. 'This is dead nice, this.'

Zoe, who'd always considered her pokey wee flat to be nothing more than . . . well, a wee pokey flat, couldn't help feeling a pang of guilt. Did this girl think she'd brought her here to rub her face in her creature comforts?

'What's yer name?' she asked.

'Mandy.' Spoken with that same defensive *what's it to you?* undertone.

'Well, Mandy, I'm Zoe, and if there's one thing I cannae thole, it's folk standing on ceremony, so park yer arse on that seat or I'll think ye've got anal warts or something.'

Reluctantly, Mandy did as she was told, while Zoe headed back to the kitchen, where the milk was just coming to the boil.

'Ye live round here, then?' she called through.

'Naw, I'm fae Rutherglen.'

'Long way fae home, then. Whatcha come way out here for?'

'Ma boyfriend.'

'Oh, right. Work locally, does he?'

'Something like that.'

*My, aren't we chatty.*

Zoe finished making the hot chocolate, emptied the saucepan into a mismatched pair of mugs and headed back through with them. She found

Mandy on her feet again, holding the recently framed photo of Victor, turning it this way and that as she studied it.

'That's—' she began.

'I know who it is,' said Mandy quietly.

Zoe's expression hardened. 'Aye? You 'n' everyone's dug. Whit's it tae ye?'

She was used to reactions like this: the wide-eyed stares, the meaningful looks people gave one another, the still-audible whispers of *did you know she's the Kelvingrove Killer's sister?* Total strangers gossiping about him, gawping over his likeness, thinking they were entitled to an opinion about him, to own a piece of him, just because his face was in the news six years ago. It was partly why she'd stuffed all the pictures of him into a shoebox in the hall cupboard. Easier just to purge all record of him than to put up with the inevitable ogling.

She slammed the mugs down and snatched the frame from Mandy. 'Nosy wee cow, aren't ye? Bet ye think ye know everything there is tae know about him an' aw.'

'Sorry.' Mandy lowered her head in contrition.

She looked so utterly pathetic, standing there with her eyes downcast, that Zoe was left feeling like she'd kicked a puppy.

She sighed. 'No, *I'm* sorry. I didnae mean tae shout. Just drink yer drink, OK? 'Fore it gets cold.'

Mandy eyed the mugs uncertainly, as if she feared the contents had been laced with arsenic. Zoe was on the verge of telling her that if she didn't hurry up and drink it she'd bloody well pour it down the drain when Mandy finally lowered herself onto the sofa, took one of the mugs and began to sip gingerly.

Zoe rubbed the picture with her sleeve, wiping away the prints Mandy had left on the glass, and set it on the mantelpiece, like a parent placing the cookie jar out of reach of a child.

'Who was he tae ye anywie?' Mandy nodded at the picture between sips. 'Yer man?'

'My brother.'

'Oh, right. Sorry.' She was silent for a moment, then her nose curled again, this time in amusement. 'S'pose, be a bit weird if he *wis* yer man. I mean, he dis kinda look like ye.'

'Mean the hair? Family curse. One of our ancestors must've impugned a witch or something. 'Sides,' she went on, as Mandy took another, more enthusiastic sip, 'have ye no heard? It's scientifically inadvisable tae breed two gingers.'

'Oh aye?' For the first time, Mandy seemed to genuinely let her guard down, regarding Zoe with wry amusement. 'How come?'

'Their kids are like *turbo*-charged gingers or something. Even their skin's the colour of Irn Bru.'

At this, Mandy actually burst out laughing, sloshing hot choccy on her miniskirt. Zoe found herself smiling. It felt good hearing laughter in the house again. Lifted some of the oppressiveness that hung in the air.

At that moment, a single long, sustained blast from a car horn rent the ghostly stillness outside.

Mandy was on her feet in an instant, her mug abandoned. 'Fuck.'

Zoe watched as she hurried to the window. 'What?'

Mandy peeled back the curtain and peered out. 'Ma boyfriend.'

Zoe joined her at the window. In the spot where Mandy had been standing ten minutes ago, a flash-looking sportscar now idled.

Mandy turned to Zoe, eyes wide with unspoken fear. 'I have to go.'

'Stay and drink yer choccy. He kept *you* waiting long enough. Couple more minutes willnae kill him.'

Mandy shook her head. 'He gets mad when I make him wait.' She ducked past Zoe and made for the door. 'Thanks for inviting me in. It was nice o' ye.'

Before Zoe could object, she was gone, door slamming shut behind her. Zoe listened as her footsteps clattered down the stairs, then watched from the window as she hurried out into the street, crossing over to the car and slipping into the passenger seat. It occurred to Zoe, as she watched it pulling away, that there was something decidedly odd about a girl so obviously down on her luck having a boyfriend who could afford a motor like that. You'd think he might share some of his cash with her. Or maybe he was one of those tight-arsed types who didn't believe in the redistribution of wealth.

She took Victor's picture down from the mantelpiece and returned to the sofa, holding it close to her. He'd changed when he started going to Willow Bank – that much she knew. Subtly, perhaps, but she couldn't pretend he hadn't. He'd always preferred his own company and possessed something of a stubborn streak, but as he'd entered his teenage years, he'd become increasingly withdrawn and secretive. He'd also developed a hair-trigger temper, responding to the slightest provocation by flying into a rage, like a cornered rat fighting for its life. At the time, Zoe had just put it down to typical teenage boy mood swings. It was a phase they all went through, or so she'd been led to believe. *Boys will be boys.* But now she was facing up to what, deep down, she'd known from the moment Lucy Foster had first raised the possibility that there had been abuse at Willow Bank, and certainly since Gillian had told her what sort of students the abusers had targeted: that there was every possibility that Victor too had been one of those 'lost boys'. That, while she'd sauntered through her teenage years with no greater care in the world than which boys she fancied and whether she was going to be able to afford that new sparkle top, he'd been drowning in his own personal hell, unable to turn to the one person who, more than anyone, should have been there for him.

And there it was: the feeling that had been gnawing away at her innards day after day for weeks now.

Guilt.

Awful, soul-crushing guilt that wrapped itself around her, enfolding her in its tight embrace, making it hard for her to breathe. Was guilt one of the stages of grief? If it wasn't, it damn well oughta be. It was certainly where she was now. The 'this is all my fault' phase.

A phase she wouldn't be able to move past until she did something to atone.

# 17

# The Most Wonderful Time of the Year

*Thursday 24 December*

2015 continued its relentless death march, the skies growing ever greyer, the nights ever blacker. Zoe increasingly withdrew from the world around her, cutting her shifts at the Corner to the bare minimum, burning through all her accrued annual leave. The party season was well underway, but she allowed it to pass her by entirely, turning down a slew of invitations in favour of remaining holed up in the flat with her laptop and dark thoughts. It just didn't seem appropriate – the idea of going out on the razzle-dazzle, exchanging gifts and platitudes about peace on earth and goodwill to all men. After all, what sort of Christmas were the victims of Willow Bank and Netherfield having? On the rare occasions when she did go out – usually to buy food and other essentials – she found herself studying the men she passed in the street, searching their faces, their mannerisms for some sign as to whether they too had fallen prey to the machinations of the Adam Broadhursts of the world. How many of them were out there? And how many were like Richie Deans, suppressing what was done to him until it drove him to the grave?

She spent her days scouring the internet, reading every article on child abuse she could get her hands on. It seemed it didn't matter where you went in the world – someone somewhere was getting their kicks from exploiting the very children they'd been entrusted to protect. Schools, orphanages, the Catholic Church, the British state broadcaster – the list ran on. And, each time, the pattern was the same. Every so often, a scandal would erupt, with crimes long buried coming to light and anyone who'd been in a position to do something throwing up their hands and crying, 'But we didnae *know*!' And, more often than not, those responsible – the abusers as well as their enablers – either got a slap on the wrist or were moved to another school or parish, free to prey on a fresh set of innocents. Many were acquitted in courts of law despite the mountains of evidence against them. Others were long dead, their crimes only coming to light once they were conveniently safe from prosecution. In some jurisdictions, there was even a statute of limitations, meaning that men the whole world knew were guilty as sin got to swan around, unchallenged and unpunished. It boggled Zoe's mind that there could be a statute of limitations on child rape, but there it was in black and white. The world, she concluded, was fucked in the head.

At various points over the last fortnight, she'd attempted to reach out to Gillian Crowley, whom she regarded as the one genuine ally she had in all of this. But her emails went unanswered, and attempting to access the 'Justice for Conor' blog now returned a generic landing page advertising the domain name as being for sale. The last email she'd sent had bounced completely, returning an 'address not found' error. Though a part of her did wonder whether Gillian had been 'got at', she knew the most likely explanation was that she really had been serious about putting all this misery behind her and heading out to Australia to join her sister.

The seventeenth of December, her thirty-fourth birthday, came and went. Another year older, and fuck-all to show for it. Once upon a time, she'd have marked the occasion with an absolutely banging party, surrounded by all her favourite people, dancing till her feet ached and getting absolutely blootered. Alcohol had been an essential component in her life since she'd been of legal age (well, all right, since considerably earlier than that), both as an aid to letting her hair down and for drowning her sorrows when the need arose. Of late, though, she'd found that, like sex with another actual person, it had lost much of its lustre. Instead, she spent the evening lying on the sofa with her pants around her knees and her vibrator between her legs, trying in vain to stop thinking about child abuse for long enough to make herself come.

Christmas Eve rolled around – not with a bang but a whimper. She came to in the middle of the morning, still in the clothes she'd had on yesterday and feeling sticky and crusty all over. Dragging herself out of bed, she made her way over to the window and gazed out at Dumbarton Road. She looked up at the overcast sky and wondered if the temperature would drop low enough for the faint drizzle currently pattering against the window-pane to turn to snow. There was, she noted, a distinct lack of Christmas cheer all round, both in the street outside and inside the flat. She hadn't even bothered putting up any decorations this year, concluding that there was no point. What difference did it make to her whether it was Christmas? It was just a day like any other, and it wasn't as if she had anyone to share it with.

She cast her mind back to the dim and distant past, to Christmases in the house on Astley Street with Victor and Granny. They would always get up bright and early and troop downstairs to the living room to open their presents together in front of a blazing fire. Then, in the afternoon, more often than not Anna would come over. Christmas wasn't a fixture in the Scavolini household, but the Callahans always included her in the festivities, and Granny always remembered to get her a present – nothing fancy, but enough to make sure she didn't feel left out. In retrospect, Zoe recognised that their efforts had probably been a bit patronising, not to mention highly presumptive, as if a lack of Christendom in one's life was a deficiency that had to be corrected. Still, if Anna had minded, she'd never let it show. Most likely, she'd recognised and appreciated the well-meaning intent behind the gesture. Granny had been good that way. And Victor too, who'd always had a bit of a thing for Anna, though he'd never had the courage to tell her. Deep down, Zoe had always suspected he'd looked forward more to the doorbell ringing to announce her arrival than to his own prezzies.

*Victor.* She reached, as she so often did these days, for the framed photo of him and gazed down at it. Her finger gently traced the outline of his peaceful, sun-kissed face, the untold mysteries beyond those enigmatic features lying agonisingly beyond her reach. She desperately wished there was some way she could communicate with him – to ask him to confirm or deny her darkest fears about what had happened to him. Shutting her eyes, she imagined the picture coming to life in her hands, the motion returning to the passing countryside behind him like a paused video resuming. His nostrils flaring slightly as he inhaled a breath while he slept.

She imagined herself reaching into the frame and shaking him gently by the shoulder, saying, *Victor, there's something I need to ask you . . .* But when she opened her eyes, the picture remained frozen in time, Victor and his secrets still beyond her reach.

Heading over to the sofa, she booted up her laptop. The pointer did its spinning thing for a bit, then returned her to the last page she'd visited the previous night. It was the online telephone directory, showing the search results for all the residences in Glasgow registered in the name of Broadhurst. The only 'A Broadhurst' on the list lived on Balvicar Drive in the Southside. She switched to another tab, which showed a Google Maps street view image of a nice-looking townhouse on the outer circle of Queen's Park, within a stone's throw of both the local Baptist Church and the Church of Scotland – perfect, she imagined, if you were religiously minded but felt like hedging your bets. She wasn't sure whether Broadhurst was that way inclined – but then, as her research had shown her, a personal relationship with the Almighty didn't appear to preclude you from being a pederast. In fact, it might even be seen to actively encourage it.

She emerged from the flat in the early afternoon and crossed the road to the nearby bus stop, where she caught a number three heading east. As it trundled along Dumbarton Road towards the city centre, she spread herself across the empty back seat, got out her compact mirror and examined her reflection. She looked awful. Her hair was greasy and unwashed, her face even paler than normal, accentuating the dark bags under her eyes. She wasn't sure how much sleep she was getting, what with all those late-night Googling sessions, but she was fairly sure it wasn't enough. Oddly, though, she wasn't tired. In fact, she felt strangely alert and awake for someone so sleep-deprived. She assumed she must be running on pure adrenaline.

Just then, she caught a flash of something reflected behind her in the mirror. Without turning her head, she angled the compact to get a better view of the car directly behind the bus. It was a grey Fiat – a 12-reg. She was sure this wasn't the first time she'd seen it. True, grey Fiats weren't exactly uncommon, but the last one had been a 12-reg too, which lengthened the odds somewhat. She racked her brains, trying to dredge up where she'd seen it. Given how limited her movements had been of late, there couldn't be that many options. She tried to get a look at the driver, but the Fiat's tinted windshield, coupled with the low sun shining behind her, made it impossible to make out more than a vague shape. She rummaged in her bag for a pen and scribbled the licence plate number on an old Fruit Pastilles wrapper.

As they neared the city centre, the traffic grew heavier, and eventually the Fiat got left behind them at a set of lights. It didn't catch up with them again, and by the time Zoe disembarked outside the Stag & Thistle on Pollokshaws Road, there was no sign of it. Telling herself her paranoia was getting the better of her, she zipped her parka up to her chin and set off for Balvicar Drive.

As the Broadhurst residence came into view, she slowed. Straight in front of her, framed by the large bay window on the ground floor, was a scene straight out of a cheesy Christmas movie. Broadhurst, wearing a check shirt and knit cardigan combo, sat in a low recliner, while a tall woman in a coat, about thirty years his junior, bent down to embrace him. As she straightened up, two small boys, no more than five or six years old, came tearing into view. They leapt onto the recliner like eager little puppies, flinging their arms round the old man, who wrapped them both in a doting embrace.

Zoe stared at the scene unfolding before her in abject horror. *Grandsons.* Why had she never considered that he might have *grandsons*? She took a few unsteady, shuffling steps backward, reversing to the other side of the road. She felt dirty. Contaminated. She wanted to hurl – wanted to expel everything to cleanse herself of the filth that festered inside her.

A new desire took hold: a desire to march into that house right this instant and confront Broadhurst about what he'd done. She could picture it now: her storming into the living room, asking Broadhurst's daughter if she knew her old man had a thing for interfering with boys not much older than the grandweans sitting in his lap.

But she couldn't do it. It didn't matter how many years had passed; how many times she told herself she was an adult now and he an old man who probably had to get up multiple times a night to take a piss. As soon as she tried to put one foot in front of the other and cross the road, she was fifteen years old again, knees knocking together as she trembled before him in his office – the same office where he'd made Joshua Manning wank himself off for the camera. This must be how his victims felt, and why none of them had come forward over the years: because no matter how much time had passed, no matter how many of them had gone on to have jobs and wives and kids of their own, deep down they were all still just scared, frightened wee boys.

With her shoes scraping clumsily on the ground, she stumbled into Queen's Park, following the path in front of her as it wound uphill, putting as much distance between herself and that nauseating scene as possible. She needed to think. Needed to come up with a concrete plan of action.

Out of nowhere, a single, crystal clear thought sprang into her head: *Anna.*

She'd call Anna. Tell her everything. Let her take charge. Anna would know what to do. She always did.

# 18

# The Fade

Anna stirred, blinking heavily, and realised she must have dozed off again. For the last couple of weeks, her sleep had been unsettled and sporadic. The back and pelvic pain that had troubled her since the start of December always seemed to get worse at night, and on top of that, the baby had settled into a pattern of being at its most active during the wee hours, the inconsiderate little bugger.

She became aware of a dull pressure and looked down to find her steering wheel pushing into her swollen belly. She swore it had to have expanded in size since she'd last looked.

As she levered the seat back as far as it would go before it became impossible for her to reach the wheel, she sensed movement out of the corner of her eye. She looked up as, some forty metres further along the road, Clive Sullivan emerged from the tenement at the top of Gardner Street and headed down the garden path to the street, an empty reusable shopping bag tucked under his arm. She checked the time on the dashboard clock. 2.30 p.m. Right on cue. Keeping the sun visor down and her head low, she watched as he set off down the slope.

For the first two weeks following the memorial service, Vasilico had, true to his word, set a watch on Sullivan, tasking a handful of trusted underlings with keeping an eye on the flat and tailing him on his occasional excursions. From the brief phone calls they'd exchanged during that time, Anna had gathered that Sullivan's existence was one of routine: daily mid-afternoon trips to the Stop 'n' Shop to buy his milk and copy of the *Daily Post*, a larger shop once a week at the Morrisons next to Partick Station, and occasional visits to his allotment – a small plot of land on a site off Maryhill Road, about three miles away. There, Vasilico had informed her, he tended to his vegetable crops and pottered in and out of the ramshackle wooden shed that overlooked them. 'The man's life's as dull as ditchwater,' Vasilico had said – then added, with audible disappointment, 'but that in itself is no crime.' By the end of the second week, he'd thrown in the towel and called off the surveillance, no longer able to justify frittering away resources on an unsanctioned operation that showed no sign of bearing fruit.

The writing, it seemed, was on the wall for the official investigation too. Operation Griffin was being gradually wound up, with each passing week heralding further reductions in both funding and manpower. Soon, Anna knew, it would be shelved alongside the other 0.5% of missing persons investigations that remained unresolved – to be dusted off for the occasional review but, for all intents and purposes, a cold case. It worried away at her, like an eyelash in her eye or a bit of food stuck between her teeth, and the more she picked at it, the more it irritated her. It was unfinished business, and she hated leaving a job half-done.

Mind you, she'd had plenty of unfinished business of her own to be getting on with over the last fortnight – so much so that, on several occasions and for hours at a time, she'd actually been able to forget all about the Derek Sullivan and his strange, emotionally crippled father. The countdown to the end of term and the start of her maternity leave had entered its final stretch, and there were umpteen loose ends to tie up before she downed tools. Much of her time had been spent drawing up detailed teaching plans for the next semester. A couple of her most capable postgrad students would be taking on the bulk of her lectures, and a desire to make their lives easier, coupled with her inability to relinquish control completely, had made her determined to leave nothing to chance. When Friday the eighteenth had arrived and she'd vacated the office with her personal effects in a cardboard box, her desk cleared for the lucky soul who was going to have use of it in her absence, it had been difficult not to feel like the end of an era had arrived.

*It's just for six months,* she'd told herself. *You'll be back again before you know it.*

Before leaving, she'd finally accepted – with some reluctance – Sophie

Hennessy's longstanding offer to fulfil the role of birthing partner. At least she knew she could rely on Sophie to be level-headed and practical – a safe pair of hands. It was just that she couldn't help but think that a birthing partner was meant to be so much more than that.

For the first few days of her mat leave, she'd tried doing all the things she'd been led to believe other expectant mothers got up to while they awaited the inevitable: reading, watching TV, even loading up her iPad with some of the mindless games she'd seen her students playing on their phones. But it was no use. She hadn't the patience or thumb dexterity required for *Angry Birds*, the TV was even lousier than usual this year, and she never had been an avid reader of fiction. In times past, she'd have put on her gear and gone for a run, but that was out of the question now. She'd tried going for walks, but found she could only manage about ten minutes before running out of puff, and she'd quickly grown fed up with seeing the same half-dozen streets again and again. It was no exaggeration to say that she loved her work, and everything that went with it: the camaraderie, the friendly rivalries, the cut and thrust of scrapping for her fair share of the ever-diminishing research funding pot, even the fact that there were never enough hours in the day to get everything done. It defined who she was, and without it, it felt like she was somehow less whole.

Hence why she'd come to be sitting on Partickhill Road watching Clive Sullivan's flat on a chilly Christmas Eve afternoon. It had started innocently – and civic-mindedly – enough, with a drive out to Cranhill to drop off some old clothes at a women's refuge where a friend of hers volunteered. On the way home, and without giving it conscious thought, she'd found herself turning off Hyndland Road early to take a detour past Sullivan's flat – almost as if she was just checking it was still there. With nothing more stimulating awaiting her back at the house, she'd decided to kill some time sitting there, parked next to the bowling club grounds, the flat conveniently in view just in front of her. Just for fifteen minutes, she'd told herself. Just until she'd finished listening to the current affairs programme on the radio. But the programme had ended and she still hadn't moved, and then fifteen minutes had become half an hour, and then an hour. And then, before she'd known it, two hours had passed and she still hadn't moved from her ideally situated vantage point.

Not for the first time, she wondered how this must look to an outside observer. She was acutely aware (though she'd been trying her best not to think about it) that her current behaviour undoubtedly merited the label of 'obsessive', and that obsessive-compulsive behaviour had, in the past, been one the warning signs that she was heading for a manic episode. She'd been here before, fixating on a particular topic or task to the exclusion of all others – often something she had no business involving herself in. She told herself she was being overanxious – that, when she'd experienced manic episodes in the past, they'd been preceded by a range of other symptoms, and that, if any of these had manifested themselves, she would have recognised them by now.

*Would you, Anna? Would you really?*

She could see Sullivan now, turning up the path to the front door, his shopping bag now weighed down by his newspaper and bottle of milk. She sunk lower in her seat, but he didn't even glance in her direction. To look at him, you'd think he was nothing more than a frail old pensioner grieving the loss of his son in his own quiet, dignified way. But Anna refused to believe that was all there was to it. She didn't yet know where her suspicions ultimately led, beyond a gut feeling that there was something thoroughly dubious about the man's apparent eagerness for the world to accept his son as dead. Vasilico had felt it too, though she sensed that his anger at Sullivan's failings as a parent had largely blinded him to the possibility that there could be another, more sinister, explanation for the show the old man had staged that day at the church for the media and police top brass.

As Sullivan disappeared inside, Anna's phone hummed in her pocket, causing her to start in surprise. She retrieved it and checked the screen. It was a text, the sender going by the familiar moniker of 'RED MENACE'. She tapped it open.

**Hey doll, meet me at top of Queens park? Im there now**
**XOXO**

Well, if that wasn't the strangest thing . . . Zoe hadn't been in touch for ages, and now, out of the blue, here she was issuing Anna with a summons. And a summons to somewhere that was miles from either of their regular stomping grounds at that. Anna thought about texting her back, telling her she couldn't make it, that she had something else on. But she knew she couldn't – not without feeling like an absolute heel. Anyway, was she seriously contemplating blowing her best pal off in favour of spending the rest of the afternoon sitting outside an old man's house waiting for him to do something incriminating?

Her mind made up, she tapped out a response, saying she'd be there in forty-five minutes, then fastened her seatbelt, fired the ignition and set off, her vigil abandoned.

She drew up at the edge of Queen's Park shortly before four o'clock. In spite of the earlier drizzle, it had turned into a bright, clear winter's day. The grass sparkled with dew and white frost, and the sun glowed pale and sickly on the horizon, casting long shadows from spindly trees that had long since shed their summer coats. It was as quiet as the proverbial grave, not even birdsong breaking the silence.

Taking it slow, Anna followed the path towards the hill in the centre of the park. As she reached the top, the red-haired woman standing near the flagpole turned to her with a shriek that sent the crows nesting in the nearby trees into panicked flight.

'Oh my *God*! Ye're as big as a fuckin' *hoose*! Ye sure that isnae a baby elephant ye've got in there?'

And then, before Anna had time to utter a word, Zoe flung her arms round her, enveloping her in one of her trademark squeeze-the-life-out-of-you hugs. It was, perhaps, more forceful than was advisable for someone in Anna's condition, but she was so fed up with folk tiptoeing around her bump, drawing attention to it through their determination to treat it like an unexploded IED, that she couldn't help but feel grateful for Zoe's total lack of regard for pregnancy etiquette.

They made their way over to a nearby bench facing the northwestern edge of the park. Anna gratefully sank down, her back and ankles practically groaning with relief. Together, they gazed out at the expanse of the city before them.

'So when's D-Day?' Zoe nodded to Anna's stomach, as if there was any question as to what she was referring.

'January sixteenth, give or take.'

'Well, rather you than me, doll. Hope ye know what ye're letting yersel in for. I mean, no tae beat about the bush, but yer vadge is never gonnae be the same again.'

'Thanks for the heads-up.'

'I'm just saying, squeezing a thing the size of a watermelon out a hole the size of a slide-whistle? Gonnae dae things tae it.'

'All *right*, Zoe! Message received!'

Zoe grinned and leaned back, kicking her legs out in front of her. 'Aye,' she said, with an air of satisfaction, 'it's come to something all right when Anna Scavolini's all knocked up and gearing up for life as a single mum. I'd never've credited it.' She nudged Anna. 'Here – mind how we always used to kid on that, if one of us ever ended up wi a bun in the oven, we'd buy a massive big hoose somewhere and raise it the gether?'

Anna laughed. 'God, I'd forgotten about that. I'm pretty sure we even made a pinky promise. Course,' she added with a sly smile, 'I think we always assumed it'd be you up the duff rather than me.'

Zoe gave a dry chuckle. 'Aye – if I was a betting man, I know which horse I'*da* backed.'

'Just you wait – it'll be your turn before you know it.'

The smile faded from Zoe's lips. 'Uh-uh.' She shook her head. 'I've decided – I'm no having any kids.'

Anna looked at her in surprise. The topic of children was one they'd never discussed beyond the sort of jokey, throwaway remarks they'd made as teenagers, but she'd always assumed Zoe was someone who at the very least wouldn't rule out the possibility that she might someday end up in the family way.

'What, never?'

'Nope.' Zoe's tone was adamant. 'Last of the Callahans, me. Actually, I've been thinking I might get my tubes tied.'

'Whoa.' Anna straightened up, turning to face Zoe with a look of concern. 'That's a pretty massive step, Zo. You don't wanna do something you'll regret later on. I mean, you're still a young woman. You never know – in time you might—'

'Did ye no hear me?' Zoe snapped. 'I said I'm no having any.' She fell silent, slumping forward and leaning on her knees. 'Beats me how anyone'd wanna bring a wean intae this world anywie,' she muttered, more to herself than to Anna.

Anna continued to eye her uneasily. This wasn't the Zoe she knew or remembered – the loud, exuberant party girl she'd grown up with and had known, off and on, since she was twelve. Of course, there'd been a whole lot of water under the bridge since then, and Zoe had been dealt a crueller hand than most – all of which would have caused even the most intractable of people to change. And yet it wasn't just that. There was something about Zoe's present comportment that went beyond mere change – something Anna couldn't put her finger on. Something about her very essence.

She stirred, feeling a sudden, pressing need to banish the heavy mood that had descended over the hill. 'I almost forgot,' she said brightly. 'I know it's a few hours early, but Happy Christmas.'

She reached into her coat pocket and produced a small, square box, badly wrapped in Christmas paper.

'For me?' Zoe both looked and sounded genuinely taken aback. 'Aw, ye shouldnae've.'

She took the present from Anna, tore off the paper and lifted the lid to reveal the two small silver bracelets contained inside, each with an inscription engraved on the outer face.

'"True friends are never apart . . . ",' she read, lifting one of them up.

'" . . . perhaps in distance but never in heart",' Anna finished. 'Each one has half the quotation on it. The idea is we each wear one, and that way we never forget one another. I know it's a bit cheesy,' she added, a touch sheepishly, 'but I thought it might be fun.'

'It's . . . it's lovely.' Zoe's voice sounded curiously hoarse. She stared at the bracelet, turning it this way and that, then turned to Anna, eyes wide and faintly moist. 'Thanks, pal. Ye really didnae have tae . . . '

'Don't be daft. It's nothing.'

'I mean it. I don't deserve ye.'

She drew Anna in for another hug, but one that was far less effusive than the last. Anna, resting her head on Zoe's shoulder, felt a stab of guilt. In truth, the bracelets had been a last-minute idea, picked up at a gift shop on her way to Queen's Park after realising she hadn't remembered to get Zoe anything for her birthday the previous week – hence the thoroughly shoddy attempt at wrapping them, done in the car with some repurposed sellotape and a pair of nail scissors. She'd meant them as a sincere demonstration of her commitment to their friendship, but also as a bit of a joke between mates – a callback to their teenage years. She hadn't anticipated Zoe having such an emotional response to them.

Zoe relinquished her grip on Anna and fastened one of the bracelets round her wrist. To show willing, Anna took the remaining one and did likewise. Zoe looked at her and grinned.

'There. Now we're like twins.'

She still *seemed* like the old Zoe: goofy, endearingly immature, and utterly deaf to social niceties. And yet there was something somehow performative about it – as if she was just doing what was expected of her, wearing the old, boisterous Zoe like a costume, to be promptly shed once there was no longer anyone around to see her. Anna could think of no other way to explain it than that there seemed to be less of her there. Not in the sense that she was losing weight (though now that Anna thought about it, she *was* looking more than a little drawn about the cheeks these days). It was as if, like the daylight itself, she was fading; as if, with each passing day, a little more of what made her Zoe had disappeared. Anna racked her brains, wishing there was something she could say or do to perk her up – something to take her back to her happy place, before the world turned cruel and took away her innocence.

'What you doing tomorrow?' she asked. 'Up to much?'

'*Aye!*' Zoe's relief at having something to respond to was palpable. 'Got this banging party I'm gonnae check out the night. Ye know the drill: booze, tunes and cheesy dancing, toast the arrival of our Lord and Saviour at the stroke o' midnight, then rinse 'n' repeat till we finally pass out at sunrise. Come to at midday, dust ourselves off and start all over again. Should be absolutely mental.'

'Sounds it, yeah.'

She was glad to hear it. The prospect of Zoe spending Christmas alone, especially given the mood she seemed to be in, didn't bear thinking about.

'Unless' – Zoe cast Anna a wary sidelong look – 'ye fancied getting the gether and daein' something, just the two of us.'

For a brief instant, Anna was tempted to say yes, before cooler heads prevailed.

'No, no,' she said hurriedly, 'you've got plans. You don't need me cramping your style.'

That was one reason, certainly. The other, unspoken one she couldn't

quite explain, beyond the rather shameful realisation that she didn't particularly *want* to spend the day with Zoe. It was an oft-unacknowledged truth
that the act of reconnecting with someone you hadn't seen for a long time,
of readjusting to the old dynamic you used to enjoy, was often a lot more
difficult than it seemed on paper. It required less effort just not to bother
– which, she supposed, went some way towards explaining why they'd
fallen out of touch for so long.

'Ye sure?' Zoe sounded doubtful.

'I'm sure. Besides, I've kinda got plans of my own.'

'Aye?'

'Yeah – the neighbours are having a bit of a soirée. You know – mulled
wine and nibbles, bit of the old Bing Crosby on the record player. Probably
dead naff, but I said I'd show my face.'

This was what was known in the trade as a bald-faced lie. Her next-door
neighbours, Jim and Arianne, had indeed invited her round for Christmas
Eve drinks – an invitation that she suspected was born purely out of pity
for the lonely spinster next door, and which, for that selfsame reason, she'd
already turned down, citing other (non-existent) arrangements. She told
herself she'd make more of an effort in the new year. For now, though, let
Zoe enjoy her drunken Christmas shenanigans with her current crop of
friends – friends who, she suspected, were less likely to remind her of the
past and the pain associated with it.

Zoe pulled a wry face. 'Living life on the edge there, doll. But aye,
s'probably for the best. Don't want ye going into premature labour on
account of having too much of a good time.'

Anna laughed. 'Fat chance! I'll probably be in bed by ten.'

'Oh, here.' Zoe shifted gears, her mind doing that thing it sometimes
did of moving onto another subject without stopping to make sure everyone
else was keeping up. 'I was clearing out the hall cupboard the other day
and I found a buncha photies. Y'know, fae the old days.'

'Uh-huh?' Anna wondered where she was going with this.

'There was a few of you in there. Fair took me back, so they did.
'Member how ye used to have that dead long wavy hair?'

'I used to spend ages straightening and blow-drying it, didn't I? Hardly
seems worth the effort now. This is much less hassle.' She gestured to her
utilitarian shoulder-length bob.

'If ye like, I can let ye have some o' them.'

'Yeah?'

'Aye – come round the flat sometime and ye can pick out yer faves.'

'I'll do that,' said Anna, secretly relieved that Zoe hadn't pressed her to commit to a date then and there.

'Aye, there was stuff in there I'd completely forgot about. Like, mind that trip to Blackpool we all took that one summer? We went down for the week – you, me, Victor and Granny. She rented a cottage by the beach.'

'It rained the whole time,' said Anna with a grin. 'We spent the entire week inside. Was your granny ever pissed! The weather man had promised her nothing but clear skies.'

'And that wallpaper.'

Anna mimed dry heaving. 'Oh, *God*, the wallpaper! And the carpets, and the bedcovers! Brown and orange diagonal stripes!'

'Pure vomit colours! What sick basturt dreamt *that* up?'

And for a moment, just a moment, Zoe was her old self again – *really* herself, not putting on some elaborate performance. It lasted a few more seconds, then the light seemed to dim from her eyes.

'Aye,' she said quietly, 'good times.'

They fell silent, seeming to have run out of things to say to each other. Zoe's smile slowly faded, leaving behind only a trace, like the faint residue that remains on a TV screen after displaying the same image for too long. A distant look came into her eyes, as if her mind had taken her to some place far away. Anna watched her, puzzled and more than a little concerned to be witnessing what looked for all the world like a dissociative episode.

She eyed their surroundings. It was cold and desolate out here, the park a far cry from its summer splendour, when the trees were in full bloom and the sounds of children playing echoed far and wide.

'What are we doing out here, Zo?' she said. 'We could've met in a café or something, somewhere closer to home. Why'd you bring me all the way out here?'

Zoe nodded into the distance. 'For that.'

'What?'

'*That.*'

She nodded again, and this time Anna followed her gaze, looking out at the view of the city unfolding before them. It was the magic hour, the sandstone tenements on Balvicar Drive on the park's northwestern edge glowing red in the late afternoon sun, the spires of the two churches looming side by side like twin sentinels.

'It's beautiful, in't it?' said Zoe softly. ''Specially this time of day.'

'It's nice,' said Anna, still wondering if there was something she was missing.

'I've lived here my whole life,' Zoe went on, her voice a low, almost singsong murmur, 'and I've always just took it for granted. Like, I never appreciated how good I had it, getting to grow up here. Never appreciated how lucky I wis. It was always just . . . there. It's like they pictures I found in the cupboard. These . . . moments, they pass so quickly. Like, if ye're no on the ball, ye miss 'em completely. And then, before ye even know it, the light's already fading.' She turned to face Anna imploringly, her eyes glowing in the late sun. 'Dae ye no see it?'

Anna shifted uncomfortably. She wasn't used to this sort of introspection from Zoe, whom she'd always regarded as something of an open book.

'It's just a city, Zo.'

'Aye, but it's *our* city. It's where we came fae. S'what made us who we are.'

As she spoke, the last light of the sun sank behind the hills far off to the west, plunging the buildings into shadow.

'See what I mean?' said Zoe. 'Gone in a flash.'

Anna said nothing. It was as plain as day that something was seriously up with Zoe – something that was beyond her skill to tease out. She wondered just how long Zoe had been sitting here on her own, staring out at the skyline, before she'd arrived. She told herself there was no point in pressing the matter – that, if Zoe wanted her to know what was going on, she'd tell her when she was good and ready. In the meantime, whatever was going on inside that flaming red head of hers, she was going to have to figure it out herself.

So Anna kept her own counsel. But she wondered, and she worried.

# 19

# Traces

*Thursday 31 December*

'Dave's been such a godsend,' said Janice. At least Anna *thought* she was Janice. She could just as easily have been Jacqui or Jodie. 'Whenever I need something, he's there with it before I even have to ask. I've never known him to be so attentive.'

'You're lucky,' replied Sharon – or was it Karen? 'My Barry hasn't so much as lifted a finger for me since he got me up the duff. Have to do everything myself. It's like having a great big wean in the house already.'

Anna sipped her anaemic decaf coffee as the other mums-to-be continued their brain-numbing conversation, her mind wandering. You'd think, given that she shared something fairly significant in common with them all, that it would be easy to make small talk. In reality, she'd exhausted every possible conversation topic within the space of five minutes and found herself fading into the background as the other women prattled away happily about whether it was ever appropriate to dress a boychild in pink and why a natural birth was the only way to go. She hadn't even wanted to join them for coffee, but after class that morning the one she thought was called Janice had practically backed her up against the wall and *demanded* that she accompany them to the little café on Hyndland Road. And now here she was, firmly wedged between two other women with her back to the wall, making escape impossible. So she gritted her teeth and sipped her disgusting decaf and resisted the urge to tell them that the natural birth industry was just repackaged misogyny, ennobling and

175

romanticising women's suffering as some beatific act of purity, rooted in the notion that they required and deserved to feel pain.

Someone was saying her name. She looked up. 'Sorry?'

Sharon/Karen smiled patiently. 'We were all just wondering whether it's a boy or a girl you're having?'

Six eager pairs of eyes stared at her, awaiting an answer.

'Well,' Anna said, after the very definition of a pregnant pause, 'it's definitely one or the other.'

'Oh, a surprise!' One of the other women clapped her hands in delight. 'What a lovely idea! It must be so exciting not knowing.'

This kickstarted a spirited debate about whether or not it had been better in the olden days, when it wasn't possible to tell in advance and you had to just wait and see what popped out on the day. Anna once again found her mind drifting, only to be seized by a sudden, sharp flare-up of pain in her lower abdomen. It lasted for around half a minute, during which she had to bite down on the inside of her cheek and make a concerted effort not to cry out. In the week since Christmas, she'd been experiencing these attacks on and off, along with a persistent, throbbing headache which no amount of paracetamol would cure. On Boxing Day, she'd availed herself of the emergency out-of-hours GP service, only to be assured that every-thing was fine and that the pain would pass. But it hadn't, and as December wound its way to a close, the abdo pains had only grown worse and more frequent.

The wave passed, and the women's conversation, which the pain had all but obliterated, came back into focus. Watching them, each and every one of them revelling in their status as mothers in waiting, she wondered why those same rosy maternal feelings she'd been promised stubbornly refused to materialise in her, and whether it was possible that she was somehow irretrievably broken.

It was almost an hour and a half later when she finally managed to extricate herself from their company. Spurred on her way by a chorus of good wishes for the imminent blessed event, she left the café and headed up the pavement to collect her car. She was driving everywhere now, even what would once have been a five-minute walk back to Clarence Drive now beyond her ability. It still didn't quite seem real that her due date was just over a fortnight away. As recently as a few weeks ago, it had still felt as if she had loads of time, and yet the big day was now rushing towards her with all the speed of an express train. In a strange way, it reminded her of the long summer holidays of her childhood. At the start, they always seemed to stretch out endlessly before you, the notion of nearly two whole months of freedom almost too great to even quantify. And yet, as surely as night followed day, the weeks flew by in the blink of an eye, and suddenly it was Sunday night and you were packing your schoolbag, your uniform freshly ironed and laid out for you to wear on Monday.

As she pictured her younger self standing in front of the mirror, knotting her tie emblazoned with the Willow Bank crest, she suddenly realised why it was that she'd refused the repeated overtures from midwives and obstetricians to enlighten her as to her baby's sex. It wasn't, as the other women so naïvely assumed, because she was saving it as a nice post-labour surprise. It was because, consciously or otherwise, she'd been trying to ensure that the baby remained as intangible as possible, without it developing characteristics and becoming a 'he' or a 'she'. She wanted it to remain, for as long as was feasible, an abstraction. An 'it'.

As she halted next to her car and rummaged in her bag for the keys, out of the corner of her eye she caught sight of a figure emerging from the general store a little way up the road. Something familiar about its gait and posture caused her to look up. She stood and watched as Clive Sullivan paused at the kerb to wait for a gap in the traffic, his arm weighed down by the heavy contents of the large carrier bag he was holding.

In the week since Christmas Eve, Anna had made a serious effort to avoid allowing Sullivan to intrude on her thoughts, forcing herself to put aside her pretensions of cracking the case in favour of becoming the expectant mother she was supposed to be. Now, though, as she watched him waiting for the traffic to clear, the old bloodhound's instinct was kindled in her once more. Hyndland Road wasn't his usual patch, and she couldn't think what could possibly have brought him to the Costcutter here that he couldn't have got at the Stop 'n' Shop on Dumbarton Road. Unless, she thought, he didn't want anyone who might recognise him to see what he was buying. She studied the bag containing his purchase. A large, rectangular bottle, judging by the shape of it.

A gap finally appeared in the traffic. Moving surprisingly quickly for a man of his age, Sullivan crossed the road and halted next to an aged beige station wagon, where he shifted his carrier bag to his other hand while he unlocked the door. Until now, Anna hadn't even realised he owned a car – though, as her eyes took in the station wagon once again, she realised she recognised it from her Christmas Eve vigil on Partickhill Road, where it had been parked a little further along on the opposite kerb.

As Sullivan got into his car and shut the door, Anna's instincts took over. Fumbling to unlock her own vehicle, she scrambled inside and buckled her seatbelt, stretching it over her protuberant belly. Somehow, she managed to fit the key into the ignition with her shaking, clammy hand, and, as Sullivan's station wagon pulled out into the traffic, she gunned the engine and set off up Hyndland Road, hot on his tail.

At first, she had no idea where they were headed. However, as they passed through Kelvindale and continued north along Switchback Road, she began to get an inkling of Sullivan's ultimate destination. Her suspicions were confirmed as, around a mile later, he circled Canniesburn Roundabout and doubled back along Maryhill Road, finally pulling into the gravel track just past the science park, which led up to the sprawling cluster of allotments where, Vasilico had told her, Sullivan owned his little plot of land.

She looked around. There was nowhere for her to park the car on the busy main road. She chewed her lip pensively, then accelerated and drove on till she came to the turnoff to Dawsholm Road some four hundred metres further along. She left her car there, tucked out of sight round the bend, then hotfooted it back up Maryhill Road as quickly as she could.

She was breathless and drenched in sweat by the time she reached the allotments. She made her way up the gravel track, constantly on the lookout for Sullivan. She found his station wagon a little way up the track, in an otherwise empty parking area, and was glad she hadn't been foolish enough to follow him in there in her car.

She turned to face the allotments – a patchwork of little city gardens stretching out east as far as the eye could see. It took her a moment to spot Sullivan, tramping up the narrow path running through the middle of the fields with his back to her. He was still carrying his shopping bag, but had now augmented this with a mop and bucket. He kept walking till he reached a plot about a hundred metres along the path. Anna, sheltering from view behind a hedge, watched as he unlocked the door to a small wooden shed – which she recognised instantly from the picture she'd seen on his mantelpiece – and headed inside with his various accoutrements.

She picked her way along the path, sticking as close to the various huts and sheds that lined it as possible, until she came to the allotment adjacent to Sullivan's. There, she ducked behind a tin shack, thanking her lucky stars the place was deserted. Only the truly mad, she surmised, would think to come out here for a spot of gardening in the middle of winter – which only made Sullivan's activities seem all the more suspicious.

For the next half-hour or so, she watched from behind the shack as he laboured inside his shed with his mop and bucket, emerging periodically to empty the latter and refill it from a communal tap at the end of the row. There could be no question about it: he was performing a deep clean of the shed. When he finally downed his tools and stepped out into the pale sunlight, his breathing was laboured and he was stripped down to his shirtsleeves. He paused in the doorway to stretch his evidently aching back, then set off back down the path towards the car park. Anna scarcely had time to get out of sight behind the shack before he passed her, his movements now considerably more laboured than earlier.

As his footsteps receded, she racked her brains, trying to decide on her next move. Should she follow him? The fact that he'd left his equipment and overcoat behind suggested he planned on returning. Plus, as far as she could tell, he'd left the shed unlocked. This might be her only chance to get a look inside. Her decision made, she darted across the allotment, ignoring the frost-encrusted crops she trampled along the way, and slipped inside.

The stench of bleach hit her the moment she crossed the threshold. The entire place had been scrubbed spotless, the bare floorboards wet and glistening. Despite this, the shed was in a sorry state, the wood rotten and heavily warped in places, while the glass of the solitary window was caked in a layer of mould. The various tools that lined the far wall were rusted and notched from heavy use. Only the bare lightbulb hanging from the ceiling appeared new and relatively unspoiled.

*What* happened *in here?* she wondered, ignoring the voice at the back of her head that was telling her it required little imagination to guess.

In the corner nearest the door, a now-empty bleach bottle sat next to the bucket, the mop protruding from it with Sullivan's coat hanging from the handle. Next to these was the carrier bag in which Sullivan had transported the bottle, now bulging with what appeared to be a large, rolled-up piece of fabric. Keeping as close to the doorway as possible to avoid leaving footprints on the wet floor, Anna reached across and tilted the bag towards her, peering inside.

As she took in its contents and processed the significance of what she was seeing, a crow shrieked outside, followed by a flap of wings as it took flight, evidently disturbed by something. Abandoning the bag and its contents, she slipped over to the window and peered out. Sullivan was making his way back up the path towards her. She dropped to a crouch, her heart in her throat. Realising her only other option was to wait here for him to find her, she dived out of the shed and plunged out of sight behind it, grateful that the view from the path was blocked by the tin shack in the neighbouring plot of land.

Peeking round the corner, she watched as Sullivan headed back inside, carrying what appeared to be a portable dehumidifier. He emerged shortly afterwards, minus the humidifier but having collected his coat, mop, bucket and the bulging carrier bag. He paused to lock the shed door, then set off down the path once more. Continuing to crouch low, Anna watched until he disappeared from view. Still she didn't move. A few minutes later, she heard the revving of a car engine and tyres on gravel, and knew that the coast was clear.

This time, she took her time making her way back to her car. She knew that attempting to give chase would be useless at this stage; Sullivan had a considerable head-start on her and she had no idea even of which direction he'd gone in.

Back behind the wheel, she pondered her next move. She contemplated calling Vasilico, but decided against it. He'd already been warned off Sullivan by his superiors, and as such she was loath to involve him in any way that might rebound negatively on him – not until she had the final proof to back up her suspicions. Besides, she was damned if she was going to risk exposing herself to potential ridicule until she'd made sure she wasn't barking up the wrong tree.

She assumed that, his clean-up mission now complete, Sullivan would, sooner or later, head for home. Either way, that was where she was now headed. As she turned the key in the ignition and set off for Gardner Street, she felt a sense of euphoria in the pit of her stomach . . . or perhaps the baby was just on the move again. One way or another, she felt, the truth was within her grasp.

## 20

# Game's Up

Fifteen minutes later, Anna pulled to a halt at the top of Gardner Street. Sullivan's station wagon was parked on the other side of the road. As she clambered out of her car, she was once more hit by a blinding burst of abdominal pain. She gritted her teeth and leant on the hood, waiting for it to pass. As the pain and lightheadedness subsided and her vision came back into focus, she lifted her head and gazed up towards the third floor of the sandstone tenement. She could still back out now, she told herself. She could turn around and get back in her car and go home and mind her own business like any sane, normal person.

Fat chance.

As she hauled herself up the stairs, pausing at each landing to catch her breath, she steeled herself for the confrontation ahead. She didn't think she was in any immediate danger from Sullivan, but she still felt better about confronting him here, within earshot of multiple neighbours, rather than out on a deserted allotment. Nonetheless, she readied her keys as a makeshift weapon, blades protruding between her clenched knuckles – an old technique she'd learned at a self-defence class. She came to a halt outside flat 3/2, waited for her breathing to settle, then rang the bell.

A moment later, the door opened. As he took in the sight of Anna, Sullivan appeared briefly surprised, then, very quickly after that, thoroughly pissed off.

'You? What do you want?'

'I thought we might have a little chat,' said Anna, opting for the bull-dozer approach.

'I've got nothing to say to you.'

As he made to close the door, she stuck her foot in the gap. She winced as the door collided with it, but she held firm.

'Move or I'll call the police,' Sullivan snarled.

'I think we both know that's the last thing you're going to do.'

He gave her a surly look. 'What's that supposed to mean?'

With one hand, Anna gripped the edge of the door in case he tried to close it again. With the other, she continued to grip her keys, hidden just out of sight inside the sleeve of her coat.

'We can either do this out here or we can do it inside,' she said. 'Your choice.'

For a moment, Sullivan seemed to be considering his options. Then, with a defeated sigh, he relented and stood aside to let Anna pass, swiftly shutting the door behind her as she crossed the threshold.

'What's this all about?' he demanded, turning to face her with a look of pure poison. 'I deserve an explanation for this . . . this incursion.'

'I think you know exactly what this about,' said Anna, unmoved by his self-righteous indignation. 'It's about Derek. Your son – remember him?'

Sullivan met Anna's gaze unblinking, refusing to respond to her provocation. 'My son,' he said stiffly, 'is dead.'

'That's what I thought at first. For a while, I even wondered if you'd killed him.'

*That* got a reaction. *'Killed?'* Sullivan spluttered, eyes practically bulging out of their sockets. 'But why . . . why would I . . . ?'

'Would it matter? People murder their loved ones every day for the most trivial of reasons. And you have to admit, right from the start your behaviour looked like that of a man who had something to hide.' She began to recite, counting the reasons off on her fingers, 'There was your indifference when he went missing. Your failure to disclose his mental health condition, despite it vastly increasing the odds of him being at risk. The continued refusals to participate in any media appeal.'

Sullivan huffed and puffed, but he had no comeback to any of this other than noisy indignation.

'And then there was that business with the windbreaker. If you ask me, it was all just a bit too convenient. Derek goes missing in September, there's not so much as a sniff of him for weeks on end – and then suddenly, just after the investigation is ramped up, an item of clothing belonging to him happens to materialise, ideally placed to be found, at a location so infamous as a hotspot for suicides it's almost a cliché at this stage.'

'I don't have to listen to this . . . this drivel.' Sullivan had found his voice at last. 'I was given assurances I'd be left alone.'

'And then there was the memorial service. In the blink of an eye, you went from shunning all contact with the media to holding what amounted to a press conference proclaiming your son's death. Why? Why work so hard to convince everyone Derek was dead – unless it was somehow in your interest for people to believe there was no point looking for him?'

Sullivan shook his head. 'You're out of your mind.'

'I thought that too for a while. But not anymore.' She moved closer to him, forcing him to reverse up the narrow corridor until his back was to the door. 'I've been to the allotment,' she said, leaning in, giving him nowhere to hide from her words. 'I followed you there this morning. I watched you doing your deep clean.'

At this, Sullivan seemed to quail before her eyes. 'You're mad,' he said, but it sounded halfhearted, like he was just going through the motions now.

'Here's what I think,' said Anna, straightening up and backing off slightly to give him room to breathe. 'I think Derek hid in your shed for a time. I think you either knew from the outset, or else at some point you discovered him there and, for whatever reason, decided to continue sheltering him there. I imagine you brought him food and bedding and whatnot. The sleeping bag?' she suggested. 'The one rolled up in that carrier bag you took away with you? You got rid of it on the way home, I imagine. Tossed it in a skip or something like that.'

'You haven't a clue what you're talking about,' said Sullivan, his voice growing shriller with each subsequent denial. 'You come barging in here, throwing mud at the wall, hoping something sticks—'

'Oh, I'll admit some of it's supposition,' said Anna, almost breezily. 'And I admit I could have got the wrong end of the stick entirely. It wouldn't be the first time.' She shook her head. 'But I don't think so. I think I've got the main bits right, more or less, even if I can't *begin* to fathom what your motive was.' She paused. 'And if I'm right, then there's something else I can be pretty confident about.'

'What?' said Sullivan, in a voice that suggested he had no desire to find out but also knew it was inevitable.

'That you know where he is now.'

For a few seconds, Sullivan said nothing, staring at her in defiance. As she continued to meet his gaze, Anna heard the sound of a door creaking open behind her. Sullivan's expression faltered, a look of apprehension entering his eyes.

Anna turned to see a figure facing them from a doorway at the far end of the corridor. He'd lost weight since she'd last seen him, his hair had grown considerably, and where once his cheeks had been smooth and clean-shaven, he now sported an unkempt, scraggly beard. But his face had haunted her thoughts for so long that she'd have recognised him from his eyes alone.

'Hello, Derek,' said Anna. 'Remember me?'

## 21

# Into the Void

Anna followed Derek into the living room and shut the door, conscious all the while of the elder Sullivan's presence behind it – ready, she guessed, to come bursting in the moment he deemed it necessary to intervene. The curtains were drawn, a sliver of pale mid-afternoon light filtering through a gap between them. She sat watching Derek as he paced in little circles, worrying at the back of his scalp with his fingernails. His clothes were mismatched and ill-fitting, his dishevelled appearance so at odds with the pristine nature of his surroundings that he might as well have been transplanted from another planet. His circles grew ever wider, his movements increasingly frantic.

'How d'you feel about sitting down, Derek?'

He glanced at her briefly, gave a quick, furtive head-shake and continued pacing. He was muttering something to himself, his lips quivering, the words – if words they were – little more than a low hum.

'Do you remember who I am?'

Another glance; this time a barely perceptible nod, accompanied by more scalp-scratching. His muttering was growing louder and more intense, the words spoken too quickly for her to make them out.

'What's going on, Derek? You can tell me. I'm here to help.'

'Can't help. No one can help.' He broke off his muttering, or chanting, or whatever it was, just long enough to address those six words to her, then continued as before.

'I'm sure that isn't true. Are you in some kind of trouble?'

'Trouble, yes. Double, double, toil and trouble.'

'Trouble with who? Your colleagues? Were they making life unpleasant for you?'

He glanced at her long enough to deliver a derisive snort. Not that, then.

'Talk to me, Derek. Whatever it is, I'm sure the situation isn't unsalvageable.' She gazed up at him imploringly. 'Perhaps you could start by telling me why you ran away.'

'Message.'

'What message?'

He gave a short, sharp shrug, almost like a tic.

'You mean like a phone call? An email?'

She knew his phone and email records had been trawled extensively and that any suspicious communications would have been identified by the police months ago. Given his state of mind, it seemed far more likely that his 'message' had come to him in the form of an upside-down horseshoe or something written in the clouds.

'What did it say?'

Sullivan made a sudden, angry noise and abruptly collapsed into a nearby armchair. He sat, hands clasped behind his head, forearms pressed against his ears. Rocking back and forth, he began to sing in a soft, reedy voice:

> *I left my baby lying there*
> *Lying there, lying there*
> *I left my baby lying there*
> *To go and gather blaeberries.*

It didn't take a trained psychologist to tell that his mental health had seriously deteriorated in the months since he'd been missing. Had it been this bad from the start, Anna wondered, or had the symptoms gradually built up during his long incarceration in that shed, alone for weeks on end with only his own mind for company?

> *Ho-van, ho-van gorry o go,*
> *Gorry o go, gorry o go;*
> *Ho-van, ho-van gorry o go,*
> *I've lost my dearest baby-o . . .*

She got to her feet and slipped out, leaving him to his nursery rhymes.

Out in the hallway, Sullivan was doing some pacing of his own. As Anna emerged, he turned to face her, a look of desperate anticipation on his face, as if he was waiting for her to issue some pronouncement that would solve all his problems.

'Well,' she said, 'that made about as much sense as a conversation with a wind-up doll.'

Sullivan performed a convincing impression of a deflating balloon. 'I'd wondered if perhaps a familiar face . . . '

'Oh, I sincerely doubt he knows me from Adam.' She shot him an acidic look. 'I'm going to take a wild stab in the dark and assume he hasn't been receiving any medication.'

Sullivan's silence said it all.

'Well,' she said, making no attempt to hide the venom in her voice, 'I seriously hope you're proud of yourself.'

Sullivan glowered at her. 'Whatever you think of me, just know that everything I've done, I've done with his best interests at heart.'

'I don't doubt that's what you believe.'

Sullivan lowered his eyes, unable to withstand her gaze. There was contrition in his expression, but a hint of defiance also. In spite of all the evidence in front of him, he still seemed unable to acknowledge the folly of his actions.

'So what happened?' she said.

Sullivan let out a defeated sigh. 'You already worked out most of it yourself. Back in October – in fact, not long after the night you showed up at my door – I went to spend some time at the allotment. It'd been a while since I'd been out there. As you can probably imagine, I'd had other things on my mind. I went into the shed, and there he was.

'From what I was able to make out, he'd been holed up there since the night he went missing. He was in . . . a bad way. He'd been living off fruit and veg from the allotments and water from the shared tap, as best I could gather. He was half-starved. And his state of mind . . . He begged me to let him continue to hole up in there. Begged me not to give him up.'

'And you went *along* with this?' spluttered Anna, unable to believe what she was hearing.

'I thought it might give him time to straighten himself out,' Sullivan snapped. 'And I thought, if I could support him – bring him food and bedding and whatnot – then at least it was better than leaving him to his own devices.' He looked at Anna almost in desperation. 'You didn't see him then. He was filthy, living in his own muck like some sort of animal, ranting and raving like a man possessed.'

'He has a *mood* disorder!' Anna all but screamed at him. 'It's not something you can cure by locking him up with a vomit bowl while he goes cold turkey!'

Sullivan said nothing. In the silence that ensued, Anna suddenly realised something.

'This is about pride, isn't it?' She shook her head, almost laughing in utter incredulity. 'Oh my God, it actually *is*. Vasilico was right. You were so ashamed of the state he'd gotten himself into, you'd rather let people believe he was dead than a nutter.'

'You know nothing!' Sullivan snapped. 'Absolutely nothing.' He lowered his voice to a hiss, his eyes flaring angrily. 'You think I did this for myself, but I did it for *him* – to spare him the shame of people seeing the mess he was in. People who'd expended vast resources on his behalf, hunting high and low for him, convinced he'd come to genuine harm, when all that time he was safe and sound under their very noses.'

'Oh yes.' Anna's voice dripped sarcasm. 'Truly selfless behaviour on your end. Real "father of the year" stuff.'

Sullivan flinched at her words but made no further attempt to defend his actions. Anna wasn't sure whether he realised they were indefensible or had just concluded that there was no point trying to convince her otherwise.

At length she spoke again, attempting a more conciliatory tone. 'And how long's he been here with you?'

'Since the twenty-fourth,' said Sullivan, with a heavy sigh. 'I went out there late in the afternoon – you know, to bring him food and a change of clothing. I spent some time with him. We talked for a bit, though I doubt either of us was able to understand the other overly well. But then, when it was time to go, I found I couldn't just leave him there. It was perishing cold, even with the portable heater I'd brought him, and he'd developed this cough . . . and I thought, since it's Christmas . . . ' He looked at Anna with something that almost resembled eagerness. 'And you know, I honestly believe it's done him a power of good. He's made some real progress over the last week, compared to where he was.'

*Bully for you*, Anna thought, unable to muster even a pretence of entertaining his delusion. 'Have you any idea what he's afraid of?' she asked instead.

Sullivan merely shrugged. 'You'd have to ask him, I'm afraid.'

'Believe me, I tried.'

'I don't suppose it makes much difference, does it? One way or another, it's all in his head.'

Anna contemplated this for some time. 'It's real to him,' she said eventually, 'and I suppose that's ultimately what matters.'

Sullivan didn't look especially convinced, but he didn't argue with her. 'Would you mind if I used your bathroom?'

Sullivan glanced up, blinking. 'Hmm? Excuse me?'

'The bathroom.' She shrugged sheepishly. 'Pregnant woman? Urgent urge to pass water?'

'Oh. Right. Down the hall and to the left.'

She left him leaning against the wall, as if the very effort required to remain upright had become too much.

When she emerged from the bathroom a few minutes later, there was no sign of Sullivan, but from the clacking of crockery coming from behind the adjacent door, she concluded that he was indulging in a spot of therapeutic housekeeping.

She headed back to the living room, where she found Derek in much the same position as before: sat in the armchair, rocking back and forth, continuing to recite his poem.

> *Ho-van, ho-van gorry o go,*
> *I've lost my dearest baby-o . . .*

She shut the door, making as little noise as possible for fear of attracting Sullivan's attention. As she sat down, the creaking of the sofa's springs caused Derek to look up sharply, falling silent.

'It's OK,' she reassured him. 'It's just me.'

He gave her a long, hard look, seemingly puzzled to see her. 'Did *they* send you?' he said, his voice an urgent whisper.

'"They"? Who's "they"?'

He scoffed and shook his head, as if this was the stupidest question he'd ever heard.

'Come on, Derek. Who's "they"? Who are you scared of?'

'Bad men. Bill and Ben, flowerpot men.' He shook his head, thighs pressing together, squeezing his tightly clasped hands between them. 'Ashes to ashes, shapes and shadows. Men who hear everything. *See* everything. No room for secrets – not from them, no, no.'

'And what is it you're afraid they'll do?'

Derek slapped the side of his head so hard Anna flinched. 'They want my brain, and my eyes.' He let out a sudden, high-pitched giggle. 'And my ears,' he continued, in a singsong voice, 'and my fingers, and my toes. They'll take yours too, if you make them angry.'

'*Who*, Derek?'

Derek looked left and right, then leaned in towards her and uttered three solitary words in a low, strained hiss.

'*The Shadow Men.*'

The uneasy silence which followed was broken by the sound of a car pulling up outside. In the brief moment before the engine was killed, she recognised the smooth purr of Vasilico's Porsche. *Bloody hell,* she thought, *that was quick.* She tried not to react, not wanting to tip Derek off in any way.

Too late. Derek was already on his feet, darting over to the window. He peered through the crack in the curtains, then drew in a sharp breath and leapt back as if he'd been stung. He turned to face Anna with a look of utter disbelief.

'What did you *do*?' he hissed.

The doorbell sounded in the hallway. Derek's head snapped in its direction.

'It's OK,' said Anna, getting to her feet, hands raised reassuringly. 'We just want to help you.'

Derek said nothing. He just stared at her with wide, accusing eyes, his expression that of someone who'd just been stabbed in the back by their closest confidant.

Anna heard the creak of the front door, followed by voices. She recognised Sullivan's, haughty and aggrieved, and Vasilico's, curt and officious. There was an indignant 'Hoi!' from Sullivan, then the sound of feet entering the flat – multiple pairs, advancing at speed towards the living room.

As Derek backed up against the far wall, crouching low like a cornered animal, the door swung open and Vasilico stepped in, a uniformed officer close behind him. Anna could hear Sullivan loudly protesting, presumably being restrained in the corridor by another officer.

'Now then, Derek,' said Vasilico, advancing cautiously into the room with both hands raised, palms open to show that he was unarmed, 'you're not going to do anything daft, are you?'

When she'd called Vasilico from the bathroom, Anna had resigned herself to the fact that, when the time came, Derek was unlikely to go down without a fight. In reality, however, it was over remarkably quickly and with minimal fuss. He capitulated almost instantly, not putting up even the token resistance his father had offered. Perhaps, deep down, he was relieved it was finally over. He was almost docile as the uniformed officer took hold of his arm and led him out of the living room, Anna and Vasilico bringing up the rear.

In the hallway, they found Sullivan waiting, a second officer by his side, one hand on his forearm. As the little procession drew level with them, Derek stopped and turned to face his father. For a moment, they looked at one another in silence, then Sullivan raised his shoulders in a fatalistic shrug.

'Yes, well,' he said quietly.

Derek gave a small, sad smile. Sullivan lifted his hand almost imperceptibly, and for a moment Anna thought he was going to hug his son or shake his hand or brush his cheek or at least do *something* to show that he cared, but instead he let it fall to his side again, and then the moment passed and the officer escorting Derek ushered him on towards the door.

As she and Vasilico stood on the landing outside the flat, watching Derek being marshalled down the steps like a condemned man being taken down, Anna experienced the sudden, visceral feeling of having done something truly awful. The look of utter betrayal in his eyes as he'd realised she'd turned him in was seared into her mind like a branding iron.

'What'll happen now?' she said.

'We'll take him to the Western for a check-up,' Vasilico said. 'He'll need to be assessed, both physically and mentally. Our main priority is obviously his wellbeing. But there are questions to be answered too. We need to get to the bottom of why he did what he did.'

'Well, don't expect to get much sense out of him. And go easy on him. He's been through a lot.'

As Vasilico opened his mouth to respond, shouts and sounds of a struggle broke out on the landing below. He and Anna rushed to the bannister in time to see Derek throwing all his weight against his minder, driving him into the wall. As the winded officer struggled to catch his breath, and even as Vasilico sprang down the stairs towards him, Derek's eyes alighted on the window behind him. Anna watched with painful helplessness, knowing what was going to happen even before it did, as he backed himself up, then charged straight at it. The sound of shattering glass rang in her ears as Derek Sullivan hurtled into the void.

## 22

# A Cup o' Kindness

It had been Zoe's first shift at the Corner in almost a month. She'd tried to wriggle out of it, but Malcolm Malcolm wasn't having any of it. 'I need you tonight, Red,' he'd snarled down the phone line, 'no ifs or buts.' She'd toyed with the idea of pretending she was sick – or, alternatively, just telling him to jump on a spike. It would certainly have given her no small amount of satisfaction, and she had a feeling she wasn't long for the job anyway, so there was a certain logic to getting the inevitable dismissal over and done with. But in the end she'd agreed to honour her shift, for old times' sake if nothing else.

It had actually turned out to be surprisingly enjoyable: a chance to forget about Victor and Broadhurst and the rest of it – for a few hours at any rate. There'd been almost a feeling of mass euphoria in the air, born out of a shared recognition among the staff that they might as well make the most of the night in lieu of the various Hogmanay parties they were all missing. So they'd taken it in turns to sneak down to the basement to raid the liquor supply, getting as tipsy as they dared without arousing the suspicions of Malcolm Malcolm. She'd even given Craig, who was made up to see her again after so long, a little Christmas peck on the lips behind the wine racks, though she'd made sure it went no further than that.

Once they'd seen off the last of the customers and shut up shop for the night, Malcolm Malcolm gave them all a surprisingly generous cash-in-hand bonus and wished them a healthy and prosperous 2016, and for a brief instant Zoe almost managed to believe that, in another life, she might have actually liked the guy. As she turned her back on the restaurant and set off to catch her train, she found herself experiencing a deep and aching sense of loss. Somehow, she knew she wouldn't be back.

As the virtually empty train wound its way homeward, Zoe's phone pinged a text alert. It was from her pal Gemma, asking if she'd got out of work yet and saying there was still time to join her and the others in George Square for the countdown if she wanted to change her mind. She deleted the message and switched her phone off.

She wondered what Anna was up to right now. Tucked up safe in bed, if she had any sense. It'd been nice seeing her on Christmas Eve, chatting away to her about this and that. She'd realised, as soon as she laid eyes on her, blooming with new life and looking ready to drop, that she couldn't burden her with the knowledge of Broadhurst and the abuse. The last thing she wanted was a bloody miscarriage on her hands. So she'd kept schtum about the reason she'd dragged her out to Queen's Park in the first place and spouted a whole lot of guff instead about photos and childhood holidays and whatnot. She might have veered towards the maudlin at times, but by and large she'd managed to keep a lid on the emotions bubbling below the surface – even if those friendship bracelets Anna had produced had just about threatened to set her off. Anna had meant well, obviously, but if ever a present had been tailor-made to remind Zoe what a lousy pal she'd been in recent years, it was that. She'd worn hers ever since, keeping it on day and night, almost as a penance – a reminder of her selfishness and inadequacy, like a hair shirt or belt of nails.

As Zoe turned onto Dumbarton Road, she spotted a familiar figure standing at the kerb: a young, dark-haired woman in a denim jacket. She slowed her pace, not relishing another encounter with the girl – not least because she knew she'd feel compelled to invite her in again, and she really wasn't in the mood for entertaining. But she knew she couldn't get into the flat without Mandy noticing her, and she was damned if she was going to let her walk the streets until 2 a.m. or however long it would take her twat of a boyfriend to pick her up.

Hearing Zoe's footsteps, Mandy turned to face her. The first thing Zoe noticed was the black eye she sported – a dark, swollen-lidded shiner of the walked-into-a-door variety. The second was that Mandy wasn't alone. A small girl, who until now had been hidden out of sight behind her, stood clutching her hand. She must only have been about four or five, with the same dark hair as Mandy and a paint-spatter of freckles across the bridge of her nose that was all her own. She stared up at Zoe with the wide-eyed suspicion of someone who had learned from experience that not every adult she encountered had good intentions.

In the five seconds or so that it took Zoe to process the sight of them and assess their situation, her mind was made up.

'Come with me,' she said. 'The pair o' yese.'

Neither Mandy nor the girl offered a word of objection – or, indeed, a word of anything – as they followed Zoe up the stairs. The girl looked dead on her feet, only still awake by dint of having nowhere to lay down her head. Zoe directed them to the living room, turned the thermostat up full and fetched a spare blanket and pillow from the bedroom. She returned to find the two of them on the sofa, the girl lying with her head in Mandy's lap. Mandy, stroking her hair mechanically with a thumb, looked up.

'Normally the lady next door watches her for me in the day,' she said. 'But she's gone tae her family for New Year's. I couldnae leave her alane in the flat . . . '

'It's OK,' said Zoe. 'Ye don't have to explain.' She turned to the girl with a friendly smile. 'Well look at *you*. Heh, ye've got nearly as many freckles as me.'

The girl stared up at her from Mandy's lap with the same wariness as before.

'Sorry.' Mandy winced apologetically. 'She isnae aw that trusting o' strangers.'

*Smart kid,* Zoe thought.

Between them, they made up the sofa and got the girl bedded down. Once she was asleep (it didn't take more than a few minutes), they headed through to the kitchen, where Zoe made them each a strong coffee with heaps of sugar.

'She yer sister?' Zoe asked, leaning against the countertop, watching Mandy take long, slow sips at the kitchen table.

'Ma daughter. Ruby. She's five.'

'Bit young tae be wandering the streets on New Year's Eve.'

'Aye, well, like I said, didnae hae much choice.'

'Lemme guess – yer boyfriend's picking yese up.'

Mandy gave a brief, curt nod.

'He dae that tae ye?'

There was no need to specify what 'that' meant. Mandy, staring resolutely into her mug, said nothing.

'Ye shouldnae be wi him if that's the way he treats ye,' said Zoe – aware, even as she spoke, that she was most likely on a hiding to nothing.

'It's . . . complicated.'

'It aye is. But I'da thought having the wean would make it pretty simple. She ever see him laying intae ye?'

'It's no like that.' Mandy's head shot up, eyes flaring at the implied criticism of her parenting. 'I make sure she isnae aroon when I see him. Anywie, this is the first time he's ever done something like this.'

There seemed little point in going down the Spanish Inquisition route. As like as not, Mandy would just get defensive or clam up totally, neither of which would help matters. Anyway, there were other ways to be an ally besides imploring her to cut all ties with the bastard.

'Well,' Zoe said, circling round the table to Mandy's side, 'just so's ye know, if yese ever need someplace tae go – tae get away fae him or just tae get outta the cold – yese can always use this place.'

'Aye?'

Mandy stared up at Zoe, suspicion etched on furrowed brows. She was probably trying to work out what the catch was – what would be expected of her in return.

Zoe shrugged like it was no big deal, even though she knew perfectly well that folk didn't normally offer complete strangers the use of their home – which, now that she thought about it, possibly went some way towards explaining why the world was in the state it was in.

Mandy said nothing. As she sat there, nursing her mug in both hands, her eyes strayed past Zoe to the fridge at the far end of the kitchen. Zoe turned, following her gaze. At first, she assumed Mandy was hungry and was on the verge of offering to fix her a sandwich when she realised that her attention wasn't on the fridge itself but a photo pinned to the door. It was another of the ones of Victor she'd found in the shoebox. He was sitting on the living room sofa at the old house on Astley Street, rolling a joint, head bowed in concentration. It would have been about a year before his death – possibly even the last one of him she'd ever taken.

'D'ye miss him?'

Mandy's voice brought Zoe back to the present. She stirred. Nodded.

'Don't wonder at it. 'Specially this time o' year.'

Zoe arched her shoulders, trying to appear unshaken. 'Aye, well, disnae get any easier, I'll tell ye that much.'

Mandy gave a sad little smile. She seemed to understand. Zoe couldn't help wondering what sort of grief *she'd* experienced in her own short life.

'Talk to me about him.'

'Huh?'

'Go on. I'd like tae hear about him. I don't mean the shite they wrote in the papers. I mean what he was really like.'

In six long years, it was the first time anyone had ever asked her that. No one had seemed to have any interest in getting to know the person behind the headlines – not the cops, not the so-called friends who'd sold their stories to the tabloids, certainly not the journos who'd hounded her for a juicy 'my brother the killer' quote. This was her chance to tell someone the true story. To wipe the slate clean.

So she started to tell Mandy all about him – his shyness, his sensitivity, the way the tips of his ears used to turn pink whenever he got teased. And she told her about the wonderful, unexpected acts of kindness he was capable of – like the time at primary school when she'd been banned from the trip to Alton Towers after she'd punched Scott Campbell in the nose and called him Smellybollocks, and Victor had dug his heels in and said that if his big sis couldnae go, then he wasnae goin' either. She told Mandy about all the bad parts too – the mood swings, the sullenness, the endless rows about petty nothings. Bits that contributed, in their own essential way, to her memories of him and which, despite all the grief they'd caused at the time, she wouldn't change for the world. That was the thing about Victor: he hadn't been perfect. Who ever was? He'd been a complex, maddeningly flawed human being, but he'd been her brother, the only one she'd ever had and ever would, and she cherished each and every one of those memories, warts and all.

She continued to talk and Mandy continued to listen. And then, before she had the presence of mind to stop herself, she found herself telling

Mandy about the abuse, about Broadhurst and the DVD, and the list of suspected abusers she had and how it included names of people from every pillar of the Establishment. She told her about the botched investigation into Netherfield, and the dark forces that had leant on Cadogan to make sure the case collapsed and nobody was charged. She talked about her fears about Victor – about how afraid she was that he'd been one of the victims and that it accounted for why he'd gone so badly off the rails, and how it was her fault for being such a shite big sister. She was letting it all pour out, using Mandy as a sponge to soak it all up because there was no one else to turn to.

'There's some right bad people in the world,' said Mandy, when Zoe finally ran out of steam.

'Aye.' Zoe nodded soberly. 'There is that.'

They fell into silence, lost in their own thoughts. Mandy sipped her coffee, making loud slurping noises that would have been funny under different circumstances.

At length, Zoe stirred. 'Mind if I go take a slash? Been on the hoof aw night.'

She took herself to the bathroom, locked the door and stared long and hard at her reflection in the mirror, wondering what the hell had possessed her, blabbing all that stuff to a virtual stranger.

She slapped herself hard across the face. 'Get a hold of yersel, Callahan,' she snarled. 'Ye're losing the heid.'

She remained there for a few more minutes, trying to collect her composure. Eventually, having left it as long as she felt she feasibly could, she splashed some water on her face, took a deep breath and headed back to the kitchen.

Mandy wasn't there. She wasn't in the living room either, and neither was Ruby. Only the pillow and blanket, lying in a crumpled heap on the sofa, served as proof that they'd ever been there. She hurried to the window and peered out, but the street below was empty.

Mandy marched up the pavement, carrying the still half-sleeping Ruby in her arms, her short, sharp breaths leaving little clouds of vapour in the cold air. As she passed the library, an ominous concrete block looming over her in the darkness, she heard the hum of a car approaching behind her. She kept walking, but a bolt of icy fear coursed through her. She knew the sound of that engine. Would recognise it anywhere.

Her fears were confirmed as the detective's flash sportscar drew alongside her, slowing to match her pace. As she continued to pound the pavement, the window slid down.

'Well now, *someone's* in a hurry tonight. What's the matter? Late for a New Year's party?'

Knowing the game was up, Mandy stopped and turned to face her tormenter. He brought the car to a standstill and stepped onto the pavement, forcing her up against the shopfront grille behind her. He towered over her, more than a foot taller, so close they were almost touching, his expensive cologne making her want to gag.

'You abandoned your post.' His smooth purr belied the underlying menace to his words. 'That wasn't part of the arrangement.'

'I'm done.' She forced the words out between teeth that remained clenched to stop them from chattering. 'Ye can find someone else tae dae yer dirty work.'

'Is that so?'

'Aye. Ye can knock me aroon aw ye like. Disnae make a difference. Bigger men than you've done worse.'

The detective said nothing. He continued to gaze down at Mandy, eyes drilling into her, making her feel like she had nothing on. She met his gaze defiantly, even though her knees were shaking and her stomach was doing belly-flops. Slowly, his gaze shifted from her face down to Ruby, asleep in her arms – or pretending to be.

'Cute kid.'

There was no need for him to spell out what he was thinking.

'Ye wouldnae.'

'Wouldn't I?'

'She's only a *wean*.' The words came out as a strangled hiss.

'And, as her mother, any harm that were to befall her would ultimately be your responsibility. I'd hate for you to have that on your conscience.'

Tears filled Mandy's eyes. 'Bastard,' she hissed.

The detective smiled. 'It has been said. So do we have an understanding?'

Mandy lowered her eyes and nodded.

The detective's smile broadened.

*   *   *

Fifteen minutes later, Mandy was once again stomping up the street, Ruby's head on her shoulder. Her lungs burned, but she didn't stop. She just knew she had to put as much distance between herself and that creep as possible.

As she turned onto Dowanhill Street, she noticed an elderly man sitting in the doorway of the Oriental Takeaway, a weather-stained rug about his shoulders. A handwritten cardboard sign at his feet announced him as one of the city's sizeable homeless population.

She came to a halt. He raised his head, looking up at her with cloudy eyes, the hope long ago snuffed out of them.

'Here.'

She held out the crisp £50 note the detective had given her – payment for services rendered. The man stared at her and it, as if wondering if he was hallucinating – or, perhaps more likely, if this was a cruel joke and she was going to snatch it away the moment he reached for it.

'Go on.'

He took it, pocketing it instantly in case she changed her mind. He stared up at her wordlessly, no doubt taking her for a madwoman – which perhaps she was. After all, she could have put it to good use. It would have paid for a hearty meal for her and Ruby, and a bed for the night somewhere warm and safe. But she knew she couldn't profit from what she'd just done – not without feeling even dirtier than she already did.

The man continued to stare up at her. 'You feeling awright, hen?'

Mandy didn't respond. She just turned and ran, Ruby bouncing up and down against her chest as she fled into the night.

Zoe stood by the window, gazing out into the dark, empty street. Wherever Mandy and her daughter had gone, she hoped it was someplace warm.

Somewhere outside, a clock struck twelve. A few isolated fireworks popped and fizzed.

It was the first day of the new year.

## 23

# Room Temperature

Anna stirred and rubbed bleary eyes. She wasn't sure if she'd actually been asleep or if she'd just briefly zoned out. She glanced at the digital clock/thermometer on Vasilico's desk. Almost midnight. Far too late. 24.7 degrees. Far too hot. No *wonder* she'd drifted off. She wondered how they justified keeping the heating running. The place was all but deserted – a combination, she presumed, of the late hour and it being Hogmanay.

The door swung open. At last – Vasilico. She'd have leapt to her feet if her condition hadn't made it physically impossible. She settled instead for an abrupt 'Well?'

'He's alive,' said Vasilico, shutting the door behind him. 'Stable, but in a critical condition. The surgeons operated to remove a clot on his brain. They're keeping him in an induced coma for now.'

It was both worse news than she'd hoped for and better than she'd feared. When the paramedics had scooped Derek off the pavement at the top of Gardner Street, she'd been convinced he was dead. Sullivan had been too, judging by the rage with which he'd flown at Vasilico – this latest turn of events, it seemed, having finally stirred a genuine emotional response from somewhere in the depths of his soul.

'I suppose I'm in the shit,' she said with a rueful grimace, 'for making a delicate situation worse.'

'Quite the opposite, actually,' said Vasilico. 'I've just been briefing the ACC – hence my being held up. I made it abundantly clear I'd hand in my badge on the spot if there was even the slightest sniff of action being taken against you.' He laid a hand on her shoulder. 'You solved the case while the best and the brightest of the Major Investigations Team were chasing their tails. This is your moment.'

As victories went, it seemed an incredibly pyrrhic one, and try as she might, Anna couldn't derive any sort of satisfaction from her role in the day's events.

Vasilico seemed to sense what she was thinking. 'Hey.' He put a hand under her chin, gently lifting her head to meet his eyes. 'You're not to blame, so don't even think about flagellating yourself over this. If what happened is on anyone, it's on that utter arse of a father for entertaining the poor lad's delusions and exacerbating his condition. I still haven't ruled out pursuing charges against him.'

Anna shook her head. 'Don't. Just imagine what must be going through his head right now. The guilt he must be feeling. That's punishment enough, surely?'

Vasilico gazed at her in silence, lips pursed. 'You're probably right,' he sighed after a moment. 'You do have a certain knack for appealing to my softer side.' He cocked his head and smiled at her. 'So be it. I shall forego my thirst for punitive justice to spare your liberal blushes.'

Anna briefly returned the smile, but her mind was already elsewhere. She was rerunning her conversation with Derek. Most of what he'd said had been obvious gibberish – the deluded outpourings of a seriously unbalanced mind. But there had been one phrase in particular that, for all its apparent nonsensicalness, had nonetheless left her with a vague and inexplicable feeling of unease.

Vasilico seemed to sense her disquiet. 'What?'

'I was just thinking . . . ' She considered leaving it at that, then decided he might as well hear it. 'While I was waiting for you to arrive, Derek said something strange to me. He said "the Shadow Men" were after him.'

For a moment, Vasilico said nothing. Then he shook his head and laughed. 'The Shadow Men? And who are they when they're at home?'

She shrugged sheepishly, regretting even mentioning it. 'I've no idea. But whoever he thought they were, he was frightened to death of them.'

'"The Shadow Men",' Vasilico repeated, testing the words in his own mouth. 'Nope, 'fraid I've never had the pleasure.' He stroked his chin pensively for a moment, then snapped his fingers. '*I* know what'll pep you up.'

Anna watched as he crossed over to the other side of the office and opened the top drawer of one of the numerous filing cabinets that lined the wall. After rummaging inside, he produced a bottle of store-brand champagne and two mismatched mugs.

'I know it's not entirely appropriate now, but I was saving this for when we cracked the case. Seems a shame to let it go to waste.'

Anna grimaced and patted her stomach. 'I can't . . . '

But Vasilico was unfazed. Heading over, he leaned past her to open one of the desk drawers, from which he produced a can of Coke. She was about to remind him that caffeine was off-limits as well, then stopped herself. *Oh, why not?* One wasn't going to hurt – and besides, she couldn't bring herself to burst his bubble. Not with him looking so pleased with himself.

She popped the tab on the can while Vasilico poured himself a measure of champagne.

He raised his mug in toast. 'Here's to success.'

They clinked beverages and drank.

Anna feigned a smile. 'Mm, room temperature.'

As she put the can to her lips once more, somewhere outside a clock struck twelve. A few isolated fireworks popped and fizzed.

It was the first day of the new year.

# 24

# January Blues

*Friday 1 January 2016*

Anna was woken by a hand on her shoulder, shaking her gently. As she stirred and opened her eyes, the young police constable who'd roused her hastily withdrew his hand and stepped back.

'Sorry,' he stammered, as if he was afraid she was going to hit him for disturbing her slumber, 'but I thought you'd be wanting to be wakened. It's past nine.'

Anna eased herself into a sitting position on the sofa, rubbing her stiff neck. She'd refused to go home the previous night, insisting that she wanted to be there to hear any news about Derek's condition firsthand. It had been Vasilico who'd suggested she bed down in the break room, promising to come and find her the moment he heard anything.

'Where's Vasilico?' she asked, turning her head this way and that to work out the crick in her neck.

'The DCI got called away on other business,' said the officer. 'He said I was to drive you home.'

She supposed she might as well take him up on the offer. Bracing herself, she dragged herself to her feet, waiting for the sparks to stop dancing in front of her eyes before she risked moving.

'Has there been any news about Derek Sullivan?' she asked as she followed the officer down the stairs.

'No change as far as I'm aware,' he replied with an apologetic half-shrug.

\* \* \*

The journey back to the West End took a little over ten minutes. The roads were quiet, the traffic lights in their favour. Anna, seated in the back, humoured her driver's attempts at small talk, but she wasn't really in the mood for it. Her mind was still on Derek, on the sight of his lifeless body lying on the pavement at the top of Gardner Street, surrounded by shards of glass from the window he'd leapt through, and on the look of horrified betrayal in his eyes as he'd realised she'd brought the police to his door.

'*Come on, Derek. Who's "they"? Who are you scared of?*'

'*The Shadow Men.*'

She stirred, glanced out of the window and realised they were nearing Zoe's flat. The gold-lettered façade of Caffè Monza passed them by to the left; up ahead, the railway bridge leading into Partick Station loomed above the road. A sudden impulse to drop in on Zoe took hold of her. She craved company, and right now the idea of crawling into bed with her and spending the morning snuggled under the duvet together having deep, searching conversations about nothing, just like they'd done after many a sleepover in their youth, appealed to her more than just about anything else she could imagine.

She leaned forward and tapped the driver on the shoulder. 'This is fine. You can drop me here.'

As the police car's tail-lights receded into the distance and its engine died away into nothing, the eerie silence of the normally busy street was almost deafening. She reminded herself that it was 9.30 a.m. on New Year's Day and that the whole city was currently nursing its collective post-Hogmanay hangover. The only people currently abroad would be the handful of oddballs like herself who hadn't spent the previous night bevvying.

She headed into the tenement block that housed Zoe's flat and climbed the stairs to the first floor, hoping Zoe wouldn't mind her calling so early in the day. She knocked on the door. No answer. She knocked again, this time louder: Zoe was a notoriously heavy sleeper. Still no response.

Of course, she'd made the naïve assumption that Zoe would be in. Now that she thought about it, it was entirely possible that she'd found some party or other to go to last night and, having spent the night downing her own body weight in alcohol, was currently lying unconscious on the floor of someone else's flat. Yes, that was the most likely scenario. Well, let her sleep it off. She abandoned any thought of trying to get Zoe on her mobile and set off back down the stairs, feeling disappointed and rather dejected.

Stepping out into the street once more, she pondered the odds of her being able to summon a taxi on New Year's Day in anything approaching a timely manner, and the steepness of the resulting fare. She was just about to get out her phone and try her luck with one of the local firms when she remembered that her car was still parked at the top of Gardner Street, a stone's throw from where she now stood. She even briefly entertained the possibility of calling on Sullivan while she was at it to find out how he was doing, before swiftly concluding that, under the circumstances, it would be wise to give him a wide berth – for the time being, at any rate.

She made her way along to Gardner Street and began the arduous trek up the hill. She regretted her decision almost immediately. It was enough of a slog that she'd normally avoided it even in her pre-pregnancy days. In her current state, she might as well have been attempting to scale Ben Nevis. Halfway up, she was forced to stop to catch her breath, leaning against the nearest wall. The pale sun beat down on her mercilessly, making her feel clammy and dizzy, and wishing she hadn't wrapped up quite so warmly the previous day.

Just then, the sound of singing reached her ears, faint and far-off. A little way down the hill, an elderly woman was pottering around in her garden with a rake. As Anna listened, she recognised the lyrics as the same ones Derek had chanted to himself the previous day.

> *Ho-van, ho-van gorry o go,*
> *I've lost my dearest baby-o . . .*

*What an absolutely horrible poem,* she thought. The singing continued, the words made all the more haunting by the woman's quavering, melancholic voice. Anna shuddered and, steeling herself, set off once more.

She hadn't gone more than a few metres, however, when the pain in her abdomen, such a constant in her life now that she'd almost ceased to notice it, suddenly and without warning ascended to new heights: a rending, shredding sensation which caused her to double over, ripping the breath from her lungs. As she remained frozen to the spot, trying to breathe through the pain, she felt something warm and wet trickling down her leg. *Great,* she thought. *I've gone and pissed myself.*

But it wasn't that. As she opened her eyes and looked down, she saw the puddle of dark blood collecting at her feet, expanding outwards and running down the slope behind her, like some twisted parody of a shadow.

## 25

# One Job

The years had not been kind to the house on Astley Street, though it was still standing – after a fashion. No one, it seemed, had wanted to live in what had once been the home of Glasgow's most notorious serial killer of the twenty-first century. A few years ago the Council had identified structural faults during a routine check and, seeing little point in spending money doing up a building with a worse reputation than Dr Terror's House of Horrors, had simply allowed it to fall into ruin. The weeds in the garden were chest-high, most of the windows were boarded up, the front door had long ago been reappropriated, and a spray-painted scrawl on the pebbledash wall informed passersby that *THE KELVINGROVE KILLER BURNS IN HELL*. Zoe wondered if the artist was a fan of *Carrie* or if they'd just stumbled on those words by chance.

She stepped gingerly over the threshold and made her way upstairs, in constant dread of one of the steps giving way under her. It didn't happen, though, and, having reached the top, she headed straight to Victor's old room. It had long since been gutted; she'd either binned or taken his belongings with her when she moved out, and passing thieves had no doubt helped themselves to anything of value that had remained. His bed was still there, though – stripped and stained with mildew and God knows what else, but otherwise intact. She made her way over to it and, choosing a corner that looked comparatively sanitary, sat down.

She wasn't sure why she'd made the trek out here. It wasn't as if she'd expected to find Victor's ghost still haunting the place, on hand to offer sage advice. But something had called her here, and as she sat, ignoring the boarded-up windows and the grot and grime, she found that she could see the room as it once was: floor strewn with discarded items of clothing, shelves above the bed crammed with graphic novels, walls adorned with posters. And, if she shut her eyes and concentrated hard enough, she could just about hear Victor's footsteps clomping up the stairs and along the corridor, the sound of the door flying open and slamming shut behind him, his schoolbag landing on the floor as he tossed it aside.

Her mind continued its journey into the past, back to a time before Willow Bank, before Astley Street, back to that sunny autumn day when her parents had made the fateful decision to take the new car out for a spin. The twenty-ninth of September 1987. She'd been five, Victor three. They'd been on their way back from wherever it was they'd been to, winding their way along one of those innumerable country lanes north of the city. She and Victor had been side by side in the back, both on the verge of falling asleep when their mum's sudden, frantic shout – 'JOHN, LOOK OUT!' – had jolted them both awake. She remembered vividly the sight of the thick trunk of the oak tree hurtling towards them, as if it was moving and they were stationary. The sight of her dad's shoulders bracing as he spun the wheel, trying desperately to correct their course back onto the road. The moment of impact, the seatbelt fastened securely across her chest crushing the air from her lungs.

And then, silence. She and Victor, both strapped into the back, had escaped with minor bumps and bruises. Their parents were both killed instantly. A problem with the pinion system on that model of car, she'd later heard. The company that made them had issued a mass recall and made changes to the design to ensure it wouldn't happen again. Which, funnily enough, was of little comfort to her.

She didn't remember a whole lot of what had followed – just individual moments, like snapshots that had once been part of a much larger picture album. She remembered a room with floral wallpaper and brightly coloured cushions, and a woman – she must have been a social worker – talking to her and Victor, telling them not to worry, that their granny would be there soon. She remembered Victor crying non-stop – loudly at first; then, once he'd worn himself out, just a sustained sniffling as he sat next to her, his little legs dangling over the side of the seat, not quite reaching the floor. She hadn't cried – she remembered that too. She wasn't sure why not. It wasn't as if she hadn't understood what was happening. Victor certainly had, and he was nearly two years younger than her. She supposed, on some level, she must have seen it as important to put on a show of bravery, for both their sakes. The social worker woman had picked up on that, in fact, telling her she was very grown-up.

'He's going to need you looking out for him from now on,' she'd said, nodding to Victor, still mewling quietly in the background. 'Know why?'

Zoe had shaken her head.

'Because that's what big sisters do.'

In that moment, Zoe had reached for Victor's hand, taken hold of it and squeezed it tightly, determined that she would never let anything bad happen to him. Ever.

She opened her eyes. She was back in Victor's old room, surrounded by mould and damp, the state of the place a grim reminder of everything that had happened since that day nearly thirty years ago.

She found herself thinking back to another fateful but far more recent day: the day in December six years ago when her phone had blinged the text message alert that, for the second time in her life, had upended her entire existence forever. She'd been in bed with Carol at the time, basking in the aftermath of a dirty afternoon quickie at her place, back in the days when they still hadn't gone public yet. And then Victor's text had come through – a farewell message confessing everything he'd done, and what he was about to do to Gavin Price at the top of the university bell-tower. And she hadn't even hesitated. Not for more than an instant. Within seconds, she'd dialled 999 and told the police everything: who, why, when and where. Less than half an hour later, Victor had been dead, shot by a police marksman as he moved in for the kill, his blood staining the snow in the West Quadrangle while Zoe screamed at them, over and over, *Bastards! You fuckin' bastards! You fuckin' killed him!*

Except it hadn't been them who'd killed him. Not really. One of them might have pulled the trigger, but they wouldn't have had the opportunity if she hadn't shopped her own brother to them. And for what? For killing a bunch of unrepentant rapists? A bunch of sick perverts who'd deserved worse than death?

She knew now what she should have acknowledged from the start. She'd failed to protect Victor from all the evil in the world, and now he was dead, killed under circumstances she'd actively facilitated, and nothing she did was going to bring him back – so what was the point in even trying?

*You had one job . . .*

One job, and she'd failed.

Boy, had she ever.

She emerged blinking into the pale sunlight, clutching the sides of the doorway to steady herself. As she reached the pavement, she spotted the familiar grey Fiat parked at the end of the street. Same licence plate as before. No way in hell was it a coincidence. Well, let them follow her, whoever they were. If this was how they got their kicks, they could knock themselves out.

She set off in the opposite direction, half-listening for the hum of the Fiat's engine following her. As she slid her hands into the pockets of her jeans, her fingers brushed against something. Slowing to a halt, she took out the dog-eared list Gillian had given her: name after name of suspected abusers – all of whom, she knew, would never face justice. As she gazed down at it, an intense anger welled up inside her. *Screw you, Gillian,* she thought, *for dumping this in my lap, then fucking off and leaving me holding the baby.*

She scrunched the list into a ball and was about to toss it with all her strength when, out of the blue, her phone began to ring. For a moment, she stood there, frozen on the spot, listening to its jaunty, incongruous jingle. Then she came to her senses, dug it out and checked the caller ID. *Number withheld.*

Somewhat apprehensively, she put the phone to her ear. 'Who's this?'

'Zoe Callahan?' A woman's voice – one she didn't recognise.

'Aye . . . ?'

'My name's Debbie Christie. I'm a midwife at the Western—'

And, in an instant, she understood.

Anna.

It was about Anna.

## 26

# Fragments

Anna remembered the events which followed as a series of fragmented vignettes, the moments in-between lost to the ether. She remembered keying '999' into her phone. She remembered lowering herself into a sitting position on the pavement, propped up against a nearby telecoms box. She remembered the wail of sirens, and the paramedics approaching her at a canted angle – which told her that, by that time, she was no longer upright. She remembered snatches of the journey to hospital: the harsh fluorescent lighting which irritated her eyes; the sharp scratch as they fitted a cannula to the back of her hand; the oxygen mask being placed over her face. And then she was being wheeled down a corridor, the overhead strip-lighting zipping by like runway lights. A young woman in blue scrubs kept pace, asking her when was the last time she'd felt the baby move. She couldn't respond – partly because she couldn't catch her breath, and partly because she didn't know the answer.

She wasn't sure how much time passed, or indeed how many changes of location she experienced. A seemingly endless stream of medical professionals came and went, undressing her, putting her into a gown, drawing blood samples, attaching electrodes to various parts of her anatomy. She was aware of them performing an ultrasound, and of a small, middle-aged man with owl glasses and a shiny head introducing himself as Mr Kumar and telling her she'd suffered a placental abruption and that it was imperative they got the baby out immediately by caesarean section. And Anna, who'd spent the last eight months researching every facet of pregnancy, everything that could possibly go wrong, was forced to acknowledge that the subconscious part of her mind had known all along what was wrong, ever since the pain had first started.

*This isn't supposed to be happening,* she thought. Her birth plan – drawn up with Sophie Hennessy during a series of gruelling plenary meetings – was in tatters, her hospital bag still lying under the table at the front door, ready to go.

But she didn't say any of this to Mr Kumar, who she had the presence of mind to conclude didn't need to be troubled with such details. She just confirmed that yes, she understood and consented to the procedure, and then Mr Kumar was gone and the woman in blue scrubs was asking her if there was anyone they could call to be with her, like perhaps her partner.

Anna opened her mouth, Sophie's name on the tip of her tongue, then stopped. She had a sudden moment of perfect clarity, more tangible and sharply defined than anything she'd experienced since collapsing on Gardner Street.

'Zoe,' she said. 'I want Zoe.'

How Zoe made it in time, she had no idea. She was convinced it was a fool's errand – that the best she could hope for was that Zoe would be there for her coming round afterwards. They were actually prepping her in the anteroom next to the operating theatre when she became aware of a commotion outside. She recognised Zoe's voice instantly, uttering a string of indignant obscenities as someone attempted to bar her way. Then the doors burst open and she came charging in. She hurried over to Anna, squeezing her hand and stroking her face, while the anaesthetist and surgeons watched helplessly, baffled by this flagrant breach of protocol.

'You came,' said Anna.

Zoe shrugged like it was no big deal. 'Course I came.'

'Get out!' Kumar exclaimed, practically hopping up and down with apoplexy. 'You can't be in here.'

'Have a heart,' said Blue Scrubs. 'Give her a minute with her partner.'

Kumar looked like he'd swallowed a wasp. 'Thirty seconds,' he said eventually, with all the grace of an injured pheasant.

As the medics withdrew to a respectful distance, Zoe turned to Anna with a grin. 'She thinks we're an item,' she said, as if the very notion was inherently hilarious.

Anna wasn't smiling. A fresh panic gripped her, different and more acute than before. She reached out and grabbed Zoe's hand.

'I can't have a baby, Zo,' she jabbered. 'I'm not ready.'

But Zoe merely beamed and squeezed her hand. 'Ah, don't sweat it. Ye'll do grand.'

Before Anna could respond, the surgical team had surrounded the trolley once more, and she was aware of Zoe being bundled out of the room. And then the anaesthetist was talking to her, and she was counting backwards for him, *ten, nine, eight, seven, six, f—*

## 27

# Alone Again (Naturally)

Someone was saying her name, repeating it over and over and shaking her shoulder – rather more roughly than necessary, she thought, which seemed awfully rude of them, especially when she just wanted to sleep. She tried to tell them as much, but the words came out sounding like gibberish.

She must have drifted off again, because when she next came round, there were no voices or intrusive hands – just a steady beeping sound. She felt as if she'd slept for a week, and was dimly aware both of having a sore throat and of feeling vaguely queasy. She looked around, blinking through scrunched-up eyes. She was in a single room, with walls so white they hurt to look at. Light from a low afternoon sun shone through a nearby window.

'Hey,' said a voice.

Zoe leant over her, bending down with a smile that extended from ear to ear.

'Hey,' Anna replied faintly. 'How long have I been asleep?'

'Docs brought ye round 'bout a half-hour ago. Ye've been drifting in and out since then.'

Anna screwed up her features. 'Feels like longer.'

Zoe grinned. 'Aye, well, ye wouldnae believe some of the mince ye were coming out wi.'

Anna winced. 'Did I disgrace myself?'

'Well, ye did sort of accuse the nurse of stealing yer pants. 'Part fae that, nothing ye wouldnae repeat tae a wean.'

And then it all came back to her: the PV bleed on Gardner Street, being blue-lighted to the Western and prepped for emergency surgery . . . Panic gripped her, the only outcome she could conceive of being the worst one imaginable. She tried to sit up, and immediately felt a dull but heavy pain in her lower abdomen.

'Careful, careful.' Zoe eased her back down. 'Mind yer stitches.'

'Is . . . is . . .'

'It's fine,' said Zoe firmly. '*He's* fine.'

'H–he?'

'Aye – all six pounds, seven ounces of him.'

'A boy? I've . . . I've had a boy?'

'That's right.' Zoe beamed with such pride you'd have thought she'd had something to do with it. 'I mean, I know they've got cooties and they smell, but we'll no hold that against him.'

As Zoe spoke, Anna's eyes alighted on the cot a few feet away by the window. A sense of nervous anticipation gripped her as, straight away, her mind began to churn with all the things that could be wrong.

'Wanna hold him?'

Should she? *Could* she? Was it safe? Was it allowed?

Taking matters into her own hands, Zoe headed over to the cot and scooped out a little bundle wrapped in duck-egg-blue blankets. Holding the tiny parcel close to her chest, she approached the bed. Anna got herself as upright as she could and received it into her trembling arms. Heart hammering, she gently brushed the blanket aside to reveal the tiny pink face beneath it.

In that instant, a rush of emotions engulfed her, like the bursting of a dam. So many conflicting feelings that she couldn't identify all of them. Above all, though, she felt an overpowering sense of helplessness, like she was drowning in an endless sea. The knowledge that she held another life in her arms, that she was responsible for it – that she'd *created* it – was too much to bear.

'H–hi, baby,' she whispered tearily.

The little creature stirred in her arms, kicking feebly as it began to mewl.

'Ugly little bugger, in't he?' said Zoe, grinning like a proud dad. 'I mean, everyone says all babies are dead gorgeous, but did *you* ever see one that didnae look like a bug-eyed wee alien?'

Anna stared up at her, eyes welling at the utter powerlessness of her situation. 'What . . . what am I going to do?'

Zoe blew a dismissive raspberry. 'Ah, ye'll figure it out. Ye always do.' She jerked a thumb over her shoulder. 'Look, I better go get the docs, let 'em know ye're back in the land of the living. I'll leave yese to it – get a bit of one-on-one wi E.T. here before yese're inundated wi well-wishers.'

As Zoe retreated towards the door, Anna had to suppress an overwhelming urge to call after her. *Don't go. Don't leave me to deal with this on my own.* Clutching her bundle, she watched as Zoe slipped out, leaving her to her own devices.

The next half-hour, or however long it was, passed in a blur. She was visited by Kumar, who seemed much more cheerful now compared to when she'd been brought in, and by a succession of nurses who took her and the baby's temperature and gave her toast to eat and sugary tea to drink. It was important, they said, that she keep her strength up. Kumar assured her there had been no unexpected complications, and that there was no reason to believe she couldn't have further children in future. *Hold your horses,* she thought. *I'm still getting over having this one.*

She was finishing off the last of her tea, baby asleep in the cot once more, when there was a knock on the door.

Vasilico poked his head round. 'Up to receiving a visitor?'

Anna struggled upright, suddenly acutely conscious of her bed hair and the toast crumbs on the front of her hospital gown. As she tried to brush them away, he slipped inside, shutting the door behind him softly.

'How you bearing up?'

She grimaced. '"Bearing up" about sums it up. How did you . . . ?'

Vasilico grinned. 'Police radio. Picked up some chatter about a pregnant woman in the Partick area being taken in by ambulance and figured I'd come for a look-see. I'd've brought flowers, but apparently they don't allow that anymore.'

'Spoilsports,' said Anna, though she couldn't think what practical use she'd have for flowers right now.

Vasilico moved over to the cot and inspected its contents, nodding approvingly. 'Looks like you've got a fine specimen there. Dare I say he has his mother's eyes?'

'His eyes aren't even open.'

'Touché. Well, I count two ears, a nose and a mouth, so as long as there isn't a vestigial tail I don't know about, I'd say he came out pretty much spot-on.'

'You've got a real way with words, you know that?' she said, but without malice. 'So come on – what's with the in-person visit? Or do we have to keep pretending either of us believes you came all this way just to check up on me?'

'I like to think of it less as checking up and more satisfying my own natural curiosity. Though as it happens, your powers of deduction are, as always, on point. This isn't entirely a social call.'

He perched himself on the end of the bed, his expression growing sombre. 'I thought you'd be better off hearing this from me than reading it in tomorrow's fish-wrappers. Derek Sullivan died a few hours ago.'

Anna's throat tightened. 'What? How?'

'Catastrophic bleed on the brain, I'm told. Docs tried their best, but it was a lost cause.'

Anna said nothing. She felt terrible for Derek, of course, and for his father, but those feelings were somehow less acute than she suspected they would have been had she received the news a few short hours earlier. It felt more distant, less intensely personal – as if, in the grand scheme of things, it suddenly wasn't all that important.

Vasilico reached out, touching her hand lightly. 'This is not on you, OK? It's . . . ' He shrugged helplessly. 'It's just one of those things. I don't imagine you're the type who believes in reincarnation and what have you, but even *you've* got to admit, there's something to be said for the whole "as one life ends, another begins" philosophy. My advice is, put the last few months out of your mind and concentrate on what really matters.' He glanced across at the cot. 'Something tells me that little bundle of goodness is going to be demanding all your attention for the foreseeable.'

'What about you?'

'Me?'

'Are *you* going to be able to put the past few months out of your mind?'

Vasilico rubbed behind his ear. 'That's the other thing I wanted to tell you. I've decided to clear out for a bit. I've got a shedload of annual leave owing, and I figure now's the time to take it. Means I won't be around for the next month – maybe two. These batteries are in serious need of recharging.'

'I'll bet. Know where you're going to go?'

'Not yet, but I'll be sure to send you a postcard.'

In the cot, the baby stirred and began to cry – a feeble, gravelly mewl that hit Anna right in the solar plexus. She looked at Vasilico helplessly.

'Can you pass him to me?'

With a deftness she wasn't expecting, Vasilico scooped the baby up and deposited him in her arms. As she tried in vain to shush him, Vasilico gave a knowing nod.

'He wants feeding.'

'Done this before, have you?'

'No, but I was around when both my uncle's sprogs were this age. You get to know the sound.'

She gazed up at him. He didn't move. She raised a questioning eyebrow.

'So, what – you're waiting for a show, or . . . ?'

He laughed, utterly unfazed. 'Quite right, quite right. I'll leave you to your own devices.'

She smiled. 'Take care of yourself, Detective. I hope you manage to recharge those batteries.'

He bade her farewell with a dip of his head and ducked out, leaving her in peace.

Alone once more, Anna gazed down at her baby, continuing to squirm and whimper in her arms. *Oh well, going to have to get the hang of this sooner or later.* Reaching behind her back, she undid the drawstring, lowered her gown and offered up a puffy nipple to the baby's lips.

It wasn't easy, but after several false starts, both mother and baby seemed to get the hang of things – to the extent that, by the time Zoe reappeared some twenty minutes later, Anna was feeling if not exactly comfortable then at least like she had things more or less in hand.

Zoe nodded approvingly. 'See? What'd I tell ye? You're a natural.'

Anna grimaced. 'I swear it's like he already has a full set of gnashers.'

'Aye, fair play tae ye, doll. Yer nips'll be tough as old boots by the time he's ready for solids.'

'I'm going to have to start paying by the hour for all this reassuring counsel.'

Zoe merely grinned and plonked herself on the end of the bed, watching as the baby continued suckling contentedly. If it had been anyone else, Anna would have been absolutely mortified, feeling like an exhibit in a zoo. With Zoe, though, it was oddly comforting to have her there, treating it like none of this was any big deal – like it was perfectly normal to be sitting having a conversation with your boobs out and an hours-old baby in your arms glugging colostrum.

'Called yer mum yet?'

Anna grimaced. 'One step at a time, yeah? Gonna take some time before I figure out how to have *that* conversation.'

'Aye, right enough. Decided what ye're gonnae call him?'

Anna thought about it. 'Jack. I'm going to call him Jack.'

'Short for Giacomo?'

'No, just Jack.'

'Jack.' Zoe tested the name, chewing it over like a tough piece of meat, then gave an approving nod. 'Aye, good name. Nice, easy to spell, nae bull-shit.' She winced and covered her mouth. 'Sorry – shouldnae've said that in front of the wean.'

For the first time since she'd come round, Anna laughed. 'I think if the worst he ever gets exposed to is a bit of the old sailor-talk, I'll have done all right by him.'

Zoe wagged a warning finger at her. 'Just you wait. He'll be drinking tins o' Tennent's and getting baked before ye know it. Ye'll need to be on the lookout for his hidey-holes. Mind how me 'n' Vic used to keep our stash in the space behind that loose tile in the bathroom? 'Member, the house on Astley Street?'

'Yeah – to hide it from your granny. Bet you anything she knew about it all along, though.'

Zoe chuckled. 'Aye, prob'ly. She always was a shrewd one.' A wistful look came into her eyes. 'She'd've been fair made up for ye. They both would've.'

Anna smiled. She glanced down at Jack. 'I think he's done. Can you . . . ?'

Zoe obliged, holding him while Anna covered herself up again. As she took Jack back into her arms, she felt an overwhelming sense of . . . well, *something*. An all-consuming desire to protect him from all the bad things in the world; to hold him close to her and never let go. Were these the elusive maternal feelings she'd been repeatedly promised would kick in? She couldn't say, but one thing was for sure: she was responsible for this little life, and she knew she was prepared to go to the wall to protect it.

She looked up to see Zoe pulling on her parka. 'You're not staying?'

Zoe shook her head. 'Nah. Got some business tae take care of.'

'Somewhere you need to be?'

'Something I need to do. Just wanted to make sure ye were OK – that ye didnae need anything.'

'I'm all sorted,' said Anna.

And she meant it. She knew that, before long, she'd need food, clothes, all the usual boring necessities. But right now, with Jack in her arms, fed and contented, it felt like she had everything she could possibly need.

Zoe looked hard at Anna, studying her. 'Aye. Ye look it.'

Then, to Anna's great surprise, she leant in and kissed her on the forehead. 'What was that for?'

Zoe shrugged. 'Y'know. S'no every day yer bestie becomes a mammy. Guess that makes me an auntie now, dun't it?'

'Guess so,' Anna agreed, disinclined to argue with the logic of this.

She watched as Zoe zipped up her parka and turned to go. Something about this really didn't sit well with her. For reasons she couldn't articulate, she had a sense that something momentous had just happened or was about to happen. Something . . . *final*.

'Zoe.'

Zoe stopped in her tracks. 'Aye?'

'You'll be back, won't you?'

Zoe shifted uneasily. 'I might be gone for a bit . . . but ye're no tae worry, all right?'

'Zoe—'

'Promise me ye won't worry.'

Anna opened her mouth to protest, then stopped. 'I promise,' she said, wondering what she was agreeing to.

Zoe smiled – a weary, melancholic smile, but one which suggested she'd made peace with whatever it was she'd decided to do. 'Just mind,' she said, 'Astley Street.'

She flashed Anna a wink, and then was gone.

Anna sat with Jack in her arms, staring at the emptiness of her surroundings. She was left with the overwhelming feeling that everyone was leaving her. Well, almost everyone. She gazed down at Jack, at his shock of thick, dark hair – something he'd *definitely* inherited from her – and his pinched little face, his inchoate features contorting as he shifted in her arms, dreaming whatever it was newborns dreamed about.

'It's just you and me now, Trouble,' she said. 'Welcome to the world.'

As the nearly empty bus crawled south towards Queen's Park through the encroaching gloom, Zoe felt an odd sense of serenity. She didn't know what was going to happen once she arrived at her destination, but one way or another, things were about to come to a head.

It was time to put this whole sorry affair to bed once and for all.

PART THREE

# The Shadow Men

# 28

# Blur

*Tuesday 26 January*

'I must say,' the health visitor said as Anna walked her to the door, 'I think you're doing splendidly. If I didn't know better, I'd never have guessed this was your first time.'

'Thanks,' said Anna, as if a complete stranger's judgement meant everything in the world to her.

The woman turned to smile down at Jack, asleep with his head on Anna's shoulder. 'You must be pleased he's such a good sleeper. It's rare to see such a contented baby so early on.'

Jack, to his credit, waited till the woman was safely in her car and on her way before waking up and immediately beginning to exercise his lungs – that all-too-familiar crackling wail that simultaneously punctured Anna's heart and made her want to tear out her eardrums.

Those first few weeks at home had merged into one continuous, febrile blur, from which the only respite came in the form of brief, snatched moments of sleep that never seemed long enough. Gone was her carefully cultivated routine. Now, the concept of fixed, identifiable mealtimes seemed positively quaint; long, luxuriating showers were a thing of the past; her normally clockwork-like bowel movements replaced by chronic constipation. Getting a good night's rest, too, had become an alien concept. Jack slept for a good chunk of the day, but rarely for more than three hours at a time, and Anna invariably found herself unable to settle for fear of sleeping through the alarm for his next scheduled feed – or else she'd drift off, only to jolt awake seconds later, convinced she'd missed it. More often than not, though, she'd lie awake watching him sleep, her heart leaping into her throat every time the rise and fall of his chest stopped for a fraction of a second. She'd known to expect all this, but reading about it and actually living it were two radically different concepts.

And then there were all the things the baby books and antenatal classes *hadn't* prepared her for – things like the pleasures of persistent lochia, cracked nipples and the fact that all manner of actions that had once been second nature now had to be relearned so they could be performed one-handed. And she ached in all the expected places. The C-section wound was probably the least of it, all things considered, though she'd learned to dread the sharp twinges that accompanied sudden movements, and she didn't dare exert herself more than was completely necessary for fear of tearing her stitches.

At least she had no shortage of well-wishers on hand to offer to do the things she couldn't – like wheeling the bins out to the kerb or retrieving the jar of peanut butter she'd dropped the previous day but had been unable to bend down to pick up. And of course they all wanted to admire the new baby, telling her how like his mother he looked (she really couldn't see it) and how well she was doing (she really didn't feel it). It didn't help that they always seemed to turn up at the worst possible moments – usually when she'd just succeeded in getting Jack to go down. She tolerated these intrusions as best she could, though the urge to scream at them to get out of her house and leave her alone grew and grew.

Front of the queue of helpful busybodies had been Sophie Hennessy, who took it upon herself to restock the fridge, take care of the dirty dishes piled in the sink like the Leaning Tower of Pisa, and dispense her usual well-intentioned but thoroughly grating advice – stuff Anna already knew, like how to care for Jack's umbilical stump and the importance of doing her Kegel exercises. Though Sophie never articulated it in so many words, Anna sensed that she was in something of a strop over not having been present for the birth. The one time her absence had come up, Anna had told her, in as regretful a tone as she could muster, that there simply hadn't been time to call her – not letting on that, when push had come to shove, she'd chosen Zoe instead.

Where *was* Zoe, come to think of it? While every man and his dog had spent the last few weeks invading her home, intent on subjecting both her and her offspring to endless poking and prodding, the one person whose attention she'd actually have welcomed under the circumstances was conspicuous by her absence – all the more so considering that Zoe hadn't been able to get enough of Jack back at the hospital. She reminded herself that this state of affairs was simply a reversion to the mean – that, prior to her unexpected summons to Queen's Park on Christmas Eve, it had been normal for them to go for months without any contact. She'd tried ringing Zoe a couple of times, but had failed to reach her on either her mobile or her landline and decided against leaving a message, concluding that she must indeed have been serious about clearing out for a while.

*Well, good for you, Zoe. It's about time you got out of Glasgow and saw a bit of the world.*

And yet she continued to feel uneasy in a vague, indefinable sort of way.

Anna's phone began to hum in the pocket of her jogging bottoms – not that they ever saw any jogging action these days. She had the thing permanently on silent, but she still snatched it up immediately, fearful that Jack, who she'd just managed to settle after a lengthy battle, would somehow sense the vibration and start up his banshee howl again.

'Hello?'

'Oh, Anna, *hi*. It's Marion. How are you doing?'

Marion Angus, one of her former postgrad students, now terrorising the Social Sciences department at the University of Stirling. A woman chronically incapable of coming to the point, or having a phone conversation that lasted less than an hour.

'Oh, you know,' said Anna airily. 'Getting by.'

'Well, first of all, I mean *congratulations*, you know? I heard your good news the other day from Susie Gorman who got it from Jen Piesiewicz and goodness knows who *Jen* picked it up from. Me, I hadn't even realised you were in the family way, but when I heard, of *course* I had to—'

'Actually, Marion,' Anna said, one eye on Jack, settled in his rocker a couple of feet away, 'I've only just gotten him off to sleep. So if you don't mind . . . '

'Of course, of course, don't let me keep you. Bet you hardly ever get a moment to yourself these days, and here I am eating into your precious "me" time. God, what am I like, rabbiting on? If there's one thing you can never accuse me of, it's brevity of verbiage – right?'

'Right. Anyway, it was lovely to hear from you, Marion. Now, if there's nothing else . . . '

'Just a sec.' Marion's voice stopped her in her tracks, phone already half-away from her ear. 'There actually *was* another reason why I called. I was just wondering, have you been following the news about that nasty business out by Queen's Park?'

Anna hadn't so much as *looked* at the news app on her iPad in the last three weeks, or turned on the TV. 'Can't say I have.'

'Oh, it's an absolute shocker. Older fella stabbed to death in his own home, on New Year's Day of all days. His daughter found him lying dead in a pool of his own blood. They say it was a robbery gone wrong, but I mean, come on, there's just no need for that level of—'

'That's awful, Marion, but I really can't see how it involves me.'

'I'm sure it doesn't – but, thing is, I seem to recall you once mentioned you went to school at Willow Bank. It only came to mind cos I went there myself, for my sins – though obviously my time was a good while after—'

'Would you get to the point, *please*, Marion?' Anna said, her tightly stretched patience finally snapping.

'Of course. Sorry. It's just, the papers mentioned he used to be a head-teacher there – back in the nineties? That would've been during your time, wouldn't it? And I just thought, well, if Anna doesn't already know, surely she'll *want* to . . . '

Anna had all but stopped listening. She felt lightheaded, as if she'd stood up suddenly and all the blood had rushed to her feet. In the last fifteen years, she hadn't thought about her old headmaster more than a handful of times, but she could picture him now, as clearly as if it had been yesterday: a tall, imposing figure with a long stride and Rhadamanthine demeanour, sweeping the corridors of Willow Bank like an elemental force.

'What was his name now?' Marion was still rabbiting on. 'God, it was on the tip of my tongue. Oh yes! Broadhurst. That's it. Adam Broadhurst.'

Anna became very still. 'Marion,' she said, her measured tone belying the emotions racing through her, 'I'll call you back.'

Police today issued a fresh appeal for information relating to the horrific murder of a sixty-seven-year-old man.

Adam Broadhurst, a property developer and former headmaster of the prestigious Willow Bank Academy, was found dead in his home near Queen's Park on New Year's Day.

Emergency services were called after Mr Broadhurst's daughter arrived at the property in the early evening to signs of forced entry. She discovered her father on the living room floor, the victim of a savage and frenzied knife attack. She attempted to administer first aid before calling 999. Upon arrival, paramedics attempted resuscitation, but their efforts were unsuccessful and Mr Broadhurst was later pronounced dead at the scene.

Speaking exclusively to the *Standard*, Detective Superintendent Sean De Groot of the Major Investigations Team said: 'Mr Broadhurst was subjected to a brutal and sustained assault. It is imperative that the person or persons responsible be apprehended as quickly as possible.

'Extensive enquiries have been carried out and are continuing, and our team will spare no effort to ensure that justice is served.'

Police are keen to speak to anyone who was in the Queen's Park area between 4 and 6 p.m. on New Year's Day. Anyone with information relevant to the investigation is urged to contact Strathkelvin Police via one of the methods listed below.

Mr Broadhurst was awarded an MBE in 2008 for services to education.

Enquiries are ongoing.

## 29

# Worried

'I know – I can't get my head round it either.' Anna cradled the phone between her ear and shoulder, trying to simultaneously avoid dropping it and support Jack in her arms. 'It's just mind-blowing.'

In the last couple of days, she'd found herself discussing precious little else. Since Marion's call on Tuesday, two more people had rung Anna to ask if she'd heard about Broadhurst – both old schoolfriends, neither of whom she'd so much as exchanged an email with since they'd gone their separate ways in 1999. Both of them, to her surprise and no small amount of irritation, had already discovered she was a recent mother and eagerly showered her with the obligatory congratulations, in-between discussing the small matter of their murdered ex-headmaster. It seemed the old Willow Bank information network was alive and as effective as ever. Since Tuesday, she'd spent the greater part of the rare moments of peace and solitude she was afforded reading the press coverage of the murder, though most of it simply regurgitated the same scant information with varying levels of salaciousness, depending on the pedigree of the publication in question.

The doorbell ringing caused Jack, who until now had been dozing quietly in her arms, to stir and flex his limbs.

'Sorry, Claire,' said Anna, 'I'm going to have to go.'

She hung up and, transferring Jack's head to her shoulder, headed down the hallway to the front door. She opened it to find two men in suits standing on the top step. One look at them told her they were either policemen or Jehovah's Witnesses.

'Anna Scavolini?' said one – the taller of the two and, she deemed, the one in charge.

'Yes?'

'DS Douthwaite, DC Rennie. Can we come in?'

Not Jehovah's Witnesses, then – which was, she concluded, marginally preferable.

'What's this about?' She adjusted her hold on Jack as he twisted and squirmed, evidently none too pleased at being removed from the warmth of the living room and exposed to the chill from outside.

'Best if we talk inside.' The tall one (DS Douthwaite, she assumed) was already stepping over the threshold. 'You don't mind, do you?'

'No,' she said, privately thinking that yes, she very much *did* mind, particularly as they still hadn't given her any indication as to why they were here.

They strode on in, the shorter one (Rennie, by process of elimination) playfully waggling his fingers under Jack's nose as he passed. The new, compliant Anna – whose door, it seemed, was open to every stranger under the sun who wished to invite themselves in and make themselves at home – followed them through to her own living room, where, in a bid to cling to *some* semblance of control, she invited them to take a seat before they seized one of their own accord. She lowered herself into the armchair facing the sofa to which she'd directed them, *shh*-ing in Jack's ear as he squirmed and mewed.

'How can I help you, Detectives?'

'We understand you're a close friend of Zoe Callahan's,' said Douthwaite, easing himself into the sofa and spreading his legs in a way that left Anna wondering if she was supposed to be impressed.

'That's right,' she said, not altogether sure how true that actually was these days. A sudden pang of fear gripped her. 'Why? Has something happened to her?'

'We were sort of hoping *you* might be able to help *us* out there. Have you seen her recently?'

'She's not in any trouble, is she?'

Douthwaite made a noise at the back of his throat. She sensed his growing irritation. Well, he could rest assured the feeling was nothing if not mutual.

'We're eager to speak to her in relation to an ongoing investigation,' said Rennie, who had evidently been assigned the role of Good Cop.

'Does this have anything to do with Adam Broadhurst's murder?' Anna asked, then immediately wondered why she'd said that.

'We're not at liberty to say,' said Rennie.

Douthwaite shifted his weight. 'If I may make so bold an observation, Ms Scavolini—'

'Doctor.'

'*Doctor* Scavolini,' he corrected himself – though, she sensed, with gritted teeth, 'if I may make so bold an observation, you're not being especially cooperative here.'

'It's hard to cooperate when I don't know what I'm supposed to be cooperating *with*.' She moved Jack's head from one shoulder to the other in the hope that it would help him settle, but to no avail. 'No, I haven't seen her recently and no, I have no idea where she is. The last time I had any contact with her was when I was in hospital, shortly after the birth of my son about a month ago.'

By now, Jack's mewing had progressed into full-blown crying, to the point that she was having to raise her voice to make herself heard. She got to her feet, partly to see if a change of position would calm him down, partly in the forlorn hope that the detectives would take the hint and leave.

'And the last time you saw her,' said Douthwaite, remaining infuriatingly sedentary, 'did she happen to give anything to you?'

'Like what?'

Once more, a spasm of exasperation passed over Douthwaite's face. It didn't take a genius to work out that he was sitting on quite a temper. 'Like *anything*.'

'In that case, no.'

'What makes you so sure?' said Rennie, who unlike Douthwaite had taken the hint and got to his feet.

Anna exhaled loudly in exasperation. 'Because, if she'd given me something, I'd have been aware of it at the time. That's generally how the laws of physics work. Look,' she went on, as Jack's crying began to approach fever pitch, 'he needs his feed, so if there's nothing else . . . '

It wasn't actually true. This wasn't his scheduled feeding time, and the noise he was making wasn't his 'hungry' noise, but it wasn't as if these two were going to know the difference, and she figured threatening to whip out her boobs was the quickest way to get rid of them. And it seemed to do the trick, as Douthwaite finally – and decidedly reluctantly – rose to his feet.

She saw them to the door, Jack continuing to do a fine impression of a fire alarm. On the step, Douthwaite turned to face her, holding out a business card.

'This is my number. If you remember anything, no matter how trivial it seems, I want you to call me right away.'

With both arms full, Anna took the card between her forefinger and middle finger.

'You're absolutely positive she didn't pass you anything?' said Rennie. 'Is it possible she could have slipped you something without you knowing it?'

'Perhaps,' said Douthwaite, before Anna could respond, 'it would be simplest if we took a look at any items you brought home with you . . . '

'Goodbye, gentlemen,' said Anna, and promptly shut the door on them.

As soon as she'd managed to get Jack to settle, Anna headed upstairs to her bedroom and retrieved the canvas bag she'd brought back with her from the hospital. She'd had her hands so full at the time that she'd simply kicked it under the bed – dirty clothes, empty food wrappers and all. Now, however, she undertook a root-and-branch examination of its contents, tipping everything out onto the floor, going through every pocket and crevice in search of the mysterious item the two detectives seemed convinced Zoe had passed to her.

'What are they talking about?' she asked Jack as he watched the proceedings from his rocker. 'There's nothing there.'

She eased herself back onto her feet, breathing through the pain as her C-section wound registered its disapproval. The whole situation made her uneasy: Zoe's apparent disappearance; the detectives' refusal to tell her why they were looking for her; the fact that Broadhurst's death and Anna's last sighting of her appeared to coincide by a matter of hours. What was it Zoe had said to her at the hospital before she took off? *'Got some business tae take care of. Something I need to do.'*

*Stop it, Anna. You're putting two and two together and making five.*

She got out her phone and opened the Facebook app. She found her way to Zoe's 'Fanny de Bergerac' profile and scrolled down the timeline. Zoe didn't appear to have posted anything since before Christmas, and Anna couldn't help noticing that there had been a marked decrease in her activity since around mid-November. Most of the recent posts had come from Zoe's cadre of mostly younger, mostly seriously nutty friends, either tagging her into funny videos or memes or, lately, mentioning that they hadn't heard from her in a while and wanting to know what they'd done to offend her.

She switched from Facebook to the text messages app, opening up her chat history with Zoe. The last communication between them had been Zoe's unexpected request for Anna to join her in Queen's Park on Christmas Eve, followed by Anna's brief acknowledgement. Now, Anna composed a fresh message.

**Hey Zoe, hope all's well. Haven't heard from you in a while and just wanted to check you were OK. Jack is in good health and getting bigger (and louder) by the day. Let me know when you get this.**

She thought about mentioning the visit from the two detectives but decided against it. She had no great desire to spook Zoe, especially if it turned out that she was getting herself worked up over nothing. More pertinent than that, however, was an indefinable but no less powerful conviction that it would be unwise to commit anything relating to this matter to record. So she signed off with a perfunctory 'Love, Anna', hit Send and settled down to wait.

As the minutes ticked by, Anna's feelings of apprehension grew. When an hour had passed and there was still no response from Zoe, she opened Facebook again and once more navigated to Zoe's timeline. She hesitated for some time, reluctant to intrude on what she perceived as a private space for Zoe and a set of friends she knew nothing about. Eventually, though, her anxiety overrode any sense of awkwardness, and she tapped out a message.

**Hi everyone, I'm a friend of Zoe's looking to get in touch with her. I haven't seen or heard from her since the beginning of January. Has anyone had recent contact with her?**

**Please help if you can. I'm worried.**

She posted the message. Then, lifting Jack out of his rocker, she headed over to the window and gazed out into the street. It was one of those interminably dull, grey January days where it felt like winter was never going to end. A little way up the road, engineers were working on the telecom cables attached to the lamppost at the corner onto Falkland Street, one of them in a cherrypicker a good twelve metres off the ground. She frowned. Hadn't she seen them working at the same lamppost this time last week? At least, she *thought* she had. Given how hard a time she was having keeping track of the days, she wouldn't have liked to swear to it.

Her hand went absentmindedly to the friendship bracelet on her wrist. She didn't normally wear any jewellery apart from a simple wristwatch, and over the last few weeks she'd found herself unable to stop fiddling with it. Now, her fingers lingered over it for an extended spell, tracing the indentation of the engraved quotation. *True friends are never apart . . .*

'What d'you reckon, Trouble?' she said to Jack. 'Where's your Auntie Zoe got to?'

# 30

# Gone Visiting

*Saturday 30 January*

Anna made sure the pouch sling was securely fastened across her chest and that Jack was safe inside with his little hat snug on his head, then opened the front door and stepped out into the world. It felt strange, standing on the top step with the familiar sounds of the West End reverberating around her. Strange, too, to be wearing outdoor clothes, having spent most of the last month in her dressing-gown and jogging bottoms.

Since Thursday, she'd had around two dozen responses to her Facebook post, though none of them shed any light on Zoe's present whereabouts. Most simply confirmed her own experience: that Zoe had gone off the grid at around the start of the year. A few posited amusing (in their own minds, at any rate) theories that involved alcohol and wanton mayhem, though most treated Anna's plea with the seriousness it warranted. *'I'm worried 2,'* one Weejulietots McGeachy had written. *'U think we shud contact Missing People?'* Anna had assured her that she didn't think they were at that stage yet, but suggested that everyone share her message on their own pages, and to consider checking any places they could think of where Zoe might have gone.

Knowing she couldn't just sit at home while the Facebook army was out pounding the streets, she'd resolved to do some searching of her own – hence why she was now standing outside her front door, running through a mental checklist of the contents of the baby-bag hanging from her shoulder. Wet wipes, nappies, changing mat, a change of clothes for

Jack in case he got too hot or made a mess of himself, bottles of expressed milk in case she had to feed him but found herself suffering from stage-fright . . . She was pretty sure she'd covered every eventuality, though she fully expected to get to the end of the road only to realise she'd left something essential behind. Once you had a neonate on your hands, there really was no such thing as just popping out.

She set off, the bag's contents heavy on her shoulder and Jack a dead weight against her chest. She wished she was driving, but the doctor had told her that she was under no circumstances to think about getting behind the wheel till her C-section had had at least six weeks to heal.

As she made her way down Clarence Drive, she clocked the grey Fiat parked outside the house across the road. *Strange.* She was sure the couple who lived there were in Mauritius till June. She told herself it was none of her business, and that, in any event, the most likely explanation was that someone was simply taking advantage of the free parking.

She continued along Lauderdale Gardens, down the gentle curve of Banavie Road with its tall trees and big old houses, then down Peel Street past the cricket club, finally reaching Dumbarton Road fifteen minutes later. Both the walk and the fresh air had perked her up considerably, while Jack, lulled by the rhythm of her footsteps, was sound asleep by the time she arrived at her ultimate destination: the Taste of India takeaway, above which stood Zoe's flat.

She let herself in through the side entrance and tramped up the stone steps to Zoe's door. She knocked. No response. She tried again, then put her ear to the door and listened for signs of life inside. Nothing.

'Zoe?' she half-whispered, wary of waking Jack. 'You in there?'

Still nothing – though she wasn't overly surprised. If the police had come to her seeking information about Zoe's whereabouts, it stood to reason that they'd have tried and failed to get her at home first.

Supporting Jack's head, she lowered herself to her knees, pushed open the letterbox and peered inside. Not that there was much to see: the hall corridor was at a right angle from the door, giving her a splendid view of the far wall and precious little else. Nonetheless, she was able to make out a sizeable pile of mail lying on the mat – enough, she concluded, to account for several weeks.

Zoe, it appeared, was long gone.

\* \* \*

Out on Dumbarton Road, she contemplated her next move. She'd been somewhat reassured by the lack of a police presence at the flat. If they really did suspect Zoe of a crime, or that she'd come to some sort of harm, they'd surely have searched the place, if not put a watch on it – and there was no evidence of them having done either. Chances were there was nothing sinister about this at all, and she'd turn up safe and well in a few days or weeks, perhaps with a new tan or a new bloke or a new something. But if she didn't, if there genuinely *was* something untoward going on, then Anna knew she'd never forgive herself for having done nothing.

She got out her phone and scrolled through her contacts, coming to a halt at Paul Vasilico's name. He had his head screwed on properly – for the most part – and being a cop himself made him a potentially useful source of information.

She called his number. It rang and rang and eventually went to voicemail. She hung up without leaving a message and tried again. Once more, it went to voicemail. She gave up and dialled MIT headquarters. The woman who answered was eager to assist however she could but was unable to shed any light on Vasilico's present whereabouts. He was signed off on extended leave, she explained, and they didn't know yet when he'd be back. If Anna liked, she could leave a message to be passed on to him in the event that he called. Anna thought about it, but ultimately concluded that it wouldn't be right to disturb him during his much-needed downtime.

As she went to pocket her phone, it blinged a notification sound – one she hadn't heard before. She checked the screen.

**New Message Request**
**From Craig Rankine**

Her finger hovered over the unfamiliar message for a moment, then curiosity got the better of her and she tapped it. A private chat screen opened, along with a message.

**Saw ur post about Zoe. Was goin 2 reply but thot best 2 do it thru PM**

She tapped out a response.

**Who is this?**

A flashing ellipsis appeared inside a speech bubble below her message, indicating that Craig – whoever he was – was composing his reply. A moment later, it appeared.

**Friend of Zoes. We worked 2gether at the Corner in mount Vernon**

Another pause, another flashing ellipsis. Then . . .

**Cud we meet up? Might have sum info but easier 2 tell u in person**

She considered telling him to just spit out whatever it was he had to say, but in truth she was getting fed up with trying to simultaneously text and hold her phone with one hand and was minded to agree that a face-to-face exchange would be considerably easier to conduct. Over the next few messages, she established that Craig was currently at work but had a break coming up in an hour's time and, if she got herself out there by then, would be waiting for her by the service entrance round the back. She tapped out a terse 'OK', pocketed her phone, then gazed down at Jack, who hadn't stirred. His inaugural trip out of the house had passed without incident so far, and there seemed no harm in getting him used to some more new sights and sounds before calling it a day.

'What d'you say, Trouble? How d'you feel about going on a fact-finding mission?'

Within moments of boarding the train, Anna realised something she hadn't appreciated until now: that the world, and public transport in particular, just weren't designed to take into account the needs of mothers and newborns. The carriage was jam-packed, and the surrounding cacophony of voices and the grinding of the wheels on the track caused Jack to waken more or less instantly. They'd barely left Partick before he began to exercise his lungs, and she was forced to stand in the middle of the aisle clutching her howling baby, attracting all manner of filthy looks from the passengers seated comfortably in front of her. Eventually, an elderly gentleman took pity on her and offered up his seat, but she declined. He looked like he needed it more – and besides, she felt sure she and her screaming infant would just end up on the receiving end of even greater ire if she sat with him among the scowling commuters. Seriously, where was everyone going today?

Not Mount Vernon, it seemed, as she and Jack were the only ones to disembark there, to audible sighs of relief, when the train rolled into the station half an hour later. Having managed to get Jack to settle once more, she set off on foot for the Corner Bar & Grill. As directed, she headed round to the courtyard at the back, where a tall, skinny boy in his early twenties was sitting on the step outside the service door, fiddling nervously with an unlit cigarette. Seeing her approaching, he lurched to his feet and made his way towards her.

'Craig?'

'Um, yeah, uh.' He began to extend his hand, then changed his mind and scratched his neck instead. His eyes alighted on Jack. 'Oh,' he said, sounding vaguely alarmed.

'Don't worry – he doesn't bite. So you work with Zoe?'

Craig nodded, continuing to eye Jack as if he might have something contagious. 'That's right, yeah. We both started round about the same time and, um, yeah. We . . . she never mentioned me?' A hint of disappointment in his voice.

'She probably did. I'm rubbish with names.'

She wasn't sure whether she was trying to spare his bruised ego or reluctant to admit just how little contact she'd had of late with the woman who was meant to be her best friend.

'So you had something to tell me . . . ?'

'Oh yeah, sorry.' He tucked the cigarette behind his ear. Shooting for James Dean, she thought – and missing by a nautical mile. 'So like I said, I seen your post on Facebook – about how you were tryna track her down?'

'That's right,' said Anna, already convinced it was too much to hope that Craig was about to tell her he knew where Zoe was.

'Me too.' Craig lowered his head with a sheepish little smile. 'I tried texting her and that, but she never got back. Last time I seen her was when we worked the Hogmanay shift together. Since then, nothing.'

'And she never mentioned she was thinking about going away for a while or anything like that? Not even to your boss?'

Craig blew out an exaggerated breath and shook his head. 'I tell you, he was spitting mad! Kept going on about how she'd left him high and dry; how if he ever seen her again he was gonnae tan her arse the same colour as her hair.' He blushed, averting his eyes. 'Sorry. It was him who said it, not me. I mean, I don't think he'd've done it *literally*, but he's got an awful temper on him and you have to—'

Anna had reached the end of her patience. 'I'm sorry,' she said firmly, cutting him off mid-flow, 'but I thought you had information for me – or did you just bring me out here so you could tell me you don't know anything about her whereabouts?'

'Sorry.' Craig dipped his head, the picture of contrition. 'I mean, it's true, I don't know where she is, but there's more . . . ' He exhaled a heavy breath and let his shoulders slump. 'What I mean is, I'd been worried about her . . . even before she stopped coming into work, I mean.'

'Go on.'

'Well, I mean, last few weeks before New Year, she was hardly ever in. Like, she turned down loadsa shifts – and you don't *do* that, right? Not if you wanna make ends meet. And when she *was* here, she was . . . funny.'

'Funny how?'

'Distant. Moody. Like her mind was someplace else. We used to have a right laugh – y'know, coming up with funny names for the customers, making fun of Malcolm Mal— I mean, Mr Stilwell. And she was always telling me films I should watch – like, all these super-gory horror movies with cheesy dubbing and whatnot. She'd proper good taste in films. We even hung out a few times – y'know, outside work.'

Anna was slowly beginning to suspect Craig of carrying something of a torch for Zoe. She hoped that was as far as it had gone. Zoe would have eaten him alive.

'But lately . . . ' Craig shrugged unhappily. 'I dunno, sometimes it was like she'd turned into a different person. There was this one time when she—' He stopped abruptly, as if he'd had a sudden change of heart.

'What?' Anna glared at him expectantly. 'This one time when she what?'

Craig rubbed the back of his neck agitatedly. He took the cigarette from behind his ear and began to tap it against his palm. 'It was back in late November. We'd gone back to mine to . . . to hang out, and afterwards, she was all kinda subdued and quiet, and I asked her what was wrong, and she looked at me and she said, if I knew someone'd done something bad, what would I do?'

Now he had her attention. 'Something bad?'

'Yeah. "*Really* bad, like hurt a buncha people" – that's what she said.'

The uncomfortable feeling in the pit of Anna's stomach, which had been there since the visit from the two detectives, intensified. She felt Jack beginning to shift inside his sling. She bounced him up and down gently and he seemed to settle again.

'And how did you respond?'

Craig shrugged. 'Said it'd depend who they were. Like, some people, you just can't touch.'

'Did she say anything else?'

Craig frowned, thinking hard. 'Well, there was *one* other thing. She asked if I thought it was ever right to do something bad yourself to punish someone else who done something bad.'

'And you said . . . ?'

Craig looked sheepish. 'To be honest, I was getting a bit outta my depth. I said as much and we . . . hung out some more. And then it never came up again. I never really gave it any more thought, until . . . '

Anna swallowed heavily. The knot in her stomach was tightening with each passing moment. She couldn't explain *why* she was so convinced something awful had happened, beyond an unshakable feeling that all these events – Zoe's recent turn towards introspection, her disappearance, Broadhurst's murder, the visit from the two detectives – were somehow connected.

'I thought we were cool.' Craig's voice cut into her thoughts. 'But then, not long after, she stopped coming into work or answering my texts. I've been fretting about it for weeks. Keep asking myself if I did . . . I mean, if I said something wrong.'

Anna allowed herself a soft smile. It was easy enough to read between the lines. There was something oddly endearing about the fact that his combination of insecurity and ego, so typical of young men of his age, allowed him to think that all this was down to him.

'I don't think you did anything wrong,' she said gently. 'I'm sure she appreciated you being there for her as a . . . ' She considered her next words carefully. ' . . . as a friend.'

Craig bit his lower lip, unconvinced. 'I just . . . I can't help thinking she was tryna tell me something. If . . . mibby, if I'd been more on the ball, I could've said something. *Done* something.'

*You and me both, pal,* Anna thought. 'Thanks, Craig. You did the right thing telling me.' She turned to go.

'Wait.'

Craig's voice stopped her in her tracks. She turned to face him again. 'Yes?'

Craig continued to tap his cigarette against his palm, all but crushed now. 'If you find her or, y'know, if she turns up, tell her . . . just tell her we miss her and that . . . well, there's folk here who care about her.'

Anna managed a strained smile. 'If I manage to track her down, I'll be sure to mention it.'

The motorcyclist idling at the far end of the road watched, vizor down, face obscured, as Anna emerged from the courtyard and set off in the opposite direction, moving at considerable speed for someone encumbered with both a baby and a laden shoulder-bag. They continued watching until Anna disappeared round the corner, then revved the engine of the black Ducati Panigale and set off.

## 31

# Violated

By the time Anna got back to Clarence Drive, it was late afternoon and she was utterly worn out. It scarcely seemed credible how much the brief excursion had taken out of her. The grey Fiat was still parked across the street. As she passed it, she tried to get a look inside, but the windows were tinted and she couldn't tell whether or not there was anyone inside.

*Get a grip, Scavolini,* she thought. *If you told anyone about this, they'd say you were off your trolley.*

*Or off your lithium.*

That too.

As soon as she stepped into the living room, she was hit by the indefinable but unshakeable feeling that something wasn't right. She couldn't put her finger on it, but the place seemed to have *changed* in her absence. It seemed somehow . . . what? Smaller? Larger? Brighter? Darker? She couldn't say, but the hairs on her back and arms were standing on end, her breathing fast and shallow. *Something* was pricking at her subconscious.

She told herself it was nothing, that she was just feeling lightheaded from all that pounding around and because she hadn't eaten anything since mid-morning. But the feeling persisted and only intensified as she headed upstairs, carrying Jack against her shoulder. The door to her office – a bright, airy room overlooking the street – was slightly ajar, which was odd, since she always made a point of keeping it closed during the winter months to conserve heat. She pushed it open and looked in. Nothing *seemed* out of place, and yet . . .

It took her a moment to spot it. The LED light on her monitor, facing her on the desk by the window, was blinking orange. Standby mode.

She hadn't had the computer on – hadn't been in here at all, in fact – since before Christmas, and she was sure she'd switched it off as part of the grand winding down process at the start of her mat leave.

*Pretty* sure, at any rate.

She felt Jack rooting against her, clenching and unclenching his fists. And she knew exactly what that meant. *Feeding time at the zoo.*

She headed down to the living room, installed herself on the sofa and settled in for the long haul. The pain that accompanied the feeding process was less intense these days. She wasn't sure if she – and Jack – were getting better at the mechanics of it or if she was just becoming used to it, but it was no longer the endurance test it had been in the early days.

As she sat there, listening to him glugging away happily, her eyes alighted on a darker patch of hardwood flooring at the sofa's edge. It was almost as if the sofa was casting a shadow – only it was in completely the wrong direction. She suddenly realised what was so off about the room.

The sofa had moved.

It was only a few centimetres, and someone without an intimate knowledge of the room's layout would never have noticed. But she knew the place like the back of her hand. Was perfectly attuned to every aspect of its décor.

Someone had been in the house.

She lurched to her feet, ignoring the burst of pain as Jack, clearly miffed at being moved in the middle of his feed, tugged on her nipple with his hard gums. She strode across to the window with him still plugged into the mains, opened the sheer curtain a crack and peered out. The grey Fiat was gone. All was quiet in the street. Everything appeared utterly – almost banally – normal. She held her breath, straining her ears for any sign that she wasn't alone, but the only sound she could hear, apart from the faint hum of traffic up on Hyndland Road, was Jack's suckling.

Violated. That was how she felt. Violated. The thought that someone had been inside her house, without her knowledge or consent, left her feeling more vulnerable than at any point since the day she'd collapsed bleeding on the slope of Gardner Street.

The two detectives. The ones who'd spoken to her the day before yesterday. Who'd been insistent that Zoe must have given her something. Who'd wanted to look through the things she'd brought home from the hospital. Was this *their* doing? Surely the police wouldn't just invade a private citizen's home and go through her things? They needed a warrant to do that.

*Yes, Anna, because we know the cops* never *break the rules.*

She tried to remember whether either of them had shown any ID. Maybe they had; maybe they hadn't. Her head had been so all over the shop that day, it was anyone's guess.

She spotted Douthwaite's card, lying on the table where she'd dumped it without a second thought after he left. She picked it up, studied it. It looked like a normal enough business card to her, complete with his name, phone number and the Police Scotland insignia above the words 'MAJOR INVESTIGATIONS TEAM'.

She got out her phone and dialled the number. It rang a couple of times, followed by a click.

'DS Douthwaite.'

She realised her folly the moment she heard his voice. If the police *had* been responsible for breaking in, the last thing she wanted was to tip them off to the fact that she knew. She killed the call instantly.

Was she going mad? Was she totally losing the plot?

Back at the hospital, they'd tried to get her to go back on the lithium within a few hours of Jack's birth. Again and again, they'd told her it was for the best; that there was considerable risk of her developing postpartum psychosis, especially during the first few weeks after the birth. She'd understood their caution – after all, she knew all the stats that pertained to bipolar mothers, probably better than they did – even as she'd wished they'd just accept that she knew her own mind and body and let her get on with doing things her way. Because she'd decided she knew best, as always. She found herself wondering whether the pregnancy had simply been a convenient excuse for her to come off her medication – the medication she'd taken religiously since being diagnosed in her early twenties. It wasn't as if she *had* to breastfeed. Plenty of mothers didn't, for a variety of reasons. Was she now experiencing the predictable consequences of her own pigheadedness?

But then, one look at Jack, still sucking away contentedly, and she realised she wouldn't have given up this feeling, this bond, this precious link between mother and child, for anything. If she was going mad, so be it. She'd live with the consequences.

But she was pretty certain she wasn't.

Standing by the window, she watched as the light grew steadily dimmer outside, night drawing in like a suffocating veil. All afternoon, heavy clouds had been gathering overhead, and as darkness began to fall, so too did the rain.

It took Jack an inordinate amount of time to settle after his feed. Anna tried burping him. She tried walking him up and down the stairs. She even tried playing white noise on the music system, which just gave her a headache and made him cry even louder. She wondered if he was picking up on her own tense mood. She walked all around the house with him in her arms, using the opportunity to explore every nook and cranny, making sure there wasn't someone hiding in some cupboard or under a bed, waiting to pounce when her guard was down. There wasn't, but she did discover half a dozen other objects and items of furniture that showed signs of having been moved – further evidence that someone had been poking around in her absence.

It was after eight when Jack finally gave up the fight, at which point it suddenly occurred to Anna that it had been almost ten hours since she'd last had anything to eat. She'd been so stressed out by everything that had been going on that she hadn't even noticed the gnawing hunger pangs, but now they were impossible to ignore. She headed to the kitchen and was in the process of fixing herself a late meal when the doorbell rang.

Her first thought was that it was another unwanted well-wisher, turning up uninvited to poke and prod her offspring. Jack, sleeping on her shoulder, offered up only the faintest grunt of protest as she carried him through to the hallway and approached the door. She saw the shapes of two figures through the frosted glass, illuminated by the porch-light. At the sight of them, something caused her to falter momentarily. It was nothing, just the faintest twinge in her gut (more than likely a symptom of the recurring IBS she'd had since giving birth), but what remained of the walk down the corridor felt unnervingly ominous.

Her nerves were far from assuaged when she opened the door. Ostensibly, the two men standing on the step looked like another pair of plain-clothes detectives: trench coats, ties, severe expressions. But much like the furniture in the house that had been moved out of position, something about them was ever so slightly off. The one on the left had one of the tails of his shirt untucked and was sporting at least forty-eight hours' worth of stubble, while the one on the right had a long, thin face and the sort of haircut one normally associated with football hooligans or the American military. You shouldn't judge a book by its cover, but absolutely everything about these two men was sending warning signals shooting up her spine to her brain.

She kept her hand on the door, holding it half-open, and affected a look of casual indifference. 'Yes?'

'Anna Scavolini?' It was the one with the untucked shirt who spoke. 'DI Mitchell, DS Johnson.'

'Got anything to prove that?'

The other one – was he Mitchell or Johnson? – gave something that looked suspiciously like a smirk, then opened his wallet and flashed an ID card so quickly it could have been a bus pass for all she knew.

'We gather you spoke to two of our colleagues on Thursday,' said the other one – who, she noted, hadn't shown any ID.

'That's right – DS Douthwaite and DC . . . Smith.'

Neither of them seemed to notice the deliberate error. 'We've got a few follow-up questions. Just a couple of points we need to clarify.'

Anna said nothing. Every single one of the voices in her head was screaming *DO NOT TRUST THESE MEN* at her in multi-channel surround sound. Her grip on the doorframe tightened. She pressed Jack closer to her. Her eyes didn't leave the two men for an instant.

The talkative one took a step forward. 'Be better if we could talk inside.'

Behind him on the other side of the road, Anna clocked the grey Fiat back in its usual spot, passenger door slightly ajar.

Her eyes racked focus to the two detectives – if that was indeed what they were. 'Now's really not a good time.'

'It'll just take a moment.'

In the kitchen at the far end of the hallway, the oven timer started to beep. Jack chose that precise moment to stir and begin to bawl. Beset on all sides – by the cooker, by Jack, by these two thoroughly off-putting men – it was all Anna could do to maintain her composure.

The one with the stubble chuckled. 'Got quite a set of lungs on him, hasn't he?'

His companion gave an oily grin and picked at something between his teeth.

The blood was cold in Anna's veins. She found herself rooted to the spot, staring up at them without any thought in her mind other than that she must not under any circumstances allow them into the house. Not taking her eyes off them, she called, in as offhand a tone as she could muster:

'Daniel! Can you sort the oven? Dinner's ready!' She gave them a little eye-roll, as if to say, *Typical!* 'My partner. He'll be down any minute.'

The two men looked at one another. The silent, thin-faced one smiled to himself and shook his head.

The ill-shaven one nodded to the still-howling Jack. 'Wonder what the neighbours must be thinking, the racket he's making.' He gave Anna a be-seeching, *be reasonable* look. 'Why don't we just take this inside?'

As he moved forward again, putting his hand on the door handle, something stirred in Anna. Her warrior spirit was awakened, and with it an unyielding determination to defend both her home and her child.

'Are you here to enforce an arrest warrant?'

'No,' he said, blindsided by her question.

'Are you in pursuit of a criminal who you believe to have entered the building?'

'No.'

'Has someone inside the building requested your intervention?'

'No—'

'Has a member of the public reported a disturbance?'

The man merely glowered silently.

'Then, under common law and as stipulated in the Police Scotland Standard Operating Procedure Manual, I'm not obliged to grant you access unless you've applied for and been issued with a search warrant by the Procurator Fiscal or a Justice of the Peace. *Have* you been issued such a warrant?'

She was actually quite impressed that she'd managed to make that sound so authoritative, particularly with Jack still screaming his lungs out and the cooker alarm continuing to shrill.

The ill-shaven man gave a soft little laugh. 'Quite right. Young woman such as yourself, newborn baby to look after . . . You'd be a fool to let two strangers into your house on a dark, wet night just because they say they're police officers.' His eyes narrowed, all trace of mirth fading. 'And you're no fool, are you, *Doctor* Scavolini?'

'Daniel!' she called again, more plaintively this time. 'Can you get the oven?'

Across the road, the door to one of the facing houses opened and one of her neighbours – an elderly man with a well-deserved reputation for curtain-twitching – leaned out. Anna had never been more pleased to see the nosy old bastard in her life.

'That's all right, *Doctor* Scavolini,' said the ill-shaven man, his tone magnanimous but at the same time somehow mocking. 'We wouldn't want to disturb your meal for one. We'll call again at a more convenient time. Goodnight.'

The two men turned and made their way down the steps. Anna couldn't hear them over the combined din of Jack and the alarm, but she was sure they were sniggering at her. She watched as they returned to the Fiat and got in, but made no move to start the engine.

She hurried inside, slammed and double-locked the front door. Then, clutching the still howling Jack tight against her, she slowly sank to the floor with her back against the door, a prisoner in her own home.

## 32

# Siege

She retrieved the charred remnants of her dinner from the oven and binned them, her appetite having well and truly evaporated. She checked every window and door, making sure they were securely locked and bolted, turned on all the lights, then double-checked everything again. Once she'd managed to get Jack to settle – no mean feat given her own heightened agitation – she holed up in her bedroom with him in his bassinet at the foot of the bed, sitting cross-legged on the floor with her back against the door, a steak-knife within arm's reach. She didn't think the two men would try to force an entry. If they'd been going to do that, they'd surely have done it while she had the front door open. But then, it was possible they were just waiting till the rest of the street was safely tucked up in bed so they could go about their business undisturbed. And assuming it had been them – or someone in league with them – who'd searched the house earlier, they clearly had the means to get in anyway, regardless of whether she co-operated. She wasn't taking any chances.

She sat there, gnawing at the overhang on her thumbnail, and forced herself to think. There was no longer any doubt in her mind. Zoe's disappearance, Broadhurst's murder, the break-in while she was out, the attempt just now by those two men to gain entry to the house – all these events were connected in some way. She kept coming back to the first two detectives – though she was no longer at all convinced that that was what they had been – and their insistence that Zoe must have passed something to her. Whatever it was, she sensed that it was central to unlocking the puzzle.

She fingered her friendship bracelet. Shutting her eyes, she took herself back to the last time she'd seen Zoe, replaying their final conversation in the hospital recovery room. *Got some business tae take care of. Something I need to do.* They'd talked about other things too, but that was the part Anna kept coming back to.

*Business.*

But what business?

She tried to remember what else they'd discussed. There'd been the thoroughly unappealing prospect of telling her mum about Jack – a task she *still* hadn't summoned the will to tackle – and a brief reflection on whether it was appropriate to swear in front of a neonate. And Astley Street. Zoe had mentioned her old house on Astley Street. Twice. Anna remembered thinking at the time that it seemed odd, almost as if she was shoehorning it into the conversation, though she'd been too caught up in post-childbirth euphoria to give it much thought.

Had Zoe been trying to tell her something? Was there something significant about the house on Astley Street? Was there something there? Some item, perhaps, that these men, whoever they were, were looking for and mistakenly believed Zoe had given to her?

If there *was* something there, then she damn well wanted to know what it was. The question was how to get it without leading those men straight to it. If she went now, and via the back door, she might just be able to give them the slip under cover of dark. But that would involve scaling the fence behind the house, and she couldn't very well do that with Jack in tow. The thought of taking him into a derelict, structurally unsound building didn't hold much appeal either.

She suddenly thought of Sophie Hennessy. More than once in the last couple of weeks, Sophie had offered to watch Jack for her – to let her get out of the house and partake in what she quaintly referred to as 'me time'. Anna had always resisted, partly because she couldn't stand the thought of letting Jack out of her sight, and partly on the not entirely unjustified grounds that she might well return to find that Sophie had rearranged the entire house in her absence. Now, though, she had bigger fish to fry than Sophie's tendency to stick her oar where it wasn't wanted.

It was time to cash in that offer.

\*   \*   \*

By the time Sophie's car pulled up outside half an hour later, Anna was waiting for her in the front hallway, all ready to go. Jack had still been fast asleep when she'd checked on him five minutes earlier, not daring to kiss him goodbye in case he woke. She watched for the shimmering outline behind the frosted glass. Then, before Sophie had a chance to ring the bell, she thrust the door open and dragged her inside, shutting and locking it behind her.

'Anna, what the flying fuck . . . ?'

'Thanks for doing this, Soph. Really. You've no idea how big a help it is. Is Matthew watching Cosmo?'

'Of course he is. Anna, you wanna tell me what the hell this is all about? When you asked me to come over, I thought for sure something'd happened to you or Jack—'

'Jack's fine. He's fast asleep upstairs. He had his last feed about two hours ago and his next one's due in an hour. There's freshly expressed milk in the fridge, and you know where to find clean nappies and the rest. I shouldn't be gone any longer than—'

'Anna, would you please just stop and *listen*?' Sophie grabbed Anna's arm, halting her in her tracks. 'I don't know what's going on, but try and look at this from my perspective, hmm? You're acting like someone who's lost the plot.'

Anna took a deep breath, forcing herself to dial things down a notch. She knew she was speaking too fast, her movements overly animated in a way that couldn't help but call to mind someone in the grip of a manic episode. Which she kept telling herself she wasn't.

'Sophie, I wish I had time to explain, but I don't. I just need you to do this for me.' She shook herself free from Sophie's grasp and looked at her imploringly. 'I know how it looks. But I need you to trust me, OK?'

For a moment, Sophie looked like she was on the verge of protesting. Ultimately, though, she gave a resigned sigh and a look that was clearly meant to convey her disapproval in the strongest possible terms.

'Thank you,' said Anna. 'I'll be back as soon as I can.'

Then, not waiting to give Sophie a chance to change her mind, she turned and headed for the back door.

She let herself out, locked the door behind her and crossed the grass to the low wall bordering the lane at the back of the house. She hauled herself over the top, clenching her teeth against the searing pain in her abdomen, then dropped to the ground on the other side. She glanced in both directions. No sign of anyone. So far, so good. She turned and gazed back at the house, the warm glow of its lights beckoning to her. She prayed Sophie and Jack would be safe till she got back. She was banking on the belief that, if the men watching the house thought there was more than one adult inside, they'd be less likely to try anything. Another reason why it was imperative that she slipped away unnoticed.

The taxi she'd called was waiting for her next to the church on Hyndland Road.

'Parsons?' she said, as the driver wound his window down.

'Aye.'

She got into the back. 'Astley Street, near Ruchill Park.'

The driver nodded and spun his wheel, pulling away from the kerb.

'One other thing . . . and I know how this is going to sound, but if a grey Fiat follows us, I need you to lose it.'

The driver shook his head, clearly convinced he'd picked up a nutter. 'Right enough, hen.'

Anna sank low, taking deep, deliberate breaths to settle her pounding heart. After a minute or so, she risked raising her head to peer out the back window. No sign of the Fiat.

She turned to face forward again, failing to notice the black Ducati motorbike falling in behind them as they headed north towards Great Western Road.

# 33

# Hidden Places

Ten minutes later, the taxi pulled over at the end of Astley Street. Not knowing how long she was going to be, Anna paid the driver, tipping him handsomely for his trouble, then waited till he'd driven off before making her way up the pavement to number 58.

The old Callahan family home was a grim sight to behold. Unoccupied, unmaintained, unloved, it stood as a stark reminder of the fate that befell things people no longer cared for. As she stepped over the threshold, using her phone to light the way, she knew that the odds were thoroughly stacked against her finding what she was looking for, and would have been so even in broad daylight. She had no idea where it was, what it looked like, or indeed if it was actually here – assuming there even *was* an 'it'. But the gut feeling that had brought her this far remained as strong now as it had when she'd first hatched this crazy scheme.

It took her the better part of half an hour to comb the house from top to bottom, exploring every nook and cranny with the beam of her phone's torch. Not that there were many nooks left, and even fewer crannies; the place had long since been ransacked of all its furniture, and what little remained was in an advanced state of decay. She spent the bulk of her time in Zoe's old room, concluding that if Zoe *had* hidden something in the house, then that was the likeliest place. But the most interesting thing she found was a deposit of mouldy rat droppings in the cupboard where Zoe used to keep her sizeable shoe collection.

Her last stop, the bathroom, was, if anything, in an even worse state than the rest of the house. The old porcelain tub was still there, though the toilet and sink were long gone, and a steady patter of rainwater dripped down from a crack in the ceiling. Worn out from her efforts, she perched on the side of the tub to recover her strength.

As she sat there, listening to the rain pattering on the floor and the howling wind outside, she remembered something else about her and Zoe's conversation in the recovery room. The reason they'd got onto the subject of Astley Street had been Zoe's swearing in front of Jack. Anna had said he'd be doing well if the worst thing he ever encountered was the occasional profanity. She found herself mouthing Zoe's response in time to the voice she now heard in her head, as clearly as if Zoe was perched next to her.

'Just you wait. He'll be drinking tins o' Tennent's and getting baked before ye know it. Ye'll need to be on the lookout for his hidey-holes. Mind how me 'n' Vic used to keep our stash in the space behind that loose tile in the bathroom?'

Anna swung around, training her phone on the olive-green tiling on the wall above the bath. Could it be . . . ?

She stepped into the tub, holding onto the still-attached towel-rail for support, and felt along the wall, fingers tracing the outlines of the tiles. *Five down, twelve across*, just like a crossword puzzle. Crazy that she could barely remember what she'd had for breakfast but could recall that detail perfectly. She came to the tile in question. Pressing her fingers into the grouting on either side, she prised it out.

The hollow space beyond was a dark void of nothingness. She shone her phone inside it, but the beam was too weak to reach all the way to the back. Steeling herself, she plunged her hand into the unknown. She thought perhaps she might find a bag of forgotten contraband – or, if she was particularly unlucky, the decayed corpse of some unfortunate creature that had crawled in there and been sealed inside, *à la* Poe's Black Cat. Instead, she felt something rectangular and flat with corrugated edges and a papery surface. Grabbing hold of it, she pulled it towards her, bending it slightly to fit it through the hole.

It was a padded envelope, a little damp around the edges but otherwise intact. There was nothing written on the front, but she could feel the shape of something hard and flat inside. She opened it and withdrew the contents:

a Sony re-recordable DVD, its label as blank as the envelope, and a small bundle of photographs held together by an elastic band.

Setting the DVD and envelope aside, she began to flip through the pictures one-handed, training the light on them with the other. They were all photographs of teenage boys – a mixture of professional portraits and run-and-gun-style candid snaps. One, a dark-haired boy with glasses, looked vaguely familiar, but she wouldn't have liked to swear to it. The rest, as far as she could tell, she'd never seen before in her life.

That was until she came to the last picture and found herself gazing down at the thick freckles and ginger curls of Victor Callahan.

She swallowed heavily, gripped by a sudden, horrible fear that she couldn't put into meaningful words. Her eyes drifted to the DVD, lying in the soap tray where she'd set it down. Something told her that whatever was on it wasn't going to be pretty.

She emerged from the house, the envelope containing the DVD and pictures jammed out of sight inside her waistband. She looked both ways. The coast was clear.

She headed east along Astley Street, scrolling through the contacts on her phone for the number of the taxi firm she'd used earlier. Before she could get to it, however, she spotted a cab idling a few hundred metres up the road, the light on the roof indicating that it was open for business. Eager not to spend a minute longer than necessary in the cold and rain in this inhospitable part of town, she quickened her pace towards it.

'Hyndland Road,' she said as she collapsed into the back.

The driver, a short, heavyset man completely dwarfed by his headrest, grunted a nod and pulled out into the road.

They headed south, their surroundings eerily quiet for a Saturday night. Not that Ruchill was party central at the best of times, but normally you could expect to see a few groups of wayward teens roaming the neighbourhood. She supposed the rain must be keeping people indoors. Apart from the purr of the engine, it was as silent inside the cab as it was outwith it, the radio bereft of the usual low-level chatter between the various cabbies and their dispatcher.

'Quiet tonight,' she said. She wasn't normally one for making small talk in taxis, but the near-total silence was unnerving her.

'Aye,' the driver agreed. 'Not many folk out.'

They continued to the bottom of Tamshill Street and turned right onto Ruchill Street.

'What brings you out here on a night like this?'

'Just visiting an old haunt.'

'In Ruchill?' He sounded strangely amused. 'Wouldn't've guessed – nice, well-spoken girl like you.'

'Takes all sorts.'

Silence descended once more. They continued west along Ruchill Street, over the bridge that straddled the canal and on towards Maryhill Road.

'Was it what you were expecting?'

'Sorry?'

'This old haunt of yours. Changed much since you were last here?'

'Bit, yeah.'

She sunk lower in her seat, kicking herself for striking up a conversation with him in the first place.

'Find anything interesting in there?'

'Like what?'

'Howsabout you tell me?'

She caught his eyes in the rearview mirror. Noticed the sheen of sweat on his forehead. As their eyes continued to meet, she was aware of them sailing on past Kelvindale Road.

'You missed the turn-off,' she said, still clinging to the forlorn hope that it had been an honest mistake.

'Thought we'd go for a little drive. Give us time to talk.'

'Stop the car,' she ordered, trying to ignore her rapidly contracting guts.

'You're not going to be silly now, are you? They told me you were an intelligent woman.'

*Who's 'they'?*

She felt the outline of the DVD being pressed against her still-tender abdominal flesh by the tightness of her waistband.

'Did you hear me? I said "stop the car".'

'I will, just as soon as you hand over what you found in that house. Come on.' He tried to adopt a more conciliatory tone. 'You're in way over your head here. Believe me, it'll be a relief when you give it to me. I bet you *want* to, really.'

'I don't know what you're talking about,' she said feebly, as they continued to roar up Maryhill Road, through the tunnel and up the hill towards the desolate stretch of ground overlooking the old locks.

'Come on,' the man snapped. 'Just give me the list and this can all be over.'

*List?*

As they reached the top of the slope, Anna made her move. Lurching forward, she jammed the sharp blade of her house-key into the driver's neck, right next to his jugular vein.

'Stop the car!' she yelled.

The taxi slammed to a halt so suddenly it was a miracle she remained upright. Silence fell once again, not even the hum of the engine now disturbing it.

With her free hand, Anna reached for the handle of the back door. Locked.

'Open it,' she hissed.

'You're making a mistake.'

She pressed the key harder into his neck. 'I don't intend to repeat myself.'

The man raised both hands to shoulder level. Keeping his right aloft, he slowly moved his left over to the dashboard controls.

'Look,' he said, keeping his voice level, 'if you work *with* us, I'll be in a position to make sure no harm comes to your friend when we find her. And believe me, we *will* find her.'

'Shut up.'

'If not . . . ' He shrugged. 'Well, it's no skin off my nose.'

'Open the *fucking* door.'

'Your choice – but believe me, the next lot of people they send won't ask so nicely.'

He flicked a button on the dashboard. She heard the locking mechanism disengaging. When she tried the door again, it swung open.

Slowly, she slid across the back seat, continuing to press the key against his neck until her arm wouldn't stretch any further. She counted to five, then withdrew the key and scrambled out, slamming the door behind her and backing off as fast as she could. The cab took off almost instantly, roaring through the red light up ahead and turning off down Cowal Road, where it quickly disappeared from view. Anna gave herself a couple of seconds to steady her breathing, then fumbled for her phone.

Even as she did so, the roar of an approaching car reached her ears. She turned as a black Ford Escort rounded the corner. Her immediate impulse was to flag it down, and she'd even taken a few steps towards it before her brain kicked in, telling her this was a profoundly unwise idea. Her worst fears were confirmed as it came to a stop about fifty metres away from her and two men stepped out. Not the ones who'd tried to get into her house by posing as detectives. These men were bigger, tougher and altogether meaner-looking. The sort of men who got called in to do the jobs no one else was willing to do. They advanced towards her at a leisurely stroll, which somehow only reinforced the hopelessness of the situation. She cast around. There was no escape route, and she knew she hadn't a hope of making it to one of the nearby flats and raising the alarm before they reached her.

Just then, she heard the roar of yet another approaching vehicle. She turned as a motorbike crested the slope and came to an abrupt stop. It remained stationary for a moment as the cyclist, wearing black leathers and a flip-front helmet, appeared to size up the scene unfolding in front of them. Then, without warning, they revved the engine and gunned the bike towards Anna. The two heavies gave charge, making for her as well.

It all happened so quickly that Anna had no chance to form anything approaching a coherent thought. The bike roared to a halt beside her, the cyclist lifted their visor, and Anna found herself staring into a pair of wild, intense eyes – eyes belonging to a woman she'd never in a million years dreamed she'd see again.

'Get on!' snarled Fin.

Anna hesitated for barely a second before springing to life. She scrambled onto the pillion, looping her arms round Fin's waist. Fin spun the bike around and they took off at top speed, roaring back down Maryhill Road, leaving the thugs sucking exhaust fumes behind them.

# 34

# Lockup

Anna clung on for dear life as Fin roared through the rainswept streets at full tilt, ducking and weaving between the traffic, cutting through alleyways and side-roads. The heavy rain battered her face. The wind whistled in her ears. She could feel her coat-tails billowing out behind her and was utterly convinced that, any minute now, they'd become tangled up in the rear wheel, bringing them to a sudden and quite possibly fatal stop. That, or Fin would lose control on a sharp, rain-slick turn and they'd both be thrown headfirst over the handlebars. But mercifully, neither happened, and, after they'd been travelling for some time and Anna had lost all sense of geography, Fin pulled onto a narrow cobblestoned lane and into a lockup under one of the arches of a disused railway bridge.

The moment they came to a standstill, Anna scrambled off, her feet almost giving out under her as they touched the floor. She tottered a few steps, thighs burning, legs like jelly, before promptly dropping to a crouch for an extended dry-heaving session. Between heaves, she lifted her head and watched through watering eyes as Fin, now *sans* helmet, strode over to the entrance and hauled down the overhead door, shutting out the night and any potential pursuers. She wandered nonchalantly back to her bike and leaned against it, making no attempt to hide her amusement at Anna's state. Anna gave one last futile heave, spat a mouthful of frothy saliva onto the concrete, then straightened up to face her unlikely saviour.

'What the fuck?' were the first words out of her mouth.

'Hey, don't mention it,' said Fin, looking smug.

Anna just stared at the woman standing before her, lost for words. She was a little thinner about the cheeks, perhaps, which gave sharper definition to her features, and her dark hair, previously cut short and fashioned into thickly gelled spikes, now reached past her shoulders. In all other respects, though, she was clearly the same infuriating, sardonic Fin who Anna had briefly encountered at Monklands Hospital in the early hours of a July morning three years ago. It had been bucketing then too, she recalled, and the stakes had been no less high than they were now – all of which made Fin's sudden unheralded reappearance seem strangely appropriate, if no less inexplicable.

Anna took a few unsteady steps towards her, wishing she had something to hold onto to steady herself. 'What are you doing here?' she said, finding her tongue at last.

Fin rolled back her shoulders and uttered a single word.

'Zoe.'

'Zoe? Have you heard from her? Where is she?' The words came pouring out of Anna's mouth like verbal diarrhoea.

Fin raised her hands for calm. 'Easy, Professor. Don't give yerself an aneurism. No, I ain't heard from her, and no, I dunno where in the seven hells she is. But I figured she needed my help.'

'What . . . how?' Anna spluttered. Events seemed to be unfolding at a level her brain wasn't equipped to make sense of.

'Wouldn'ta thought it'd be rocket science to a brainiac like yerself. I keep an eye on the old social media – y'know, making sure she's living her best life, all that jazz. And yesterday I chanced on that screed of yours on her Facebook, and I figured, "Looks like old Bright Eyes has got herself into a mighty pickle". Seems I got here just in time. Case you hadn't noticed, you've had a tail on ya all day.'

'I . . . I have?'

'Aye, like a second shadow – and I'm not talking about me. I mean, I *was* following ya, but I wasn't the only one. I figured you weren't traipsing all over the city with the littl'un in tow for shits 'n' giggles, and that if it turned out you were on her trail, I oughta be on hand case ya ended up leading those goons straight to her. On the subject of which, who the fuck *are* they? And where do they get off staging a kidnapping at the top of Maryhill Road in the middle of the night?'

Anna eyed Fin warily, not sure how much she actually cared to confide in her. She knew maddeningly little about the brash, delinquent Irish-woman, other than that she'd helped Zoe out – if you could call it that – three summers back, and that she had what might charitably be described as an ambivalent relationship with the law. If it had been up to her, Fin would have been far from her first choice of ally – but she was hardly in a position to pick and choose. At any rate, it was clear that they had at least one thing in common: concern for Zoe.

She unbuttoned her coat and retrieved the envelope from her waistband. 'I'm not sure who they are, but I think this is what they want.'

Fin pulled off one of her riding gloves with her teeth, then took the envelope and rifled through the contents. Setting the DVD to one side, she flicked through the bundle of photos before coming to a stop, as Anna had done before her, at the one of Victor. She held it up, looking at Anna almost accusingly.

'That's her brother, innit?'

'Yes. And I'm assuming, whatever this is all about, the answers are on that disc.'

'No time like the present, then.'

Fin handed the photos back to Anna and moved off, disappearing behind the rusted shell of a car that had evidently been stripped for parts. They were in a garage of some sort, Anna realised – though whether Fin was actually renting the place or had merely appropriated it in the owner's absence was anyone's guess. Going by past behaviour, she was strongly inclined to suspect the latter.

Fin returned a moment later, clutching an ageing brick of a laptop. Setting it down on a nearby workbench, she loaded the DVD into the drive and began to paw at the trackpad.

Anna headed over to join her. 'The man who picked me up on Astley Street – the one posing as a taxi driver – he mentioned a list. I'm guessing that's what's on the disc.'

Fin shook her head. 'No list. Just a movie.'

'Play it, then.'

Fin tapped the trackpad and the file expanded to fill the screen. At first, there was nothing – just a blank image. Then it gave way to a wall of video noise, before finally getting to the movie itself. A movie of a half-naked teenage boy standing in a room with pastel-tinted walls.

'The feck is this?' said Fin.

It wasn't long before they found out. It took less than fifteen seconds for Anna to recognise the offscreen voice addressing the boy as that of the recently deceased Adam Broadhurst, and only slightly longer to figure out where things were headed. Fin, evidently a little slow on the uptake, continued to stare at the screen with a look of perplexity until Broadhurst started talking about masturbation, at which point the penny finally dropped.

'I'm turning this off,' she said, reaching for the trackpad. 'I don't need to see this shit.'

Anna offered no objection. As the screen returned to the desktop, she once more felt weak at the knees. She leant against the worktop to steady herself, the room around her spinning.

Fin turned to her with an accusatory look. 'Just what the fuck have yous two got yourselves mixed up in?'

Anna didn't respond. Her mind was churning. Broadhurst's murder; Zoe's disappearance the same day; her random summons to Queen's Park a few weeks earlier; the photos of the other boys, including Victor . . . She found herself reeling as the various jigsaw pieces finally slotted into place.

'I think,' she said after a moment, slowly and carefully, 'I think Zoe got her hands on evidence that our old headmaster had been abusing his pupils, and . . . ' A wave of nausea gripped her. 'Oh, Christ . . . '

'What? For the love o' God, shit or get off the pot.'

Anna swallowed heavily. 'I think she might've killed him.'

She could scarcely bring herself to believe it was possible, and yet there could be little denying how it looked. Correlation didn't necessarily imply causation, but there came a point in every study when the evidence pointed so firmly in one direction that the result became a foregone conclusion.

Fin's eyes narrowed. 'That what you think happened?'

'It's certainly what it looks like.'

'I didn't ask what it *looks* like. I asked if it's what you *think*.'

Anna shrugged helplessly. She found herself unable to meet Fin's eye.

Fin made a disgusted noise at the back of her throat and shook her head. 'You're something else, you are. That's what you think of her? Thought yous were meant to be besties.'

Anna felt a surge of anger coursing through her at the thought that her loyalty to Zoe was being questioned – and by someone who, as far as she was concerned, didn't know the first thing about either of them. She was about to say as much when she stopped to consider just *why* she was so furious. Could it be because, deep down, she knew Fin had a point?

'The police seem to think she has questions to answer,' she muttered feebly.

Fin snorted. 'That a fact? F'ya think those geebags were cops, I got a big-ass old bridge to sell ya. Leastways, if they *are* the filth, they sure as hell ain't doing any of this above the radar.'

It was what Anna had suspected for some time now, and any lingering belief in her mind that this was a sanctioned police operation had been thoroughly kiboshed by the incident in the taxi. But she couldn't bring herself to concede even this point.

'She'd have killed Dominic Ryland if you hadn't stopped her,' she said quietly.

Fin shook her head firmly. 'No she wouldn't've. She mighta thought about it. Might even've come close to doing it, but when push came to shove, no way in hell would she've been able to go through with it. And if you can't see that – well, ya got no business calling yourself her pal.'

Once more, rage welled inside Anna. Where the hell did this woman, who'd spent all of a fortnight in Zoe's company, get off on issuing proclamations about the nature of her psyche? She bit her tongue, certain that, if she didn't, she'd only end up saying something she regretted.

'So what's all this about a list, then?' Fin said.

Anna shook her head. 'I've no idea.'

'Names of victims, maybe?' Fin gestured to the stack of photos in Anna's hand. 'Maybe *that's* the list.'

Anna looked at the bundle. It didn't wash for her. 'No – I think, whatever this list is, it's something else. Something we haven't found yet. I reckon it's something only Zoe knows the answer to.'

Fin worked her bottom lip back and forth against her upper teeth, mulling it over. She turned her head towards the door, listening to the teeming rain outside. 'Well, if she's got any sense, she'll've got herself to someplace far away. Someplace dry 'n' hot, preferably.'

'She hates the sun,' Anna retorted. As petty as it was, she found she was still trying to score points in the 'who knows Zoe best?' sweepstakes.

'Well, North Pole, then. Point is, if she wanted to vanish off the face of the earth, she'd've put as much distance between herself and this podunk as possible. S'what I did.'

'I don't even think she has an active passport.'

Fin gave a knowing smirk. 'There's other ways to skip the country.'

'And you think Zoe's got the wherewithal for that?' Anna sighed, trying to moderate her tone. 'Look, here's the thing about Zoe. She's . . . well, she's uncomplicated. I'm not saying she's not intelligent in her own way, but she's got a pretty straightforward way of approaching things. She's not got the resources to spirit herself out of the country under the radar, and I doubt she'd have the first clue where to start.'

'Jaysus, woman, would ya check yerself?' Fin spread her arms wide. 'Since you stopped dry-heaving, you've been doing her down non-stop. Zoe wouldn't do this, she's not resourceful that way. She wouldn't think of that, she's not smart enough. But stabbing a bloke to death in his own living room? Oh yeah, sure, no problemo. Forget judge 'n' jury – let's just slap her with a big old "guilty" sentence and bang her up for life.' Her expression softened somewhat, though her words continued to cut. 'You think you're being all level-headed and whatnot, but all you're doing is proving what a low opinion ya got of her. Oh, and FYI, yer udders are leaking.'

Anna looked down, feeling the twin damp patches on her blouse almost before she saw them. The sight caused two thoughts to enter her head more or less simultaneously. The first was that she didn't have her breast pump or a change of clothes with her. The second was Jack.

An icy fear gripped her. Hard as it was to believe, until now she'd managed to forget all about him. Immediately, all manner of horrifying thoughts flooded her mind as to what might be happening back at the house.

'I've got to get back to him,' she muttered – as much to herself as to Fin.

'And what good's that gonna do, huh? C'mon, Professor – engage yer brain.'

Anna stopped halfway towards the door and turned to face Fin impatiently. 'You can't keep me here,' she said – aware, as she spoke, of how petulant she sounded.

'True, but say you go waltzing back up to yer digs right now – what d'you think's gonna happen? You reckon they'll let ya just climb back in the bathroom window and get on with playing happy families? Yer feet wouldn't even touch the ground.'

'What else can I do? I can't just sit here twiddling my thumbs. What if they do something to my baby?'

Fin shook her head. 'Ain't gonna happen.'

'How can you be so sure?'

'Cos they're banking on you coming back for him. And, long as you and they both know where he is, he's the perfect bait. Face it – if it's the little man you're worried about, you're better off keeping as far away from him as possible.'

It made sense. It was hardly reassuring, but she couldn't pretend she didn't see the logic in it.

'Well, in that case, I have to at least ring Sophie and let her know what's going on. She'll be having kittens.'

'Scrawny bird with the long neck? Bad idea. Whatcha gonna say to her? No matter how ya dress it up, odds are she'll just panic and do something stupid like call in the filth.' She shrugged. 'I mean, s'your call. Maybe they'll come roaring in, sirens blaring, clear this whole sorry mess up before first light. But supposing they *are* mixed up in this . . . well, ya really wanna take that chance?'

Slowly, Anna shook her head. Her shoulders sagged. Her head felt heavy on her neck. She couldn't remember a situation so hopeless, or one in which she'd ever felt so powerless.

Fin pulled off her remaining glove. 'We'll sort something out in the morning. Meantime, I dunno 'bout you, but I'm for turning in. I'm bushed.' She gave what Anna assumed was the closest thing in her repertoire to a reassuring smile. 'Don't be fretting about yer littl'un. He'll get by without his mammy for a few hours yet. Get yerself some shut-eye. We got a big day ahead of us tomorrow.'

# 35

# Sanctuary

*Sunday 31 January*

Fin dragged out an old mattress and flopped down on it, arms folded behind her head, settling in for what remained of the night. Anna, meanwhile, took herself over to a secluded corner and went through the ignominious process of hand-expressing the contents of her leaking boobs. Having cleaned herself up as best she could, she headed back over to the mattress and gingerly lowered herself down next to Fin, leaving as much space between them as the mattress allowed. Drawing her coat tightly about herself, she lay there in the dark, listening to the gentle sounds of snoring behind her.

The next few hours were among the most miserable in Anna's life. This was, she realised, the longest she'd been separated from Jack since he'd been born. Before tonight, he'd never been more than a few feet away. Miles now lay between them, and she couldn't even pick up the phone to check that he was OK. All through the night she lay awake, imagining all the worst possibilities, torturing herself with her own powerlessness. She heard the rain outside subsiding to a light patter, then stopping completely; felt the distant rumble of the first early-morning train; saw the first hint of daylight seeping in via the gap under the door.

Fin continued to sleep on, undisturbed by the growing sounds of life outside. Anna was on the verge of rousing her when, a little after 8.30, she finally stirred, stretched luxuriously and sat up, tilting her head in various directions to work out the tension. She turned and looked at Anna with a frown, as if she couldn't remember how they'd come to be sharing a mattress, then flashed a crooked grin.

'Right then, Mama, what's say we see about getting yer sprog back?'

The St Enoch Shopping Centre was mobbed, which suited Anna to a T. The bigger the crowd, and the more public the location, the better. On Fin's instructions, she set herself up at a table in the ground-floor food court, ordering coffee and a croissant to get the barista to stop pestering her. The nearby soft play area was full to bursting with children and their parents, their delighted shrieks and shouts mingling with the infuriatingly upbeat teenie-pop being pumped out on the tannoy.

She'd been there for just over half an hour, her food largely untouched, when she finally spotted Sophie striding through the crowd towards her, wearing Jack's sling across her chest. She was lugging the baby-bag over her shoulder and had a face like spoiled meat.

Anna was already on her feet, ready to scoop Jack into her arms, but she stopped dead as her eyes drank in the sight of him, slumbering peacefully within the folds of the sling. Somehow, she'd managed to convince herself that he would have visibly aged, despite only a few hours having passed since she'd last seen him. But to her surprise, he actually looked even smaller, even more vulnerable than she'd remembered – which only served to compound her guilt at having left him in the first place.

'Well then,' said Sophie, eyes flaring at Anna, 'this is a merry dance you've led us.'

'Thanks for coming.'

'Oh, don't mention it. This is exactly how I'd planned on spending my Sunday morning – *after* spending the whole night babysitting a newborn whose mother saw fit to abandon him.'

'Soph—'

'Do you know how sick with worry I've been?' Sophie snapped, so abruptly that several nearby diners turned to look in her direction. 'You couldn't even bring yourself to pick up the phone and let me know where you were.'

'Sophie,' Anna raised a weary hand, appealing for amnesty, 'I haven't the energy to argue. Just believe me when I say I really didn't have a choice in the matter.'

'I don't know what's got into you, Anna, but I have to tell you I *really* do not like what I'm witnessing. What was I supposed to think when you didn't come home last night? And didn't answer your phone. *Anything* might have happened to you. Before you called, I'd been *this* close to ringing the police . . . '

Anna wasn't listening – at least, not fully. While Sophie was speaking, she'd noticed two men leaning on the balcony rail a couple of floors up, doing a less than convincing job of pretending not to be watching her. She recognised them immediately as the two 'detectives' who'd come to her door the previous night. So far, so predictable. She'd anticipated that they'd follow Sophie here – though, as yet, she hadn't figured out how she and Jack were going to shake them.

'Are you even listening?' Sophie's voice, strident and maddeningly self-righteous, cut through. 'Whatever's going on, you need to deal with it before it starts affecting Jack. He needs a mother who makes him her number one priority, not one who's willing to palm him off at the drop of a hat so she can do . . . ' She shrugged, exasperated. 'I don't know, whatever it is you've been doing for the last twelve hours.'

'I'm fine,' said Anna absentmindedly.

'Oh yes, because this is all totally normal behaviour. I still don't understand why you had me hoof it all the way out here with him . . . '

Deciding not to even acknowledge Sophie's sarcasm, Anna gave what she hoped passed for a look of contrition. 'Thank you for looking after Jack last night. I'm sorry if I inconvenienced you.'

Sophie's expression softened. She sighed, her shoulders sagging as the fight left them. 'You haven't inconvenienced me. I'm just *worried*, Anna. Worried and tired and bloody confused.'

Anna gave a penitent's shrug. 'I'm sorry I can't explain everything right now. One day, when all this is over, I promise I'll give you the full lowdown. Until then, just trust me when I say that I'm not losing the plot.'

As she spoke, she realised she wasn't only saying this for Sophie's benefit. On some level, *she* needed to hear it too.

Sophie looked far from convinced, but at length gave a curt nod. 'Sounds like that's as good as I'm going to get right now.'

'It is.'

'Right, then. Shall we do this?'

There followed a game of pass-the-parcel as Sophie transferred Jack, and the sling, to Anna – a manoeuvre that required no small amount of coordination between them, and made the fact that Jack didn't stir once something of a minor miracle.

'I changed him before I set out,' Sophie said, depositing the baby-bag on an empty chair as Anna adjusted Jack's position against her chest, 'and gave him a feed, so he should be good for another couple of hours. I've put what was left of the expressed milk in the bag. Oh, and I noticed he's got the beginnings of a nappy-rash. Did you not spot that?'

'No,' said Anna, feeling even more thoroughly inadequate.

'Well, I've put on some barrier cream, but you'll want to keep an eye on it in case it gets worse.' Sophie took a deep breath and rolled her shoulders back. 'I think that's you fully up to speed. Now, if you'll excuse me, I'm going to go and enjoy what's left of the day with my *own* son.'

As soon as Sophie was gone, Anna did the one thing she'd been dying to do since the previous night: she scooped Jack up into her arms and held him close, convinced she'd never be able to bring herself to let go of him again. She buried her face in his neck, breathing in the smell of him. It wasn't a *pleasant* smell per se, but it was *his* smell, and it re-energised her more than an entire night's sleep could have hoped to.

'I'm sorry, Trouble,' she whispered. 'I don't mean to be such a fuck-up.'

She gazed up to the second floor, where the two men remained at their vantage point. She wondered how the hell she was going to shake them. It would have been a tall enough order if it was just her on her own, but with a young child to protect, the task seemed insurmountable.

*A child to protect . . .*

An idea began to form in her mind. She sat there awhile longer, letting it play out in her head, then grabbed the arm of a passing barista.

'Excuse me,' she said, as the girl stared down at her with the sort of wide-eyed look of panic folk tend to get when accosted by a crazy mother, 'I don't mean to be a pest, but those two men up there have been watching the play area for ages now. Look, I'm not one of those people who sees child predators everywhere, but there's something not right about them, and as a mother myself . . . '

The barista did a legitimately impressive job of clocking the two men without making it obvious. She gave Anna a low-key nod, then headed back into the café at a brisk clip. Anna remained seated, waiting to see what would happen next.

She didn't have to wait long. Within five minutes, two security guards appeared on the upper floor. A moment later, another pair arrived from a different direction, all four converging on the two men at the balcony. Anna watched with some satisfaction as a terse exchange ensued. She couldn't hear the words, but she saw the aggrieved protestations of her two pursuers and their lack of impact on the stony-faced mall cops.

She waited till she was satisfied the two men wouldn't be going anywhere anytime soon. Then, leaving a tenner on the table to cover breakfast, she took off with Jack, walking as briskly as she dared without drawing undue attention to herself.

She left the mall via the back door and took a circuitous route up to the mouth of Mitchell Lane, where she found Fin waiting, clutching a bulging shopping bag and looking almost unrecognisable in a parka, beanie and a pair of thoroughly unseasonable shades. If they hadn't arranged the spot in advance, Anna would likely have missed her – which she quickly realised was the entire point.

'Here.' Fin handed her the bag. 'Get this on ya.'

Anna inspected the contents: a puffer jacket with a fur-lined hood. Not her usual choice of attire at all, but she took the point that, like Fin, she needed to change her appearance – and sharpish. So she handed Jack over to Fin and changed into the jacket, stuffing her own coat, caked with dried rainwater and mud from last night's impromptu motorcycle ride, into the nearest bin. As she took Jack back, he stirred and began to cry.

'Shh, shh, shh.' She rocked him back and forth, trying to settle him. 'It's OK . . . '

Fin shook her head impatiently. 'You're holding him all wrong. Here.' She adjusted Jack's position, tilting his head a little to one side and repositioning Anna's hand. 'There. No wonder he's crabby.'

Anna had to bite her lip to stop herself from telling Fin that she was the last person she planned to take lessons in parenting from. The fact that Fin's intervention actually seemed to have left Jack more contented only made it worse.

'Right, then,' said Fin, 'shall we shake a leg?'

\* \* \*

They set off, moving at a far brisker pace than Anna felt comfortable with – though, feeling inadequate enough already, she gritted her teeth and passed no comment on the matter. Ten minutes later, they were on Trongate, tramping up a narrow staircase to the floor above one of the many bars that populated the Merchant City. Fin drew up in front of a red-painted door, rapped on it and waited.

'What are we looking for here?' Anna asked, trying to conceal her breathlessness.

'Sanctuary,' was Fin's cryptic reply.

Footsteps sounded beyond the door. It opened to reveal a slight, pale young woman of South-East Asian extraction. She wore a kimono the same colour as the door, her dark hair in a loose beehive.

'*Nom de Dieu!*' she exclaimed in a rich, fruity drawl that came from somewhere deep at the back of her throat. 'You have some nerve!'

Fin shrugged amiably. 'Hey, Reiko. How's tricks?'

Reiko cast a brief, disinterested glance at Anna, then turned both barrels on Fin. 'You do not write, you do not call, for more than two years I am hearing nothing of you. What am I to think? I worry that you are hit by a bus or small asteroid – and now you are here at my door, unscathed, unmolested, making the shrugs and saying, "Hello, Reiko. How are the tricks?" *Quel culot!*'

Fin winced sheepishly and shifted her weight to her other foot. She struck Anna as uncharacteristically taciturn in the presence of this spirited Gallic woman – even intimidated.

Reiko folded her arms, continuing to give Fin the evil eye. '*Eh bien, quoi?* What do you want?' She cast another brief, and this time rather suspicious, glance at Anna. '*Et c'est qui, ça?*'

'We kinda sorta need a place to crash,' replied Fin, before Anna could say anything. 'Just a night or two. A week tops.'

Reiko raised her eyes to the heavens and sighed in exasperation. 'Oh, *tu me prends la tête!* Always with you it is the same, Euphemia. You never give – only take, take, take. Anyway,' she added, with a dismissive little flick of her wrist, 'perhaps now is not so convenient for me, hmm?'

'Ah, sure you'll hardly notice we're here.' Fin was clearly trying for a bit of her usual roguish charm, but it landed like a damp squib in the face of

Reiko's scowl. 'Reiko, Reiko, help an old mucker out. I wouldn't be asking ya if I wasn't desperate.' She nodded in Anna's direction, lowering her voice. 'C'mon, she's got a tiddler.'

Reiko leaned past Fin to look at Anna again. For the first time, she appeared to notice Jack, shifting and squirming in her arms.

Instantly, her whole demeanour changed. She clapped her hands together, practically bouncing up and down in delight. 'But why are you not saying? *J'adore les bébés! Entrez, entrez!*'

Taking Anna's arm, she practically hauled her over the threshold. Then, before Anna had a chance to object, she'd whisked Jack out of the sling and was bouncing him up and down in her arms, cooing at him and talking to him in what sounded, to Anna's untrained ears, like a mix of French and Japanese.

'She used to talk to *me* like that,' Fin muttered to Anna as she joined her inside.

Reiko shot Fin an acrid look. 'It is very, *very* fortunate you are arriving now. Just ten minutes previously, I am saying goodbye to an *extremely* nice girl. Only recently she is accepting and embracing her predilections, but already she has a voracious appetite.'

Anna got the distinct impression this revelation was intended to make Fin seriously jealous, or at the very least convey to her that Reiko had been getting on just fine without her.

With Jack nestled against her shoulder quite contentedly, Reiko strode past Fin and looped her free arm through Anna's. 'Come! I will show you to your room, and you will tell me everything about *le petit*. What is his name? He is how many weeks? Oh, *comme il est joli!*'

Feeling slightly overwhelmed, Anna allowed herself to be led down the corridor, while Fin, evidently surplus to requirements, remained behind, kicking her heels.

Still carrying Jack, Reiko ushered Anna into a bedroom which, like her kimono and the front door, was decorated from head to toe in red – wallpaper, carpet, bedclothes, even the ceiling. A walk-in closet housed an array of saucy negligées, while the dresser on the other side of the room showcased several very large and complicated-looking strap-ons. Before Anna could even avert her eyes from the collection of oversized phalluses, Reiko casually swept them into an open drawer. Anna wondered just what this woman did for a living, but didn't have the nerve to ask. Besides, it seemed churlish to quibble, given that she was providing them with shelter.

Reiko studied Jack's features intently. 'He has your nose, I think.' She turned to Anna again. 'And which of you is the biological mother?'

It took Anna a moment to realise what Reiko was asking. 'Oh!' she exclaimed, feeling herself flushing red to match her surroundings. 'I'm not . . . I mean, *we're* not . . . I mean, he's mine.'

'Ah.' Reiko sounded almost relieved. 'So you and the errant Mademoiselle Finlay are not *en couple*. This is probably good, I think. She is . . . not reliable.'

'So I gather,' said Anna, as Reiko handed Jack back to her.

'But, eh, perhaps we are making allowances for her, hmm? After all, she has had a – how you say it? – a difficult upbringing.'

'Oh really?' In spite of herself, Anna found her curiosity piqued. So much about Fin remained shrouded in mystery that she couldn't help but be intrigued.

Reiko shook her head ruefully. '*Ah oui, c'est une tragédie.* Deserted by her *papa*, maltreated by her *maman*, abandoned to the state before age of eight . . . ' She shrugged. 'They say such experiences teach one to be self-sufficient – to take what one can get.'

'I can see how that would be the case,' said Anna.

'*Et maintenant, écoute.*' Reiko fixed her with a severe look. 'You will not repeat a word of what I am telling you. She would be most displeased to learn that we are discussing her private affairs behind her back.'

'I promise,' said Anna. 'Not a word.'

Reiko held her gaze for a moment longer. Then the moment passed and she made a grandiose sweep of the room with her hand, her earlier flamboyance once more to the fore. '*Et bien, voici ta chambre.* I am guaranteeing you will be most comfortable in here.'

'But isn't this *your* room?' said Anna. 'Where will you sleep?'

'Ah, *mais non!*' Reiko seemed most amused by the idea. 'This room I use only for the entertaining. For the sleeping, I have other arrangements.'

'And Fin,' Anna ventured, 'where will she be sleeping?'

Reiko made a dismissive noise with her lips, like blowing as raspberry. '*Pour elle, la chaise longue.* That way, she will not be having *ideas.*'

Reiko remained in the room awhile longer, clucking around like a mother hen, rearranging this cushion and putting that sex toy out of sight, before finally leaving Anna to it. Anna immediately sank onto the bed with Jack in her arms, holding him close, relishing being alone with him for the first time since the previous night's activities.

It didn't last long, however. She felt the envelope jammed into her waistband, digging into her flesh, and knew she couldn't continue to carry it around on her person indefinitely. Still holding Jack, she performed a sweep of her new lodgings, searching for an appropriate hiding place. Eventually, she concluded that the dildo drawer was as good a spot as she was going to find, though she had to admit she was largely relying on any potential intruders being too prudish to go rooting around among the strap-ons and other assorted pleasure devices.

She paused to examine the incision in her abdomen. There had been a little oozing, and the skin on either side had turned an angry red, but it was frankly a relief not to find it split open. Still, it was hard not to regard her various leaking appendages as yet more evidence of her loss of control over her own body. While she was at it, she took the opportunity to undress Jack and give him a thorough examination of his own. Everything was as she'd expected to find it, and she could see no sign of the rash Sophie had described. Anna wondered what the hell she'd been wittering on about.

She'd just finished putting him back into his baby-grow when Fin poked her head in.

'Settling in OK?'

Anna nodded.

'How's the little man?'

'He's fine, all things considered. But if we're going to be spending more than a day or so here, I'm going to need supplies: nappies, clothes, wipes, et cetera. The baby-bag's only going to keep us going for so long.'

'We can pick all that up while we're out.'

Anna frowned. 'Out? Why, where are we going?'

Fin looked at Anna as if she'd just descended from the Planet Zombo-tron. 'To prove old Bright Eyes innocent, of course.' She clapped her hands together like a troop-master rallying her charges. 'Boots 'n' saddles! Chop chop!'

## 36

# Watcher

There were few things Anna would have liked more than a shower, a change of clothes and – if she was very lucky – an hour's shut-eye, but Fin was in no mood to delay. It pained her to leave Jack behind so soon after she'd been reunited with him, though she took Fin's point that he'd only encumber them and that their pursuers would be on the lookout for a woman with a newborn in tow. At least she could be confident that Reiko, delighted at being asked to babysit, would lavish him with plenty of attention – though she had a mental image of them returning to find that she'd given him one of her many sex toys to play with.

'You know I've checked here already?' she said as Fin led the way up the steps to Zoe's flat on Dumbarton Road. 'It was pretty much my first port of call.'

She could have phrased it less acerbically, perhaps, but she was tired and in pain, not to mention thoroughly pissed off with Fin's lack of forthcomingness as to the nature of their mission.

'Yeah,' said Fin, as they arrived at Zoe's door, 'but did ya actually go in? Or did ya just stand outside knocking the door like a prize chook?'

'Oh, sure.' Anna rolled her eyes. 'Cos I was totally going to break the door down. Can't see how that could *possibly* have ended badly.'

Fin scoffed, not even dignifying Anna's sarcasm with a response. Then, kneeling on the floor, she took out a long metal implement that looked vaguely like a nail-file with a tapered point, and set to work on the keyhole.

*A lockpick. Of* course *she'd be carrying a lockpick.*

Anna shifted uneasily, convinced that at any moment someone would come out of one of the neighbouring flats and catch them in the act. As the seconds ticked by and Fin seemed no closer to success, both her apprehension and her impatience grew. Eventually, on impulse, she reached past Fin and tried the handle.

The door swung open easily. Fin stared up at her with a look of dumb-founded exasperation. Anna couldn't resist flashing her a smug smile as she stepped past her into the flat.

On Anna's previous visit, her brief peek through the letterbox had given her the impression that the only thing that was untoward about the place was the pile of uncollected mail on the mat. Inside, however, told a different story. Like Anna's house, someone had clearly searched it. Here, however, they hadn't made even a cursory attempt to hide the signs of their presence. The living room and bedroom both looked like they'd survived an earthquake, with furniture upturned, clothes ripped off the bed and tossed in a heap, and the contents of drawers and cupboards strewn on the floor. Gazing down at the aftermath, Anna could *feel* the violence of it: the grow-ing rage and aggression as whoever had done the place over realised that they weren't going to find what they were looking for.

She emerged from the bedroom to find Fin in the hallway, rifling through Zoe's unopened mail.

'Find anything?'

'Only that she's four weeks overdue on her leccy bill.' Fin held up an envelope, the words 'FINAL REMINDER' emblazoned on it in red.

Anna headed through to the kitchen, only to come to an abrupt halt in the doorway. Lying on the table in the centre of the room were the remains of a hastily abandoned meal. There was bread and jam, a carton of milk, and plates and glasses – two of each.

Silently, she doubled back to the hallway and beckoned insistently to Fin. Mystified, Fin put down the mail and followed her. Stepping past Anna into the kitchen, she headed over to the table, lifted the milk carton and sniffed.

'Fresh as a daisy.'

As Anna opened her mouth to speak, she heard a thud coming from across the hallway behind her.

Instantly, she and Fin froze. Fin put a finger to her lips and motioned for Anna to stay put. As Anna watched, she crept out of the kitchen, her Converse-clad feet making no sound.

A few seconds later, all hell broke loose in the bathroom across the hall: a series of crashes and bangs, accompanied by what sounded like a shower curtain being ripped off its rings, and much grunting and cursing. Then, even as Anna pondered whether she should intervene, a shape passed the kitchen doorway in a blur: two figures locked in a visceral embrace, like a pair of wrestlers trying to choke the living daylights out of one another.

Anna hurried after them to the living room, where she found Fin grappling with a small, scrawny young woman who was quite clearly fighting as if her life depended on it – clawing, scratching and screaming an endless torrent of epithets of a seriously graphic nature. Eventually Fin, undoubtedly the more physically able of the two, gained the upper hand and, giving the girl a sharp left hook to the jaw, knocked her backwards onto the sofa.

The girl had a look that could only be described as feral. She lay prostrate where she'd landed, every muscle in her skinny little body tensed, staring up at her captors with wide, white eyes, lips drawn back in a snarl, revealing two rows of small, decayed-looking teeth. Fin stood over her, shaking out her fist, her own heavy breathing mingling with that of the girl.

Still shaken by what she'd just witnessed, Anna made her way over to join Fin. 'Who d'you suppose she is?' she said, not taking her eyes off the young woman on the sofa.

Fin spat and jerked her head sideways, clicking the bones in her neck. 'Whoever she is, looks like the little freeloader's been living here for a while.' She set her sights on the girl again. 'Ya got a name, *chiquita*?'

'Fuck you in the cunt!' spat the girl.

Fin raised a fist. It was more a warning than a sign of sincere intent, but it was more than enough for Anna.

'Stop!'

Placing herself between Fin and the girl, she got down on her hunkers and gave as warm and reassuring a smile as she could muster.

'You poor thing,' she said soothingly. 'It's all right. We aren't going to hurt you.'

*No more than we have already,* she thought, noting the red welt on the girl's jaw where Fin had lamped her.

She hadn't been expecting any dramatic or immediate results from her intervention, but the act of hearing a kindly voice seemed to cause the girl to relax a little. Her shoulders untensed, her lips reverted to a less animalistic position, and her breathing grew easier. Buoyed by her success, Anna reached out and stroked the girl's greasy hair gently, as if she was petting a frightened dog.

'See? Everything's OK.'

With a sudden twist of her head, the girl sank her sharp teeth into the flesh between Anna's thumb and forefinger. Anna yelped and whipped her hand away. The girl was already on her feet, hurtling towards the door.

But Fin was too fast. Diving after her like a rugby player going for a ball, she brought her to the ground with a crash. Then, without giving the girl time to recover, she hauled her upright, dragged her across the room by the scruff of the neck and manhandled her into a dining chair by the window, where she held her in place, one arm wrapped round her neck.

'Ya wanna get that looked at,' she said as Anna got to her feet, gingerly inspecting her injured hand. 'Never know what the little skank's carrying.'

Anna carefully flexed her stinging hand, the jagged imprint of the girl's teeth stencilled into her flesh. She hadn't actually broken the skin, which was somewhat reassuring, but Anna knew she was going to have the bruise to end all bruises in the morning.

Fin, meanwhile, grabbed a pair of curtain ties and bound the girl's wrists to the back legs of the chair, securing her in place. Satisfied that she wasn't going anywhere, she circled round and stood before her, feet parted, fists balled.

'Right then, talk. What ya doing here?'

'I don't have tae tell you *shite*!' said the girl.

Fin responded by grabbing an umbrella from the stand by the fireplace and whacking the girl hard across the shins. She screamed and howled – a dreadful, animal sound that Anna felt deep in her gut. She strode over to Fin, grabbing the brolly.

'What the hell are you playing at?'

At the same moment, the cupboard door of the TV unit on the other side of the room burst open and a shape came hurtling out like a ballistic missile: another dark-haired girl, but considerably smaller and younger.

She launched herself at Fin, striking out with her little fists. As she continued to pummel Fin's legs like a punchbag, Fin burst out laughing.

'Ah, get a loada this! Xena Warrior Princess eat yer heart out!'

'Leave her alone!' cried the one who'd bitten Anna.

At the sound of her voice, the infant ceased her assault on Fin's legs and ran over to her, flinging her arms around her and burying her head against her side. Anna saw the way the pair of them were together and instantly recognised the familial resemblance. Her stomach lurched at the thought of this tiny child, barely more than a toddler, cowering inside the cupboard, listening to her mother, sister or whatever she was being violently assaulted. Even Fin appeared to be experiencing some level of remorse for her actions – though, from the way she kept clenching and unclenching her fists, Anna could tell that a part of her was just itching to get stuck in again.

Preempting a fresh assault, Anna made her way over to the two girls and, maintaining a safe and respectful distance, cleared her throat.

'Truce?'

The older girl lifted her head and gazed up at Anna with still-brimming eyes. The look in them was one of pure hatred, but coupled with a sense of resignation, as if she was so used to being ground down that she knew better than to expect anything else.

'We won't hurt you anymore,' said Anna. 'I promise. Just answer our questions and you can go – both of you.'

The child raised her head and turned to look at Anna. Her eyes were wide and uncomprehending, reflecting an innocence that, unlike the older girl, had yet to be ground out of her. She had a heavy dusting of freckles across her nose and cheeks, Anna now noticed, which couldn't help but make her think of Zoe.

'Is she your daughter?' she asked.

The older girl glowered at Anna some more, then nodded. 'She's *five*,' she added pointedly.

'I've got a son. His name's Jack. Only he's a whole lot younger than her.'

The older girl, unmoved by this act of sharing, said nothing.

'My name's Ruby,' said the child in a slow, singsongy sort of voice.

Anna smiled, wishing she had the natural ability to talk to children that so many of her friends and colleagues seemed to possess. 'That's a nice name.'

Ruby bit her bottom lip and gave a little half-smile, clearly confused by the kindly words coming from the mouth of one of her mother's abusers.

Anna turned to the girl's mother again. 'What's *your* name?'

'Mandy.' Delivered in the same tone as *fuck you*.

'Are you going to do anything daft, Mandy?' She gestured to the curtain ties. 'Or am I safe to undo these?'

Mandy gave a sullen shrug. 'Ye kin dae whit ye like.'

Anna hesitated. She glanced back at Fin, who was leaning against the fireplace, watching the proceedings with barefaced contempt. One look at her was enough to tell Anna what she thought of this idea. Well, tough. Violence hadn't got them anywhere so far.

She moved behind the chair and untied Mandy. Immediately, Ruby leapt into her mother's lap and flung her arms around her – a move which Mandy was only too eager to reciprocate, clinging to her daughter for dear life. Anna gave them as much time together as she felt she could – too little, she was sure – before clearing her throat again.

'About those questions . . .'

Mandy clung to Ruby for a little longer, then whispered something in the girl's ear. Ruby withdrew her arms from around her mother and shuffled into a sitting position in her lap. Mandy lifted her head and met Anna's gaze with tired resignation.

'G'wan, then.'

Anna decided to start with the most pertinent question – the one Fin had tried and failed to get an answer to.

'What are you doing here?'

'*She* said we could stay here.'

'Who? Zoe?'

'Aye. She wis *nice* to me.'

She shot a venomous look in Fin's direction as she spoke. Fin bared her teeth and said nothing.

'She said you could stay in her flat?' said Anna. 'Just like that? Forgive me if I find that slightly hard to believe.'

'Don't care whit ye believe,' said Mandy sulkily. 'She's proper decent, so she is. Took us in when we had naewhere else tae go. Made Ruby up a bed on the sofa an' aw.'

It still sounded farfetched, though Anna wondered if that was simply because *she* would never have considered doing anything like that. With Zoe, all bets were off. Too warm-hearted for her own good.

'When did you last see her?'

'Night before New Year. Night she took us in.'

'And you've been staying here all this time?'

Mandy shrugged. 'Last coupla weeks, jist. Mibby a bit mair. I havnae been keeping track. She was already gone when we got here.'

'And this' – Anna gestured to their ransacked surroundings – 'was this how you found the place?'

'Aye!' Mandy sounded genuinely hurt. 'It wisnae *me*.'

'I'm not suggesting it was. But d'you have any idea who *did* do it?'

Mandy said nothing. She lowered her eyes and clutched Ruby tighter.

'Mandy? Is there something you're not telling me?'

Mandy steadfastly avoided Anna's gaze.

Anna folded her arms and watched her, saying nothing. She knew from experience that, more often than not, the best way to loosen a reluctant tongue was to give it a silence to fill. Most people, conditioned to respect the normal ebb and flow of conversation, would struggle to remain mute for long. And so it proved with Mandy. After only a few seconds, she caved.

'Aww, *fuck*! I wis told tae watch yer pal, OK? Tae keep an eye on her, see where she went, who she spoke to. I didnae want tae, but he never given me any choice. And after she left, he said tae watch the flat – y'know, case she came back.' She shrugged petulantly, as if challenging Anna to do something about it.

Fin was already moving towards her, an ugly look in her eyes. 'You little sneak . . . '

Anna stalled her with a raise of her hand and a warning glance. 'Who's "he"? The one who made you do all this.'

'A cop. Detective something-or-other. Mid-thirties, no bad-looking. Wears flashy suits, drives a posh motor. Porsche, I think, or a Jag. He done me a coupla times for hooking or shoplifting. S'how he got me tae spy on yer pal. Said if I didnae, he'd gie me the jail and Ruby'd get taken into care.

I didnae have a choice.' She lowered her voice to a whisper. 'He was gonnae hurt Ruby.'

Fin made a disgusted sound at the back of her throat. Anna, though, could understand Mandy's compulsion to protect her daughter only too well.

'This man,' she said, 'this detective. You don't happen to remember what his name was?'

'Cannae 'member cos he never telt me. We werenae exactly on social terms.'

'*That's* convenient,' said Fin.

Anna shot Fin another warning look, then fixed her attention on Mandy again. 'And did he ever give you any sort of feel for *why* he had you watching Zoe?'

Mandy glanced uncertainly at Ruby, still perched on her knee, hanging on her and Anna's every word. 'On ye go, muffin. Mummy needs tae do grown-up talking.'

Instantly, Ruby clambered down and made her way to the other end of the room, where she plonked herself down on the floor with her back to them and sat cross-legged, covering her ears with both hands. Anna got the distinct impression that this was something she was used to doing, and wondered just how many different activities came under the umbrella of 'grown-up talking'.

'I figured it had something tae dae wi the abuse,' said Mandy.

Anna's ears pricked up. Behind her, she sensed Fin standing up a little straighter.

'What do you know about that?'

Mandy shrugged. 'Said she'd found out a buncha kids'd been interfered wi back in the nineties. Boys fae good families going tae good schools. And then, outta the blue, someone stuck a package through her door. Photies of a buncha boys and a DVD of some old perv making a boy tug hisself aff. That bloke who got kilt a few weeks back. Broad-something.'

'Broadhurst,' said Anna quietly.

'Aye. I'm no saying I'd of done what they done tae him, but ye cannae tell me he didnae deserve it.'

Anna offered no opinion on that particular line of thought. 'You said "schools" plural. So this isn't just about Willow Bank.'

'She said it was aw different schools in aw different places – Glesca, Lanarkshire, Stirling . . . Said it went on for years. There was even a big investigation intae wan o' them. That boys' school that was in the news way back.'

'Are you talking about Netherfield Academy?' said Anna. She'd been living in Rome when the story had broken, but it had been a big enough deal that even the Italian press had covered it.

'S'right. Said someone'd telt her the whole thing was sunk fae the inside. That the cop in charge got leaned on – that there was folk working tae make sure naeb'dy saw the inside of a jail cell. Dark forces, she called 'em.'

'"Dark forces"?' Fin echoed, incredulous. 'Tinfoil hat wearers of the world unite!'

Mandy glowered at her. 'That's what *she* called 'em. I'm jist telling yese what she said.'

'I know you are,' said Anna. 'Go on.'

With some reluctance, Mandy wrested her eyes away from Fin. 'She said, "Cadogan knows the truth". That was his name: Cadogan. Said they'd leant on him tae make sure the whole thing fell apart. Dinnae ask me whit the truth is or how come he knows, cos I'm no a fucking psychic, right?'

'Ya don't say,' snorted Fin.

Mandy paused to give Fin another long, hard glare before turning back to Anna. 'She had a list of names too. The folk who done the abuse. Big, important people. Like politicians, lawyers, even folk aff the telly. That Broadhurst – he wis oan it.'

*The list.* The list the taxi driver had tried to get Anna to hand over. And presumably what the people who'd searched her place and Zoe's had been looking for.

'And the detective you were working for – did you tell *him* about this list?'

'I wisnae *working* for him,' said Mandy adamantly. 'I wis *coerced*.'

'That's an awfy big word for a silly wee lassie,' Fin remarked. 'Bet ya still took his thirty pieces of silver all the same.'

Mandy pulled back her lips in a snarl, and for a moment Anna thought the pair of them were going to fly at one another again. But instead, Mandy turned to Anna once more, with a look that somehow succeeded in conveying both sullenness and contrition simultaneously.

'Aye,' she said, 'I telt him. And I'm no proud of masel. But I had tae put Ruby first. She's all I've got.'

Anna glanced across at Ruby, still sitting cross-legged on the floor with her hands over her ears, and knew there was no way she could hold any of this against Mandy. A month or so ago, she almost certainly would have. But she was, in so many respects, a different person now.

She turned back to Mandy. 'This detective. Have you got . . . I don't know, a phone number for him?'

Mandy scoffed. 'Aye, right. Like he'd want *me* calling him in the middla wan of his important meetings an' embarrassing him.'

'Then how d'you keep in touch?'

'*He* keeps in touch wi *me*.' Mandy rolled her eyes, clearly resenting having to explain herself. 'In the beginning, I'd report tae him every coupla nights – same time an' place each time. But after me 'n' Ruby moved in here, he said there wis nae need for that anymair. Now he drops in unannounced – so's he kin check up oan me, he says. Make sure I'm behaving masel. I havnae seen him since Friday. Dunno when he'll be here next.'

'And you've no idea where Zoe might have gone?'

Mandy shook her head. 'Nuh. But wherever she is, I hope she's awright.'

Anna gave a small smile of agreement, then turned to Fin with a weary sigh. 'Let's go. She's told us everything she knows.'

Fin looked dubiously at Mandy. 'Ya sure about that?'

'I'm no fucking lying!' snarled Mandy.

Anna, who didn't fully trust Fin not to attempt one last round of her own personal style of interrogation, placed herself firmly between the two of them.

'I'm sure.'

Fin opened her mouth to object, then scoffed and shook her head. 'All right. But mark me,' she jabbed a finger at Mandy, 'you work for us now. If Bright Eyes comes back here, or you get word from her at all, you tell *us*, not them. You'll find us at the flat above Maggie May's on Trongate.' She turned to Anna. 'Give her yer number.'

She watched, arms folded, as Anna and a thoroughly reluctant Mandy exchanged phone numbers.

'Remember,' she said, once they were done, jabbing her finger at Mandy again, 'that detective comes back, you come and find us. Hear *anything*, you come and find us.'

'Aye, I'll dae it,' muttered Mandy, eyes on her shoes.

'Make sure ya do, else I'll come and find *you*, and I swear I'll break every bone in yer skanky little body.'

'Let's *go*,' said Anna firmly.

She took hold of Fin's arm and practically dragged her towards the door. As they stepped out into the hallway, Mandy's hesitant voice piped up behind them.

'I can still stay here, though – right?'

Fin's only response was a disgusted noise at the back of her throat as she strode out.

Anna turned to look back at Mandy, standing in the living room doorway with one arm around Ruby, who clung to her mother, both arms wrapped round her legs. She gave them one last apologetic wince, then hurried after Fin.

# 37

# This Much We Know

It was dark by the time Anna and Fin got back to Reiko's flat. They'd stopped off on the way to pick up various provisions: food, spare clothes and various items Jack would need over the coming days. To Anna's irritation but no great surprise, Fin had happily watched her pay for everything.

Reiko was waiting for them, in obvious high spirits and, if possible, even more flamboyant than before. She and Jack had had a *gorgeous* time together, she said, and now he was *tout fatigué*. She showed Anna through to the red room, where she found Jack asleep in a makeshift crib fashioned from a laundry basket lined with blankets. Anna managed to fight the overwhelming urge to pick him up and hold him to her, and left him in peace and quiet.

'He is a fine specimen,' Reiko informed her. 'He will grow into a very big boy, I think.'

'Oh good,' said Anna, because what else *was* there to say?

Despite Anna's protestations that she'd already done too much for them, Reiko insisted on making dinner, stating that it was *tout mon plaisir* and roping a sullen-looking Fin into assisting. Anna, banished to the sofa, listened to Reiko bustling around the kitchen, pausing every so often to upbraid Fin for getting in the way or making a dog's dinner of the salad.

Afterwards, they ate together in the living room, perched on cushions around the coffee table. Anna and Fin dutifully made small talk with their host until, shortly after nine, Reiko announced that she too was *toute fatiguée* and bade them goodnight, bending down to kiss Anna on both cheeks and giving Fin a surly look, before departing with a swish of her red kimono.

'She's always been an early bird,' Fin explained as Reiko's bedroom door clicked shut behind her. 'In bed by nine and up at first light. Could never understand it myself.'

Not for the first time, Anna tried and failed to picture Fin and Reiko as an item in a previous life.

'And tell me, was she always this . . . exuberant?'

Fin chuckled. 'Believe me, you ain't seen nothing yet. She's not actually French, y'know. She was born in Coatbridge. That's just a character she plays.'

'Seriously?'

Fin smiled enigmatically, leaving Anna no clearer as to whether or not she was pulling her leg.

'But she's solid as a rock,' she went on after a pause. 'Long as you're under her roof, no harm's gonna come to you – or the tiddler.'

'Good to know,' said Anna.

She wished she felt so confident about Reiko's ability to successfully hold even a single determined intruder at bay, solid as a rock or not. So far, they'd managed to keep under the radar, but she wasn't remotely optimistic about this state of affairs lasting indefinitely. Every moment that passed, the odds of their pursuers tracking them down multiplied. Which meant that, if they were going to get to the bottom of whatever Zoe had got herself mixed up in, the clock was most definitely ticking.

'So,' she said, 'where do we go from here?'

Fin thought about it, scratching her belly from a reclining position on the sofa. 'Well, let's start with what we know for sure. We know old Bright Eyes got her hands on evidence that boys were being abused at a buncha schools during the nineties . . . '

'Including her brother.'

Fin raised a warning finger. 'Gonna chalk that one up as a maybe. A photo on its own ain't proof. What we *can* say for certain is someone *wanted* her to think he'd been interfered with – by a bloke who just so happened to turn up stabbed to death the very day she did her vanishing trick. Hella convenient, dontchathink?'

'You think she was set up?' said Anna, wishing she could believe it. 'That someone wanted to make this look like a revenge killing?'

Fin shrugged. 'Dunno. But looks like they'd been keeping tabs on her for a while – since well before old Broadarse carked it. And I reckon if she had the presence of mind to stash the evidence and drop a few well-placed hints about its whereabouts to yer good self, she had enough of an inkling something wasn't right to make contingencies. I'm telling ya, she's cannier than ya think.'

'OK,' said Anna, refusing to take the bait, 'but who's spearheading all this? You say it's not the police, but remember, Mandy said the guy who got her to spy on Zoe had arrested her before. And if we take her at her word—'

'*I* wouldn't.'

'*If* we take her at her word,' Anna said firmly, 'then it means at least one bona fide police officer is involved in this.'

Fin shrugged. 'Rogue operative? Someone with a vested interest? Or someone they've got over a barrel? World's fulla bent cops in hock to crims. And it's not like *he's* playing by the rulebook. I mean, c'mon – using a clapped-out hooker as yer eyes 'n' ears? F'ya ask me, whoever's doing this is (a) desperate and (b) got finite resources at their disposal. I say we find that list of names and we'll be a good step closer to finding out who's pulling the strings.'

'You think it's someone on the list?' said Anna, frowning in surprise. 'One of the abusers?'

'Someone,' said Fin, 'or a whole buncha someones. Resources might be stretched, but I bet yer bottom dollar this ain't just one guy's pet project.'

Anna thought about it, saying nothing. Her mind turned to Mandy's description of her handler, as it had done on various occasions throughout the evening. While she doubted that there was any great shortage in the CID of good-looking, well-dressed men in their thirties who drove flash sports cars, if there was one thing the events of the last few days had taught her, it was that coincidences should not be taken lightly.

'What I don't get,' she said, after a lengthy pause, 'is if the people behind this are the abusers themselves, why kill Broadhurst? Why bump off one of their own?'

Fin shrugged. 'Who can fathom the ways of the pervert mind? Doubt this lot've got too many scruples 'bout doing over one of their own. Maybe someone was using Bright Eyes to settle an old debt.'

Once again, Anna was silent for several moments as she digested this. 'It still doesn't mean she didn't do it,' she said eventually. 'OK, I can buy the whole "setting her up" angle, but that doesn't necessarily mean they framed her. For all we know, they gave her just enough of a dunt in the right direction, then sat back and watched her do their bidding for them.'

Fin sighed. 'We back to this again? Jaysus, woman, you're like a dog with a bone! I'm telling ya, she's not the sort.'

'So you keep saying. And maybe you truly do have some unique insight into her character because of some shared experience the two of you had a few summers back. But I've known her a lot longer, and I'm telling you, she loved her brother with every bone in her body, and if she thought someone had done something like *that* to him, I shudder to think what she'd have been capable of. Believe me, I want her to be innocent just as much as you, but wanting and being aren't the same thing.'

Fin stared back at Anna obstinately. 'Believe what you like. But when you've been around the sort of people I've been around, you get a feel for what folk are capable of. Some people, you just *know*, OK?'

Anna sighed and shook her head. What it must be to have absolute certainty in the face of so much powerful evidence to the contrary!

'OK,' she said after a moment, 'so you're saying one or more of Broadhurst's fellow abusers decided to bump him off and frame it to look like Zoe's doing. Why didn't they go the whole hog, then? I mean, they presumably had a plan to implicate her. Why haven't they put it into action? Why isn't she murder suspect number one right now?'

'Cos she cleared out before they had a chance?' Fin manoeuvred herself into a more upright position. 'Roll with me here. Somehow or other, she gets wind of what's going on and she skedaddles before they can fit her up. And now she's laying low, biding her time or whatevs, and she's got this list of names, and they're pulling out all the stops on the down-low to get their hands on her and it 'fore she blabs to the wrong people. Look at the mess they made of her gaff. To me, that doesn't say "all going according to plan". That says "everything went tits up and we never had time to cover our tracks".'

It sounded halfway plausible, though once again it was predicated on

Fin's unshakeable conviction that Zoe couldn't have done it. But Fin clearly wasn't going to be persuaded otherwise.

Anna groaned and rubbed her eyes. Her brain was fuzzy from lack of sleep, and the warm air in Reiko's flat wasn't making her any more lucid.

'So what now?'

'Now?' Fin gave her a long, severe look. 'Now it's beddy-byes time for you, Mama. Go on – ya look beat.'

'What about you?' Tired though she was, Anna was reluctant to throw in the towel with Fin still wide awake and plotting.

'Oh, I'll turn in in a bit. Meantime I'll put out the feelers – make some calls to people, ask 'em to keep their eyes peeled for any red-haired strangers who've suddenly popped up in their neck of the woods.'

'What sort of people?'

Fin bared her teeth. 'The sort a proper laudy-daw like yourself needn't concern herself with.' She jerked her head towards the door and clicked her tongue. 'Go on, beat it. You've done well to keep yer head up. I'm well impressed.'

With some lingering reluctance, Anna got to her feet. As she reached the doorway, she stopped and turned.

'Fin.'

Fin lifted her head and gazed over the back of the sofa.

'You're really convinced she's innocent?'

Fin was silent for a long moment. 'I'm here, ain't I? And that's a mighty big risk to be taking, me having unfinished business with the local constabulary and all. So aye, I'm convinced.'

It was as good an answer as Anna was going to get. She nodded good-night and sloped through to the red room, where she found Jack still fast asleep in his makeshift crib. She didn't think he'd ever slept uninterrupted for this long before. Whatever Reiko had done with him had well and truly knackered him. Feeding schedule be damned – she'd just have to trust him to let her know when he was hungry.

Before turning in, she got out her phone and composed a text to Zoe.

**Zoe, please get in touch. Things are happening here that I don't fully understand. Whatever trouble you're in, I'm sure we can sort it if we work together.**

She hesitated for a moment, then added:

**At least let me know you're OK.**

She hit Send. Then, with what little energy remained, she loosened her grubby, sweaty clothes and crawled under the bedcovers. She was asleep almost before her head touched the pillow.

# 38

## Mama Duty

*Monday 1 February*

Anna awoke with a start, as if someone had pegged her nose in her sleep and caused her to choke. She looked around, blinking her eyes into focus. Daylight streamed in through the open curtains. She heard the sounds of traffic in the street below. With mounting disbelief, she realised she must have slept through the entire night – something that hadn't happened since Jack had been born.

*Jack.*

Instantly, a million awful thoughts flooded her mind, most powerful of all the fear that someone had taken him. No way could a four-week-old baby have slept through the night and on into the morning. He should be bawling.

Dragging herself out of bed, she stumbled over to the makeshift crib. Her worst fears were confirmed as she stared down at the empty space where he should have been lying. As she stood there, blind panic over-whelming her, the noise of jaunty music and crash-bang-wallop sound effects reached her ears from across the hall. She heard Fin's familiar throaty cackle. On shaky legs, she hurried out of the bedroom and stumbled through to the living room.

There on the sofa, perched in Fin's lap with the back of his head resting against her chest, was Jack. He was stark naked and looking thoroughly content with this state of affairs as he stared, transfixed, at the Tom and Jerry cartoon on the TV. As the double-barrelled shotgun Tom had been attempting to use to blow Jerry away rebounded on him and obliterated the top half of his own head, Fin roared with laughter, then turned and looked up at Anna with a broad grin.

'Back in the land of the living, are ya? I tell ya, Prof, if sleeping was an Olympic sport, you'd get the gold medal.'

'But what . . . when . . . ?' Anna spluttered.

'He woke up a coupla times in the night. I took care of things. You were out for the count so I figured, shame to wake ya. I used the boob juice from the fridge.'

'Uh-huh?' said Anna, half-dazed. 'What's with the full frontal nudity?'

'Messed himself once or twice. I got fed up putting clean nappies on him, so I decided why not let him run free like nature intended? Plus, he's got a bit of a rash down there. Thought it'd be good to give it an airing.'

*Why am I the only one not seeing this rash?* Anna thought.

'Well,' she said, rather uncharitably, 'don't come crying to me when he unloads in your lap.' She looked around. 'Where's Reiko? Thought she was an early riser.'

'Ah.' Fin stood up and, perhaps motivated by the talk of unexpected bowel movements, deposited Jack into Anna's arms. 'Cleared out first thing. Strode in with her bags all packed and announced she was *goeeng to stay weeth one of her lovers.* Said she didn't know what the pair of us had got ourselves mixed up in, but that she planned on keeping her schnoz clean.'

*So much for 'solid as a rock'.*

Fin shrugged disarmingly. 'So you 'n' Junior got the whole place to yourselves.'

'Why? Where are *you* going?'

'Aberdeen.'

''*Scuse* me?'

'Been waiting so I could tell ya: contact of mine came good. Eyewitness sighting: red-haired girlie in her early thirties been working in a café in Dyce last coupla weeks. Could be nothing, but the description and timeframe check out. I'm gonna go have a look-see. Means you're on mama duty.'

Fin set off, zipping up her motorcycle leathers on her way out the door. And then it was just Anna and Jack once more, a return – of sorts – to business as usual. Anna couldn't help noting that Jack appeared to have adapted quite readily to life on the lam, and indeed had been a good deal more settled during the last twenty-four hours than at any point since they'd left the hospital. She wasn't sure what that said about her parenting skills, but she supposed she should be glad the recent disruptions to his routine didn't appear to have had an adverse effect on him.

He nodded off fairly quickly, and on top of a full night's sleep Anna was able to enjoy both an actual sit-down breakfast and her first proper shower in nearly a month. Afterwards, she returned to the living room, having helped herself to one of the numerous silk gowns in Reiko's wardrobe, and settled herself on the sofa with her phone. There had been no response to the text she'd sent Zoe the previous night, though she wasn't overly surprised. It was becoming increasingly apparent that, even if Zoe *was* out there somewhere, alive and well, she was either unable or unwilling to respond to Anna's attempts to make contact. All their hopes, it seemed, rested on one of Fin's mysterious sources coming good – a state of affairs that left Anna feeling pathetically small and powerless. Still, she was damned if she was just going to mooch around Reiko's flat all day while Fin was roaring up the A90 on a mission that, however forlorn, was at least a proactive one. Besides, there *was* something she could be doing – something ideally suited to her own particular skillset. *Research.*

Over the course of the next couple of hours, Anna set about plugging the gaps in her knowledge of the Netherfield investigation. She read all about the missing evidence; the failure to interview key witnesses; the public shaming of Tom Cadogan, the DCI who'd led the investigation. She gazed down at the picture of the massive, jowly figure stumbling bleary-eyed out of the Old College Bar on High Street and wondered just how credible this talk of a cover-up really was.

*Never ascribe to malice that which is adequately explained by incompetence,* as one dead pundit or another had once said. And perhaps it was true. Perhaps the failure to prosecute a single person in the biggest institutional child abuse scandal Scotland had ever seen really was just down to the industrial-strength ineptitude of one man. But if there was more to it than that – if, as Zoe had evidently believed, he really *had* been leant on to ensure that the perpetrators were protected – then he might just be the key to unlocking the entire mystery.

There was just one problem: like Zoe, Tom Cadogan had dropped off the face of the earth. The last public record of him was in an article published in November 2003, stating that he had been demoted by two ranks and bumped back to uniform following a tribunal into his conduct during the Netherfield affair. She checked the online phone book, but there wasn't a single Tom or Thomas Cadogan registered in Glasgow, or indeed anywhere else in Scotland. Nor could she find any deaths recorded in his name on the ScotlandsPeople website – which suggested that, unless his records had somehow been erased or he'd left the country, he was still very much alive . . . somewhere.

She rolled her shoulders back and massaged her stiff neck. Spending all this time reading screeds of text on her phone's tiny screen was far from ideal. She wished she had her iPad, or better yet her computer, but needs must.

As it happened, it was in part because of the limitations of the eleven-centimetre screen that she initially failed to spot what was staring her in the face. One of the articles about the Netherfield case – a lengthy special on the fall of Cadogan, published in the *Caledonian* following his tribunal – featured a number of photos of the man himself, including the widely circulated one of him staggering out of the boozer, as well as a handful that showed him as a younger man. Someone had even managed to dig out his police graduation photograph, showing around forty newly inducted probationers arranged in three rows outside Tulliallan Castle circa the mid-seventies. Cadogan himself had helpfully been circled – considerably less overweight back then than he'd been in the more recent photos but still an imposing figure, towering half a head higher than everyone else in his row. It wasn't until Anna, re-reading the article in case she'd missed something, scrolled past the image for a second time that she spotted it. Or rather, the unconscious part of her brain did. Her breathing quickened. She pinched the screen to enlarge the image, zooming in until only the faces of Cadogan and the two men standing on either side of him were visible.

It was the officer to his right that had caught her attention. She zoomed in even further, expanding the image until his face filled the screen. The resolution was poor, the individual pixels giant blurry squares more reminiscent of a mosaic than an actual photograph. But it was enough.

Even as she continued to squint at the man's face, it seemed to gain definition, her memory filling in the gaps where no detail existed. Like Cadogan, he'd been a young man then – more than three decades younger than when she'd encountered him herself six years ago, and with a whole lot more hair on his head. But it was definitely him. The likeness was unmistakable.

Of course, she had no idea whether he and Cadogan had kept in touch after graduation or had simply gone their separate ways as soon as the photo had been taken, never to cross paths again. And yet everything she knew about the police told her that the ties that bound them together were unusually strong – like those of family, as Vasilico had once told her. And even if these two particular officers hadn't remained penpals for these rest of their careers, the police grapevine was such that word was bound to have got around as to what had become of the detective who'd presided over the Netherfield fiasco.

The point was, she had history with this particular officer. History and leverage. And as such, he was her best lead.

# 39

# Good Cop

The bus came to a halt on a neat suburban street in the Shawlands area, some three miles south of the Clyde. Anna disembarked and set off, Jack nestled snugly against her in his sling. She kept the hood of her puffer jacket up, though it went against every instinct she possessed. She wasn't sure whether it was something that stemmed from her own experiences or simply an awareness, afforded by the work she did, of just how vulnerable women actually were in public spaces, but she detested hoods and the effect they had on her peripheral vision. Now, though, she reluctantly concluded that the anonymity it afforded her outweighed the fact that it also made it much easier for someone to creep up behind her unnoticed.

She turned up the driveway of a nice-looking bungalow, all neatly trimmed hedgerows and crazy paving, and rang the bell. A moment later, the door opened to reveal a short, pot-bellied man of about sixty. He was suffering from an aggressive onset of male pattern baldness and had the sort of leathery, careworn face one tended to associate with people who'd spent most of their lives exposed to the elements. It wasn't an unkind face, but it didn't look like the sort that did much smiling.

'Can I help you?'

'Hello, Detective,' said Anna. 'Remember me?'

Former Detective Inspector Bill Norton continued to stare at her uncomprehendingly. Then, as she lowered her hood, recognition dawned on his craggy features.

'Dr Scavolini.'

In a strange way, he didn't seem surprised to see her.

\* \* \*

'After we tied up the Kelvingrove case, I stayed on for a bit, pitching in here and there where there was a use for me, but it ended up being my last major investigation.'

Anna sat in the living room, listening to Norton's raised voice coming from the adjacent kitchen. Porcelain ornaments covered virtually every available surface; the mantelpiece above the hearth was lined with framed photographs, many of them showing Norton with a stout, ruddy-cheeked woman of around the same age. It was, in every respect, the polar opposite of Clive Sullivan's cold, austere home.

'I collected my pension just over a year later. It was long overdue, and every man and his dog was saying I should call it a day. I like to think they had my best interests at heart, but I fancy the truth is they were just sick of the sight of me.'

Anna looked up as he appeared in the doorway, carrying a laden tea-tray.

'D'you miss it?' she asked.

'Sometimes. By the time I left, I felt I'd done about as much as I realistically could.'

He set the tray down on a side table and poured tea and milk into two matching cups. He motioned to the sugar jar. Anna shook her head.

'You don't always notice it's happening,' he went on, 'but there comes a point when you've no option but to conclude that the sheer number of brick walls you run into, the sheer number of doors you find locked when you try to go through them, aren't mere coincidences. For whatever reason, your face doesn't fit. You're too "this" or not "that" enough. You begin to feel that you're a rat in a maze – that there's only one possible path open to you: the one its maker chose for you.'

He eased himself into the chair opposite her. 'It's mostly the little things I find myself hankering after – like the late-night pizza run when we were knee-deep in a case and we knew no one would be getting home that night, or doing the *Tribune* crossword with Billy Martin in the canteen. I miss the people. I don't miss the institution.'

He gestured to the nearest framed photo – one of himself and the woman Anna had already concluded was his wife. 'It was really Moira who made the decision for me. She saw what all the backbiting and the politics were doing to me. "Bill," she said, "either you get out now or you'll drive yourself into an early grave". I think she was probably onto something.'

'And Moira,' Anna ventured, 'is she . . . ?'

'Oh, she's still alive and kicking,' said Norton. 'Plays bridge on a Monday, otherwise I'm sure she'd have been delighted to meet you and the little one. Congratulations, by the by.'

'Thank you,' Anna said automatically. She was becoming more accepting of people saying it to her. It no longer seemed quite so patently absurd now that they were reacting to something tangible.

'We weren't able to have any ourselves,' Norton said, with a note of regret. 'But we make do with our lot. I sometimes wonder if the officers who called me "sir" weren't something of a substitute for having kids of my own. Lord knows, they needed taking in hand often enough.'

'Officers like Detective Sergeant Murray, you mean?' said Anna.

Norton stiffened, his cup halfway to his lips. For a moment, he didn't move. Then slowly, deliberately, he took a sip. 'Amongst others.' He set the cup down. 'And now, as pleasant as it is to be sitting here reminiscing about the bad old days, shall we turn to business?'

Anna looked at him in surprise.

'Come now – you know as well as I do that you didn't just drop by to say "how-d'you-do".'

Carefully, Anna lowered her own cup and set it on the side table. 'I'm trying to track down a man who seems to have effectively ceased to exist. A former colleague of yours, I believe – a DCI Tom Cadogan.'

Norton swallowed, his facial muscles tightening. 'I'm not sure if I—'

'Oh, I know for a fact that you do. I have photographic evidence that you were in the same graduation group. Besides, I doubt you could have failed to notice the prominent coverage he received in the media a number of years ago.'

'Now listen.' Norton raised a warning finger in Anna's direction – a finger that she now noticed had a slight tremor. 'Whatever it is you're doing, you need to stop it right now. No good will come of digging up the past.'

'Who said anything about digging up the past? I haven't even told you why I'm looking for him.'

'No, but I can guess what this is about. The only thing anyone ever wants to talk to Tom Cadogan about.'

'Netherfield,' said Anna quietly.

The pain in Norton's eyes was palpable. 'Just let it go,' he said.

Anna had been prepared for this reaction. It was why she'd deliberately laid the groundwork by mentioning DS Murray earlier.

'You know,' she said, 'at the time, I let myself believe you were doing me a favour, making the charges against me disappear in exchange for my not taking the way your sergeant treated me any further. That was certainly how you presented it to me back then. But I've had ample time to think about it over the years, and I now realise it was actually the other way round. I was the one doing *you* a favour – sparing you and your employers the PR nightmare of a public investigation into one of your own man-handling and ill-treating a detainee.'

'I see,' said Norton, his expression stony. 'And as a result, you now feel I owe you.'

Anna said nothing, preferring to let her silence do the talking.

'I dealt with him, didn't I?' said Norton, his temper revealing itself for the briefest of moments. 'His career hit the skids once I'd made sure word got round about the sort of man he was. Last I heard, he's directing sheep in some godforsaken corner of the Outer Hebrides.'

'And I'm sure the residents of the Outer Hebrides are profoundly grateful for your intervention – but it doesn't stop me being right, does it?'

Norton shook his head. He seemed more disappointed than angry. 'You're as obstinate as ever.'

'I prefer "determined".'

'That too.' He sighed in resignation.

Sensing that they'd come to an understanding, Anna leaned forward. 'So,' she prompted him, 'Netherfield.'

Norton shook his head. 'That was a shameful, shameful series of events. None of it turned out the way it should have.'

'The official account is that it was a botch job from start to finish. Cadogan messed up and paid the price.'

'No.' Norton's finger shot up. 'Those *boys* paid the price. They never saw justice done. They put their trust in us and we failed them.'

'*He* failed them, you mean? I've read the press coverage. I know all about the missing statements. The liquid lunches.'

'The press always did like a neat, cut-and-dried story. They wanted a sacrificial lamb, and that's what they got. I'm not saying he wasn't at fault,' he added, before Anna could respond. 'He was a drunk, he was fond of cutting corners, and he had a reputation for taking backhanders. Most of what they said about him was true. But there was an awful lot that didn't get printed. A lot of names left off the roll of dishonour. A lot went on behind the scenes that no one got to hear about.'

'Are you saying the investigation was sabotaged from the inside?'

Norton pursed his lips tightly. 'I'm not saying that,' he said carefully. 'I'm just saying that there were other men besides Tom Cadogan who should have been at that tribunal, answering for their actions.'

She was beginning to tire of all these riddles. She wasn't sure how much Norton knew himself and, for whatever reason, wasn't telling her, and how much he was merely surmising. One thing was for sure: most of the answers she sought would need to come from the horse's mouth.

'Do you know where he is now?'

Norton gave her a long, hard look. 'You have to understand how hard this all was on him. The media hounded him relentlessly. And then there was the public reaction. The only thing folk hate as much as a paedophile is a paedophile enabler, and as far as they were concerned, that's what he was. In the end, it got so bad he had to change his name.'

That would explain why all record of him had suddenly dried up.

'To what?'

Norton looked at Anna sharply. 'I hope you're not planning to make life hard for him. He's had a tough time of it. It would be a kindness to let him live out his last days in obscurity.'

Anna met his gaze without wavering. 'I just want to ask him some questions. I'll work it out myself eventually, you know. Now I know he changed his name, it's just a matter of accessing the right records. Somewhere or other, there's bound to be a paper trail. Might as well tell me now and save me the legwork.'

She wasn't sure this was actually true. If Cadogan hadn't done it by statutory declaration, there was every chance he really would have been able to slip under the radar.

'I won't mention that it came from you,' she went on, as Norton continued to say nothing. 'After today, you'll never see me again.'

Norton fixed her with the same deep, probing gaze she remembered so well.

'Gil,' he said eventually. 'He calls himself Gil McLaren.'

## 40

# Bad Cop

Several areas in Glasgow had what might be termed a reputation, but they all paled in comparison to Summerhill. It had long topped the league tables for both deprivation and criminal activity, and rumour was that the authorities, having failed to get a grip on the situation, had effectively ceded control to the local gangs, on the grounds that they commanded more respect from the inhabitants and were therefore more likely to actually be obeyed. Oddly enough, this gave Anna some measure of comfort. She had a feeling this was the last place her pursuers would look for her.

All the same, she kept her hood up and an arm coiled protectively around Jack, snug against her in his sling, as she stood across the road from the cluster of high-rises that comprised the Ardmore Estate, watching a hulking, dishevelled figure slowly making his way along the exposed stretch of pavement on the other side of the road. He was in his late fifties, sporting a weather-beaten trench coat that reached his knees. A heavy shopping bag hung from each hand. Surreptitiously, she compared him to the photo on her phone.

As he turned onto the overgrown footpath leading to the flats, she crossed the road and strode after him.

'Mr McLaren!'

They were on an exposed spot at the top of a hill, and the eddying wind drowned out her voice. She tried again, louder this time.

'Mr McLaren, can I have a word?'

This time, he heard her. He glanced briefly over his shoulder, then carried on, quickening his pace. She did likewise.

'I really need to speak to you. Please, Mr McLaren . . . or would you prefer it if I addressed you as DCI Cadogan?'

That made him stop. He remained stock-still with his back to her, shoulders rising and falling in time with his breathing. As she came to a halt, he slowly turned to face her.

'What do you want?'

'I have some questions for you. Questions about a case you were involved with in the early 2000s.'

His eyes were distrustful, but there was a hint of something else in them too. He swayed slightly from side to side, breathing heavily through his half-open mouth, his tongue thick and slightly protruding.

'I've nothing to say to you.'

He turned to go.

'I can see this wasn't a good time,' said Anna, raising her voice after him. 'Maybe you'd prefer I came back later – perhaps with some members of the press in tow.'

He turned to face her once more. This time, there was no mistaking the look in his eyes: pure, unadulterated fear.

She continued towards him. 'I'm sure they'd be *very* interested to hear where the detective who bungled the Netherfield investigation was living, and under which assumed name.'

Cadogan/McLaren's eyes burned with fear and hatred in equal measure. He towered over her, huge in every sense of the word. It occurred to her that, if he wanted to shut her up, he probably wouldn't have too much difficulty. And would probably be left in peace to do it, too, in this godforsaken place.

'So who are you?' he demanded. 'You're obviously not a reporter. And you're not old enough to be one of those boys' mothers. Are you someone's wife? Girlfriend? Sister? Why are you here? What's Netherfield to you?'

'That doesn't concern you. All you need to know is that I'll be out of your hair a whole lot quicker if you hurry up and answer my questions.'

McLaren's shoulders slumped, his will to fight fizzling out.

'Not out here,' he said.

McLaren's eleventh-floor flat was cramped, grubby and smelled strongly of mildew. Anna followed him into the living room and watched as he sank into a deep armchair in the corner with a sigh that sounded every bit as pained as it did weary. She heard the clink of glass bottles as he set his bags on the floor.

'D'you mind if I take a seat?' she said.

'Don't suppose I've much choice in the matter,' McLaren grunted uncharitably.

Anna shifted some old newspapers from the sofa and sat, supporting the still slumbering Jack with one arm. A low coffee table lay between her and McLaren, a couple of old battered paperbacks propping up one of the legs.

'Well?'

McLaren sighed. 'What do you want to know?'

'Everything. I want to know everything.'

'With a remit like that, I'm not sure where to begin.'

'Then let's start with what I know already. I know about the original investigation. I know it collapsed under your watch; that the whole thing was a complete dog's breakfast. What I don't know is whether that was purely down to incompetence on your part or if there was something more sinister about it.'

McLaren scowled. 'I did what I could for those boys, you know. It might not have counted for much in the end, but I tried to make sure they felt supported. That they were believed.'

'So what happened?' Anna shrugged expectantly. 'If you cared so much, why did it turn into such an almighty bin-fire? Why did so much evidence go walkabout? Why did you spend hours in the pub getting blitzed when you should have been out there bringing the perpetrators to justice? That's not the behaviour of someone who cared.'

McLaren didn't respond. Realising she was going to have to incentivise him to loosen his tongue, Anna took out her phone.

'One call and every media outlet in the country will be banging on your door. I mean, that *is* why you changed your name, isn't it? To hide from the mob baying for your blood?'

McLaren continued to meet her gaze in stony-faced silence. Slowly, deliberately, he reached into one of the shopping bags and took out a bottle of supermarket-brand whisky. Anna watched as he retrieved a cloudy-looking tumbler from the table and poured himself a generous measure, most of which he knocked back in a single gulp. He paused to swallow the rest and set the glass down on the table next to the bottle. Then, after a deep, laboured intake of breath, he finally began to speak.

'I can already tell you're not going to believe me, but it wasn't supposed to turn out like this. When they gave me Netherfield, I knew straight away it was going to end up being the most important case of my career. I was determined to do everything by the book. Determined to see justice done. It was the least those boys and their families deserved. But certain people had other ideas.

'They came for me one night as I was leaving work, a few weeks into the investigation. They cornered me in the car park, told me it had come to their attention that my work was straying into *inconvenient territory*. That certain individuals risked being exposed who would prefer very much to stay out of the limelight. I was given an ultimatum: "Sink the case or we'll sink *you*".'

'Sink you how?'

McLaren gave Anna a withering look. She wasn't sure whether this was because she'd interrupted him or because she'd asked a question that he deemed worthy of contempt.

'It's not unheard of for cops to pick a vice or two, especially ones who've been in the job for a while. The drinking had been an open secret since forever, but I had other . . . *interests* . . . that weren't so widely known. I'm not talking about anything like what went on at Netherfield,' he added, preempting whatever judgement he imagined was forthcoming from her, 'but there'd been various . . . indiscretions over the years. I thought I'd been careful, but they had chapter and verse on me. It would have been more than enough to end my career and leave me with nothing if any of it got out.'

'These people who threatened you – who were they? What were their names?'

McLaren laughed mirthlessly. 'That's not how it works. You don't blame the postman when he hands you a court summons. They were only ever messengers. The real instigators, the ones pulling the strings, they always got others to do their dirty work. There's such a thing as plausible denia-bility, you know.'

Anna's patience was frayed to breaking point. 'So who were the instigators? Enlighten me. Or would you like me to add "indiscretions" to the list of charges against you when I ring the *Evening News*?'

'You really want to go down this route? Believe me, there are some things you're better off not knowing.' He nodded in Jack's direction. 'Think about your little one.'

Anna's stony glare was her only answer.

For a long time, McLaren was both deathly silent and deathly still – torn, it seemed, between fear of exposure and some other fear, far stronger and more deep-rooted. At length, he appeared to reach a decision. Leaning forward, he began to speak in a low voice.

'There's a group,' he said, 'inside the Strathkelvin Police Force. An inner circle. A police force within the police force. High-ranking cops scratching each other's backs, drawing a veil over each others' transgressions. Officially they don't exist, but there's not a single officer who hasn't heard of them, even if they think it's just a bogey story dreamt up to put the wind up new recruits. Officially, they don't have a name, but among the uninitiated they're known as the Shadow Men.'

A chill ran down Anna's spine as she realised she'd heard that phrase before, and who had spoken it.

'But who *are* they?' she asked, her own voice instinctively dropping to a whisper to match McLaren's.

McLaren poured himself another measure of whisky before continuing. 'In the mid-eighties, three men – Monkhouse, Glackin and Campbell – all rose to senior positions within the Force. They got there through a mixture of ruthlessness, politicking and a not insignificant amount of plain old-fashioned luck. For close to two decades, they ruled as a triumvirate, with Monkhouse as Chief Constable, Glackin as his deputy, and Campbell as Assistant Chief Constable for Crime. During that time, they assembled a handpicked cabal of enforcers – folk loyal to them, for one reason or another – and used them to commit some of the worst abuses of power you can imagine.

'At first, there were only a handful of them – a dozen or so men who could be relied on to apply the right sort of pressure to the right people and clear up any inconvenient messes. But as the years passed, the monster they'd created grew and grew and took on a life of its own, until it had its tentacles in every unit, from Fraud to Vice to Major Investigations. Officers who were on their books started running their own books, and in turn the officers on *their* books started running books of their own. I couldn't give you an exact figure, but it's been said that, at the peak of their power, they had more men on their payroll than not.'

'Jesus,' Anna breathed.

'Let me tell you a little something about corruption,' said McLaren. 'It's a contagion, spreading from officer to officer like a virus. The ones that are more susceptible are invariably drawn to the ones with a reputation for being bent, and because there's such an emphasis on learning on the job, on new recruits being mentored by old hands, bad habits get passed down like family heirlooms. As for the rest – the so-called "good cops" – never underestimate the lengths a man will go to to remain ignorant of something when his continued wellbeing depends on it.'

He paused to finish what was left in his glass. 'Those on the periphery were mostly involved in low-level offences: shaking down sex workers, skimming off drug busts, that sort of thing. But those at the top of the food chain were up to their necks in heavy, heavy stuff: falsifying evidence, fitting up innocent people . . . There were even rumours of a black site where they'd beat confessions out of suspects. And yes, some of them had a hand in what went on at Netherfield.'

Anna said nothing. As the scale of what McLaren was describing slowly sank in, so too did the scale of what she herself was up against. She felt Jack shifting against her and realised her grip around him had become vice-like.

McLaren poured and downed yet another measure of whisky, this time in a single gulp. He was steadily working his way through the bottle, Anna noticed. If it loosened his tongue, she wasn't minded to stop him.

'So after they threatened you, what happened then?'

'I did as I was told. Took the fall for the investigation's collapse on the understanding that I'd get to hang onto my career. Oh, I had to take a public flogging. They needed a face for the inevitable scandal, and mine fit the bill. And of course they had to be seen to take my transgressions seriously – to mete out the appropriate punishment. A demotion and a return to uniform. But at least I'd still have my pension, they said, and a chance to work my way back up the ladder again. "Play your cards right," they told me, "and in a few years you'll be back where you are now, like none of this unpleasantness ever happened".' He gave a sour smile. 'That's not how it ended up playing out, but I'm man enough to admit that that's on my head rather than theirs.

'After the tribunal and the demotion, I was confined to desk duties – to keep me out of the public eye, you understand. Back then, Netherfield was still fresh in a lot of folk's minds, and the press were forever on my case. But it didn't do a lick of good. They found out where I lived, showed up at my door, printed pictures of my house. And then it was only a matter of time before the pitchfork-wielding masses descended as well: parents of boys who'd been abused at Netherfield as well as a bunch of hangers-on who decided to make what happened to someone else's kids their business.' He glanced up at Anna, eyes flaring. 'Have you ever been spat at in the street? Ever had dog excrement pushed through your letterbox?'

She hadn't, but she wasn't interested in entertaining his self-pity.

'I had one woman who hounded me relentlessly – the mother of a young lad who committed suicide after the investigation broke down. She was on my case day and night – showing up on my doorstep, accosting me in public places, calling me a paedo lover. Eventually, I realised the only way I'd get any peace was if I became someone else. I was christened Thomas Gilbert Cadogan, so it was straightforward enough to start using my middle name on correspondence and official documents. But to be absolutely sure, I knew I had to go the whole hog.'

'Why McLaren?'

He gave a rather sheepish smile. 'After the racing car. When I was a wee lad, I was obsessed. Had pictures of it all over my bedroom wall; told myself, when I was older, I'd make a ton of money and buy one and drive it to work every day. When I needed a new name, it was the first one that popped into my head. By then, I figured it was the closest I'd ever get to achieving that dream.'

He was silent for a moment, the faint glow of nostalgia in his eyes as he gazed off into a distant past. 'Eventually, the hue and cry died down and it was deemed safe enough for me to return to the front line. Folk have awfully short memories, and in a few years Netherfield went from the biggest scandal in Scottish education since Brandon Lee to barely a blip in the public conscious. It wasn't how I ever envisaged my career playing out, I can tell you that. Still, I'd made my peace with it – seeing out my days in Traffic, counting down the days till I could draw my pension. I thought what had happened at Netherfield was dead and buried; that the ghosts had all been laid to rest. But then, last summer, everything blew up.'

Anna looked up sharply. 'What do you mean?'

McLaren's eyes snapped to hers. She got the distinct impression that he hadn't, until now, realised he'd spoken the last part aloud. As he continued to hesitate, her eyes strayed to the open whisky bottle on the table in front of her. Reaching across, she slowly, deliberately, refilled his glass. Their eyes met again, and an understanding seemed to be reached. McLaren took the glass and drank deeply before beginning to speak.

'A couple of years back, I was assigned to mentor this young probationer. A bit feckless, and seriously green around the gills, but basically a good kid. He hadn't made too many friends, but I always got on with him well enough. After he'd done his stint in Traffic, we went our separate ways, though our paths still crossed from time to time. I'd nod hello if I saw him, but that was the sum total of our interaction – until one night in July when he rang me up out of the blue and said could he talk to me? Told me he'd found something he wasn't sure what to do with. I wasn't really in the mood for playing agony aunt, but something in his voice told me he'd got himself involved in something heavy, and I couldn't in good conscience tell him to take a hike, so I arranged to meet him in a quiet little pub safely out of the way.

'When I arrived, he was there waiting for me – and I tell you, he was as white as anything. He hummed and hawed for a bit, but eventually he came clean about what was going on. His uncle had died recently, and he'd taken responsibility for seeing to the old man's effects. Among the various odds and ends, he found a whole pile of old tapes. He was going to chuck them out, but then he thought perhaps they might be old home movies – you know, something with sentimental value. So he hung onto them and, first chance he got, popped one into the VCR and gave it a spin.'

McLaren swallowed heavily and shook his head. 'What he found . . . well, I don't intend to dwell too heavily on it. Suffice it to say, it involved a teenage boy and two considerably older men. I don't imagine I need to spell out what sort of material I'm talking about.'

'No,' said Anna quietly, 'you don't.'

'Well, at first he thought . . . ' McLaren shrugged. 'Quite honestly, I don't know *what* he thought. Anyway, he went through the other tapes, and every one of them contained more of the same. Worst of all, in one of them, his uncle was clearly visible, doing things to a boy no adult should ever do to a child. You can imagine what it did to him. Bad enough those boys having their innocence taken like that – but for it to be his own uncle doing the taking?'

Anna could feel her heart pounding against Jack's head. She'd long since put two and two together in her own mind. She just needed the final confirmation.

'This young officer – was his name Derek Sullivan?'

McLaren looked at her sharply. 'How do you know that?'

'It's not important. Go on.'

'Well,' said McLaren, a tad doubtfully, 'if you know the young lad was Derek Sullivan, then you'll also know who his uncle was and why that made the discovery such an absolute powder-keg. I mean, *the* Hugh Sullivan – the man who led the response to the Excelsior Hotel bombing in 1996, among other shining glories. The man's considered a bloody hero. If word got out, the damage to the Force's reputation would be incalculable.'

'I can see why that could have been inconvenient,' said Anna starchly.

'It wasn't about inconvenience,' McLaren snapped. 'The lad was scared, and for good reason. He knew he couldn't take this to his superiors. Hugh Sullivan had a lot of friends and admirers on the Force. He knew it'd get brushed under the carpet, and that he'd be blackballed for besmirching the legacy of a hero. His life wouldn't be worth living. And he'd heard enough rumours about the Shadow Men and what happened to those who fell foul of them to know that being cold-shouldered was the least of his worries.

'He said there were other cops on those tapes as well. Ones he recognised. Some were retired, but many of them were still active in senior roles. From what he told me, the entire Strathkelvin Police Force was riddled with these . . . these *animals*. Another reason why he couldn't go through the official channels with what he'd discovered. But he was determined to find some way of bringing it to light. He talked about handing them over to the press – you know, posting them anonymously to the *Tribune* or STV. But I counselled him against doing that. Too many uncertainties; too much risk of them falling into the wrong hands. Then I remembered Matt Pinnock.'

'Who?'

'A couple of months earlier, this bloke rang me up out of the blue. Said he was an investigative journalist doing an exposé on the abuse at Netherfield and that he wanted me to go on the record about my role in it. How he'd managed to track me down, I have no idea. Over the next couple of weeks, he kept ringing, leaving messages, but I ignored them and eventually they stopped. To be honest, I'd more or less forgotten all about him till Sullivan came to me with his predicament. And then I thought, *Maybe there's a way some good can come of all this.*'

'Why?' said Anna. 'You were perfectly content to keep quiet about Netherfield for nearly fifteen years. What suddenly changed?'

McLaren hesitated, looking pained. 'It wasn't just tapes Sullivan found. There were a bunch of notebooks too. Diaries, with dates and times and names of various schools. St Christopher's was one, and Willow Bank Academy, and a bunch of others. I asked him, and he told me Netherfield was in the mix as well. That was when the true extent of what I'd done all those years ago hit me. I'd thought it was just a handful of cases at Netherfield I'd helped cover up. But I realised then that I'd effectively provided cover for what, in all likelihood, amounted to hundreds of crimes committed at more than a dozen different schools. And I knew, if anyone was in a position to do something with this information, it was Pinnock. I got the impression he wasn't afraid to poke the beehive. So I gave Derek his number, told him to ring it and tell Pinnock what he'd told me. He said he'd think about it, and we went our separate ways.'

'And then?'

'After that, I didn't hear from Derek for a few weeks. Then, just when I'd begun to assume he'd got cold feet and burned the tapes or dumped them at the bottom of the Clyde, he rang me and said he'd done it. He'd met with Pinnock, told him everything. He was absolutely chuffed to bits with himself. Kept saying, "I've done it, Gil, I've actually done it". He said he was going to hand over the tapes and diaries that very night. They'd arranged a time and a place and everything. This was the eighth of September – the night it rained cats and dogs. I wished him luck, said I hoped something positive came of it, but that I didn't think it was wise for us to continue to communicate about it. He agreed and rang off.

'Just before one in the morning, I got called out to an incident on the

M8. A car had gone off the road, killing the driver. When I got there, I recognised him immediately from his pictures online. It was Pinnock.'

Anna swallowed hard. 'And you think his death was—'

'Too much of a coincidence to actually *be* one? I'm certain of it. I figure, if he was fishing around for quotes about Netherfield, it wouldn't have taken long for word to get back to the Shadow Men about what he was up to. One way or another, they found out he was sticking his nose where it wasn't welcome and took appropriate action to shut him up.'

'Appropriate action? Just so we're clear, we're talking about premeditated murder here.'

McLaren said nothing, just nodded.

Anna let out a long breath. She felt numb and queasy. She'd dismissed Derek as a paranoid delusionist, convincing herself that his fears of sinister forces out to get him were a product of his fevered imagination, brushing off his frantic attempts to communicate the very real danger he was in. She of all people should have known better.

'This order to shut him up,' she said, finding her voice, 'who would it have come from? Monkhouse and the rest aren't still calling the shots, are they? They must be positively ancient by now.'

'The old guard are long gone, if that's what you mean. Campbell died back in 2004, and Glackin retired soon after, though Monkhouse held on for as long as he could. Couldn't bear to let go of what he'd created, I suppose. But before he stepped down, he groomed a successor – a protégé who, when the time came, would step into his shoes and keep the old ways alive into the next generation.'

'Who?'

'The current Assistant Chief Constable – Peter Strickland.'

Anna wondered how many more revelations this day had in store. She remembered her own brief encounter with the little man with the hang-dog eyes and diffident manner and tried to picture him as the head of a clandestine ring of corrupt police officers. The cognitive dissonance was overpowering.

'What happened next?' she asked.

'I figured it was only a matter of time before it came to light that Pinnock had been in touch with Derek, which meant it was only a matter of time before the Shadow Men came looking for *him*. As soon as I could, I rang him and told him he needed to drop everything and clear out. "Don't even think about going home to pack a bag," I said. "Wherever you are, you start walking *now*". And he did. A few days later, I heard he'd failed to report for work and had been listed as a missing person. That was the last I heard of him till I woke up on New Year's Day to the news he'd thrown himself out of a window in the process of being apprehended by the police.'

*And I led them right to him,* thought Anna. She wondered if it really had been a bleed on the brain that had ultimately finished him off or if that too had been the work of 'dark forces'.

'All these calls between you and Derek,' she said, forcing herself to save the self-recriminations till later, 'why weren't they picked up when the police accessed his phone records?'

'He had a burner phone,' said McLaren. 'One of those cheap pay-as-you-go numbers. Used it to communicate with me. Pinnock too, I'd imagine. He was canny like that.'

*Just because you're paranoid . . .* 'And have you any idea what became of the tapes?'

'Like I said, the night Pinnock was killed, he and Derek were supposed to meet so Derek could hand them over. I've no idea whether that meeting ever took place. Either it did, and Pinnock had the tapes on him when he died, in which case they're almost certainly in the Shadow Men's hands now, or—'

'Or Derek took them with him when he ran.'

'Or he dumped them first, *then* ran. If he was anything like me, he'd have wanted shot of them as quickly as possible.'

*But he wasn't like you,* Anna thought. She could hear Clive Sullivan's words replaying in her head: *I taught him to do what was right and to never shirk his responsibilities.*

'Pinnock's car,' she said. 'Whereabouts on the M8 did it crash?'

'Near the A814 overpass.'

'And which direction was it going in?'

'Sorry?'

'Was he heading into town or coming back out?'

McLaren thought about it. 'Heading in,' he said, after a moment and with some conviction. 'He was heading into town.'

\* \* \*

After that, there wasn't much more to tell. Jack was becoming restless and irritable – and that, Anna concluded, was as good an indication as any that it was time to go. McLaren saw her to the door.

'I'm not proud of what I did, you know,' he said, as she stepped out into the stairwell. 'You can think what you like about me, but there's not a day gone by that I haven't wished I could turn back time and do things differently.'

'I'm glad to hear it, but I'd say it's a little late in the day for regrets, wouldn't you?'

He said nothing. She thought they were done, but as she turned to go, he piped up again.

'I'm dying.'

She turned to face him, wondering where this had come from and why he was telling her now. 'I'm sorry?'

'End-stage liver disease. Brought about by my fondness for the bottle, so I've only myself to blame – but still. The docs have given me a few months tops. They offered to consider me for the transplant list.'

'Well, that's good. I hope—'

'I turned them down.' McLaren's tone was blunt. 'Couldn't bear the thought of taking up the place of someone who actually *deserves* a second chance.' He offered a limp shrug. 'I'm not asking for your pity. I know I don't deserve it. But if I was allowed one wish, it's that, before I go, some good might come of everything that's happened.'

Anna fixed him with a steely look. 'You covered up the institutionalised abuse of children. There's not a thing in the world that can make that right. But I'll do what I can with the information you've given me.'

As she turned to go again, she thought of something else. Something that had been worrying away at the back of her mind ever since Sullivan's involvement had come to light – and, if she was being honest with herself, since some considerable time before then. Since her and Fin's encounter with Mandy in Zoe's flat.

'The detective who led the hunt for Derek,' she said, 'was DCI Paul Vasilico.'

'I know.' McLaren's expression was inscrutable.

'How much do you think he knew? Is there a chance he was' – she found herself lowering her voice to a whisper – 'in on it?'

McLaren looked at her for a long, hard moment. 'You do know who he is, don't you?'

'No. Who?'

'He's Strickland's nephew.'

'His *what*?' Anna all but spluttered.

'He doesn't shout it from the rooftops, but it's basically an open secret. It's why he's able to get away with half the things he does: bending the rules, giving his superiors cheek. They used to work Vice together, and then, when Strickland made ACC, he moved Vasilico over to Major Investigations – putting him right at the heart of the action. Believe me, the two of them are as thick as thieves. There's not a word reaches the nephew's ears that doesn't find its way back to the uncle.' He scoffed drily, as if in amusement at Anna's gaucheness. 'Why else would Strickland have put him in charge of the investigation?'

# 41

# Forget

It was mid-afternoon by the time Anna reached Partick. Until now, Jack had been almost preternaturally well-behaved, spending his time either sleeping or watching the world go by from his sling. But now, as she descended the stairs at the railway station, he stirred and began to bawl.

It was an ear-splitting, rasping cry – one which caused everyone around her to turn in her direction, their accusing eyes boring into her, judging her, resenting this disruption to their peaceful commute. She could hardly blame them. She knew she'd done exactly the same thing countless times in the past when she'd been in the vicinity of a screaming baby. And her first thought had always been the same: *bad mother*. Babies didn't just cry for no good reason, and if one was distressed enough to create that level of noise, the blame must surely lie with the parent. Through negligence or cruelty or just plain incompetence, the child had been brought to the brink of despair and was expressing itself in the only way it knew how.

*So which is it with* you, *Anna? It's not cruelty, which only leaves negligence and incompetence.*

Wincing apologetically to the multiple judgemental onlookers, she hurried down the steps and out into the open air, where she tried desperately to calm Jack down. She attempted everything in her repertoire: rocking him back and forth; bouncing him up and down; offering him The Breast, in full view of a trio of adolescent males who made animal noises and videoed her on their phones. She even tried singing to him, though she couldn't hold a tune to save her life – an old Yiddish song her grandmother used to sing, and which was the only one she was able to call to mind. But it was no use. Jack wasn't happy, and he was determined that everyone should know it.

He continued to bawl as she hoofed it up Gardner Street – the very hill that had brought him prematurely into the world a few short weeks earlier. She reached the top, panting, entered the sandstone building on the corner, dragged herself up the steps to the third floor and hammered on Clive Sullivan's door.

Sullivan was about as pleased to see Anna as she'd been anticipating. Pre-empting his attempt to slam the door in her face, she pushed forward, twisting her body sideways to shove her head and one shoulder into the gap between door and doorframe while still keeping Jack at a safe distance from any potential collision.

'Please don't shut the door on me, Mr Sullivan,' she said wearily, raising her voice over Jack's screams. 'This will only take a few minutes.'

'This is harassment,' spluttered Sullivan. 'Get off these premises right this minute or I'll call the police.'

Ignoring the hollow threat, Anna pressed on. 'I found out what your son was mixed up in. He discovered tapes showing your brother and other high-ranking police officers committing acts of child abuse, and he went on the run because the journalist he was working with to bring it to light was murdered and he was afraid he'd be next.'

'You're insane,' said Sullivan, but without much conviction. He sounded like someone going through the motions, protesting not because he antici-pated it having any effect but simply because it was expected of him.

'I've no idea how much you knew,' Anna continued, 'and frankly, I don't much care. But I'm going to go out on a limb here and surmise that whatever possessions Derek took with him when he went on the run were either here in the flat or out at your allotment at the time of his death.'

Jack's cry was like a siren now, so loud and high-pitched it made Anna's ears ring. It was a wonder the neighbours hadn't come to make sure someone wasn't slaughtering an animal in the stairwell. And that was to her advantage because she knew that, if *she* was thinking it, chances were Sullivan was too. And the last thing he would want was a gaggle of nosy neighbours prying into his affairs.

'I'm not asking you to sign a full and frank confession as to what you knew,' she said, raising her voice even higher. 'We both know that's not in your nature. All I'm asking is for you to let me take a look at his belongings.'

For several long, agonising seconds, Sullivan met Anna's gaze in silence, the veins on one side of his forehead pulsating with cold fury while Jack continued to wail. At length, the old man sighed and let the door swing open, stepping back to allow Anna into the flat.

'Well?' she said, once she'd crossed the threshold and shut the door behind her.

'Everything,' said Sullivan.

'Excuse me?'

'I knew everything.'

Several seconds passed, punctuated only by Jack's cry. With a sudden, aching sense of clarity, Anna understood.

'You weren't hiding him out of shame. You were protecting him.'

Sullivan lowered his eyes. He looked spent, ground down by grief and months of carrying this secret.

'When I found him hiding in my shed, he was still relatively lucid. He came clean to me then and there; told me the whole story. The abuse, my brother, the ring of corrupt officers – everything. He told me they were hunting for him – that, if they found him, he'd end up the same way as that dead reporter.'

'That's why you staged his suicide.'

Sullivan nodded. 'I needed some ruse to throw them off the scent. Believe me, I took no pleasure in pretending to the world that I'd written him off. Ours had never been the model of an ideal father/son relationship, but to stand there in front of all those people and claim that . . . ' He trailed off, a heavy breath racking his chest.

Jack was still crying, but more softly now, as if he'd realised it wasn't getting him anywhere. The knowledge that her baby was in distress and she was doing nothing to comfort him pierced Anna's heart like a dagger.

'How much did you know about your brother's activities?' she asked, doing her best to force these thoughts from her mind.

Sullivan lifted his head and gazed at her with weary, sorrowful eyes. 'I didn't *know* anything – not until Derek told me what he'd seen. But that doesn't mean I didn't have my suspicions. I'd always had a hunch he'd been involved in some dubious activities – that his conduct hadn't always been befitting of an officer of the law. As to the specifics, I didn't ask, and he never told me. But *child* abuse?' He shook his head vehemently. 'If I'd even had the slightest inkling . . . '

Anna wondered whether he really would have said or done anything or whether, like so many others before him, he would simply have closed his eyes and ears to the evidence in front of him, convincing himself it wasn't true.

'Derek's belongings,' she said, circling back to her original mission. 'Where are they?'

Sullivan shook his head. She couldn't tell whether he'd heard her or not. 'Why would you want to trouble yourself with this? You've seen what happens to those who poke their noses where they don't belong.'

'Tell me,' said Anna, through gritted teeth. 'I'm not afraid of them, even if you are.'

'Well, maybe you should be,' said Sullivan, his tone half-contemptuous, half-pleading.

Anna glared at him, refusing to stand down. 'He was determined that the truth would come out. That those men be held accountable for their actions. Tell me – to honour his memory if nothing else.'

At length, Sullivan quailed and, no longer able to withstand her gaze, looked away.

'The allotment,' he said quietly. 'I buried those tapes under the crops. Them and the diaries.' He shot Anna a barbed look. 'You're welcome to them.'

'Thank you,' said Anna. It had been like getting blood from a stone, but she finally had what she wanted. She turned to go.

'Do you know something?'

Sullivan's voice stopped her in her tracks. She turned to face him.

'I wish he'd never offered to see to my brother's effects. I wish he'd never found those tapes. I wish none of this . . . *unpleasantness* had ever come to light. He'd be alive today if he'd just let things be.'

'I think he was just trying to do the right thing,' said Anna weakly.

Sullivan laughed humourlessly. 'The right thing? And what's that when it's at home? The right thing would have been not getting mixed up in affairs that were no concern of his. The right thing would have been leaving well alone.'

'Is that really what you'd have done in his shoes? Ignored evidence of widespread child abuse and carried on as if it had nothing to do with you? That was his uncle on those tapes. Your *brother*.'

'Why should I care? Folk do unspeakable things to each other every moment of every day. Yes, it's dreadful what happened to those boys, but in the grand scheme of things, so what?'

Previously, Anna had thought Sullivan incapable of shocking her further. She'd thought wrong.

'You don't believe that,' she said, stunned by his cynicism.

'Don't I?' Sullivan's features contorted into an ugly sneer. 'Here's what I believe: if the price for having my son back alive and well was the rape of every other child on this earth, I'd gladly pay it a hundred times over.'

She could see she wasn't going to change his mind, and she wasn't sure she'd be doing either of them any favours by trying. Rather than waste any further breath on him, she turned on her heel and left the flat.

'Don't come here again,' she heard him say behind her as she set off down the stairs. 'I don't want to know what happens. I just want to forget.'

## 42

# Flesh and Blood

By the time Anna reached the foot of Gardner Street, Jack's crying was once more gaining momentum. As she stepped onto the concourse outside Partick Station, she slowed to make another futile attempt to placate him. As he continued to gurn and whine, she heard, less than twenty metres behind her, the sound she'd lived in constant fear of for the last two days.

The sound of someone calling her name.

'Anna!'

She decided to ignore it, hoping whoever it was would conclude they'd mistaken someone else for her. Quickening her pace, she continued towards the terminus.

'Anna, wait!'

This time, the voice was followed by footsteps hurrying after her. She kept going, each stride longer than the last, her breath coming out in frantic gasps. She felt a firm hand on her shoulder, and then Paul Vasilico was stepping in front of her, blocking her path, grinning at her like a demented Cheshire cat.

'I *thought* it was you! Didn't you hear me? Now where would you be off to at such a furious pace?'

His cluelessness would have seemed amusing if it weren't for the utter dread that now overwhelmed her.

'I just got back into town yesterday,' he went on, chattering away to fill the void left by her silence. 'I called round at your place, but you weren't in. Fancy us running into each other here!' His eyes alighted on Jack, his smile broadening further. 'And is this the little man? Well now, aren't *you* growing up big and strong?'

His sudden interest in Jack spurred Anna into action. 'Get the fuck away from him!' she snarled, turning sideways to shield him with her body.

Vasilico stared at her uncomprehendingly, his smile slowly receding as he realised something was seriously amiss. 'What's wrong, Anna? What have I done?'

'You tell me,' she snapped, eyeing him guardedly.

'What's that supposed to mean?'

'If you can't figure it out, you could always ask your *uncle*.'

All trace of mirth left Vasilico's face as understanding finally dawned. 'So you know about that,' he said quietly.

'Believe me, that's only the *start* of what I know.'

By now, Jack was wailing full tilt, forcing Anna to raise her voice as she continued to give Vasilico both barrels.

'I know he heads up a secret ring of senior police officers that cover up each other's lawbreaking and corruption. I know he's had people killed. That he protects child molesters and their friends. That he'd abdicated every oath he ever swore to uphold the public good.'

'Come on, Anna.' Vasilico laughed nervously. 'You're upsetting the baby.'

'Do *not* use him to try to shut me down.' It came out as a low, guttural snarl. 'I know you're up to your neck in it as well, so don't even *try* to deny it. Or are you going to tell me it was just a coincidence you were assigned to lead the hunt for the man who'd found out what was going on and was going to blow the lid on it? That he just *happened* to die in hospital on your watch, conveniently taking his secrets to the grave?'

'Are you talking about—'

'I'm talking about Derek Sullivan!' She was yelling now, and she didn't care who heard her. The more of a racket she made, and the more attention she drew, the less likely Vasilico was to try anything. 'It always *was* going to end that way, wasn't it? I mean, that's why Strickland put you on the case: so you could find him and shut him up.'

'No!' Vasilico sounded genuinely aghast. 'I mean, it wasn't . . . I mean, I . . . I don't *know*.' He pinched the bridge of his nose, eyes screwed shut as he tried to keep a lid on his emotions. 'Yes, my uncle put me in charge of the Sullivan case and tasked me with making it my number one priority to find him. You know that already. But what you're suggesting – that he had Sullivan killed, or that . . . or that *I* would have had anything to do with that – well, it's absurd. More to the point, it's offensive. This is my uncle we're talking about. My own flesh and blood. You honestly expect me to believe he'd . . . '

He shook his head adamantly, but there was a hint of something in his eyes when he opened them: a creeping doubt, a sense that he was beginning to replay certain past interactions in his mind, reassessing their meaning.

Anna said nothing. She merely glowered at him with narrow, distrustful eyes. Jack continued to howl.

Vasilico's shoulders sagged. He smiled once more, trying a more conciliatory tack. 'Anna, come on. It's me. You know me.'

'I *thought* I did,' she muttered, lowering her own eyes to avoid his.

'Talk to me. We can sort this out together.' Vasilico moved towards her, reaching out to lay his hand on her shoulder.

She reacted instantly and instinctually. 'Get your fucking hands off me!' she roared, wrapping her arms round Jack to shield him.

Vasilico instantly withdrew his hand, taken aback by her ferocity. Not waiting for him to regain the initiative, she swerved around him and took off across the car park like the clappers, Jack howling at the top of his lungs as he bounced in her arms.

# 43

# Dig

Anna embarked on a long, roundabout trek across the city, choosing her route at random but sticking to areas that had a sizeable presence of other people. Every so often, she stopped to look over her shoulder, but there was no sign of Vasilico following her. Nonetheless, her phone pinged constantly with a stream of texts from him, asking her where she was and entreating her to let him know she was OK. Eventually, she got fed up jumping out of her skin at each successive ping and blocked his number.

By the time she and a seriously unhappy Jack made it back to Reiko's flat, the sky was dark and teeming with rain. Having made it safely inside, she locked the door and drew all the curtains, before dedicating herself wholly to the Herculean task of placating her child. He seemed determined to punish her for the last few hours, and she could hardly blame him. It wasn't supposed to be like this. This was meant to have been quality mother/baby bonding time, warm and safe in their house on Clarence Drive. Eventually, after alternating between wailing and screeching himself hoarse for what felt like several lifetimes, he grew quiet and, having utterly exhausted himself, drifted off to sleep in her arms.

As she carefully laid him in his makeshift crib, a loud, impatient rap sounded on the front door. She froze, her blood chilling as she stared in its direction. A moment passed, then there was another rap, followed by an exasperated hiss.

'Fucksake, open the door! Think I wanna spend all night out here?'

Practically gasping with relief, Anna hurried to unlock the door. A drenched Fin swept past her and stormed into the living room, where she began to peel off her motorcycle leathers with a ferocity that suggested they'd personally done something to offend her.

'Well?' Anna demanded.

Fin turned to her with a face like boiled piss. 'Polish! She was fecking *Polish*!' She rolled up her trousers and hurled them at the floor. 'Answer me this: do Polish and Weegie sound remotely similar to you? Mind you,' she raised a qualifying finger, ''s'pose I'm not being entirely fair. After all, she *was* a redhead. Only slight catch is the colour came out a fecking bottle!'

Anna knew better than to try to placate her. Mentally, she'd already prepared herself for the purported sighting being a bust, so she was less crushed by disappointment than Fin. But then, she wasn't the one who'd spent the day biking to Aberdeen and back on a wild goose chase.

With a final, emphatic '*Fuck*sake!', Fin flopped onto the sofa, stripped down to her vest and a pair of men's briefs, her leathers discarded in a sodden heap on the floor. Stepping around them, Anna lowered herself onto the other end of the sofa, maintaining as respectful a distance as possible from her still volatile companion.

For a while, they sat side by side in silence, lost in their own individual thoughts. At length, Fin glanced across at Anna.

'So then,' she remarked in a disinterested tone, 'you 'n' baba get up to any fun while I was gone?'

By the time Anna reached the end of her tale, all trace of lethargy had left Fin. She was on her feet, pacing the room in her undies, a powder-keg of pent-up energy in need of an outlet. Even as Anna finished speaking, she snatched up her soaking trousers and began struggling into them.

'Why the hell didn't you say something sooner?' she demanded as she hoisted them up to her waist. 'Tell ya something for nothing, I'm not sitting here twiddling my pubes while there's work to be done.'

She zipped up her trousers and grabbed her jacket. There was a renewed sense of determination and purpose to her actions, though it was clear she was running on fumes.

'Come on.' Anna rose to her feet. 'You've been on the trot all day. You must be shattered. Besides, it's chucking it down outside. It'll keep till morning.'

'Bull*shit* it will!' Fin yanked the zip on her jacket up to her chin. 'You don't dump a hot mess like that in my lap, then say, "All right, Fin, time for beddy-byes". You tuck yerself in with a hot cocoa if you like, Professor. I got me some tapes to dig up.'

She grabbed her helmet and slammed out of the flat, footsteps receding down the stairwell. A moment later, Anna heard an engine being gunned. She reached the window in time to see Fin roaring off up the street on her Ducati.

Anna tried in vain to settle, but she found herself fizzing with the same nervous energy as Fin – except, unlike Fin, she had nowhere to channel it. She paced and fretted, wearing out the living room carpet. Outside, the rain fell in torrents, soaking the pavement and the pedestrians hurrying to and fro in the street below.

To give herself something to do, she got out her phone and spent some time reading up on Monkhouse, Glackin and Campbell – the 'triumvirate' that McLaren had claimed made up the Shadow Men's original inner circle. None of what she read was particularly surprising. They were all highly decorated career cops: men who'd joined the police straight from school and worked their way up through the ranks, excelling in every posting, enjoying long and distinguished tenures before retiring with their heads held high.

From there, she moved onto the current puppet-master, Strickland. His trajectory had been similar to that of his predecessors, though in keeping with the graduate-oriented ethos of modern policing, he'd gone down the university route first, picking up a First Class Honours degree in Law and Psychology. From there, he'd climbed through the ranks of the Strathkelvin Police Force before heading down south in 1994, where he'd spent several successful years with the Met, eventually returning to Glasgow in 2003 to head up the newly created East End Vice Squad – and ultimately, it seemed, the Shadow Men.

And then there was Vasilico. Anna tried not to think about the extent to which she'd allowed him to worm his way into her confidence over the last few months. The extent to which she'd trusted him – even *liked* him. She remembered him telling her his uncle had taken him in following his mental breakdown and effectively raised him as his own. That would have given Strickland ample opportunity to mould the younger man in his own image. What was it Vasilico had said? *I owe him everything.*

The only remaining question mark, as far as she was concerned, was over how directly he was involved with both the Shadow Men and the events of the last several weeks and months. One thing was for sure: she was more convinced than ever that Mandy's description of the good-looking, mid-thirties detective who'd blackmailed her – who wore flashy suits and drove either a Porsche or a Jaguar – fit him to a T. The one nagging seed of doubt in her mind was the look in his eyes when she'd confronted him about his uncle's activities. He'd seemed genuinely shocked, even horrified, the very idea of what she was describing too much to comprehend. If it had just been his verbal denials, then she doubted whether there would be even a shred of uncertainty in her mind as to his complicity. But there had been a spark of something in his eyes that she didn't think could be faked – not unless he was an even more gifted performer than she'd given him credit for.

But if he *was* involved, if he *had* been working hand-in-glove with Strickland throughout, then every interaction she'd ever had with him – right up to the moment when she'd summoned him to Clive Sullivan's flat on Christmas Eve and effectively handed Derek over to him – had played directly into the Shadow Men's hands, and that thought was enough to make her want to retch.

Those fears were still gnawing away at her when she heard the front door opening. She looked up as Fin appeared in the doorway. She was drenched from head to toe, covered in mud and breathing heavily, and looked for all the world like she'd just clawed her way out of a freshly dug grave. In one hand, she carried a rucksack, every bit as mud-caked as her – but not so much so that it obscured the white Adidas logo emblazoned on the back pocket. She let it fall to the ground with a thud.

As Anna rose to her feet, opening her mouth to speak, Fin firmly raised an open palm.

'First things first: a shower.'

Somehow, Anna resisted the urge to look inside the rucksack while Fin was off getting cleaned up. It was like waking up early on your birthday and having to force yourself not to open your presents till the whole family was assembled – only she knew the rucksack's contents were unlikely to bring joy to either herself or anyone else.

When Fin finally returned, hair still dripping and wearing a silk robe purloined from Reiko's collection, they emptied the rucksack onto the coffee table. In total, the contents amounted to sixteen VHS cassettes and half a dozen A5 notebooks.

Anna opened one of the latter and began to flick through it. As McLaren had described, it contained a series of dates and times, and the names of various schools. *Willow Bank, Whitecraigs, Maxwell Park, Netherfield . . .* All these and numerous others appeared on page after page, each entry accompanied by what at first appeared to be a string of random letters: *JB KS RL, EE AB, HS BM RL* and so on. It wasn't until she noticed the repeated coinciding of *Willow Bank* and *AB* that she realised *AB* stood for 'Adam Broadhurst' and that the letters were, in all likelihood, the initials of those who'd been present on each occasion.

'Why?' she said, more to herself than to Fin. 'Why create a record? Why incriminate themselves?'

'Insurance,' said Fin flatly. 'Case anyone ever decided to rat the others out. All for one, one for all. Same reason they made these, I s'pose.'

Anna followed Fin's gaze to the videotapes stacked on the table. Her stomach pitched as she thought about what was on them. She turned to find Fin, seeming to have guessed what she was thinking, looking at her in horror.

'I can't,' she said helplessly.

'It's fine,' said Anna. 'I'll do it.'

Fin shook her head. 'You don't have to. I mean, I'd say we can take it as given it's not reruns of *Coronation Street*.'

Her words were lighthearted, but her eyes were wide, silently beseeching Anna not to subject herself to this.

'I do,' said Anna, then added, after a moment, 'I have to know if Victor's on there.'

'Why?'

'Because unlike you, I'm still not convinced of Zoe's innocence, and if her brother *is* on one of those tapes, then it might make me feel a little better about the idea of her murdering Adam Broadhurst in cold blood.'

'And that makes a difference, does it? How does him being abused tip the moral scales when a hundred and one other boys having the same thing done to 'em doesn't?'

Anna shrugged helplessly. 'I don't know, but it does.'

Fin looked at her long and hard, her brows contorted into an uncomprehending furrow. 'I don't get it.'

Anna felt a stab of annoyance. She was sick of Fin's obstinacy; her seemingly deliberate refusal to see what, to Anna, was implicit, even if she couldn't actually articulate it.

'Well,' she said evenly, 'I guess that's because I know what it means to have a family, and you don't.'

For several seconds, Fin neither moved nor broke Anna's gaze. As those dark, brooding eyes bored into her, Anna grew increasingly uncomfortable, until at last the tension was unbearable. Then, in a sudden, wordless movement, Fin lurched to her feet, turned and strode out of the room.

Watching her go, Anna felt an urge to call after her, to apologise to her for striking such a low blow, but she couldn't find her voice. And besides, she doubted there was anything she could say to take back the cruelty of her words. Instead, she steeled herself and turned her attention to the task before her.

As a criminologist, and one specialising in violence against women, Anna had read her fair share of harrowing accounts of sexual abuse, but none of them had remotely prepared her for what was on those tapes. It was one thing to read about it – reduced, through layers of abstraction, to cold, uncaring theory. But to see it playing out in front of her in living colour was another matter entirely. The footage on the DVD she'd found at the house on Astley Street seemed mild in comparison. At least it had featured no direct physical contact between victim and abuser. She quickly learned that this had been very much the exception to the rule. In most of the recordings, the men – and they *were* all men – were very much active participants, their flabby bodies almost constantly in frame, often dwarfing those of their victims. She watched on fast-forward and with no sound. That, she supposed, created something of a barrier between herself and what she was seeing – but only a very thin one. Throughout it all, the same thought kept running through her head, like a record stuck on repeat: *These aren't just movies. This actually happened to those boys.*

Most of the footage was dated and timecoded. In many instances, it was therefore possible to tie each segment to a corresponding diary entry, and to match the men appearing on camera to the initials on the page. The quality was variable and in many cases clearly multiple generations removed from the original recording, but none of it had degraded sufficiently to prevent the identification of those appearing in front of the camera – both the abusers and their victims. The initials *AB* featured in a dizzying number of diary entries pertaining to Willow Bank, though Broadhurst himself never actually appeared on camera. He'd been far too careful for that. On a couple of occasions, when she slowed the footage down to regular speed and turned up the sound, she heard a man's voice issuing commands to either his fellow abusers or their victims: 'Turn him that way', 'Touch him there', 'Swallow it'. These orders, if they did indeed come from him, were the only trace of Adam Broadhurst to exist on the tapes.

On the other hand, one man who wasn't remotely shy about appearing on camera, and did so frequently, was listed in the diaries as 'SDG'. His appearance had changed sufficiently in the intervening years that it took Anna until she'd seen him in three different 'episodes' to realise that he was none other than the now head of the Major Investigations Team, Detective Superintendent Sean De Groot. He'd been less potbellied back then and hadn't yet started sporting a beard, but once she recognised him there could be no question of it being anyone else. She wondered if, like Strickland, the Shadow Men had earmarked him from early on for a future leading role within their group, and if these recordings had been stored up as leverage to encourage him to play ball when the time came.

By 3 a.m., she could take no more of it. She'd waded through five tapes, wherever possible noting down the identities or suspected identities of any men who appeared on camera. She'd recognised three boys from her Willow Bank days whom she'd known by name, and another two who appeared familiar but whose identities she couldn't place. As yet, however, there had been no sign of Victor – though that didn't prove anything one way or the other. The tapes were unlabelled and the footage had been copied onto them in a seemingly random order, with a single cassette often covering several years, judging by the burned-in dates. She'd seen footage as old as March 1991 and as recent as September 2002. And, with a further eleven tapes to go, there was still ample time for him to put in an appearance. But not tonight. For now, she'd done enough. She'd begin again at first light.

She dragged herself through to the bedroom and gazed down at Jack, fast asleep in his crib, blissfully unaware of the horrors that had been playing out in the adjacent room. His innocence and vulnerability hit her square in the solar plexus, and she felt tears welling behind her exhausted eyes. She tried to imagine what she'd do to anyone who sought to do him harm, to say nothing of—

No. It didn't bear thinking about. Murder seemed too lenient a response.

She crawled into bed, still half-dressed. Bone-weary though she was, she doubted she'd be able to sleep – not with the images she'd just subjected herself to still seared into her mind. However, even as she drew the covers over herself, she felt her eyelids beginning to droop. Drawing on the last dregs of her energy reserves, she reached for her phone and composed a text to Zoe.

> I still have questions, but I think I'm close to piecing everything together. I know what you were looking into and have a good idea who's been pulling the strings.
>
> If you're out there, please give me some sign that you're OK. You have people here who care about you and are working flat out to help you.
>
> Whatever you've done, I'll stand by you.

She wavered for a moment, wondering whether to include the final sentence. She'd originally intended to write *I still believe in you*, but had realised, when push came to shove, that she didn't know *what* she believed anymore. Perhaps it was more accurate to say that her position on Broadhurst's murder had now evolved to the point that she could no longer regard it as morally indefensible. Where that left Zoe, and her guilt or innocence, she couldn't say.

Her fingers strayed for the umpteenth time to her bracelet. As they brushed over the engraved quotation, an idea came to her. Reaching for her phone once more, she deleted the final line of her message and replaced it with the words *True friends are never apart*, then hit Send, put the phone on the nightstand and lay down to sleep.

# 44

# Pure Vomit Colours

*Tuesday 2 February*

She knew she was dreaming, but that neither came as a surprise nor seemed much to matter. She was back in the old house on Astley Street, preserved as it had been back when she was a teenager and it had been her bolthole after school and at weekends: the place where she and Zoe had spent so much of their time whiling away their adolescence.

The lights were off and she sensed that it was night-time, but she was able to see where she was going, the house cloaked in a sort of grey half-light that stripped her surroundings of colour but still allowed her to see their overall shapes. She moved from room to room, not so much walking as gliding – an act which required no effort on her part, though she knew she was fully in control of both the pace and direction of travel. The house had assumed an oddly fluid quality, its geography malleable and ever-changing, but regardless, she knew exactly which doorway opened onto which room. More to the point, she knew what she was looking for. Somewhere in the house, Zoe was waiting for her, though she didn't yet know where.

Eventually, she came to a part of the house she didn't recognise: a long, narrow corridor leading to a dead end – though why anyone would build a corridor that went nowhere was anyone's guess. At its end stood a full-height mirror. As she halted in front of it, she saw herself reflected in the dust-mottled glass. Standing next to her was Zoe. She turned, but there was no one there.

Turning to the glass once again, she beheld the two figures facing her – one short and dark, the other freckled and red-haired. They stood side by side, posed identically, like facsimiles of one another. But who was real and who was the shadow?

She reached out and touched the mirror. The reflection disintegrated like rippling water. When it settled once more, Anna's own reflection remained, but Zoe's was gone.

A sudden terror gripped Anna. She felt a tightening in her chest; the sensation of being unable to breathe. She tried to call to Zoe, but no sound came out. As she opened and closed her mouth helplessly, the walls seemed to close in around her, while Zoe's voice echoed around her, distant and unplaceable: *Come and find me, come and find me, come and find me . . .*

Anna woke with a start as her phone, lying on the nightstand, buzzed a notification, illuminating the entire room like an atomic blast. She fumbled for it, blinking sleep from her eyes. Slowly, the words 'ONE NEW MESSAGE' came into focus. The sender was 'RED MENACE'.

She tapped the link, opening up her conversation history with Zoe. An unread reply was waiting for her, timestamped 3.22 a.m. No words, just a picture. She tapped the screen again, enlarging it to full size. It showed a bracelet lying on top of a duvet: a simple silver band, unadorned but for a short inscription on the outer face. At first, she had no idea what she was looking at or what it meant. Then, as the scales of sleep fell away from her eyes, she understood.

'FIN!'

Before her feet even touched the ground, Fin had appeared in the doorway, wearing nothing but her vest and armed with a table lamp, minus its shade. Wordlessly, Anna turned the phone towards her.

Fin set down the lamp and took it, squinting, tilting it this way and that, then turned to Anna with a shrug. 'So?'

'It's hers. I gave it to her. Look.' She raised her arm, showing her own matching bracelet. 'It's *her*.'

Fin continued to study the picture, seemingly unaware – or perhaps simply unconcerned – that she was still standing there with nothing on below her waist. Eventually, she lowered the phone.

'Could be. Or could be someone *wants* ya to think it's her.'

Anna shook her head vehemently. 'Look at the inscription. Read it.'

Dubiously, Fin looked at the screen again. '" . . . perhaps in distance but never in heart",' she enunciated slowly.

'It's the second half of a quotation: "True friends are never apart, perhaps in distance but never in heart". Mine has the first part; Zoe's has the second. Before I went to sleep, I texted her my half. Now she responds with hers.' She gazed beseechingly at Fin. 'No one else would have understood the significance of that quotation. It's *her*, Fin – I know it is.'

Fin continued to study the picture, her face a mask of scepticism. 'OK, so it's her. Doesn't get us very far, though, does it? Tells us she's alive, but she could be in Timbuktu for all we know.'

She held the phone out to Anna. Anna took it, saying nothing. Throughout their exchange, something had been gnawing away at the back of her mind. She squinted at the screen, zooming the image in, scrolling this way and that, searching for the clue that her subconscious had picked up on. To all intents and purposes, it was just a bog-standard photo of a bracelet lying on top of a duvet.

*The duvet.*

Brown and orange diagonal stripes. The most distasteful décor she'd ever had the misfortune to clap eyes on.

*Pure vomit colours.*

She felt her gut contracting. She lifted her head and stared at Fin, heart pounding.

'I know where she is,' she breathed.

## 45

# Homecoming

For the third time in twenty-four hours, Fin scrambled into her leathers and prepared to set off. She was ready to go in the space of five minutes, by which time Jack was, of course, wide awake and bawling. He'd come to when Anna had shouted to Fin after receiving Zoe's text – though Anna, to her eternal shame, hadn't noticed his crying until Fin had left to get dressed. She was pacing to and fro in the corridor with him in her arms when Fin emerged from the kitchen, a slice of toast clenched between her teeth.

'Fin.' Anna moved to head her off.

Fin removed the toast from her mouth. 'Yeah, yeah, I'll drive carefully.' She turned to go, then stopped, seeing the imploring look in Anna's eyes. 'I know. I'll bring her home safe.'

And with that, she strode from the flat.

Though it was still the middle of the night, there seemed little point in going back to bed. Anna doubted she'd be able to get Jack to settle, and in any event she was too wired herself to even entertain the thought of sleep, though she must have had all of fifteen minutes of it before Zoe's text had woken her. She considered texting Zoe back to let her know help was on the way, before concluding that such a course of action could easily end up doing more harm than good. If Fin got there to find that Zoe had fled the scene, they'd be right back at square one. Desperately wishing there was something more she could be doing to help, Anna retired to the sofa to give Jack his first feed of the day.

It was growing light outside when Jack finally dropped off again, after several hours of intermittent crying, feeding and crapping, with the three merging together in a seemingly endless sea of bodily fluids. Once he was safely tucked up in his crib, sleeping the sleep of the innocent, Anna knuckled down to the grim task of completing her slog through the tapes.

The content had become no less gruesome in the cold light of day, but even so, she sensed that the constant bombardment of images was beginning to have a numbing effect on her. At first, every minute she'd watched had seemed worse than the last, each fresh piece of footage plumbing new depths of depravity. Now, though, she felt a growing and depressing sense of inevitability about the scenes unfolding before her. You could only endure so much exposure to the worst aspects of human behaviour, she supposed, before your natural defence mechanisms began to kick in, shutting off the parts of your brain that governed normal emotional responses to unspeakable things. She wondered if those who'd willingly participated in the cover-up – McLaren and all the other people who must have turned a blind eye for this to have continued for so long – had gone through a similar process, their capacity to care being increasingly blunted until, one day, they simply stopped giving a shit.

Then, about halfway through the third-to-last tape, she saw something that forced her to hit Stop and spend the next several minutes sitting there in stunned silence. Once her hands had stopped shaking sufficiently to work the remote again, she started up the tape, winding it back to make doubly sure of what she'd seen. She pressed Pause and spent over a minute staring at the image frozen on the screen, studying it until she was satisfied that she hadn't been mistaken.

She sat in silence for several more minutes, her insides churning, her hands clammy in her lap. Then, forcing herself to focus, she once again hit Play and moved on to the next victim.

By early afternoon, the task was complete – or at least as complete as it could ever be. Of course, she had no way of knowing whether the tapes constituted the sum total of what had actually been filmed. Certainly, the diaries appeared to be incomplete, with a number of pages torn out and a period of several months unaccounted for. And all that was assuming that the perpetrators had diligently recorded each and every act of abuse they'd committed. For all she knew, the material captured to tape merely scratched the surface.

And what now? Going to the police was out of the question. Twenty-four hours ago, she *might* have considered it, but her conversation with McLaren, and her growing realisation of the sheer scale of the Shadow Men's infiltration of the organisation, had put paid to that. Even taking the matter to a different local police authority seemed profoundly unwise, given that she had no idea how far the Shadow Men's reach extended. From the way McLaren had talked, it sounded like it was contained within the Strathkelvin force, but that was an awfully big assumption. And if her experience of the academic community was anything to go by, the world was a tiny place and shrinking by the day. You never knew who'd worked together in the past and still kept in touch, or who was a friend of a friend of a friend – or who valued solidarity with one's fellow officers over doing what was right.

The afternoon dragged by. For much of it, Jack was grumpy and unsettled – still mad at her for what she'd put him through the previous day, she imagined. She couldn't help thinking that a brief stroll would do him a world of good, but she didn't dare risk it. Her chance encounter with Vasilico at Partick Station had put the wind up her, hammering home just how much of a gamble she was taking each time she set foot outside the flat.

Shortly after nightfall – and shortly after Jack, finally exhausted from an afternoon of near-constant bawling, had dropped off to sleep – she heard the familiar hum of a motorbike approaching outside. She listened, not even daring to breathe. An eternity seemed to pass, then she heard footsteps in the stairwell, followed by a soft, understated knock. Anna, already at the door, drew back the bolt and wrenched it open.

There on the mat stood Fin and another woman with messy black hair, hacked off just below her ears in what looked suspiciously like a DIY job. Her head was low, her eyes downcast, an overwhelming sense of melancholy and hopelessness exuding from her every pore.

'Look who's here,' said Fin.

Anna stared at the other woman in slack-jawed amazement as recognition finally dawned.

'*Zoe?*'

Zoe raised her head to meet Anna's gaze with dull, tired eyes that were devoid of either hope or purpose.

'What . . . the *fuck* . . . have you done to your hair?' Anna spluttered, articulating the one coherent thought that was currently going through her head.

With a great effort, Zoe mustered a sad, mournful smile in response.

## 46

# Stronger

Anna tested the water's temperature, then turned to Zoe, who stood beside the tub, wordlessly awaiting instruction.

'Lift up your arms.'

Zoe obeyed this and each subsequent command unquestioningly as Anna undressed her. It was immediately obvious that she'd lost a frightening amount of weight. She'd always been one of those infuriating people blessed with the ability to stuff her face with as much food as she wanted without ever seeming to retain any of it, but now there was virtually nothing of her. Her collarbone and ribs protruded through her skin, and there was a sizeable gap between her thighs of the sort Anna associated with half-starved runway models, their eyes as dead and directionless as Zoe's.

Anna forced an encouraging smile. 'There now. All set.'

She helped Zoe into the bath and began to wash her with a sponge, adopting the same methodical approach she did with Jack. The water quickly turned dark and murky. Whatever Zoe had been doing with herself for the last month, it clearly hadn't included basic self-care.

They'd been like that for a solid ten minutes – Anna kneeling on the floor, sponging Zoe's back; Zoe staring glass-eyed at the far wall, knees drawn up to her chin – when, as if the act of the accumulated layers of grime being washed away had had a loosening effect on her tongue, Zoe finally began to speak.

She told Anna how it had all started for her, with Richie Deans' funeral and her chance conversation with Lucy Foster. She spoke about her initial forays into investigating the abuse at Netherfield, discovering Gillian

Crowley and learning from her about what had gone on at Willow Bank. As to what came next, Anna had already worked out much of it herself, but she let Zoe continue, sensing that the act of telling her story was serving as a much-needed form of catharsis for her. Zoe's tone remained flat and monosyllabic throughout, as if she was reporting dispassionately on something that had happened to someone else. She continued her tale until Mandy and Ruby's disappearance from her flat late on Hogmanay, then fell silent.

'What happened?' Anna asked, when the silence had gone on for well over a minute. 'The night Broadhurst was killed – what happened?'

For a long time, Zoe didn't respond, and Anna began to wonder if she'd even heard her. However, just when she was about to prompt her again, Zoe finally broke her silence.

'I was scared of him, y'know.' She barked a short, humourless laugh. ''Magine – me a grown wumman, scared of an ex-schoolteacher. The number o' times I thought about just marching up to his door and asking him straight out if he done it. Y'know, if he . . . if he hurt Victor. But I couldnae. Not till I seen Jack.'

'Jack?' Anna lifted her head in surprise at this apparent non-sequitur.

'He looked so . . . ' Zoe gave a helpless shrug. 'I dunno – *pure*. And helpless, and innocent. It was like the kick up the jacksie I was needing. Like, here was this perfect wee bundle of new life who couldnae dae a thing for hisself, and here I was faffing around about Broadhurst cos I was still caught up on that one time he called me intae his office and gave me a bollocking. I cannae really explain it. It just put it into perspective, somehow.'

'Did you . . . ?' Anna couldn't bring herself to actually say it.

'I went to confront him. I was gonnae dae what I shoulda done weeks ago: chap on his door and say to him, "Did you abuse my brother, yes or no?" I dunno what I'd've done if he'd said yes. I didnae exactly go there wi a plan. But I never got to find out, cos when I got there, I found someone'd beat me to it.'

Anna stared intently at Zoe, the sponge hanging limp in her hand.

'The front door was lying wide open. I shouted his name, and when I got no answer, I went on in.' She drew in a deep breath, hugging her legs tighter against her chest. 'He was lying there on the living room floor.

Someone'd done a number on him – stabbed him all over, a whole buncha times. There was blood everywhere. I just froze. I couldnae move. Couldnae think. Couldnae *anything*. And then, just like that, it all made sense. The video, the photos, the feeling I'd had for weeks that I was being followed. *They're setting you up,* I thought. *They're gonnae pin this on you.* Then I heard a creak on the stair and I didnae stop to see who it was. I turned and bombed it outta there like my arse was on fire.

'I knew I couldnae go back to the flat. I figured they'd be waiting for me there. So I ran straight into town and jumped on the first train heading down south. Didnae matter where. I just knew I had tae put as much distance between me and them as possible.'

Anna said nothing. She felt hollowed out. Of *course* Zoe hadn't killed Broadhurst. The very fact that she'd ever allowed herself to even consider it shamed her beyond all measure. Fin had called it right from the start: what sort of so-called friend wrote off her best pal at the drop of a hat?

'I 'membered the beach cottage in Blackpool,' Zoe went on, mercifully unaware of the thoughts going through Anna's mind. 'Weird, in't it? It was our chat up on the hill put me in mind of it. I figured it'd be way off anyone's radar, and it wasnae like anyone'd be using it in the middle of winter.' She gave a little shrug. 'Good a hiding-place as any.'

'And you've been there all this time?'

'Aye. I hopped a coupla trains on the way there – trying tae shake any tail I mighta had. But I don't think anyone was following me. Reckon they werenae expecting me tae bolt like that. I think, in all that confusion, I managed tae gie 'em the slip.'

'You could have come to me,' Anna said helplessly. 'I'd have helped you. Together, we could have . . . '

Zoe shook her head. 'Couldnae dae that tae ye. Not now's ye had Jacko tae think of. I knew neither of yese would be safe as long as I was hingin aroon like a bad smell. Though I thought . . . ' She paused to draw in another deep, mournful breath. 'I thought mibby, if some harm *did* come to me, mibby someday you'd pick up the trail and do what I wasnae able tae. S'why I kept banging on about Astley Street. I'd hid the evidence there, in case . . . ' She trailed off, leaving it unsaid. 'I was worried I'd been a bit too subtle, but then I figured, "Anna's a right brainbox, she'll work it out".'

Anna gave a sheepish smile. 'Took me a bit longer than it should've, but I got there in the end.'

Silence fell once more. Anna could feel tears pricking at her eyes and feared she was just a hair-trigger away from a full-on blubfest. To give herself something to do, she took down the shower-head and began to rinse Zoe's hair. It was tragic what she'd done to it. Her hair had always been stunning – long, lustrous and brilliantly red. Now, when Anna looked at it, all she could think about were the charred remnants of a doused fire.

'I kept waiting on my face turning up in the papers,' said Zoe. '*Zoe Callahan: wanted for housebreaking and murder.* I couldnae figure out why it never happened.'

Anna cleared the thickness in her throat. 'Fin worked that part out. She figured the real killers couldn't risk a nationwide manhunt. If they plastered your face all over the media, there was no guarantee they'd get to you first. That's why they tried to keep it under the radar – tailing me, trying to get me to tell them where you were. Because they figured if you'd confided in anyone, it'd be your old pal Anna, right?' She laughed feebly to cover her own sense of shame.

Zoe said nothing. She rested her chin on her knees, her bony back hunched forward as Anna squeezed shampoo into her ruined hair and began to work it in.

For a while, they carried on in silence, Anna massaging Reiko's luxury shampoo into Zoe's scalp, Zoe lost in her own thoughts. Anna knew there was something she needed to say. She wasn't sure how it would be received, but she knew her conscience would never again be clean if she kept it to herself.

'I had doubts, Zo,' she said. 'About you. Fin never gave up on you, but there were times when I let myself think you *might* have done it.' She shook her head. 'What am I saying? There was no "might have" about it. I thought you *had.*'

'I shoulda,' said Zoe quietly. 'If I was any sort of a big sister, I'da done it weeks ago, 'stead of faffing about on the internet and skulking in the shadows, watching him playing wi his grandweans. But I'm no strong enough. Havnae got that . . . *killer instinct.*' As she spoke those words, her voice turned into something ugly and guttural.

'Not strong?' Anna stared at her incredulously. 'Are you kidding? Just think about everything you've been through. Losing your parents at age five. Your own brother shot dead by police. Dominic Ryland. This. All of it. No matter what life throws at you, no matter how many times it knocks you down, you dust yourself off and get back up. You not having a killer instinct – it's not a sign of weakness, it's your *strength*.' She laid a hand on Zoe's shoulder. 'You're the strongest person I know. Way stronger than I'll ever be.'

Zoe didn't respond. Anna could tell she wasn't convinced by this paean to her courage and indefatigability. Not that she'd expected her to undergo a sudden radical change of heart – to leap out of the bath reinvigorated, raising a fist to the ceiling and crying, 'I am woman, hear me roar!' But, like her earlier confession about her doubts as to Zoe's innocence, it was something she'd felt compelled to say.

She stirred and exhaled a heavy breath. 'All right now, shut your eyes or you'll get soap in them.'

Wordlessly, Zoe complied, and Anna reached for the shower-head.

She rinsed Zoe's hair, dried her off and put her into one of Reiko's dressing-gowns, then guided her through to the red room and got her into bed. Then, perched at the foot of the bed, she told her side of the story – everything that had happened since Zoe had fled Glasgow, and everything her own investigations had turned up: Mandy, McLaren, Sullivan, the tapes, Strickland, the Shadow Men.

'I've been through the tapes,' she said, after a silence. 'Victor's not on them.'

'Aye,' said Zoe, 'but that disnae *prove* anything.'

Anna said nothing. She'd hoped telling her this would set her mind at ease, but deep down she'd known Zoe wouldn't be assuaged so easily.

'They sent you a video of another boy,' she pointed out, 'and just a picture of Victor. I know as well as you do what that was designed to make you think. But look at the balance of probability. If Victor really *was* abused, why not give you solid proof instead of trusting to luck you'd join the dots?'

Zoe shrugged. 'Mibby they lost the tape. Or mibby there never *was* a tape in the first place.' She looked at Anna plaintively. 'Balance of probability isnae enough. I need tae *know*. It's the only thing I have left to care about.'

'Zoe . . .'

'I'm serious. Just put me in a room wi they creeps for five minutes.' A thought occurred to her. 'That prick who's been pulling all the strings. Strickland. Just let me talk to him. Let me get my answer, then I can die happy.'

Anna shook her head softly. 'You know I can't do that.' Shuffling across the bed, she took Zoe's hand in hers. 'What I *can* do is stand by you, come what may. Whatever lies in store, no matter how powerful these forces are, we'll face them down together. I'm here for you, and I'm not going anywhere.'

Zoe lowered her eyes and tugged her hand free. 'I dunno why ye're so dead set on helping me. I mean, we both know how this ends. Same way it always does. I fuck up, and all the folk close to me get hurt. If ye had any sense at all, ye'd get as far away fae me as possible.'

Anna shook her head with fierce determination. 'I'm not going anywhere,' she repeated.

Zoe didn't appear to have heard her. 'I dunno – mibby I'm . . . like, cursed or something. See, I used tae believe ye make yer ain luck in the world.' She shook her head. 'But that's bullshit. Way I see it, yer card's marked fae birth, and there isnae a thing ye can do tae change it.'

Anna considered this. 'I think maybe it's a bit of both,' she said after a moment. 'You can't choose what life's going to throw at you, but you *can* choose how you respond to it. Life might deal you a seriously crappy hand, but you're not out of the game till you've played your last card.'

Zoe sighed and shook her head, tiring of Anna's stubbornness. That, or her tortured analogies. 'Fuck*sake*, Anna! Get this intae yer thick skull, will ye? I'm damaged goods. Ye need tae keep yer nose clean. It's no just you anymore. Ye've got family now, and family comes first.'

Anna laughed drily. 'Get with the programme, Zo. You're my family, every bit as much as Jack is. You're his Auntie Zoe, aren't you?'

There was a flicker of a reciprocal smile in Zoe's expression, though it went as quickly as it had come. 'This isnae your fight,' she said, with a weariness that suggested she knew she wasn't going to win this.

'You're wrong. It *is* my fight. It's my fight because I choose to make it mine. I'm not going to be a bystander in this, OK? I'm not going to let those crimes go unanswered.'

Zoe sighed and shook her head, but she made no further attempt to argue. She lay there, picking listlessly at the skin around her fingernails, Anna's continued presence seemingly neither here nor there.

At length, Anna stirred and got to her feet. She headed through to the bathroom and began to gather up Zoe's discarded clothes. The same clothes, Anna now realised, that Zoe had been wearing in the hospital the day she disappeared. She turned the T-shirt the right way round and rummaged inside the pockets of her jeans, making sure they were empty in preparation for putting them in the wash. In the back pocket, she felt something. It was a scrap of paper – grubby, battered, folded over multiple times, the corners softened through constant friction.

She unfolded it. It was a list of names. The famous list, she realised, that Gillian Crowley had given Zoe and that the Shadow Men had been prepared to move heaven and earth to get hold of. She spotted Broadhurst's name instantly, and De Groot's as well, though she doubted the latter had meant anything to Zoe. A couple of others she recognised as former Willow Bank teachers. Most, however, were so far-fetched as to be ridiculous. Politicians, celebrities, footballers, a Hollywood movie star whom she knew for a fact had been domiciled in the States since the 1970s . . . If the Shadow Men had known that all it amounted to was the febrile speculation of an overactive imagination, they'd probably have happily let Gillian and Pinnock publish it and destroy their story's credibility in the process.

And yet, despite it all, Zoe had somehow stumbled across that rare breed of conspiracy that wasn't just the product of the deluded fantasies of a bunch of shut-ins who spent too much time inhabiting their own echo-chambers. There might not be a nationwide plot involving the most powerful figures in Scotland's Establishment using prestigious schools as their personal playgrounds to indulge their sick predilections, but the reality, though more banal, was hardly any less horrific. Men at the top of the Strathkelvin Police Force had known this was going on and done nothing to stop it, and in some cases even participated in it.

She returned to the bedroom to find Zoe asleep, lying on her side in a foetal position, looking more innocent and helpless than Anna had ever seen her. Exhaustion, seemingly, had finally caught up with her. Shutting the door softly, Anna made her way through to the living room, where she found Fin on the sofa, bouncing Jack on her knee, coo-cooing at him.

She watched them for a moment from the doorway, enjoying this unconventional scene of domestic bliss, then headed in.

Hearing her approach, Fin turned and looked up at her. 'Well?'

Anna shook her head. 'She's in a bad state. I've known her since she was eleven years old and I've never seen her like this before. Not even when her brother died.'

Fin nodded soberly. 'Aye. She's had a tough time of it. S'why we gotta be ready to fight her corner, right?'

'Right,' said Anna.

Long after Fin had thrown in the towel and sloped off to bed, Anna remained in the living room with Jack in her arms, ruminating on the choices that lay before her. Truthfully, she had no idea if there was any way back for Zoe from any of this. It was all very well telling her that she was strong and that she was loved, but those words needed actions to back them up. Otherwise, they were just empty platitudes.

At length, she made a decision. It would be a massive gamble – one which, if it failed to pay off, risked jeopardising everything. But she knew it was time to trust her own instincts and judgement of character. And more to the point, she knew that it was the only realistic path available to her; that there was only one person who was in a position to help her.

She got out her phone and began to dial.

PART FOUR

The Early Days of a Better Nation

# 47

# Trust

*Thursday 4 February*

Vasilico sat on Reiko's sofa, flicking through one of the diaries from Hugh Sullivan's attic. Every so often, he stopped to shake his head in disbelief. Anna watched him from the opposite end of the room, studying his face intently – the pursed brows; the cheeks that, over the last few minutes, had all but drained of colour. Though he hadn't said a word as she'd laid out what she, Zoe and Fin had collectively discovered, his face told her everything she needed to know about what he was thinking.

Zoe and Fin had let her do all the talking, but she'd made sure they remained on standby to answer any questions that might arise, and to add a certain moral heft to her narrative. Their scepticism about Vasilico had been palpable from the outset, and Anna still sensed their doubt and distrust – more overtly from Fin than from Zoe, who remained withdrawn and uncommunicative and, Anna suspected, had simply decided to accept whatever fate threw at her.

Vasilico shut the diary and set it on the table next to the others. He looked up at Anna, skin taut around his eyes.

'I just can't . . . ' he said feebly.

'There's the tapes too,' said Anna. 'If you need more proof . . . ' She gestured to the stacks on the table.

He looked positively nauseous at the thought. 'That won't be necessary,' he said quietly.

Slowly, he rose from the sofa, the eyes of the three women tracking him intently.

'All right,' he said, after a moment, 'I believe you. I didn't want to, but I . . . ' He trailed off with a limp wave of his hand. 'You made the right decision coming to me.'

Anna didn't dare look at Fin. She could imagine her expression all too well.

'What happens now?' she asked.

Vasilico rubbed the bridge of his nose and exhaled heavily. 'I'm going to have to move carefully. "Sensitive" doesn't even begin to cover it. So many figures at the top of the organisation are implicated in this, and that's just the ones we know about. The number of people I can trust is limited to say the least. But I have to show due diligence here. I can't just go barging in and affect the arrests of scores of senior officers without building an airtight case first.

'The tapes alone should be enough to convict anyone who appears on camera, and the diaries should provide reasonable grounds for bringing in those we suspect of being the names behind the initials for questioning – though that on its own wouldn't stand up in a court of law. But if we're going to get the ones at the very top of the conspiracy, we're going to need McLaren onside. His testimony will be key.'

'And if he refuses to talk?'

'We're just going to have to hope I haven't lost my powers of persuasion, aren't we?'

'What about Strickland?' said Zoe quietly.

Anna thought she saw something akin to a spasm of pain crossing Vasilico's face. 'My hope,' he said, after a lengthy pause, 'is that, if he *is* the one who's been calling the shots, one of the others will be prepared to rat him out in exchange for a more lenient sentence.'

'Sounds dead cosy,' said Fin glibly.

As Vasilico glanced sharply in her direction, Anna swiftly cut in. 'When's the soonest you can make a move?'

Vasilico held Fin's gaze for a moment longer, then turned to Anna. 'We can't do this by half-measures. We can't risk one of the conspirators tipping off the others. We either nab them all in one go or the best we can hope to end up with is a bunch of low-level pawns while the rest scarper for the hills.'

Anna nodded soberly. She saw the sense in this, though she feared that what he was describing would take weeks to set up, if not longer. What was to happen to her and Zoe and Jack? Were they to wait in limbo, holed up in Reiko's flat or in some safe-house, spending every moment in constant dread of being discovered?

'What should we do in the meantime?'

Vasilico considered the question. 'For now,' he said eventually, 'the three of you are just going to need to sit tight for me. I'll be in touch as soon as I have anything more concrete for you.'

Anna assisted him in gathering the evidence into a couple of large carrier bags and saw him out with them.

'You know,' he said, as they reached the door to the flat, 'if I go through with this and it all comes to nothing, I'm going to be finished.'

'It won't come to that,' said Anna, with more conviction than she felt.

'Of course, to a certain extent it's academic. Regardless of whether we win or lose, my name's going to be dirt to a significant proportion of the Force.'

'Can you live with that?'

Vasilico was silent for a long moment, brows pinched in thought. 'Yes,' he said slowly. 'Yes, I think so.'

He looked to be on the verge of leaving when he suddenly turned to Anna, an intense look in his eyes.

'This is the bit I can't get out of my head,' he said in a strained whisper. 'All this, going on right under my nose, and I never . . . I mean, deep down, I always knew my uncle wasn't squeaky-clean. But *this* . . . '

'I know,' said Anna quietly. She'd experienced similar feelings herself over the last few days: the self-reproach, the soul-searching, wondering whether she should have noticed anything and whether there was something she could have done.

'I had doubts, you know,' said Vasilico. 'Not about . . . *this*. I swear to you I knew nothing about any of it. But that night in my office, when you told me Derek Sullivan had said the Shadow Men were after him, I started to wonder. Started asking questions of myself – who I was really working for, things I might have turned a blind eye to over the years.'

'I don't think they *were* onto him,' said Anna. Over the last couple of days, she'd had plenty of time to think, to run through the various possibilities in her head, and had grown increasingly convinced of the theory that had developed in her mind. 'The approaches to tracking him and Zoe down are just too different. With Zoe, they've clearly been at pains to keep the fact that they were searching for her out of the public eye, whereas with Derek they went in all guns blazing, circulating his likeness far and wide, broadcasting his status as a missing person from the rooftops. It was your uncle who ordered the efforts to be stepped up. He wouldn't have done that if he knew what was really behind his disappearance.' She shrugged helplessly. 'I honestly think they just saw him as a bog standard missing person.'

'In which case, his death was even more of a fucking waste,' Vasilico said morosely.

Anna reached out and gave his hand the lightest of squeezes. His skin was cool to the touch. 'Don't think that right now. Just focus on making sure these men face justice.'

Vasilico's expression hardened. 'Don't you worry. They're going to get what's coming to them.'

His grip tightened on the carrier bags. As he turned to go, Anna realised something was still troubling her – a last loose end she needed to tie up.

'Vasilico.'

He stopped and turned to face her.

'Mandy. The girl who was told to watch Zoe. She described her handler as a good-looking detective in his thirties who wears expensive suits and drives either a Porsche or a Jaguar.'

It took Vasilico a moment to cotton on. 'You don't seriously think . . . '

'I don't know what to think. I just know I have to ask.'

Vasilico looked at her for a long, uncomfortable beat. There was no anger or hurt in his eyes, but Anna nonetheless found it difficult to meet his gaze.

'Is there anything I can say to you to convince you it wasn't me?'

Anna shrugged helplessly, not knowing how to answer that.

Vasilico was silent for some time, seemingly deep in thought. 'Plessis,' he said eventually, and with an obviously heavy heart. 'The only other person in the Strathkelvin Police Force I know who fits that description and drives a Porsche is Detective Inspector Carl Plessis.'

*Plessis.* The cocksure detective who'd made the off-colour remarks about Derek's sexuality during the briefing at MIT HQ. Anna pictured him sitting at the table, leaning back in his seat, a schoolboy grin plastered on his face.

'You don't have a picture of him, do you?'

'Why?'

'Just humour me.'

'Feels like I've been doing a lot of that lately,' Vasilico said, more self-deprecatingly than unkindly. He fished out his phone, tapped the screen a few times and handed it to Anna. 'Here.'

Anna glanced briefly at the photo on the screen. It showed Plessis at some night out or other, turning to the camera with a look of inebriated surprise, one arm draped carelessly across the shoulders of a significantly younger blonde who looked like she couldn't wait to make her excuses. She transferred the image to her own phone and handed it back to Vasilico.

'I guess I'll wait for your call,' she said.

He left, Anna shutting the door after him. She locked and bolted it, then turned to find Fin leaning against the living room doorframe, arms folded.

'Hope ya know what you're doing,' she said. 'Cos, way I see it, there's a slightly greater than fifty-fifty chance you've just extended an open invitation to yer man there to fuck us all six ways from Sunday.'

# 48

# Loose Ends

*Friday 5 February*

'Right then, Trouble.' Anna gazed down at Jack with a look of remonstration. 'Let's see if we can get through this without either of us getting pee in their eye.' The stream produced by infant males, she'd learned, was nothing if not unpredictable in its direction of travel.

As she set to work unfastening the soiled nappy, Zoe leaned through the doorway, Anna's phone in her hand.

'It's that detective. He's asking for ye.'

To say that Anna currently had her hands full would have been an understatement. As she hesitated, torn between seeing her current task through and finding out what Vasilico wanted, Zoe moved alongside her.

'I'll do that.'

'You ever changed one of these before?'

'S'no exactly quantum physics, is it?'

More relieved than she cared to admit, Anna swapped places with Zoe and ducked out into the hallway with her phone.

'Vasilico?'

'I'm at McLaren's flat.' Vasilico's voice was crackly, the signal poor. 'Looks like he's cleared out. His car and a bunch of his clothes are missing and none of the neighbours have any idea where he's gone.'

*Shit.* 'Where does this leave us?'

'Up the proverbial creek. Without his testimony, the ringleaders walk. Simple as that.'

'You could still pull them in,' Anna said, conscious of the shrill of desperation in her voice. 'Sweat them. Make them think you've got more than you do. Hopefully one of them will sing to save themselves. Section Fourteen of the Criminal Procedure (Scotland) Act allows you to detain anyone you have reasonable grounds to suspect of an offence punishable by imprisonment.'

'I know what the Criminal Procedure Act says,' said Vasilico tetchily. 'These powers are notoriously ill-defined. Any half-decent lawyer would make mincemeat of a gamble like that, and you'd better believe these people have access to the best in town. They'd have their clients out of custody before their arses touched their seats.'

'So what do we do? Wait and do nothing?'

'*Yes*,' Vasilico snapped. 'In your case, exactly that.' She heard him exhale a frustrated breath. 'We can't rush any of this. In case you'd forgotten, we're playing with fire here.'

With that, he rang off.

Anna headed back to the living room. From the doorway, she watched Zoe, down on her knees, playing peekaboo with Jack, lying on his back with his limbs in the air. Over the last couple of days, she'd noticed that the only times when Zoe briefly came out of her state of inertia and appeared vaguely like her old self were when she interacted with Jack. Seeing this gave her hope. Hope that, when all this was over, there might yet be a way back for Zoe – and indeed for all of them.

Reluctant though she was to bring this moment to a close, she knew she needed to make a move. Clearing her throat, she stepped into the room.

'Hey.'

'Hey,' said Zoe noncommittally, already retreating back into herself. 'What'd he want?'

'Nothing. Just double-checking a couple of details.' There seemed no need to burden Zoe with the truth. 'Did Fin leave already?'

'Aye. While you were in the shower.'

'Best make tracks myself, then.' Anna bent down to scoop Jack up. 'I'll try not to be gone any longer than I absolutely have to, but mind and keep a low profile, huh? Stay away from the windows, keep the door locked and don't answer it to anyone.'

Zoe nodded disinterestedly. 'Right enough, aye.'

'I'm serious. If anyone comes sniffing round here, you're to call me immediately, OK?'

'Aye-aye. Quit fussing. I'm no an eejit.'

'I know you're not.'

She got Jack dressed and ready to go, then tugged on her coat, secured him in the sling and shouldered the baby-bag she'd packed earlier.

'Here.' Zoe handed Anna her bank card. 'Ye'll do what we spoke about?'

Anna pocketed the card with a nod. 'I will.'

The café in Rutherglen was noisy and bustling, which suited Anna's needs just fine. Mandy and Ruby were waiting for her, perched on stools at a high table near the back, Ruby so far off the ground that Anna felt her own extremities tingling at the sight. As she clambered onto the vacant stool opposite them, a waitress approached them with a pen and pad.

'Have you ordered?' Anna asked Mandy.

Mandy shook her head.

Anna slid the menu across to her. 'Well, take your pick. My treat.'

Mandy took up the invitation all too enthusiastically, ordering the all-day breakfast, despite it being mid-afternoon. Anna, contenting herself with a coffee, watched as mother and daughter demolished the contents of the plate laid in front of them with unrestrained gusto, letting them eat their fill before turning to business.

'The two of you should leave Glasgow if you can,' she told Mandy, once she was sure Ruby was otherwise distracted, chasing egg-yolk around the plate with a piece of bread. 'At least for a couple of weeks. I can't predict what's going to go down or when, but it could get messy. It's definitely not safe for you to carry on staying in Zoe's flat.'

'How? Whit's happening?'

'It's better if you don't know. All I'll say is I hope some very unpleasant people are going to get their just rewards. But there's an awful lot of scope for things to go badly wrong. I want you and Ruby as far away from the fallout as possible.'

'You?' Mandy looked sceptical.

'Well, a mutual friend. She asked me to give you something.'

Anna took out a bundle of money – £2,000 in twenties, withdrawn from a succession of ATMs on the way there. Mandy stared at it with saucer-like eyes, as if she couldn't quite believe it was real. Anna suspected it was the most money she'd ever seen. Hell, it was the most money *Anna* had ever seen – at least as physical currency and in one place.

'Whit for?' Mandy eventually managed to say.

'For you. And for her.' Anna nodded towards Ruby. 'To see that you're both taken care of.'

She didn't mention that the money had come from her own bank account. Nor did she plan to tell Zoe.

Mandy continued to stare at the money, lying there on the counter for the taking. She looked suspiciously at Anna.

'Whit makes ye think I willnae spend it on smack?'

'I don't think you will. And if you do, that's your choice. It's yours. No strings.'

Mandy hesitated for a moment. Then, as if she feared Anna would change her mind, she snatched the money and jammed it into the pocket of her denim jacket.

'We'll get ye a new winter coat, won't we, Rubes?' she said, turning to her daughter. 'Something nice 'n' cosy for the cold weather.'

Ruby, oblivious to what was happening but sensing that her mother was happy, beamed wide. Looking at her, Anna was again struck by how much she reminded her of Zoe with her gap-toothed grin and heavy spattering of freckles. Even their hair – dark, sticky and amateurishly cut – now looked similar.

'I'm serious,' she said, turning to Mandy. 'Look after that little girl of yours. It's not like you can replace her.'

'I know,' said Mandy tetchily.

*And I know you know,* thought Anna.

'There's one other thing,' she said. She got out her phone and, calling up the photo of Plessis, passed it to Mandy. 'This man – is he the one who made you spy on Zoe?'

Mandy didn't glance at the phone for more than a second before returning it to Anna. 'Aye, that's him. Wish someone'd wipe that grin aff his face.'

'With a little luck,' Anna said, 'someone will.'

She gathered her things and got up to go.

'Miss,' Mandy called.

Anna turned, stopping in her tracks. 'What?'

Mandy stared back at her for a long, awkward moment.

'Nuttin,' she said eventually. 'Just thanks.'

Anna's second and final appointment was on the other side of the city, in the leafy boulevards of the West End. Of the two, it was the one she'd least been looking forward to – both because she knew it would be an uphill battle and because of what lay at its end.

As she sat on the bus, Jack nestled against her, she fired off a text to Vasilico – *Confirmed: Plessis is part of it*. Then, after disembarking on Great Western Road, she turned onto Carrington Street, climbed the steps to the house at the end of the row and rang the bell.

Sophie Hennessy opened the door and stared at her, first in astonishment, then in admonishment.

'I've got a favour to ask,' said Anna.

'Why am I not surprised?'

For a moment, Anna thought that was going to be it. She should have known better. Before she'd even drawn breath, Sophie was off on one, delivering her rebuke with a level of gusto that suggested she'd been waiting for this opportunity for some time.

'You really are something else, Anna Scavolini. First there's that business with you running off in the middle of the night, then you disappear for days on end, not answering your phone, leaving me imagining all *sorts* of worst-case scenarios . . . and now, out of the blue, you show up at my door looking for a *favour*?'

Anna saw no point trying to refute any of these points. None of them were, after all, untrue.

'Pretty much.'

'Well, let's hear it, then.' Sophie folded her arms, clearly relishing the prospect of saying no to whatever Anna was about to ask for.

'I need you to look after Jack for a few days.'

'I'm positive I didn't hear that right.'

Anna gritted her teeth and said nothing. *Let her do the whole foot-stamping, what-the-hell's-the-matter-with-you thing. Let her get it out of her system.*

'When was your last meeting with your psychiatrist? Because the evidence in front of me says that either you're in the grip of a full-on manic episode or else you're turning into one of those negligent mothers you read about in the papers who abandon their kids at the drop of a hat to go off gallivanting. It's not fair, you know, dropping off the face of the earth, then showing up when you need a favour and expecting everyone else to just fall into line to suit you.'

Anna bit her tongue, refusing to be goaded into a fight. She wished she could tell Sophie the truth: that she wasn't delusional, and that it was *because* she was so concerned for Jack's wellbeing that she was entrusting him to the care of someone who she knew would keep him safe in the event that anything happened to her. Sophie, meanwhile, continued to talk, expounding loquaciously about how vital it was during this early stage in a child's development to have proper mother/baby bonding, laying out each and every one of Anna's deficiencies in lurid detail.

'It's abundantly clear to me,' she said, 'that you don't actually want this child. I can't think why you even had him in the first place.'

As Sophie continued her sermon, it dawned on Anna that constantly leaning on Sophie, expecting her to jump at her every beck and call, no questions asked, would have been a whole lot more reasonable if she'd ever done *anything* to reciprocate the woman's friendship. But no – she was too self-absorbed, too wrapped up in her own priorities for it to have ever occurred to her to offer to watch Cosmo for a few hours or take her on a spa weekend or even treat her well-intentioned parenting advice with anything but seething resentment. It always *had* been a one-way street with them. Sophie might be sanctimonious and self-satisfied and holier-than-thou, but Anna, to borrow a turn of phrase from Reiko, was a user. And realising this, realising how badly she'd treated Sophie, realising the extent to which she'd taken her companionship for granted, she found herself wishing that there was someone, *anyone* else she could have turned to. But there *was* no one else – and certainly none more reliable than Sophie. And therein lay the rub. Because she knew that, however much Sophie might rant and rave, however much of a martyr she might paint herself to be, she would ultimately agree to what was being asked of her. Because she was, at her core, a fundamentally decent person – far more decent than Anna deserved.

And so it proved. Once Sophie had said her piece, once she'd got all the high-handed recrimination out of her system, she gave a deep sigh.

'I'll take him, Anna,' she said, resplendent in her magnanimity. 'But mark me, this is positively the last time I do anything like this for you.'

*And with any luck, it'll be the last time I ask you,* Anna thought.

She handed Sophie the baby-bag, then took Jack out of his sling and, pressing him close to her, breathed in deeply, as if trying to inhale enough of his essence to last her until such a time as she was reunited with him.

'See you soon, Trouble,' she whispered.

She kissed his head and deposited him in Sophie's arms. Then, not wanting to prolong the agony for a moment longer, she immediately turned and hurried down the steps, trying her damnedest to keep the tears at bay till she was round the corner and out of sight.

## 49

# The Coming Storm

Light rain pattered against the window of a ground-floor motel room on the outskirts of Lochwinnoch. Gil McLaren stood facing it as he tipped the last drops from a bottle of Glen Mhor down his throat. He'd come out here to be alone. To think. He stood for a moment, swaying on unsteady legs, then let the bottle fall to the floor and made his way over to the hard single bed that, together with the room, had set him back £17 for a single night.

He unzipped the nondescript gym bag that lay beside him, then carefully, almost reverently, drew out a break-action double-barrelled shotgun, followed by a small cardboard box containing two shells. Placing the gun between his knees to steady it, he loaded a shell into each barrel. He closed the break, then slowly slid both muzzles into his open mouth. He shut his eyes. His trembling forefinger hovered over the trigger.

For almost a full minute, he remained like that with the gun in his mouth, holding his breath until his lungs burned. In his mind, he heard the words people had used to describe him, both in the pages of the tabloids and to his face. *Lazy, incompetent drunk. Waste of space. Paedophile enabler.* They became louder and louder, one each crueller and more cutting than the last – a cacophony of insults building to a dreadful crescendo.

Then, in a sudden rush of movement, he whipped the gun out of his mouth and released his breath in a violent, strangled sob. He collapsed forward, sinking to his knees on the floor at the foot of the bed. He gulped down air, eyes and nostrils streaming, sobbing with each successive breath he took. Sobbing for the boys he'd let down, and for himself – too cowardly to stand up and fight for those who couldn't fight for themselves.

Too cowardly even to pull the trigger and finally silence those voices.

As darkness fell, Anna drew within sight of the flat on Trongate. She'd done all her crying on the subway, determined to put on a brave face for Zoe's sake. She found her in the living room, stretched out on the sofa, watching some mindless celebrity cookery show on the TV through glazed eyes.

'All right, doll?' Zoe looked up as Anna stepped into the room.

'Grand, yeah.'

'That thing I asked ye to do . . . '

'It's done.'

'And Jacko?'

'Safe.'

After that, neither of them spoke. Anna couldn't think of anything to say – and as for Zoe, who knew what, if anything, was going through her mind right now? It continued to grow darker outside, the headlights of the passing cars glancing across the ceiling, a fine mist of rain visible on the windowpane.

They were still sitting in silence when Fin got back. She stood, leaning one arm against either side of the doorframe, smiling louchely at the pair of them.

'Wow! Could cut the air in here with a shiv. No prizes for guessing who's the only one of us who got laid today.'

All through the evening, the tension continued to build like a pressure headache. Everyone was speaking in monosyllables, and long, excruciating stretches of time elapsed with no one saying a word – including Fin, who, after some initial attempts at lighthearted banter, had thrown in the towel and contented herself with matching the moody silence of the other two. There could be little doubt that a storm of some sort was coming.

After some time, Anna excused herself and took herself to the bathroom, where, perched on the side of the bath, she unbuttoned her top, fitted the cumbersome pump and set about expressing another round of milk from her swollen, aching boobs. The process was slow, the resulting yield underwhelming – a testament to her heightened state of agitation –

but she dutifully dated the bottles with a view to storing them in the freezer until she could be reunited with Jack.

The thought of him caused the pangs of separation, which until now she'd succeeded in suppressing, to bubble to the surface once again. She looked at her watch. Twenty to eight. If he was on anything approaching his usual timetable, he'd be settling into the first of his nighttime sleeps before too long. She did up her top, then got out her phone and dialled Sophie on Skype.

After ringing for an eternity, Sophie's face filled the screen, her features fish-eyed and all the more aggressive-looking for it.

'Yes?' she barked, as if she was challenging Anna to single combat.

'Just wanted to see how Jack was.'

'*Well*,' Sophie huffed, 'he's *obviously* been somewhat unsettled by today's goings-on. It's really not good, all this upheaval. Babies need stability, they need routine, they need—'

'Is he *OK*, Sophie?' Anna forced herself to keep her own voice level in the face of Sophie's singsong sarcasm.

'He's fine,' said Sophie, in a tone that suggested this state of affairs came as a disappointment to her. 'He's just had his evening feed, and he looks like he's thinking about sleep.'

'Can you put him on? I'd like to say goodnight.'

Sophie rolled her eyes. 'You know, Anna, I hardly think *Skype* is the optimal medium for a five-week-old infant to—'

'Just put him on the fucking phone, Sophie,' said Anna, her earlier feelings of self-recrimination swiftly evaporating.

Sophie huffed and puffed a bit, then her face disappeared from view and, sooner than Anna had been prepared for, Jack filled the screen. He was in Cosmo's old cot, looking drowsy but nonetheless contented. He raised an arm above his head in a jerky movement, his little fingers closing as they grasped thin air.

Anna wiped her eyes and plastered a broad smile on her face. 'Hey, Trouble. Aren't you looking cosy? You have a good night now, you hear? Sleep well, and don't give your Auntie Sophie any hassle.'

She considered leaving it at that, acutely conscious of Sophie's continuing presence at the other end of the line. Then, managing to overcome her embarrassment, she launched into an awkward, quavering rendition of the same folk song she'd sung to him outside Partick Station a few days earlier. As she warbled and trilled, she saw his eyelids growing increasingly heavy, and told herself the comforting lie that this was down to him being soothed by his mother's dulcet tones and not simply because he was exhausted after yet another day of being passed from pillar to post. By the time she finished, his eyes were closed and his chest was rising and falling gently.

'I'll see you soon,' she whispered.

She felt her eyes growing moist again. Then, as Jack disappeared from view and Sophie raised the phone to her own face again, mouth already opening to speak, she thumbed the End Call button.

As she pocketed her phone, she heard the door opening. She turned to see Fin leaning in.

'Know this stall's occupied, but d'ya mind?' She affected a theatrical whisper. 'I'm busting for a slash.'

Anna hastily scrubbed at her eyes and cleared her throat. 'Go ahead.'

'Lifesaver.'

Fin brushed past her, dropped her drawers and planted herself on the toilet.

'Cute song ya got there,' she said, as the sound of urine splashing met Anna's ears. 'What's it mean?'

'Haven't a clue,' said Anna, wondering just how long Fin had been standing outside, listening to her cringeworthy performance.

'Well,' Fin shrugged, unconcerned, 'got a nice tune to it anyway.' The flow stopped, was silent for a moment, then started again. She winced apologetically. 'Sorry. S'all this waiting around. Makes me antsy. And when I get antsy, I do a grand impression of Niagara Falls.'

Anna smiled. 'It's all right.'

It occurred to her, as she continued to perch on the bath and Fin continued to urinate, that this entire situation was seriously weird. Weird and yet, strangely enough, not in the least bit awkward. There seemed to be some unspoken appreciation on both their parts of the intimacy and camaraderie afforded by them sharing such a private moment together.

The flow petered off into silence. 'There we are. Done.' Fin reached for a wad of toilet paper. 'Gotta say,' she continued as she bent down to wipe herself, 'kinda wish someone'd sung bedtime lullabies like that to me when

*I* was a tiddler. Never know – things mighta turned out different.' She got to her feet and flushed the toilet.

Anna was silent for a time, listening to the swirl of the water in the toilet bowl. Then, as it gurgled into silence, she lifted her head.

'That comment I made the other night. About you not knowing what it's like to have a family. I was out of order.'

Fin dismissed this with a wave. 'Sure we all say things we don't mean in the heat of the moment. Forget it. I already have.'

'No, I *was*, and I'm sorry. You were right – Victor being on those tapes or not shouldn't have made a difference to how I felt about the notion of Zoe killing Broadhurst. There's no moral distinction – or at least there shouldn't be. But for some reason we're conditioned to value the lives of family members over all others.'

'Hey, don't be dissing family now. Family matters. Doesn't matter if it makes sense or not.'

Anna shrugged limply 'I guess. Anyway,' she went on, as Fin buttoned her jeans, 'I'm hardly an authority on familial relations. My relationship with my own mother is non-existent, and I'm not exactly parent-of-the-year material myself.'

'Sure ya are,' said Fin effortlessly.

Anna was silent for some time. When she finally spoke, her tone was brittle and flinty. 'Earlier today, someone told me it was obvious I'd never wanted a child.'

'What a shitbird!' said Fin, with genuine feeling. 'Who said that? Where d'they get off saying nasty shite like that?'

'Doesn't matter. The point is, they weren't wrong. Not altogether, anyway. This . . . having a baby . . . was never part of the plan. At least, not at this stage in my life.'

Fin gave Anna a puzzled look. 'So why'd ya go through with it? I mean, no offence, but you don't exactly strike me as one of the "life begins at conception" mob.'

Anna laughed hollowly. 'I'm not. Believe me, that's the last thing I am.'

'So why, then?'

For almost a full half-minute, Anna didn't reply. This wasn't a conversation she relished having with anyone – least of all someone she barely knew, far less considered a friend. Answering that question would involve reopening old wounds she'd carried with her for years without letting on to anyone – not even the people closest to her. And yet, sometimes it was easier to talk to a stranger about intensely private matters, for the very reason that you wouldn't have to face them every day thereafter with the knowledge that, in their eyes, you were no longer the person they'd thought you were. Wasn't that why so many people spent good money unburdening themselves to therapists?

She exhaled a heavy breath. 'When I was in my early twenties – in the middle of the first year of my doctorate – I ended up getting pregnant. I was in a semi-serious relationship at the time, and we'd been taking precautions, but . . . well, these things happen, don't they? And straight away, I knew I couldn't go through with it.'

She shrugged, attempting to convey indifference; that it was all water under the bridge. 'You know how it goes. I was young – a cash-strapped student determined not to rely on parental handouts – and the father was a man I already had an inkling I didn't want to spend the rest of my life tethered to.' She scoffed softly. 'Pure pragmatist, me. And on top of all that, I'd just recently been diagnosed as bipolar and was still coming to terms with all the implications of *that*. Frankly, I had enough on my plate without adding a baby to the mix. So I made myself an appointment with a clinic and went without telling anyone.

'It wasn't out of concern over being judged,' she added, pre-empting any comment to that tune from Fin. 'The circles I moved in were all overwhelmingly pro-choice, and I wasn't going to lose any sleep over what the other side thought of me. I didn't tell anyone because it wasn't their business. My body, my choice. Whatever anyone else thought about it was irrelevant. Besides, the last thing I wanted was a whole bunch of people feeling sorry for me.'

'So you went 'n' got it done,' said Fin.

'So I went and got it done. And that part of it – the procedure itself – was fine. I mean, it wasn't *pleasant*, but it was . . . ' She shrugged limply. 'You know. I felt pretty drained afterwards, but I'd known to expect that. It wasn't till some time later, when that sensation of feeling permanently empty still hadn't gone away, that I started to realise it wasn't a physical thing so much as an emotional one.

'I tried to be rational about it. Told myself the foetus hadn't been advanced enough to be viable; that it was absurd to feel like I'd lost something. So I carried on, pretending to everyone that everything was fine. Needless to say, the relationship I was in broke down pretty soon after. To this day, I still couldn't swear to whether it was because of the strain of lying to him – about the pregnancy, about the abortion, about what I was going through – or if it was headed that way anyway.'

She glanced up at Fin, with a look that bordered on accusatory. 'Have you ever pretended to be someone you're not for months on end, performing a role twenty-four-seven? It's *exhausting*. And last year, when I realised I was pregnant again, it was like history repeating itself, and I knew there was no way I could go through all that a second time. Because that's exactly what would have happened if I'd had another termination. Just like before, I'd have gone through the whole thing alone, telling no one, pretending that everything was hunky-dory. I know it, you know it, there's no point pretending otherwise. I wasn't built to share my problems with other people.'

Fin shrugged. 'Y'ain't making too bad a fist of it just now.'

Anna smiled drily. 'Here's the thing about the so-called abortion debate. Folk who're anti-choice assume those of us that are pro see it as this tiny, trivial procedure that we decide to go through with no more thought than what we're going to order for dinner. It's not true. I'll defend the right of every woman to access those services with every breath in my body, but it's still something I never want to experience again.'

She drew in a shuddering breath, the emotion unexpectedly catching in her throat. 'And as the weeks went by and it continued to grow inside me, I thought, *It might not be such a bad thing after all*. Sure, I wasn't feeling those warm, glowy feelings every other woman in my position seemed to experience, but perhaps they'd come in time. And even if they didn't, I might still be able to treat it less as a problem and more as an opportunity. There was so much about the way my parents raised me that I vehemently disagreed with. I think a part of me saw this as my chance to do it the "right" way, without making any concessions to anyone. It was a chance to prove I had my illness under control; that it didn't define who I was or what I could do. And it was a chance to give the middle finger to convention – to succeed as a working single mother in a system set up to make me fail.' She gave a dry, humourless laugh. 'That's me in a nutshell, though, isn't it? Bringing a child into the world to make a statement. Self-centred to the bitter end.'

'I've seen ya with Jack,' said Fin quietly. 'I've heard ya. No one can pretend ya aren't doing right by him. That ya don't love him.'

'Maybe. I do . . . ' Anna grasped for the right word. ' . . . *feel* things for him. I care about what happens to him. I don't want to see him hurt or unhappy. But is that enough? And is it love? I don't know.'

'Does anyone? What even *is* love? Can you catch it, bottle it, stick a label on it? Can you hell. F'ya ask me, you're setting yourself up against an unrealistic ideal.'

Anna, unconvinced, said nothing.

'You wanna've met *my* ma,' Fin persisted. 'She was a real piece o' work – drank herself dizzy, beat me 'n' my brothers on an almost daily basis. And look, I know I got my issues, but I like to think I still turned out all right, all in all. Point is, from everything I've seen, you're a million times the mum that waste o' space ever was, so I'd say yer boy's got it pretty good.' She looked Anna square in the eyes, her expression forthright and sincere. 'You don't have to get it right all the time. You don't have to be Super-woman. Just . . . y'know, a semi-decent human being.'

Anna didn't know what to say. Fin was positively the last person she'd have chosen to turn to for a pep talk – and yet, as she gazed up at her, she realised this had been exactly what she'd needed to hear.

'I think you turned out better than all right,' she said. 'I mean, you're here at untold risk to yourself, helping Zoe. Helping me. Given the choice between having you in my corner and not, I know what I'd choose.'

'Ah, spare me the adulations, Professor,' said Fin good-naturedly. 'You'll be having me blushing.'

Climbing over Anna's outstretched legs, she headed over to the sink and began to rinse her hands.

'To be honest,' Anna admitted, 'I'm slightly surprised you didn't bail yesterday when I brought Vasilico on board.'

Fin looked up from drying her hands. 'No lie – I was tempted. I mean, I thought ya were off yer trolley when ya showed up with him on yer arm. Still do, to be honest. But I guess that just makes it more important than ever that the likes of us stick around to hold the likes of him to account. Can't be letting those feckers off the hook.'

' "All that's necessary for evil to triumph is that good men do nothing",
you mean?'

'Hey, steady on. I'm no man, and I sure as hell ain't a good one.'

Anna chuckled. 'Fair point.'

'But Zoe is,' Fin went on. 'Good, I mean. That's . . . well, I guess it's
something to aspire to, innit?' She paused. 'Plus she's got an arse to die
for, 'specially in skinny jeans.'

Anna shook her head. 'Do you ever take anything seriously?'

Fin beamed. 'Nope, chronologically incapable.'

'I think you mean "chronically".'

'Well, you're the professor, I s'pose.'

Anna smiled and turned away. She was glad they'd had this conversation.
Against all her expectations, Fin had succeeded in making her feel a good
deal better about herself. It was just possible that she might get some sleep
tonight after all.

'Hey, Anna.' Fin's voice piped up behind her.

'Huh?'

'Sorry about this.'

Even as Anna began to turn, Fin came at her from behind, looping an
arm round her neck in a choke hold. Before Anna could recover from the
surprise, she felt something soft and damp, like a flannel washcloth, being
pressed against her mouth and nose. On reflex, she drew in a breath. A
nauseatingly sweet smell filled her nostrils. Her lungs burned ice-cold.
She tried to struggle, but Fin held firm.

'Don't fight it,' Anna heard her saying, though her voice sounded faint
and distant. 'Just go with it.'

Seconds passed. She began to feel lightheaded. There was a pulsating
hum in her head, growing in intensity with each moment. Her last thought,
before unconsciousness took her, was that if she was out for the count,
who was going to give Jack his 2 a.m. feed?

Fin held Anna against her until she felt her body go slack. She removed
the chloroform-soaked flannel from her mouth and carefully laid her on
her side on the floor. For a few seconds, she continued to watch her, making
sure she was genuinely out for the count.

'Sweet dreams, Professor,' she murmured, and slipped out.

\* \* \*

Zoe, sporting dark jeans and a black hoodie, was waiting for Fin in the hallway as she emerged, zipping up her motorcycle jacket.

'Take care of business?'

Fin nodded.

'Ye get what we talked about?'

'Yeah.'

Zoe held out her hand.

Fin hesitated, a look of profound reluctance coming over her. Then, slowly, she reached behind her back and retrieved a small black pistol from her waistband. She stood there for a moment, biting her bottom lip.

'You promised,' said Zoe.

'I know. I just . . . '

She sighed and shook her head, then handed the gun over. Zoe took it and weighed it in her hand, then went to slip it into her jacket pocket.

'Not like that,' said Fin. 'Here.'

She took the pistol from Zoe, spun her around and slipped it into the waistband of her jeans, pushing it down until only the handle protruded, then tugged down the back of her top to cover it.

They turned to face one another.

'So this is it,' said Fin.

'Getting cold feet?' asked Zoe.

Fin grinned wolfishly. 'Never.'

'Then let's do this.'

Together, they exited the flat and headed out into the night.

## 50

# Kiss and Tell

At 21:37, Assistant Chief Constable Peter Strickland switched off his desk-lamp, shrugged on his jacket and overcoat, and prepared to head for home. He collected his Jaguar from the car park and set off through the city centre, picking up speed as he thundered down the M8 towards Newton Mearns.

As he drove, the strains of Brahms filling the vehicle, his mind turned to the weekend. He'd packed the family off to their second home in Aviemore earlier that morning, following a decision by himself and Melanie to take the boys out of school a day early for an impromptu long weekend. They'd intended to spend some time there over New Year, but the chaos that had engulfed the organisation at that time had well and truly put paid to that idea. As it was, he'd had to send Melanie and the boys on ahead: too much to be done at the office. But now all the most pressing business had been taken care of, and the rest would keep till Monday. He'd drive up first thing tomorrow and join them for two entire days of rest and recuperation, the responsibilities accorded by his lofty position temporarily forgotten. There was only one final piece of business to take care of: a late-night visit from his nephew – their first proper catch-up since the latter had got back from his extended leave of absence. Paul had called him earlier to arrange it. Less a debrief than an informal chat, he'd said. Just a few small matters that he wanted to make Strickland aware of.

Strickland made good time, pulling into the grounds of his isolated villa on the outskirts of Newton Mearns a little before 22:05. As expected, the house was in darkness. A lot of the homes in the area had automatic timers on their lights, but Strickland had never seen the point. It was an extraordinarily safe neighbourhood, with one of the lowest recorded crime rates in the country – perfect for raising a young family, and entirely befitting of an Assistant Chief Constable. He stored the Jaguar in the adjoining garage, covering it with its protective tarpaulin, then crunched across the gravel to the main entrance.

He climbed the stairs in the dark. Normally, Melanie would have every light in the house on for him – a beacon in the dark, calling him home. But tonight it was just him, and he was a responsible citizen of the earth, supremely conscious of his carbon footprint – not to mention the electricity bill. Even on an ACC's salary, such things had to be considered – especially when one took into account all the other outgoing expenses, such as the boys' education and the mortgage on the second home. Besides, even with his eyes closed, he knew the place like the back of his hand.

He entered his oak-panelled office and headed over to the polished mahogany writing desk by the window. He set his briefcase down, tossed his keys into the ashtray that he – a lifelong non-smoker – used to store odds and ends, then bent down to switch on the vintage banker's desk lamp. Its narrow beam created a pool of light around the desk, leaving the rest of the room in semi-darkness. He glanced up and stifled a gasp.

In front of him, a woman emerged from behind the shadow of the door, a pistol pointed at him in her outstretched hand. She wore a black sweatshirt with the hood up, the dark fabric accentuating her pale skin and the freckles across the bridge of her nose. She advanced towards him, training the gun on him.

Instinctively, he reached for the desk phone. As he did so, he sensed movement behind him, and felt something hard and cool pressing against the back of his neck.

'Now then,' said a voice behind his ear, 'ya don't wanna be doing anything daft now, ya hear? 'Less ya fancy getting fifty thousand volts in yer neck.'

Strickland slowly withdrew his hand from the phone. The pressure on his neck subsided. He remained perfectly still, watching as a second woman circled around him, training a stun gun on him in much the same way that her partner-in-crime was training her pistol. Long dark hair framed equally dark eyes that had more than a hint of madness in them. She smiled at him, flashing two rows of teeth that were slightly too large for her mouth.

'Right then, Pete, ready for a little kiss 'n' tell?'

## 51

# Important

When Anna came to, she was lying on the bathroom floor, her cheek cold and tender from resting on the linoleum. She quickly became aware of two things. First, her entire consciousness was engulfed by the sort of nausea that normally came the morning after a particularly heavy all-night bender. Second, she had a pounding headache, worse than the worst migraine she'd ever experienced – so powerful she could practically *hear* it.

As the world stopped spinning and she began to regain control of her basic motor functions, she realised that the pounding was not coming from inside her head but from somewhere else in the building. She struggled upright, clinging to the side of the bath for support. Her legs were like rubber. Her eyes refused to focus. The pounding, which she now realised was originating from the front door, continued unabated.

Feeling her way along the walls, she dragged herself down the hall corridor towards the door, though answering it was practically an afterthought. She had one priority and one only: going after Zoe and Fin and stopping them. There was no doubt in her mind as to their destination and their goal once they reached it. Zoe's words played over and over in her mind, mingling with the sounds of banging. Put me in a room with that prick Strickland, she'd said. Let me get my answer and I can die happy.

Anna fumbled with her phone, her thumb slipping and sliding on the smooth screen as she struggled to navigate the address book in her current state. She was still wrestling with it when she thrust open the door to reveal Mandy standing on the mat. Mandy was in a seriously agitated state, her huge eyes even wider than usual, hopping from foot to foot as if her bladder was about to burst.

'I wasnae sure I should say anyhin.' The words came spewing out of her mouth before Anna had a chance to open hers. 'I mean I know you told me tae take Ruby and go and I was gonnae I swear I was but it's been bouncing aroon inside ma heid aw day and I was gonnae say somehin earlier but I thought mibby it'd only make hings worse but then I realised I cannae just say nothing, no when—'

'Whatever it is, Mandy, it's going to have to wait.' Anna brushed past her into the stairwell, phone to her ear, willing Vasilico to pick up.

'But ye don't understand!' Mandy hurried down the steps after her.

'No, it's you that doesn't understand,' said Anna, without turning to look back at her. 'I need to go *now*. People's lives could depend on this.'

'This too!'

Mandy grabbed Anna's arm, bringing her to an abrupt halt. Anna turned to face her in exasperation, Vasilico's voice crackly and muffled on the phone's speaker. *'Anna? Hello? You there?'*

Mandy gazed at Anna, her expression imploring. 'Ye have tae listen. This is IMPORTANT.'

## 52

# Questions and Answers

Strickland stood behind his desk, facing Zoe and Fin. 'Do you think,' he said, looking at each of them in turn, 'that it would be acceptable for me to sit down?'

His demeanour indicated neither fear nor anger – the two emotions with which Zoe had expected to be confronted. There was an odd sort of meekness about him – a malleability, a willingness to please that she found quite disorienting. He reminded her vaguely of a bellhop at one of those posh hotels, standing at the door, eagerly awaiting a tip.

'All right,' said Fin, 'but no funny business.'

Strickland raised both hands, palms outward, as a show of his good intent. Without taking his eyes off his two captors, he lowered himself into the chair behind the desk, folded his hands in front of him and gazed up at them benignly.

'Now then, ladies, how might I be of service?'

Still training the pistol on him, Zoe lowered her hood with her free hand. 'Know who I am?'

Stickland nodded. 'I do indeed. You're Zoe Callahan.'

'And why'm I here?'

'I imagine it's because you have questions – in which case, I'll do my level best to answer all of them to your satisfaction. But this will all go a whole lot more smoothly if I'm allowed to talk at my own pace and without being subjected to any unnecessary violence. Does that sound reasonable?'

Fin glanced at Zoe for confirmation. Zoe gave a shrug of acceptance.

'Aye,' said Fin. 'That sounds reasonable.'

'Good.' Strickland smiled up at them pleasantly. 'So, what would you like to know?'

It all began, Strickland said, the previous summer, when it came to his and his associates' attention that an investigative journalist, Matt Pinnock, was asking questions about the historic abuse of boys in schools across the West of Scotland, approaching victims and their families, as well as various suspected perpetrators. Initially, a decision was made to simply watch and wait.

'The wonderful thing about conspiracists,' Strickland explained, 'is that they're their own worst enemies. Most of their accusations are so far-fetched and absurd that they succeed in discrediting the few nuggets of truth buried among their rantings. Pinnock was a classic example. So much of what he peddled was blatantly nonsensical that, in some circles, he was viewed almost as an asset rather than a liability. A useful idiot, if you like.'

But as time wore on and Pinnock continued his one-man mission to ferret out the truth, several in their ranks began to express doubts as to their chosen strategy. There was a fear, particularly among those who risked being implicated, that some mud would ultimately stick, regardless of who was doing the throwing. And there was always a danger that, if he succeeded in cajoling a substantial number of complainants to go on the record, the quantity – if not the quality – of their combined testimony would be enough to persuade people that there really was no smoke without fire.

Initially, they attempted to buy him off – 'Always my preferred tactic in the first instance. I abhor violence as anything but a last resort.' Pinnock, however, proved unresponsive to such incentives, and so their next course of action was to threaten him with career suicide, impressing upon him that they had both the means and the connections to make sure he'd never work in this town – or any other – again. But once again Pinnock proved infuriatingly immovable. His journalism existed almost entirely outside the mainstream, meaning that, among the publications upon which Strickland and his associates were in a position to exert an influence, he had no real reputation to speak of anyway. And so, with some regret, the decision was taken to silence him permanently.

'Just like that?' said Fin, with barely concealed contempt.

'Yes,' Strickland agreed, 'just like that.'

Pinnock's death should have been the end of it, Strickland went on, but in late November, he received a communication which threw everything into fresh chaos: a late-night call to his personal number from one Adam Broadhurst, one of the primary subjects of Pinnock's investigation. The trouble, as was invariably the case in such situations, stemmed from Broadhurst's past transgressions. A few nights previously, he'd had a chance encounter with a former pupil – a certain Zoe Callahan, at a venue she had no reason to be attending. Then, a couple of days later, he'd been contacted by an old acquaintance – the father of another ex-pupil – who informed him that the selfsame Zoe Callahan had recently spoken to his daughter, casting around wild accusations about Willow Bank having been a hotbed of child molestation. Callahan, Broadhurst was sure, was onto him, and he wanted to know just what the hell Strickland and his lot were going to do about it.

Strickland sighed and shook his head. 'Broadhurst had been a thorn in our collective side for some time. He was forever getting himself into difficulties, then calling us and demanding we bail him out – thinking his past association with Richard Monkhouse entitled him to a lifetime membership of the proverbial club. In all honesty, I was becoming more than a little tired of dedicating precious resources to an ageing degenerate who couldn't keep his trousers done up. We all were. But then we hit on a stroke of genius. What if we could kill two birds with one stone?'

Until now, Strickland had been addressing some nebulous space between Zoe and Fin, almost as if he was reading from an autocue behind them. Now, though, he turned his gaze directly onto Zoe, fixing her with his undivided attention as he smiled almost congenially.

'We knew, of course, all about your little run-in with Dominic Ryland and your part in his, shall we say, premature exit from the political stage – even if we never *were* able to prove anything.' He gave a low, admiring whistle. 'Turning a police asset over to the crime lord he'd been informing against? That was admirably cold-blooded. So we concluded you had the requisite streak of ruthlessness to leave you open to persuasion *vis-à-vis* Broadhurst. You just needed to be given the right . . . motivation.' He gave another of his meek, almost innocent smiles. 'And what better motivation than your own dear brother?'

Zoe swallowed heavily, the mouthful of saliva she forced down like a rock in her throat.

Strickland glanced briefly at the digital clock facing him on the desk, as if he was delivering a pre-prepared lecture and was checking that he was running to time. 'Of course, we couldn't make a direct approach to you. The best we could hope to do was nudge you in the right direction by ensuring that you had access to the proper viewing materials. So we planted the seed, and we waited, and waited, and still you did nothing.' He shook his head regretfully. 'I'm sorry to say that you proved to be quite a disappointment. Prevaricating for ages, skulking around outside his house, watching and waiting, doing *nothing*. I was quite surprised, actually. I'd have thought you'd have leapt at the chance to avenge your dearly departed brother.'

'Less of that, now,' said Fin sharply, taking a few steps towards Strickland with the stun gun thrust forward as a warning.

Strickland met Fin's gaze without faltering. He held it for a moment, then once more turned to Zoe.

'Eventually, we concluded that you weren't going to act and that the only option left was to take matters into our own hands. The plan always was that you would kill Broadhurst, and then, consumed by guilt and grief, take your own life. There was even some speculation among our number that you might yet do both of your own volition. If not, we would have been more than happy to assist.

'Unfortunately, things didn't go entirely according to plan. You fled the scene before we had time to execute the operation in full, at which point it became imperative that we apprehend you as quickly and quietly as possible. We were *particularly* eager to get our hands on a list of abusers that we were reliably informed had come into your possession. Several' – he cleared his throat – 'interested parties wished very much to ensure that it remained unavailable for public consumption. Not that anyone would have been clapped in irons because their name featured on an unsubstantiated list – but still, people might start asking questions. We searched both your home and that of your friend Dr Scavolini. We thought, if you'd shared your findings with anyone, it would have been her. But there was no trace of it, and she seemed none the wiser.'

'She didn't have it,' said Zoe. 'I took it with me.'

Strickland gave a little 'ah' of understanding. The news seemed genuinely to please him, as if he'd just found the final piece of a puzzle that had been vexing him for ages.

'Anyway,' said Fin, with a touch of satisfaction, 'even if the list ain't worth shit, it doesn't matter. There's something else much more juicy. We got yer dirty videos, Petey-boy.'

'Yes, well.' Strickland sounded almost bored. 'I hardly think that disgusting DVD we sent you proves anything other than that Adam Broadhurst was a vile degenerate who shouldn't have been allowed within a hundred miles of any child.'

'Not "video",' Fin said irritably. '*Videos*, plural. Sixteen tapes, all packed from start to finish with all sortsa filth, featuring the great and the good having their wicked way with a buncha boys in no position to give consent, all in glorious Technicolor.'

A look akin to surprise and, it seemed, genuine apprehension flickered in Strickland's eyes, though he covered it up quickly. 'Is that a fact?'

'That's right. And if that ain't enough, we got the diaries as well – dates, names and locations, arranged in order for easy reference.'

'So there *were* copies made,' Strickland mused, sounding genuinely intrigued. 'I thought they'd all been destroyed, though Monkhouse did hint that he'd kept some of them – for insurance purposes as well as for private enjoyment. I tried repeatedly to get him to tell me what he'd done with them. It's always useful to have that sort of leverage in one's possession, however distasteful. But he wouldn't – not when he was still in command of all his faculties. And now – well, these days he has enough trouble with days of the week, to say nothing of the whereabouts of a series of illicit recordings.' He looked expectantly at the two women. 'Where and how did they come into your possession, out of curiosity?'

'You mind yer own fucking business,' said Fin. 'We're asking the questions.'

'Quite so,' Strickland agreed. 'Forgive my impertinence. That said,' he continued, casually tracing a line on the table, 'I wonder if there might be scope for some sort of a trade.'

'Oh aye? This should be good for a laugh.'

'It's quite simple, really. If you were to hand them over to me – the tapes, the diaries, plus any other *compromising materials* you may have acquired – then I might be in a position to make all this unpleasantness disappear.'

'That right, is it? And how's that gonna work?'

'Not to blow my own trumpet, but as Assistant Chief Constable for the West of Scotland, and the de facto head of our little organisation, the resources at my disposal are not insubstantial.' He looked at Zoe as he spoke. 'In exchange for the aforementioned articles, I would be quite prepared to call off the dogs, so to speak, and allow you to return to your previous existence, such as it was. I could even be persuaded to overlook the small matter of tonight's armed home invasion.'

Fin glanced at Zoe. 'What d'ya think, Bright Eyes? Reckon we can do business with this bozo?'

'I reckon his word's worth shite,' said Zoe quietly.

Fin turned back to Strickland with a serene smile. 'Sounds pretty conclusive to me, Pete. The lady's not for turning.'

If Strickland's spirits were at all dampened, he did an excellent job of masking it. 'Fair enough. No harm in asking.' He glanced briefly at the clock again – a barely perceptible flick of his eyes.

'So you killed Pinnock and Broadhurst,' said Fin. 'Who else?'

Strickland's face was a picture of innocence. 'I can honestly say, hand on heart, that I've personally never taken another human life.'

Fin gave a contemptuous snort. 'Aye – get yer lackies to do yer dirty work, ya pen-pushing nancy-boy.'

Strickland didn't appear in the least offended by this description. 'I'll admit that my role is largely administrative – but then, that's the nature of the beast. The further up the ladder one ascends, the less direct involvement one has in day-to-day affairs. It's the same in any profession.'

Zoe, who had been listening to Strickland's homily of self-justification with growing frustration, could remain silent no longer. 'How d'ye dae it?' she demanded. 'How d'ye live wi yersel, knowing ye're covering up for a shower of murderers and paedos?'

Strickland shook his head regretfully. 'I doubt very much you'd be able to understand.'

'Try me.'

'A lost cause, I fear. You – and I mean no offence in saying this – have, it's safe to say, lived a rather charmed existence. If you don't get up in the morning and go to work, what's the worst that could happen? You might get an earful from your boss. A few customers might complain about the slower-than-usual service. For men like me, that luxury doesn't exist. My decisions affect people's lives to an extent that I suspect is beyond your comprehension.' He shook his head again, as if this was a source of profound regret for him. 'If you had even a modicum of understanding of the stakes at play, you'd reach the same conclusion I came to long ago: that, put simply, there is no alternative.'

In the long silence that followed, Zoe glanced sideways at Fin. Judging by her expression, Fin's incredulity was every bit as acute as her own.

## 53

# The Sting

The knock on the door came just after 10.30 p.m. while Detective Superintendent Sean De Groot was brushing his teeth in front of the bathroom mirror. His wife – who, unlike him, hadn't yet changed into her nightclothes – offered to get it. He listened as her footsteps descended the stairs, thinking it rather odd that someone could be at the door at this time of night. A late delivery, he assumed. One of those private courier firms that didn't respect standard working hours.

As he turned his attention once more to his dental hygiene, he heard his wife give a cry – 'What do you—' – followed by boots pounding up the stairs. Before he could react, the door flew open and multiple pairs of hands were manhandling him to the floor, his mouth still full of toothpaste. As he lay face-down, his nose squashed against the linoleum, his hands were cuffed behind him while a voice overhead recited, in a monotone, words he knew by heart and which he had delivered himself on countless occasions.

'Sean De Groot, I am arresting you under Section Fourteen of the Criminal Justice (Scotland) Act 1995 on suspicion of multiple counts of rape and sexual abuse of minors. You are not obliged to say anything, but anything you do say will be noted and may be used in evidence.'

With an officer on either side, holding him by the upper arms in case he attempted a getaway, De Groot was marched out of the bathroom and across the landing. As they descended the stairs, his eyes fell on his wife and three daughters, herded into the master bedroom in their dressing-gowns, clinging to one another and watching in damp-eyed disbelief.

\* \* \*

At almost precisely the same moment, the night staff at the Cathkin Braes Care Home were shaken out of their torpor as a six-strong posse of officers descended on their small, exclusive establishment. With a confidence and an air of command that belied both her rank and relative youth, Detective Sergeant Kerry Hassan strode to the enquiries desk and demanded to be shown to the quarters of ex-Chief Constable Richard Monkhouse. Monkhouse, a resident since 2014, had been put to bed nearly two hours earlier by the nursing staff. Their pleas that he be left in peace fell on deaf ears and, following a heated exchange with the nurse manager on night duty, Hassan and her team were duly escorted to their destination.

Monkhouse, roused by the raised voices outside his room, was wide awake and sitting upright in bed when Hassan strode in, though his eyes betrayed no sign of comprehension as the statement of arrest was read to him.

On the ground floor of the multi-storey car park near MIT headquarters on High Street, Detective Inspector Carl Plessis strolled towards his Porsche, its lights pulsing briefly as he unlocked it remotely via the app on his phone.

As he paused to remove his overcoat, he caught sight of movement behind him, reflected on the car's polished bodywork. He turned to find a diminutive woman he didn't recognise facing him, flanked by two uniformed male officers of the 'brick shithouse' variety.

'DI Plessis?' She strode towards him, one hand outstretched, not to shake his but to take hold of his arm. 'DS Young. Would you mind coming with us, please, sir?'

As he felt her unexpectedly firm grip on his elbow, Plessis realised that this was neither an invitation nor a request.

All throughout Glasgow and the surrounding areas, similar scenes were playing out: a series of coordinated arrests against men implicated in the historic abuse of teenage boys, participation in a clandestine network of corrupt police officers, or both. The number wasn't quite as high as DCI Vasilico had hoped, but events beyond his control had forced his hand, leaving him with no choice but to act sooner than he'd planned. At least he could content himself with the knowledge that he'd been able to get several of the heavy hitters. And as De Groot was marched out of his nice detached house in Milngavie in his T-shirt and boxers, in full view of the assembled press and rubbernecking neighbours, a grim but thoroughly earned feeling of satisfaction engulfed him.

As De Groot was brought to a standstill beside a waiting police car, he caught sight of Vasilico watching from across the street. For a moment, his features twisted into a mask of sheer animalistic hatred, before the officer chaperoning him forced his head down, bundling him into the back and out of sight.

## 54

# Beyond the Curtain

Anna walked the remaining distance to Strickland's front gate, having turned the taxi away at the end of the road. Whatever was unfolding or was about to unfold up at the house, she figured the fewer witnesses there were to it, the better. She just hoped she wasn't too late.

The building was in darkness, save for a solitary light in one of the top-floor windows. The front door was locked, but the light suggested that someone was in. She considered ringing the bell, then decided against it. Announcing her presence could have all manner of unintended consequences.

Circling around the building, she found a side door lying open. She slipped inside, using the torch mode on her phone to light the way. As she moved forward cautiously, she became aware of a voice coming from somewhere above her. She couldn't make out the words, but she could tell that it was a man speaking and that his tone was calm and level.

She came to the central hallway and found herself facing a wide, thickly carpeted staircase. The voice continued to intone above her. She switched off her phone's torch and began to climb.

As she neared the top, the voice became clearer. She could now make out the actual words.

' ... for men like me, that luxury doesn't exist. My decisions affect people's lives to an extent that I suspect is beyond your comprehension.'

She progressed along the landing, following the faint glow of yellow light seeping from a half-open doorway at its end.

'If you had even a modicum of understanding of the stakes at play, you'd reach the same conclusion I came to long ago: that, put simply, there is no alternative.'

She opened the door cautiously. Strickland was seated behind his desk with two figures facing him. Even with their backs to her, Anna recognised Fin and Zoe. She clocked the stun gun in Fin's hand and what, to her horror, appeared to be a real live pistol in Zoe's, hanging limp by her side. The entire scene looked eerily similar to one she'd encountered before – six years ago, at the top of the Glasgow University bell-tower.

'I can't wait to hear *this*,' said Fin with a dry chuckle.

Anna slipped into the shadows at the back of the room, beyond the glow of the desk-lamp. Neither Strickland nor his captors appeared to notice her.

'I wonder,' said Strickland, 'whether either of you is familiar with the story that dominated the headlines throughout much of September last year? I'm going to assume you are. I doubt there was a single serious-minded newspaper in the country that didn't carry the image of the body of that poor little Kurdish boy, washed up on a beach in Turkey after he and his family attempted to seek refuge in Europe. I suspect there's a good chance that you even know his name: Alan Kurdi.'

'Aye, I remember,' said Fin tersely. 'What of it?'

'Let me ask you this: how did it make you feel, seeing that photograph, hearing his story?'

No one responded.

'Then allow me to offer some suggestions. Sickened? Heartbroken? Ashamed? Outraged by the thought that a human life – the life of a *child* – could be valued so cheaply? Desperate to do something, *anything*, to make a difference? Yes?'

'Sounds about right,' said Fin quietly.

'And how long did those feelings last? A few minutes? A few hours? A couple of days? You can be honest here. No one's judging.'

Again, no one spoke.

'Perhaps you posted about it on social media. Signed a petition calling for more humane treatment of refugees. Donated some money to the Red Cross or Stop the War. But then – sooner or later, though I'd hazard a guess it will have been sooner – something of more pressing significance to your own life took command of your attention, and you forgot all about little

Alan Kurdi – to say nothing of the countless other children washed up on beaches or blown to smithereens by barrel bombs and American drones in other parts of the world.'

Strickland shook his head regretfully. 'That's the problem with today's hyperconnected modern world. Information about events taking place thousands of miles from us is never more than a mouse-click away. If a volcano erupts on the other side of the world, we know all about it immediately – almost before it's even happened. So we share, we retweet, we voice our horror, we make ourselves ill fretting over all the injustices in the world. And we scroll. Oh yes, we scroll. We subject ourselves to an endless twenty-four-hour feed of misery and tragedy, and even though we know we should stop, we keep scrolling, because the algorithms are designed to make us crave more.

'And because we keep scrolling, the event that made us feel such a sense of injustice is forgotten in the blink of an eye – replaced by the next outrage, and the next one after that. You remember Alan Kurdi's name, but I guarantee you hadn't given him a moment's thought until I mentioned it just now. And what about all the other tragedies and injustices that have occurred over the last year? The Charlie Hebdo assassinations in January; the Germanwings Airbus crash in March; the Nepal earthquake in April; the Paris massacre in November; the ongoing refugee crisis in Calais . . . I could go on. We're not equipped to hold all that horror in our heads. Our minds aren't built for it. We only have room for so much. And if we continue to subject ourselves, day in and day out, to a never-ending diet of that sort of thing, sooner or later we become inured.'

Strickland paused to let his words settle. 'You see, I have this theory that one reason why we manage to reconcile ourselves to all the awful things that happen in the world, despite being bombarded by a twenty-four-seven loop of injustice and suffering, is that deep down we know we can't do a thing about it. No matter how outraged we become, no matter how many tears we shed, bombs will continue to fall on the Gaza Strip, people who sought nothing more than a better life will continue to wash up dead on our shores . . . and powerful men will continue to abuse vulnerable children. Oh, we assuage our consciences by periodically sending money to worthy causes, telling ourselves we're helping, that we're making a difference, when in reality all our collective contributions barely amount to a drop in the ocean. To acknowledge that dreadful truth is to acknowledge our own powerlessness.

'So we lie to ourselves. We pick our battles. We content ourselves with indulging in individual acts of goodness so we can pretend to ourselves that, by giving a few pounds here and signing a petition there, we're making a real and positive difference. And every so often we have a jolly good cry about it, and we pat ourselves on the back and convince ourselves that this means we're good people. That we *care*.' There was an unpleasant sneer in his voice as he said the word. 'At the end of the day, it all comes down to self-preservation.'

*He's stalling*, Anna thought. *He's playing for time.* But why? Had he found some way to surreptitiously raise the alarm? Or was he just stringing this out for as long as possible to delay the inevitable?

'That's bullshit,' said Fin. 'Folk cry and give money cos they *are* good people. Stop trying to justify the fact that you don't give a shit.'

Strickland either didn't hear her or chose to ignore her. His gaze was fixed on Zoe as he spoke. 'This may be hard to believe, but not only do I understand your motives in pursuing the perpetrators of the events at Netherfield and beyond – in many ways I admire you. I admire your utopianism; your commitment to the ideal of justice. I think, beaten down by all the unfairness in the world, overcome by your own sense of powerlessness to stop it, you latched onto this terrible outrage that had been committed right on your own doorstep, under your very nose. You thought, *Here's something that's within my power to fix. Here's a situation where I can actually make a difference.*' He shook his head. 'You can't. It doesn't matter what you say or do. You can't rectify what was done to those children any more than you can end world hunger or stop all wars everywhere.

'Some time ago, I made my peace with the realisation that I couldn't do anything about the acts of corruption perpetrated by members of our group. What I *could* do was manage them. I could restrict their activities to the best of my capability – ensuring that, however many innocents might have suffered, many more would be spared who would otherwise have fallen victim to the Adam Broadhursts and Hugh Sullivans of the world. Believe me, it's the same the world over. Every institution that accords its members power over other people inevitably attracts those who will seek to abuse that power. It's not a defect in the system – it's a feature.'

Fin had spent much of this soliloquy shaking her head vehemently. 'You're talking outta yer hole. It takes a special sort of person to turn a blind eye to kiddie-fiddling and be able to sleep at night.'

This time, Strickland acknowledged her contribution, with a smile which seemed almost pitying. 'You'd be surprised what the average person will accept in return for peace of mind. It's impossible to stay outraged all the time. Part of growing up – of making peace with one's place in the world – is acknowledging that. We all do it. We all compromise our morals, out of necessity or just plain old convenience – whether it's buying that new outfit you really like despite knowing it was probably made in a sweat-shop, or continuing to eat meat despite knowing where it comes from, or flying to Málaga for your summer holiday despite knowing the damage you're doing to the environment, or giving your business to companies that defraud the public through tax avoidance schemes.'

Fin scoffed. 'Like those are remotely the same.'

'Oh, I think they are,' said Strickland levelly. 'I contend that we're both morally compromised, you and I. We just happen to draw the line at different things.'

Anna had heard variations on this argument before, but she'd never before heard it used by someone in such a nakedly self-serving manner to justify their own aiding and abetting of the worst aspects of criminality. And yet, at the same time, what truly frightened her was that there was a ring of truth to it. You heard it all the time: people saying, *I don't watch the news, it's too depressing* or *I don't pay attention to politics, my vote never changed anything.* With so much awfulness going on in the world, it was easier just to ignore it. To be wilfully ignorant. To become indifferent.

'I'm far from alone,' Strickland went on. 'Plenty of people who played no active part in the abuse or the ensuing cover-ups knew only too well what was going on but turned a blind eye because the alternative would have been so much harder. Men *and* women, incidentally. Don't think for a moment that the fairer sex is without blame. That's why whatever you're planning on doing with me will achieve nothing. I don't flatter myself into believing that I'm anything more than a temporary caretaker. And there's always a danger that whoever replaces me will be far less civic-minded than I've been. At least I've reined in the worst excesses.'

*He's not just stalling,* Anna thought, with mounting incredulity. *He actually believes this.*

'We're gonna expose ya,' said Fin, unmoved. 'We're gonna drag all you bloodsuckers out into the light and watch you burn. There won't be a single place ya can hide.'

'You still don't understand.' Strickland sighed wearily, pinching the bridge of his nose – a gesture Anna recognised instantly from Vasilico and which hit her somewhere deep inside. 'What happened to those boys, tragic though it undoubtedly was, is a mere incidental in the grand scheme of things. Think of the bigger picture. To drag all that unpleasantness out of the shadows, to bring it into the open, would be like pouring petrol on a bonfire. You have no idea what you'd be unleashing. Most people think of the police as having their best interests at heart, as upholders of the public good – and by and large, they're right. Don't shatter their illusions. Don't undermine the very institution they look to to safeguard them.'

He looked at them imploringly, as if appealing to them to look within themselves and acknowledge the truth that, deep down, they knew all along. 'You may not like me. In fact, you may not like the police full stop. After what you've experienced, after what you've uncovered, I can hardly blame you. But the world needs them, and it needs people like me: the pragmatists who get things done.'

'Ever heard the phrase "Work as if you live in the early days of a better nation"?'

Anna, who had listened to the entirety of Strickland's spiel with a growing sense of fury, could remain silent no longer. As the others turned in response to her voice, she stepped forward into the light.

'Or perhaps you'd prefer "Be the change you wish to see in the world".' She moved alongside Zoe and Fin, ignoring their bewildered looks, and fixed her gaze on Strickland. 'Don't flatter yourself into thinking you're just a caretaker. That your silence, your acquiescence, has no impact. You're an enabler. It's people like you who give succour to these monsters. Who ensure the status quo is preserved.'

Strickland scoffed derisively. 'Claptrap. Naïve, simplistic, wishy-washy claptrap.' He leaned back in his seat, an unpleasant smirk on his features.

'I remember you – my nephew's latest squeeze. Your reputation for sticking your nose where it doesn't belong truly does precede you, Anna Scavolini.'

'It's all over,' said Anna. 'I handed over the tapes and diaries to your nephew. He's rounding up your co-conspirators as we speak. You'll join them in the holding cells soon enough.'

Strickland attempted a dry chuckle, but it came out sounding more like a nervous cough. 'He wouldn't. He's coming here to see me this very night. Be here any moment, in fact. And if you have any sense, you'll all be gone before he arrives.'

'Then you don't know him half as well as you think. He's not coming to save you, Strickland. He's coming to jail you.'

'Managed to pull the wool over your eyes, I see. You disappoint me. I'd pegged you as more astute than to fall for his superficial wiles. There are few things a man won't say in exchange for a spot of slap and tickle – and Paul always did have a weakness for a woman with dark hair and an above-average-sized bust.'

Anna smiled grimly. 'You can goad me all you like, Strickland. Your time's almost up, and you can either face up to your role in these events or not. Either way, I don't care.' She nodded to the gun in Zoe's hand. 'You can put that thing away, Zoe. There's no need for it now. Let's leave this impotent little man to his own devices.'

For a moment, Zoe said nothing. There was a glazed look in her eyes, like a theatregoer who'd completely lost the thread of the narrative. She gazed down at the gun, as if she couldn't figure out how it had come to be in her hand. Then her expression hardened. She turned to Strickland once more.

'I've still got one question left. The most important one.'

Strickland, who had turned a decidedly sickly colour ever since Anna had mentioned Vasilico, seemed to regain some of his composure at the sound of Zoe's voice. Collecting himself, he folded his hands on the desk and gazed up at her benignly.

'Well, it's always sensible to save the best for last. Do go on.'

'Was my brother abused?'

For a moment, Strickland said nothing. Then, slowly, his lips spread into a slow smile. 'You know the answer to that.'

'No, I *don't* know. That's how I'm asking *you*.'

'Come now. You knew him better than anyone. Look deep within your-self and you'll find you know in your heart what the truth is.'

For an agonisingly long time, Zoe said nothing. Anna could see from the distant look in her eyes that her mind was churning, delving into its darkest recesses. Strickland waited patiently. At last, an awful, aching clar-ity entered Zoe's eyes. Her gaze met Strickland's.

'Yes,' she whispered.

'That's right. And do you know how I know?'

'Zoe,' Anna began, a sense of panic rising in her as she realised where this was heading, 'let's just go.'

Zoe ignored her. 'How?'

'Because it was me. I fucked him.'

All trace of colour had drained from Zoe's face. 'No,' she whispered.

Strickland gave a parody of a regretful shrug. 'I'm afraid it's true. He was one of my favourites, actually. Not that I imagine that's much of a source of satisfaction for you . . . ' He gave a nasty little chuckle. ' . . . though I can assure you, it was for me.'

'You *fuck*,' Zoe whispered, angry tears brimming in her eyes.

'Zoe,' Anna hissed, placing herself between her and Strickland, 'don't listen to any of this. Can't you see what he's doing? He's trying to goad you. Don't play into his hands.'

'Of course,' Strickland continued, 'I doubt it was much fun for him to be on the receiving end. It may be some comfort to know that he objected rather strenuously at first – though he quietened down after a while. I think perhaps he even began to enjoy it in the end.'

Zoe didn't move. Her expression didn't change. The only indication that she was even taking in Strickland's words was the soft click as she removed the gun's safety lock.

'Zoe, listen to me,' Anna pleaded. 'He's full of shit. It was before his time. He was in London from '94 to '03. He wasn't there when it happened . . . *if* it happened.'

'Yes,' Strickland mused, as if Anna hadn't spoken, 'I imagine it was quite a formative experience for him. It might even explain his subsequent, shall we say, turn to the dark side? They do say a significant proportion of those who've experienced abuse go on to commit similar acts themselves.'

Zoe raised the gun and advanced towards the desk, brushing Anna aside in the process. Anna hurried after her, tugging at her free arm, but she failed to even delay her advance.

'He *wants* you to kill him, Zoe!' she cried. 'He thinks by getting you to pull the trigger he can escape being held to account for what he's done. Don't give him the satisfaction. He's not worth it.'

She'd used this argument before, on another Callahan sibling, and lost badly. Victor had practically laughed in her face when she'd tried to persuade him that handing Gavin Price over to the police was more just than executing him himself. And now here she was again, making the same desperate plea to someone hellbent on revenge.

Arm outstretched, Zoe pressed the barrel of the gun to Strickland's forehead. She was trembling uncontrollably, every fibre of her being straining under unimaginable pressure.

'Do it,' said Strickland. 'You'll feel a lot better.'

'Zoe,' Anna all but screamed, 'if you do this, you'll never come back from it!'

She turned to Fin, silently imploring her to speak up, but Fin appeared to be transfixed – as if, on some level, she was actually willing Zoe to pull the trigger, or at the very least genuinely curious to see whether she would.

And then Anna played her last card. She shut her eyes, picturing herself standing behind a lectern, addressing a room full of her students. Speaking loudly and clearly, projecting her voice so that it filled the room, she began to tell a story.

It was the story Mandy had breathlessly recounted to her in the stairwell outside Reiko's flat. The story of a young woman who, standing on a street corner one cold winter's night more than six years ago, had heard sounds of merriment coming from a nearby flat and, like a lost child in a fairytale forest, had followed the noise and the light, drawn to it like a moth. The place had been crowded fit to bursting, with people coming and going all the time. No one, she knew, would notice the small, scrawny girl who hadn't been invited. Besides, she was only going to stay for a few minutes – just long enough to get warm.

She told how, as the girl had stood in an out-of-the-way corner, necking from a bottle of beer, she'd been approached by a shy, redheaded young man who'd tentatively asked her who she was here with. *No one*, she'd replied, convinced he was going to summon the flat's owners and have her thrown out, but instead he'd smiled sheepishly and said, *Same*. He'd seen her from the other side of the room, he explained, and thought how lonely she looked, and in that moment she saw that he too was an outcast; a stray like her; someone who ached for companionship and human tenderness every bit as much as she did.

She told how the girl had taken him by the hand and led him next door to the bedroom. She told of their coupling; of his gentleness and the consideration he'd shown towards her, in stark contrast to the grubby punters who pawed and slapped at her; of how, after they were finished, they'd lain together, and he'd kissed her and told her she was beautiful, which no one had ever told her before or since.

And she told how, some weeks later, she'd happened to see his face on the front page of a newspaper and read that he was dead, and that he was responsible for the Kelvingrove Park Murders. She'd refused to believe it. There was no way he could have been responsible for those awful crimes – not the sweet, gentle boy who'd made love to her that night; who'd treated her as if she mattered; as if she was a person. She'd felt an aching loss for him – an awful pain deep within her soul, as if she was grieving for a loved one. And she'd continued to mourn him with each passing day, feeling nothing else – not the cold wind nipping at her flesh, nor the thrusting and grinding of the various clients who shared her bed – until the day she realised she was pregnant.

It wasn't a given that he was the father; she'd had unprotected sex with a great many men, the extra cash too good to pass up. And even when her baby had been born, it hadn't immediately been obvious. She'd just known that she was beautiful – her child, her perfect bundle of unsullied innocence. But as she'd grown older, the resemblance had become harder and harder to ignore, until it was impossible not to see his face in hers.

The years had passed, and still he'd lingered in her mind – a resource to draw on when life knocked her back; a companion to bring her comfort on long, dark nights. And there he'd remained, nothing but a memory – until another cold winter's night six years later, when a kindly stranger invited her into her home, where she'd laid eyes on a framed picture of the same boy who occupied that special place within her mind. Her one-time lover, the father of her daughter, her Ruby.

Zoe didn't speak. She felt as if she was floating far above the earth. Everything in the room seemed to melt away: Strickland, Fin, Anna, all of it, her mind shutting them out as it focused on the only thing that now mattered to her. Somehow, against all hope, a little part of her brother lived on.

Gradually, she became aware of her surroundings again. She was conscious of Strickland sitting in front of her. Of the gun pressed against his forehead. Of her outstretched hand holding it. Hatred, revulsion, rage – all the emotions that, a few minutes ago, had been coursing through her had evaporated. Now, as she gazed down at him, she felt only pity.

She laughed softly. It sounded alien in her own ears. 'Ye're right,' she said, addressing Anna, who she was dimly aware was standing behind her. 'He isnae worth it. Y'know,' she told Strickland, 'I came here expecting ... I dunno, some sort of evil genius, I guess. But ye're not. Ye're just a sad wee man in a cheap suit and a bad haircut.' She gave a small, triumphant smile. 'And my brother was worth a hunner of you.'

She lowered the gun. Strickland stared up at her, the last hope fading from his eyes as he realised his only escape route had just closed. As Zoe turned away from him, the sound of distant sirens reached the room.

They say it's a cliché, but what happened over the next few seconds really did seem to unfold in slow motion. Zoe was aware of Anna and Fin's expressions changing, of a look of horror entering Anna's eyes, of her opening her mouth to shout a warning. She was aware of a presence bearing down on her from behind. Of tumbling forward, her hands reaching out to break her fall. As she went down, she saw Fin rushing forward, only to be thrown back with such force that she landed on the ground several feet away. Then Zoe felt a heavy weight pressing down on her, and Strickland was on top of her, turning her over, wrapping his hands around her throat, squeezing hard. A wild, deranged look was in his eyes, his face twisted into a fearsome mask that no longer seemed human. Zoe clawed frantically at his hands, but he held fast, even as her nails gouged his skin, drawing blood.

Spots began to dance before her eyes. She knew the life was literally being squeezed out of her. She felt her feet kicking involuntarily – feeble little twitches, really – and she thought, *This must have been how it felt when they used to hang people on Glasgow Green.*

Her vision was becoming blurry. She'd all but given up trying to fight. Out of the corner of her eye, she saw Anna rising to her feet, holding the pistol in both hands, pointing it at Strickland. She saw Anna's lips moving, issuing some futile order to him to stop, but the roar of blood in her ears was now too loud for her to make out the words. She saw Anna shout one last warning, and shut her eyes.

BAM!!

The sound of the gun going off was both louder and more viscerally felt than anything she could have anticipated. Even as she swayed on the brink of unconsciousness, she wondered how it was possible that such a tiny little thing could have created such a powerful explosion.

She felt Strickland's grip on her neck loosen and opened her eyes to find him still straddling her, his arms hanging limp by his sides, a gaping, bloody hole in his chest. For a moment, he swayed slightly, like a puppet suspended from strings. Then, like a felled tree, he toppled backwards, hit the floor with a soft thud, and lay still.

As Zoe eased herself upright with her elbows and the fog slowly cleared from her eyes, she became aware of Anna and Fin both staring past her in stunned, wide-eyed silence. Twisting her bruised neck, she followed their gaze to the doorway, where Gil McLaren stood, soaking wet with rainwater, clutching a break-action shotgun in both hands, its twin barrels still smoking.

Slowly, Zoe turned to face Strickland, who lay unmoving, smoke rising from the wreckage of his chest. Then, as the approaching sirens grew louder and her trembling fingers traced the droplets of blood on her own face, the reality of what she was seeing dawned on her and she began to scream and scream.

# 55

# Release

Anna emerged from Strickland's house to a scene of chaos. The entire courtyard was full of police officers and their assorted vehicles, their pulsating lights illuminating the night sky. Light rain continued to fall – more of a damp mist, really, than fully formed drops.

Her attention was drawn to a minor commotion taking place nearby. She turned to watch as, several feet away, a pair of police officers slammed Fin against the bonnet of a panda car, one cuffing her hands behind her back, the other patting her down. Judging by the maniacal grin on Fin's upturned features, she was enjoying herself immensely.

'Getting a good feel back there, are ya?' she crowed at the officer who was searching her. 'Another inch and I'm counting it as a reach-around.'

A familiar Porsche came roaring into the grounds, kicking up gravel as it went. It came to a standstill and Vasilico scrambled out of the driver's seat. As he hurried towards the house, Anna moved to intercept him. They stopped and stood facing one another in silence, neither of them seemingly able to summon words that would do justice to what had transpired that night. Vasilico had the appearance of a man under whose feet the whole world had shifted, his entire perception of reality thrown into flux.

There was movement behind them. Anna turned to watch as Gil McLaren was led out of the house by two officers, hands cuffed behind his back. His expression, curiously enough, was one of indifference as he was led over to a waiting car, his head pressed down firmly as he got in – rather needlessly, in Anna's opinion, since he obviously had no intention of resisting. As he settled into the back seat, she thought he looked like a man at peace with the world.

Nearby, a fresh commotion broke out. Turning, Anna saw that Fin had succeeded in head-butting one of the men restraining her and was now being manhandled to the ground by several additional officers, amid much squirming and teeth-gnashing. As she raised her face up from the gravel into which it had been forced, her eyes met Anna's. A look of understanding seemed to pass between them. She gave Anna a slight nod, which Anna acknowledged with one of her own.

As Fin was hauled upright and bundled away, a fresh deputation emerged from the house: Zoe, chalk-white and expressionless, being escorted by a couple of female officers. No handcuffs for her – just a firm but gentle guiding hand on her upper arm.

Anna tilted her head up to look at Vasilico, who by now had joined her at her side. 'Promise me she'll be treated fairly,' she said – then added, in what might just have been the understatement of the century, 'She's been through a lot.'

Vasilico gave a slight dip of his head. 'Nothing but the best.'

He nodded to the two officers escorting Zoe. They moved her on, leading her away to another car. One got into the back beside her, while the other headed round to the driver's seat. Anna watched the vehicle until it disappeared from view.

She felt Vasilico's hand on her arm. She turned to face him.

'I'm going to need to stick around for a bit,' he explained. 'I've got various responsibilities to take care of. Plus, they're going to need a member of the family to identify the body.'

Anna, finding it difficult to meet his gaze, said nothing.

'A car will be along in a moment to take you back to HQ for questioning. I can't be there, obviously, but I can assure you, the detectives who'll be speaking to you are above reproach.'

Anna looked at him in dismay. 'I was hoping I could go home first. Jack's waiting for me. He needs his mum.'

Vasilico looked pained. 'That's not how it works, I'm afraid. You're a vital witness to a serious crime. It's crucial that we go through everything that happened with you while it's still fresh in your mind.'

'It'll still be fresh in my mind tomorrow. Then, I promise you, I'll make myself available for all the questioning you like. But right now, I need to be with my son.'

Vasilico thought for a moment. 'Can you make your own way back to Glasgow?'

'Of course.'

'Then go now. If anyone makes it into an issue, tell them you didn't know you weren't supposed to leave.'

She said nothing more, but she smiled gratefully. Then, after giving his arm a brief squeeze, she turned away from him and set off. As she passed through the throng of people heading this way and that, each with their own urgent business to attend to, none of them paid the slightest attention to the small, solitary figure heading through the open gates and off into the night.

The taxi pulled up to the kerb on the Broomielaw, next to the George V Bridge just south of Central Station. Anna watched the cab pulling away and waited till it had disappeared from view before making her way down to the waterfront. There, under the shadow of the bridge, she slid a hand into her coat and drew out the pistol, stealthily pocketed amid the confusion following Strickland's death. She approached the water's edge and, stooping down, let the gun fall, watching as it quickly sank without a trace.

She made her way back up to the main road. There, she paused to take a deep breath, inhaling the fresh, cool night air. There were no trains or buses running this late at night, and it could be ages before she managed to summon another taxi, but that didn't seem to matter. The rain had stopped and, though common sense told her that nothing had actually changed, walking alone through the city at night now seemed a less perilous prospect than it would have a few hours ago. It shouldn't take her much more than half an hour to reach Carrington Street.

She inhaled another deep, cleansing breath, then set off to find her child.

# Epilogue

In the days following the shooting, both Anna and Zoe were questioned by the police at considerable length. They both cooperated fully with the investigation, omitting nothing – save for the small detail of the pistol, which remained at the bottom of the Clyde and, to date, has never been found. Of the four people who had been present at the house in Newton Mearns and knew of its existence, only three remained alive, and all three seemed to recognise that it was in no one's interests for that state of affairs to change. After all, only one person had discharged a firearm that night, and he had already made a full and frank confession as to both his actions and the motivation behind them.

Once the police were satisfied that Zoe had told them everything she knew and had been responsible for nothing more egregious than visiting the home of the chief conspirator in a plot to frame her for murder in a desperate bid to convince him to confess his role, she was released. At Anna's insistence, she moved into the house on Clarence Drive with her and, over the next several months, slowly began to pick up the threads of her old life.

It was not, by any stretch of the imagination, a quick or straightforward process. At first, she had little interest in doing anything other than lying in bed or sitting staring into space for hours on end. Gradually, though, and thanks in no small part to the presence of Jack, hints of the old Zoe started to re-emerge. And while Anna recognised that she would likely be forever changed by her experiences, she saw hopeful signs that, in the vein of the old wives' tale that a broken bone heals back stronger, this new

Zoe, hardened and wisened by her experiences, would be stronger and more in love with life than ever before. There was a good chance, she knew, that they never would know for sure whether Victor had been one of the victims of Broadhurst and his co-conspirators. She hoped that, in time, Zoe would come to terms with that uncertainty and not allow it to define her permanently. In the meantime, it was enough to take solace in the little victories: simple things like the act of her getting out of bed in the morning and putting on clothes, or the sound of her delighted cackle when Jack did something funny.

As winter gave way to spring, the inquiry into the Shadow Men and their crimes rumbled on, the wheels of justice turning slowly but surely. Of the fifteen arrests made that night in February, nine were formally charged, among them Detective Superintendent Sean De Groot. The charges against five others were dropped due to insufficient evidence, while former Chief Constable Richard Monkhouse was deemed not competent to stand trial. In the months that followed, numerous other low-level players in the conspiracy were identified and arrested, among them the two 'detectives' who'd attempted to gain entry to Anna's home. They were, as Anna had surmised, not police officers but hired muscle: former associates of the late crime lord Jim Cottrell, relegated to taking on mercenary jobs following the collapse of his criminal empire. The identity of the person or persons responsible for the murder of Adam Broadhurst remained a mystery.

Given the sheer quantity – and indeed the social standing – of those listed in the diaries and present on the tapes, the final tally was unquestionably disappointing, but Anna had known all along that the majority of the real movers and shakers would, as was so often the case, escape the consequences of their actions. That, she knew, was why McLaren had done what he did.

On a grey morning in early May, Zoe stepped apprehensively into what was rather benignly referred to as the family hub at Cornton Vale Women's Prison. She presented herself at the desk, and, after jumping through various security hoops, was shown through to the visitors' room. It looked far more like a nursery classroom than she'd been expecting, with round plastic tables and chairs, the walls decorated with children's artwork and a large window on the far wall overlooking a well-tended garden. Where were the armed guards? The glass partitions? The shifty-looking relatives covertly spreading their legs to extract little baggies of contraband from their birth canals to pass under the table to expectant loved ones?

A solitary figure was seated at one of the tables with her back to her, dressed in a baggy grey tracksuit. As Zoe stepped into the room, she stood up and turned to face her with a limp and oddly sheepish smile.

'Howya, Bright Eyes.'

She looked tired, Zoe thought – tired and rather subdued. She faced Fin hesitantly, wondering if she was allowed to hug her. There weren't any 'no touching' signs that she could see, but you never knew. She decided to throw caution to the wind and did so anyway, drawing Fin into her embrace and holding her close. No one objected – though Fin, she noted, seemed stiff and not really into it.

'Wow,' Zoe said, once they were seated, 'this seems . . . well, *nice*.'

'Aye, true enough,' said Fin. 'S'not exactly *Prisoner: Cell Block H*. I hear the guvnor's got these newfangled ideas about rehabilitation, not retribution.'

'They treating ye awright?'

'Well, I get three square meals a day, regular gym access and as much art therapy as I can handle. I have to be back in my cell at nine, and I gotta go to these mandatory group talking sessions – but beyond that, I'm basically left to my own devices.'

'Anyone else been to see ye?'

'Reiko's been in a couple o' times. Gave me a *loooong* lecture 'bout reaping what I sow. Mind you, she said I could doss at hers once I get out. I said I'll see. Don't want her putting her life on hold for the next eight years waiting for me.'

'Eight *years*?' said Zoe, aghast. 'What did they get ye for?'

Fin laughed drily. 'What *didn't* they get me for? Let's see,' she began to count on her fingers, 'we got handling stolen goods, we got unlawful entry, we got theft by housebreaking, resisting arrest . . . The rap sheet's pretty comprehensive.'

'And all cos of me,' Zoe muttered, lowering her eyes.

'Ah, quit being a horse's arse. I'da come a-cropper sooner or later, with or without your assistance. I've been running for a while now. Sure it was only a matter of time before they caught up with me.'

'I just . . . ' – Zoe shrugged helplessly – ' . . . keep thinking, if it wasn't for me, you'd've never come back here.'

'True enough,' Fin agreed, 'but it's not as if anyone put a gun to my head and forced me. There's that "free will" thing the Existentialists are forever banging on about.'

'Disnae mean I don't wish there was something I could do for ye.'

'Well, if you fancying doing a re-enactment of that scene from *Midnight Express* . . . ' She made a show of looking around. 'I mean, dunno how easy it'll be without the old glass partition, but I'm game if you are.'

Zoe smiled softly and almost laughed, but she couldn't quite bring herself to wholly embrace Fin's words.

Fin's smile lingered for a moment, then abruptly faded. 'I'm serious. You owe me nothing. Stop worrying so much about other people and start concentrating on that red-haired cutie in the mirror.' She reached across the table and patted Zoe's hand. 'Go. Live your life, Bright Eyes.'

Zoe remained seated for a moment. Then, slowly and deliberately, she got to her feet and, leaning across the table, kissed Fin on the cheek. She straightened up, gave a lopsided smile, then turned and strode out of the room.

Summer came early that year, with the end of May heralding a spell of unseasonably warm weather. The good people of Glasgow, never ones to pass up a spot of unscheduled sun-worship, took to the city's parks and green spaces in their droves, armed with picnic food, copious quantities of alcohol and the odd illicit bottle of sunblock.

One sunny afternoon in early June, a little deputation set off for Kelvingrove Park, Anna pushing Jack in his buggy, Zoe lugging a hamper full of munchies. They found the park already teeming with people who'd had similar ideas: a couple hundred of them stretched out on the slopes of Woodlands Hill, determined to soak up every last morsel of the sun's rays.

To Anna, it was strange to think that so much of what she and Zoe had been through over the last six and a half years could be traced back to this place. Anna had been back to the park countless times since then;

working so close by made it difficult to avoid. But she knew that, for Zoe, coming here today was a big deal. It was, in many ways, a statement; a final act of laying the past to rest, of proving that it no longer had a hold over her.

Halting on the main path that led through the centre of the park, Anna shielded her eyes and scanned the sea of people before her, then spotted two familiar figures seated on a tartan rug a little way up ahead.

As they made their way over, Mandy looked up from the slice of bread she was buttering and smiled.

'Look who's here, Rubes.'

Ruby lifted her head, lowering the piece she'd been munching on, jam spread all over her cheeks. She stared up at the new arrivals with wide, vaguely distrusting eyes.

Zoe crouched down before her, smiling. 'Heya, Ruby – 'member me? I'm yer Auntie Zoe.'

Ruby smiled shyly and averted her eyes.

Zoe grinned. 'Heh-heh, lookit you, jam-chops.' She reached out and traced Ruby's sticky cheek with her pinkie.

Anna sat there on the rug with Jack settled between her legs, listening to Zoe wittering away to Mandy about nothing in particular. She tilted her head back and shut her eyes, enjoying the feeling of the sun on her face and the sounds of conversation and birdsong around her. She'd noticed that she was more attuned to the natural cycle of the seasons since she'd come off the lithium. Everything seemed that bit more connected. More vibrant. More alive.

She opened her eyes. The light had changed. The sun had partly disappeared behind a cloud, its rays now less intense. There was something else, though. A slight prickling at the back of her neck – the feeling she got when she sensed someone watching her.

She turned and gazed up the slope. At the top, on the footpath that ran parallel with the outer circle of houses on Woodlands Hill, stood a figure: a man, tall, broad-shouldered, silhouetted against the skyline. She knew, almost without having to look, who he was.

She lifted Jack up and transferred him to Zoe. 'Watch him for me for a minute, will you?'

Zoe appeared confused, though only momentarily. As she resumed the bawdy joke she'd been explaining to Mandy, Anna slipped away and made her way up the hill.

Vasilico was wearing chinos and an open-necked shirt and stood with his arms folded behind his back. For Anna, who'd never seen him in anything other than a suit and tie before, the effect was mildly disorienting. He looked different – less like a law enforcement official and more like . . . well, a regular person. Someone she could imagine going for a drink or a meal with. Or perhaps, in time, something more.

'Were you planning on standing up here all day, or were you going to come and say hello?'

'I thought about it, but you all looked so . . . well, self-contained. I felt I'd only be intruding.'

She drew alongside him. They stood side by side, looking out across the expanse of the park and the people taking their ease.

'How's life at MIT?' Anna asked.

'Didn't you hear? I'm not there anymore.'

'Oh?'

'It's for my own safety as much as anything else. This may come as a shock to you, but something tells me I'm not going to be on many of my old colleagues' Christmas card lists this year. Plus, after everything that happened, it was felt a clean sweep was in order. A fresh team; a total break with the past.'

'And how d'you feel about that?'

Vasilico's brow furrowed. 'To be honest, conflicted. I know what went on there – the crimes that were covered up, the lives that were ruined. But I'd come to regard it as something akin to home. It sounds trite, but it feels like saying goodbye to a part of yourself.'

'I get that. It's hard letting go of the past.'

'But necessary.'

They fell silent again. Somewhere, in one of the houses on the hill, someone was playing 'Caledonia' on the violin. Not particularly well, it had to be said, but some tunes were near-impossible to mangle.

'How's your friend?' said Vasilico, breaking the silence.

For a moment, Anna said nothing. She gazed down the slope, her eyes settling on her little group. Mandy was sunbathing, arms folded behind her head, while Zoe kept a weather eye on the two children like the proud auntie she was – one not flesh and blood but no less dear to her, the other a living link to Victor.

'Yeah,' she said. 'I think she's going to be all right.'

'That's good to hear,' said Vasilico. He paused for a moment. 'Um . . . this feels like a conversation we've had before, but now comes the part where I confess that this wasn't entirely a social call.'

'Oh?' said Anna, turning.

'You'll have been aware they're setting up a task-force to investigate what went on inside the Force – everything Monkhouse and the rest were involved in, going all the way back to the beginning.'

Anna smiled drily. 'Ah yes, I heard about that. The police investigating themselves. Lots of fine words about increased transparency and learning from past mistakes. I'm sure it'll make for a nice bit of PR. But you and I both know nothing will really change, don't we?' She smiled resignedly. 'It's nothing personal – it's just the way the system is.'

'Not this time. Not if I have anything to do with it.'

Anna frowned at him. 'What d'you mean?'

'Who d'you think they've asked to head it up?'

She blinked in surprise. 'Not *you*?'

He nodded an affirmative. 'And I promise you, there'll be no whitewash under my watch. I'm making it my mission to shake the whole organisation to its very foundations: leave the people who've besmirched its name with nowhere to hide; make sure nothing like the Shadow Men can ever happen again. I'm putting together a multi-disciplinary team to lead the charge. Yes, there'll be police officers on it, but there'll also be politicians, human rights campaigners, academics and laypersons. People who are genuinely critical of the police. The more critical the better.' He gave a slightly rueful smile. 'It's what you always wanted: proper independent oversight and scrutiny of law enforcement.'

Anna looked back at him, temporarily lost for words. 'I'm glad,' she finally said – and meant it. 'I'd like to believe our children will grow up to inherit a more just society than the one we did.'

'Give it time,' said Vasilico. 'It will be.'

He fell silent again. Anna turned towards the park, though she continued to watch him surreptitiously. She wanted to believe that real change was possible, and knowing that he'd be playing a leading role gave her some measure of hope.

Her mind turned to the tapes she'd handed over to him, now stored under lock and key as material evidence, and to the ruined childhoods captured on them. Some of the victims, she knew, had already been contacted by the authorities, asking them if they would be prepared to testify against their abusers. The victims or, if they were no longer among the living, their relatives. It would take time to identify and trace them all. She wondered how many of them would wish it had remained buried and forgotten, no matter how much compensation money was thrown at them. Wondered, especially, about one particular boy who appeared towards the end of the third-to-last tape she'd viewed during her trawl. A boy with a mop of sandy hair and a long, aquiline nose, so strikingly similar to that of the man who now stood beside her.

She looked at Vasilico again, and knew she'd made the right decision in not telling him. If she had, there was no telling how he would have reacted. No way of knowing how much of his own humanity he'd have been prepared to sacrifice in the pursuit of vengeance. By keeping him in the dark, she'd ensured that he'd acted with a level head and in accordance with the law. In time, perhaps, she'd sit down with him and have a conversation about what she'd seen. But now was not that time. For now, she took comfort in the fact that the younger of the two boys appeared to have been spared the same treatment as his older brother, and had made it to adulthood as a well-adjusted, caring, honourable man.

'Which brings me to the purpose of my visit.' Vasilico's voice cut into her thoughts. 'There's a place on that team for you, if you want it. I say, with no hint of either condescension or flattery, that your knowledge and expertise – and yes, your bloody inconvenient opinions – would be greatly valued. What d'you reckon?'

Anna said nothing. For a brief moment, she was genuinely tempted by his offer. The opportunity to work on a project that stood a chance of making a real and meaningful difference to the way criminal justice worked – *and, admit it, Anna, a chance to work with* him *again* – was one she ought to have leapt at. But then she gazed down once more at Zoe, Jack and the others, blissfully oblivious to this conversation, and realised her decision had already been made.

'Paul, I'm flattered,' she said. 'And perhaps, if the circumstances were different . . . But right now, my first priority is my family, and I can't let anything get in the way of that.'

Vasilico nodded slowly, as if he wasn't all that surprised. 'Well,' he said philosophically, 'family does matter.'

'It really does.'

She could tell he was disappointed, but also that he respected her decision and was in a position to understand the reasoning behind it, perhaps more than anyone else.

'Well,' he said, 'you know how to get in touch if you change your mind.'

'I do.'

He reached out and touched her arm lightly, then turned and walked off along the path. She watched till she lost sight of him, then turned to take in the view of Kelvingrove Park again. The clouds had lifted now, the sun shining down with renewed warmth. She remained there for a while, gazing across the park to the skyline beyond it – a distant, shimmering haze of mismatched buildings, somehow ugly and beautiful at the same time. Her city: the place that had made her who she was.

A light breeze stirred her hair. She shook her head, clearing it of all weighty thoughts. Then, picking her way past the pockets of sunbathers, she made her way back down the slope to rejoin her family.

# Author's Note

I wrote the first draft of *The Shadow Men* during the summer of 2019. At that time, the QAnon conspiracy theory still hadn't fully penetrated the public conscious, and the Black Lives Matter and Reclaim These Streets movements – and the broader discussions around police misconduct and brutality that they sparked – had yet to arise. Nonetheless, when revising the manuscript during 2020 and early 2021, I was struck by how much of what I'd written seemed almost eerily prescient. It says something, I think, about the enduring nature of both these issues – online conspiracies and how best to police the police – that this novel feels in many respects like a direct response to these specific phenomena.

In devising the Shadow Men and their clandestine activities, I drew some inspiration from 'The Chicago Police Files', a series of articles by *The Intercept* chronicling rampant corruption and extrajudicial violence within the Chicago Police Department. The American police system has its own unique issues and challenges, none of which can simply be transplanted wholesale onto another law enforcement body, but debates surrounding the power public institutions such as the police wield over ordinary citizens, and how to respond when that power is abused, are as universal as they are timeless.

Several of Anna's specific demands for police reform were derived from the findings of the Angiolini Report, a review commissioned by the Scottish Government in June 2018, led by former Lord Advocate Eilish Angiolini QC. The findings were delivered in full in November 2020, though this story takes place some five years prior, proving that

Dr Scavolini has long been ahead of the curve in her thinking on these matters.

Special thanks must go to my team of beta readers for helping me birth this monster – especially Ashley Lane, for pulling me out of several deep logic holes, and Caroline Whitson, for various pointers on the subject of pregnancy. (Much like Anna, I learned that certain things aren't included in the baby books.) Thanks also to Suze Clarke-Morris, Sarah Kelley, Catherine Mackenzie, Ewan McIntyre and Daniel Sardella for typo-spotting and other miscellaneous suggestions, and Pam Fox for clarifying a few matters of police procedure for me. As always, all errors, deliberate and otherwise, are mine and mine alone.

Finally, for being the inspiration for Zoe's Facebook screen name, my thanks to the original Fanny de Bergerac, whoever you really are.

The rhyme Derek Sullivan recites is a translation of the Scots Gaelic 'An Coineachan', also known as the Highland Fairy Lullaby, which first appeared in print in *An Duanaire*, ed. Donald C. MacPherson (1868).

The Tom and Jerry cartoon Fin and Jack were watching is *Mouse Trouble*, winner of the 1944 Academy Award for Best Animated Short Film.

This book is a work of fiction. No similarities should be inferred between the fictional Strathkelvin Police Force, its Major Investigations Team, the various (non-existent) schools mentioned and any of their real-life counterparts.

Discover how it all began with *In the Silence*, the first instalment in the Anna Scavolini series.

# IN THE
# SILENCE

**Anna Scavolini hasn't set foot in Glasgow for ten years – and she's not short of reasons . . .**

On her first night back in town, what should have been the start of a relaxing Christmas getaway takes a decidedly macabre turn when she stumbles upon an old flame, Andrew Foley, bleeding to death on the snow-clad slopes of Kelvingrove Park.

Who killed Foley in such a brutal manner – and why? If the police have any leads, they're keeping them under wraps. Convinced that Foley was deliberately targeted rather than the victim of a random attack, Anna begins her own investigation, and in so doing unearths a trail of long-buried secrets, leading back to a crime committed over a decade ago.

A crime so unspeakable its perpetrators are prepared to take their silence to the grave.

**AVAILABLE NOW IN PAPERBACK AND EBOOK IN A NEW, REVISED EDITION CONTAINING MATERIAL NOT PRESENT IN THE ORIGINAL PUBLICATION**

She entered Kelvingrove Park by its northern entrance at the foot of Gibson Street, leaving behind the streetlights and their reassuring sodium glow. She'd often walked through the park as a child, though only a handful of times after dark, and always with friends. During daylight hours, people walked their dogs in it, whiled away their lunch hours on the park benches and, in the summer months, even indulged in the odd stint of sunbathing on those rare sunny days. After dark, however, it was a different story. Even as a schoolgirl, word had reached her tender ears that it was the stomping ground of rent-boys and their clients, and, over the years, it had been host to several violent attacks, muggings and sexual assaults.

Which was precisely what had made her throw caution to the wind and risk her own neck. If she opened the papers the following morning to discover some poor soul had been assaulted while she and Zoe were skipping up the Kelvin Way, nonchalantly discussing trivialities, she'd never forgive herself. She slipped a hand into her coat pocket and gripped her keys, the longest protruding between her clenched fingers like a knuckle-duster.

At first, she could barely see her own feet, but after a few moments, her eyes grew accustomed to the gloom, and she was able to make out the shapes of the snow-flocked trees and the wrought iron fencing that flanked the footpath. It was less dark in the park than it had seemed from the street. True, the clusters of trees on either side of her were as black as charcoal, but the terrain itself was readily visible, the snow a dull purplish grey.

The ground began to slope steadily downwards. Using the torch on her phone, she picked her way south, following the winding trail towards the centre of the park, where all paths converged at the Stewart Memorial Fountain. Up ahead, she could just make out the imposing shape of the monument to the Highland Light Infantry, beyond which lay the stone bridge that straddled the River Kelvin.

She was perhaps four hundred metres from the fountain when she heard it: a shrill, clear wail of anguish, coming from beyond a thicket of trees up ahead and to her left. She stopped dead. There was no doubt about it. Whoever – or whatever – had made that noise was also the source of the cry she and Zoe had heard on the Kelvin Way.

She remained stock still and listened but heard nothing more. She took a few more faltering steps, then stopped once again. What she saw caused her blood to turn to ice.

Less than fifty metres away, a shape was moving among the trees. As she watched, it emerged from the thicket and stumbled onto the footpath: a man, bent over almost double and clutching his stomach. He tottered unsteadily, turning this way and that, as if trying to work out where he was.

She drew herself up to her full height – an admittedly underwhelming five foot two – directing the beam from her phone onto him. His shirt was untucked; his belt hung loosely from his waistband, the buckle trailing behind him. It crossed her mind that she might have inadvertently broken up a transaction between a client and one of the nocturnal denizens of the park who plied their trade within its confines. She began to feel slightly foolish. In fact, she was on the verge of actually apologising when she saw it.

Blood.

Large quantities of blood, trickling from a wound in his lower abdomen, covering his groin area, his shirttails and the legs of his trousers. He was doing his best to stem the flow with one hand, but it was leaking between his fingers like water from a punctured hose.

She heard herself gasping. He must have heard her too, for he turned in her direction and looked directly at her. Light from her phone picked out the contours of his face.

Her breath caught in her throat. She knew him. Gone was the cocky smile, replaced by a contorted, painful grimace, but every other aspect of that face was instantly recognisable. The strong jawline, the high-bridged nose . . .

Seemingly galvanised by her appearance, he began to stagger in an uneven line towards her. She found herself reversing, shuffling backwards, the beam of her phone's torch trembling as she trained it on him.

'Please . . . '

It was barely a whisper, but the air was so still Anna heard it with crystal clarity.

She couldn't move. Her legs refused to obey her brain, which was screaming *Help him, help him, help him* over and over. He took a few more faltering steps towards her. Her phone and keys fell from her trembling hands.

He tottered, his legs giving way under him. He fell against her, clawing madly at her, clutching the hem of her coat. She recoiled instinctively, trying to push him off, but his weight bore down on her, and it was all she could do to prevent her own knees from buckling. She found herself supporting him in her arms, each ragged breath he took reverberating through her own body.

With a last effort, he lifted his head. Their eyes met, and she knew she was looking at a dead man.

And *he* knew it too.

His lips trembled. He opened his mouth, but instead of words, a thin trickle of blood oozed from the corner of his lips. He was choking. His grip on her tightened, then loosened.

Andrew Foley went limp and sank to the ground, leaving twin vertical streaks of blood on either side of her coat. He landed face-down in the unblemished snow and lay still.

CPSIA information can be obtained
at www.ICGtesting.com
Printed in the USA
LVHW020206280921
698841LV00001B/1

9 781916 094826